Catch a Falling Knife
by Vincent deFilippo

Catch a Falling Knife

By Vincent DeFilippo

First Edition
Copyright © 2023 by Vincent DeFilippo

ViennaRose Publishing

All rights reserved. No portion of this book may be reproduced in any form without written permission from the publisher or author, except as permitted by U.S. copyright law.

This publication is designed to provide accurate and authoritative information in regard to the subject matter covered. It is sold with the understanding that neither the author nor the publisher is engaged in rendering legal, investment, accounting or other professional services. While the publisher and author have used their best efforts in preparing this book, they make no representations or warranties with respect to the accuracy or completeness of the contents of this book and specifically disclaim any implied warranties of merchantability or fitness for a particular purpose. No warranty may be created or extended by sales representatives or written sales materials. The advice and strategies contained herein may not be suitable for your situation. You should consult with a professional when appropriate. Neither the publisher nor the author shall be liable for any loss of profit or any other commercial damages, including but not limited to special, incidental, consequential, personal, or other damages.

Paperback ISBN: 979-8-9883420-4-5
Hardcover ISBN: 979-8-9883420-5-2

Printed in the United States of America

PROLOGUE

October 2009 – New York

"**I** *told you, I don't know where the fuck he is!*"

The voice was shrill, almost feminine, and echoed off every cold, hard surface on the wharf, making Jack D'Angelo wince. He had sensitive ears. Always had. They'd made his life miserable as a kid; the taunts of grade-school bullies and the scalding tones of his mother's rants were sheer hell. He scrunched up his eyes as he climbed out of the BMW, then winced anew as the shrill voice uttered an inarticulate bleat. Clearly, Rossi had started without him. Jack grimaced; say what you like about that asshole, Leo Rossi was a guy who put his heart and soul into his work.

The north side of Staten Island was frigid and depressing this time of night, at this time of year. A chill, stiff breeze blew in from the bay, and all but the security lights were off at Spiller's Launch—even though the salvage and transportation company boasted around-the-clock service. Mr. Vaccarelli had seen to it the place had closed up tonight—he and Spiller's Launch, Inc. had done business since their early days back in '77 when all they'd had were a couple of tugboats and a forklift.

It was a cold and gloomy place to die.

Jack blew into his hands and checked the block beyond Pier 7½ down the straight line of Murray Hulbert Avenue. He knew there'd be no one else around, but old habits died hard. The lighthouse museum was a little way along the shoreline, a ways beyond that the ferry terminal at St. George, and farther along still, the Yankees' minor league stadium. Out on the black, choppy water of Upper New York Bay, the Staten Island Ferry was making its final trip. Made visible only by its yellow lights, the boat was populated mostly by drunks and nightshift workers, none of whom would pay too much attention as it chugged by the Statue of Liberty, Ellis Island, and Lower Manhattan. They'd seen it all a thousand times before.

Jack opened the coupe's door wider and pulled the driver's seat forward. "Out."

He drummed his fingers on the car's low roof, an impatient tattoo counterpointed by the rhythmic lapping of the freezing water beneath the wharf. The cold didn't bother him much—even dressed only in jeans and a Metz hoodie; Jack had lived on the Rock his entire life and had felt it a hell of a lot colder.

"Please . . . ," a voice wobbled from inside the car. Edged with raw fear, it was a good octave and change higher than a grown man's really ought to be. Sniffing the air, Jack figured his passenger—a scarecrow of a guy so tall his knees had been pressed up under his chin in the back seat of the car—had pissed his pants. Wasn't his car, so it hardly mattered.

The Beemer, one of countless others like it in the city, was rendered all but invisible by its ubiquity. That made it the perfect vehicle for the job; no one would give so much as a second glance at the twelve-year-old three-piece suit of a car. Being a two-door, it was ideal for transporting reluctant passengers. Even with their hands zip-tied behind their backs, there was a chance they'd manage to wriggle free. In a coupe, there'd be no heroic yanking open the door to take their chances out on the Verrazzano-Narrows Bridge.

Jack was damned if he was going to let *that* happen again.

Scarecrow guy was shaking his head and mouthing the word "no" over and over. Jack sighed, reached into the car, caught the guy by the upper arm, and pulled. Jack may have looked slight and even boyish, but he was wiry and strong. Scarecrow came tumbling out of the car and onto the damp, freezing tarmac. Jack shoved him up against the side of the Beemer with enough force to rock the car. The guy let out a bleat of pain that pierced Jack's sensitive ears. A gag next time, for sure.

In many ways the whole sorry business went against his grain. He told himself it was payback for all the guys who'd made fun of his lack of bulk and his bull terrier persona. When you carried a gun, no one made fun of you. He had a gun—a company-issued Springfield XD-S. He pressed the muzzle hard against the Scarecrow's temple.

"Sounds like the party's started without you," he told him. "We should hurry."

He used his free hand to pull his switchblade and took some satisfaction as the skinny guy flinched and shuffled sideways on his bony ass. Jack reached behind him and used the blade to slice through the zip tie that bound the skinny wrists together; he figured he might as well afford the guy a little dignity . . . and there was nowhere for him to run.

"You've got some talking to do," Jack growled as he pulled his captive up off the ground by one gangly arm. He gave him a hard shove in the direction of the screaming.

The guy staggered, almost fell over, then limped on through a gap between a Gator and a mini excavator. "I have money—"

"Of course you do. *Other* people's money. That's what got you into this shit show in the first place."

He shoved the guy again and saw his head turn slightly to the right. Was he seriously considering making a break for it?

"I wouldn't," Jack cautioned. "Unless you think you can outrun a .22 slug. Can you?"

Scarecrow shook his head.

They rounded the corner of a spacious white equipment shed where a large wooden sign declared We Take Pride in Your Ride. Jack liked the irony in that. Beyond, between two warehouses, was a small empty courtyard. The equipment had been moved aside to create a space maybe twenty by twenty feet. An untidy array of camping lanterns, set up especially for the occasion, gave off a sickly, flickering yellow glow that made the two men already there appear jaundiced.

The tall guy gasped as his eyes lit on the middle-aged tubby white guy on the ground. Tubby wore an identical suit to the Scarecrow's, along with handmade tan brogues; he was spattered with blood, chunks of his own vomit, and dirt from the ground. A look of abject horror drained any remaining color from the tall guy's face.

"Oh, God. What the fuck did you *do* to him?"

Tubby's tormentor, Leo Rossi, was a squat, broad-shouldered man with a day's worth of dark stubble on his chin. Ignoring the question, he greeted his associate with a courteous nod.

"Giacomo."

"Hey, Leo. Sorry we're late."

"Just the one?" Rossi gave a cursory nod in the tall guy's direction and waved hello with a thirty-inch length of rebar he held in his left hand.

"Yeah. But we got two out of the four. That's fifty percent." Jack pointed at the fat guy. "He talked yet?"

"No. He says he has no idea where the others are."

"Fuck."

"Exactly. I guess we have to keep trying, though."

With a grunt, Rossi swung the rebar in an arc over his head. The thin metal sliced through the air with an audible *whoosh* and connected hard with the fat guy's arm, which was held defensively in front of his broken face. The iron bar connected with a sickening thud.

Tubby screamed and squirmed on the ground, snot bubbling from his nose. "Will you fucking stop doing that? I don't know *shit*!" Nursing his wounded arm close to his body, the man sounded more angry than hurt.

Wishing he'd worn ear plugs, Jack looked down his nose at the guy. He was in a bad way, his navy-blue suit daubed with rust, dirt, blood, and God knew what else the guy had excreted. He'd taken his beating well, way better than Leo Rossi might give him credit for.

Aside from the possibly broken arm, Rossi had obviously done other major damage to the guy's bodily integrity. In Jack's experience, these business types usually sniveled a hell of a lot more than this and sang like the proverbial canary long before things really got serious—maybe the man honestly, *genuinely* didn't know where his errant colleagues had gone.

So, maybe his partner in crime would spill the beans? Jack had picked him up from LaGuardia, all packed and ready to go. The poor guy had almost made the plane to Belize when Jack had caught up with him and bundled his skinny ass into the BMW. Up until that moment, he'd most likely thought he was home safe.

Neither D'Angelo nor Rossi knew the suits personally. They'd been given the guys' names and where they would most likely be found. They didn't much care who they were; the brief had been to round them up and use whatever means necessary to locate the third and fourth members of their quartet of scammers—those were the two the Vaccarelli mobsters *really* wanted. These guys were basically junior associates. Although this pair had been complicit in duping the Family out of a hefty slice of their admittedly ill-gotten gains, there was a specific, more personal beef with their ringleaders that neither Rossi nor D'Angelo knew much about. It was, as was always the case with the Vaccarellis, strictly on a need-to-know basis. And neither D'Angelo nor Rossi needed to know. They were paid well to do as they were told, keep their noses out of the boss's business, and seal their mouths shut.

Even so, it grated on Jack D'Angelo to be stuck out there on the wharf this late at night, especially for less than these motherfuckers made in an hour from the poor schmucks they suckered into their investment scams. He'd heard tidbits about the scam the Vaccarellis had fallen for—everybody on the island had. Some of it had even made the papers. He'd read how some had lost it all to these sharks and killed themselves, so fucking poor at the end they'd jumped in the bay so their families could collect on their life insurance. Some were fished out almost immediately, ashamed but alive, while some succumbed to the icy waters and washed up on Governors Island or

Red Hook days later. Others were never seen again. The Vaccarellis, though, they had resources—not as many as they'd once had, but enough to strike back.

Or rather, pay muscle to strike back for them.

"You." Rossi was pointing the rebar at Scarecrow. "Where the fuck did they disappear to?"

"Who?"

"Who? Penn and Teller, you miserable son of a bitch. You damn well know who. Your partners in crime."

"I don't know." Eyes never leaving that metal bar, Scarecrow trembled, and his words trembled with him. "*Honestly*, we really don't know where they've gone. Neither of them even told us they were going, just that our part in it was over. We hardly saw them face-to-face; it was all phone calls. We're just the hired help, man. Like you."

Like us? Like hell. Jack gave the Scarecrow another shove. He staggered forward to where his overweight colleague lay sobbing and bleeding.

"Take a good look at your buddy, Mr. Scarecrow. You wanna end up like that, do you?"

The guy's Adam's apple bobbed as he considered that. "Look, here's what I know . . . and it's *all* I know. One of them is a local guy —he lives somewhere on the Rock. He may still be here. I think he's got family."

"If he's still around, we'll pick him up later," Jack told him; finally, they were getting somewhere. "What about the other one?"

The tall guy shook his head. "I don't know. I only met him a couple of times—all I know is he's some bald-headed Chink; we weren't even given his name. He was just—"

Rossi gave the rebar a casual swing. The thin metal connected with the side of the guy's head and he crumpled like somebody took the bones out of his legs. He collapsed next to his partner, trying in vain to stem the steady flow of blood from his split temple.

Jack jumped. "Christ, Leo! If you knock him out, he can't tell us a damn thing!" Sometimes he thought Rossi's muscles lay mostly between his ears.

Rossi ignored him and snarled at the Scarecrow. "Where's this Chinese guy?"

"*We don't fucking know*! If we did, we would've told you already!" He was sobbing now. "He's out of the country by now; probably went back to China."

Jack shrugged his taut shoulders and studied the guy. Odds were, he was telling the truth. Scammers who did this sort of shit weren't long on loyalty. Both these guys knew they'd been abandoned by their "partners"; it was doubtful they'd be keen on protecting them. Which meant this had been a fucking wasted evening. *I could've been watching basketball.*

"Leo," Jack said. "They don't know shit. They're just scapegoats. A couple of unlucky bastards left behind to keep us busy while their 'partners' take the gate."

Having given up trying to stop the blood pouring down the side of his head, the tall guy looked up with a spark of hope in his eyes. "That's what I've been trying to tell you. We got shit on, just like whoever hired you to . . . to do this."

Jack squatted, putting him at eye level with the guy. "Okay. So let's all calm down here, and you tell us where you think your 'Chink' partner might've gone. That's highly pejorative, by the way. Racist, in fact. I mean, you wouldn't call Rossi and me *paisanos*, right? 'Cause that would be rude."

"I . . . I . . . I . . . no, I . . . I wouldn't. But this guy—"

"Regardless," said Jack quietly. "If you're gonna call him names, call him a lying, cheating son of a bitch, not a Chink."

Scarecrow nodded, his eyes never leaving Jack's face.

"Now, think. You must have ideas about where someone like him would run to. Something he said. Something you saw."

"What the fuck, Jack?" Rossi was getting seriously impatient. He lifted the rebar again.

Jack held up a hand to stop him, holding the Scarecrow's gaze. "You worked with the cocksucker long enough—he's got to have a bolt hole."

"Um, uh, yeah. I'm sure he does."

"And?"

"Probably, most likely Shanghai, or Singapore, or maybe Hong Kong. He talked about Hong Kong like he knew it pretty well."

"Mr. Vaccarelli is not going to be too happy about this," Rossi grumbled.

"No, he's not."

Jack wasn't too happy about it either. If all they got was Shanghai, Singapore, or Hong Kong, there wasn't likely to be another payday. Vaccarelli no longer had the resources for a global search-and-destroy mission, not after the fleecing his businesses had just received. It could take decades to claw the Family's fortune back to where it had been.

So.

Jack stood, lifted his pistol, and fired two quick shots—one to the head of each scapegoat. Neither even saw it coming.

Rossi glowered at him. "Fuckin' asshole. What'd you do that for? I was gonna—"

"Yeah, you were gonna." Jack slipped the Springfield into his waistband. "I don't want to waste the rest of my evening, Leo. C'mon. We get this over quick, I can get home in time to catch the last quarter."

Jack figured Mr. Vaccarelli would at least gain some satisfaction that two out of the four who'd played him for a chump in full view of the other Families had gotten what was coming to them; he was confident that if the local guy was still in New York, he and Rossi would catch up with him soon enough. Maybe they'd get a bonus for that.

Scarecrow was still twitching when they carried him to the BMW and strapped him into the passenger seat. It could have just been nerves firing—that happened sometimes—or he could have still been alive. Jack didn't care; the bay would finish the job he and Rossi had started. They stuffed Tubby in behind the steering wheel, having to push the driver's seat back to accommodate his gut.

Finally, they opened all the windows, popped the parking brake, put the car in neutral, and pushed it off the wharf. It hit with a satisfying splash and a blossom of air bubbles. With the windows open, it wouldn't take long before Tubby and the Scarecrow became part of the ecosystem—nibbled on by fish and crabs. Possibly at some point, bits of them would float to the surface to act as a stern warning not to mess with the Vaccarellis. The bay would make sure there'd be no trace of D'Angelo and Rossi. No fingerprints, no DNA, as *everything* was going in the water after the suits—the bloodied rebar, the guns, the whole fucking lot.

"Want a ride home?" Rossi asked as they watched the last bubbles from the sunken Beemer breach the surface.

"Naw, I'll catch a cab."

"Yeah? An actual cab, or a jitney?"

"I don't do jitneys. They don't call those sons of bitches pirate cabs for nothing. They're killing the cabbies, Leo. Killing 'em."

CHAPTER ONE

Ten Years Later – Hong Kong

She was going to be late.

Valentina's father had given her a mantra: *if you're not early, you're late.* He'd lived by it, and he'd died by it. She'd never been a minute late in her entire life—hell, she'd even been born two weeks early.

She'd been informed the meeting was to be at eight sharp that Friday morning—she had ten minutes—and there'd be someone waiting for her in the main reception area of Two International Finance Center, or 2IFC as she'd learned the locals referred to it. As she hurried down the street, the red heels of her ludicrously expensive, vertiginous pumps reflecting the early morning light, Valentina knew damn well she was not going to be early.

So, this was Finance Street. Six lanes wide, lined by soaring, glass-fronted buildings, and clogged with traffic—it felt almost like home to a native New Yorker. Even the rowdy mass of placard-waving, pro-democracy protesters taking up much of the sidewalk in front of 2IFC seemed to add to the New York feel of the place. Valentina's internet research had prepared her for the protests, although she'd read they were no longer the peaceful affairs they'd started out as. People were getting seriously hurt as the growing swell of anti-Chinese sentiment became a riptide. The police were far less tolerant than they'd been in the early days of unrest.

Ahead, representing some of the most expensive real estate on the planet, the two towers of the International Finance Center rose high above the street; a pair of monstrous steel and glass constructions, they were a shiny, ostentatious testimony to pure greed and the absolute power of money.

Dressed to impress, Valentina had opted to wear her best Chanel pantsuit. It was dark blue, but not too somber, flattered her trim shape, and had cost a small fortune—especially as she'd paired it with a white, pure silk blouse and accessorized it with a trim Gucci crossbody purse. Beneath she wore silk Stella McCartney underwear. She got a kick out of wearing Brazilian briefs designed by the offspring of a Beatle.

The strategically selected ensemble had cost her more than she'd paid for her first car—an old, battered, three-door Jeep that had refused point blank to start whenever the temperature dipped below thirty-five. Now that she was the top earner in her New York office, the outfit had put barely a dent in her bank balance. Valentina filled her clothes well —five-six in her bare feet, her curvy, gym-toned figure was a perfect complement to the exquisitely cut suit, and she carried the whole professional-chic look with confidence to spare. With her chestnut, shoulder-length hair, flawless olive skin, and deep brown eyes, Valentina Vittorio couldn't have better represented her Italian-American roots if she'd tried.

The working day began early in the city, and although it was not yet eight, the streets were alive and bustling. The temperature was already in the mideighties and sticky, but Valentina caught nothing more than the sweet scents of clean bodies, fragrant soaps, and colognes—a refreshing change from the stale aroma of the disheveled and unwashed back in New York.

Valentina had stepped off the nonstop flight from JFK earlier that morning, but it felt like a lifetime ago. She was lodged at the Four

Seasons, which was the next tower along from the IFC, and connected by a curved, glass-covered walkway. She'd checked into the plush twelfth-floor suite the company had booked for her, grabbed a quick shower, and slipped into her power suit. Mercifully, she was not prone to jet lag. She'd decided to enter IFC from the street level rather than taking the walkway. Hence, her self-created time crunch. A miscalculation on her part—one she vowed not to repeat.

The trip had been very last minute. She'd received a call from Mai Lin in Human Resources at the head office a little under a week ago. Ms. Lin had advised Valentina she'd been summoned to Hong Kong to work on a brand-new initiative headed by Mr. Jimmy Wen himself, for which her exceptional aptitude as a salesperson renowned for bringing in lucrative new clients was much needed. The trip had also been very hush-hush; she wasn't to breathe a single word to any of her colleagues at the Wall Street office, nor speak of it to her family or friends.

Ms. Lin had gone on to make it crystal clear to Valentina this was not a polite request or a job offer to be considered—she was to hand her portfolio over to her New York team, discreetly sort out her personal affairs, and be at JFK airport with her bags packed in six days.

Valentina had been hoping for such a call for a long time. It was what she'd been angling for, the culmination of her ten-year plan. She'd spent a decade working her way up through the ranks in investment banks and stock brokerages, manipulating everyone of use around her, and all for the sole purpose of pinging Jimmy Wen's radar. Valentina's ruthless prowess on the sales floor, her instinct for big money, had earned her a formidable reputation even before she joined the ranks of JM Wen Limited's Wall Street office. Now Wen had summoned her to the inner sanctum of his Hong Kong headquarters.

She was elated. She was triumphant. She was filled with grim purpose. Her visitor status gave her ninety days in Hong Kong, which she told herself would be more than enough time to do what she'd come here to do.

She was also vaguely uneasy. She had no idea how, but JM Wen Limited had either managed to have her visa application fast-tracked or had begun the process some time before requesting her presence in

Hong Kong. Her new documents had simply appeared in her mailbox, and they'd used the photograph she'd had taken upon joining Wen's Wall Street office a little over six months before. That pricked her well-honed sense of suspicion. She'd wanted to attract Wen's attention, but now that she had it, she was wary of her own success.

She shook herself free of the irrational unease and gave her watch a quick glance. In a few minutes she would be *officially* late. She quickened her step the best she could, given the busy street and the height of her heels, and wove through the tiny gaps in the crowd. The last obstacle between her and the gleaming glass-and-steel facade of 2IFC was the crowd of protesters that had accumulated on the sidewalk right outside the entrance to IFC Mall, the upscale shopping destination that spanned the long block between 2IFC and the Four Seasons.

The protestors jostled and shoved her, as if actively to prevent her from reaching the mall entrance. A man, his face crimson with anger or zeal, thrust a placard into her face and screamed at her in his native tongue. She'd studied Cantonese enough to get the gist of it: She was feeding the demon, heedless of the innocent lives it destroyed.

Can't be helped.

Reflexively, barely breaking her stride, Valentina grasped the man's elbow, curled a foot around his ankle, and surreptitiously winged his shoulder with her own. Arms flailing, the protester toppled among his compatriots. Valentina knew she would be safely inside the mall before they got him back to his feet. She reached the mall's main doors and strode through them. It was precisely five minutes to eight. A left turn past the mall's oval atrium and a walk down the gleaming concourse brought her at last to the Level 1 lobby of 2IFC.

The lobby was opulent, its polished surfaces gleaming with morning sunlight and indirect light from overhead fixtures. A pair of long receptionists' desks were positioned along the curving rear wall of the huge room. Over each one hung a huge flat-screen TV displaying the suite and floor addresses of the occupants. Glancing up at the display over the rightmost desk, Valentina found JM Wen International on the menu with floor number and an arrow directing her toward the elevator bank to her right. She'd been issued a visitor's pass by mail, courtesy of Mai Lin, so at least she wouldn't need to get one at reception.

Turning toward the elevators, she paused in momentary consternation. Between her and the elevators was a security check complete with metal detectors and a half-dozen security guards in beige uniforms and blue, peaked caps. They formed a human barrier as they busily rummaged through briefcases, purses, and backpacks. A few even had disgruntled businessmen turning out the contents of their pockets into gray plastic trays. Some, they beckoned straight through the checkpoint with a nod and a smile—no doubt the same faces they saw day in, day out, and knew they could trust. Valentina hoped she'd soon be one of those. She sighed and joined the short queue.

"Next, please."

One of the security guards beckoned Valentina with a cursory nod toward her purse. His round baby face sported the fuzzy beginnings of a moustache and an absent half smile. Valentina stepped through the metal detectors, slipped her purse's thin strap from her shoulder, and held it in her hands. She hated the intrusion of bag searches with a passion, but having grown up in post-9/11 New York, security searches had become just another part of everyday life. She sighed again and stepped forward to put her purse on the guard's table.

Where's the damn cavalry when you need 'em?

"That won't be necessary. Miss Vittorio is with *me*."

Right on cue. Exactly as the officious Mai Lin from HR had promised, one of JM Wen's myriad executive assistants had arrived to greet her. The young woman wore the seemingly standard uniform for Hong Kong's women of business: black, formal blazer with matching midthigh skirt, plain white shirt with a modest V-neck, white hose, black patent shoes with heels that were barely an inch and a half tall, and an air of determined efficiency.

The guard grunted and peered at Valentina and her expensive purse. With a shrug, he waved her through. She thought he looked disappointed.

"Anita Kwok." The young assistant stuck out a hand as a formal greeting. "Welcome to Hong Kong, Miss Vittorio. I apologize for the additional security, but I'm sure you can appreciate the need, given the political situation."

Valentina firmly shook the woman's hand. It felt small, smooth, and dry in hers. "Valentina, please. And, I understand completely. Thank you for rescuing me from the indignity."

Anita wore her iridescent black hair in a precisely trimmed bob, which was a perfect frame to a round face almost devoid of makeup—nothing more than a breath of powder and a lick of pale pink lipstick covered her flawless, milky skin or touched her lips. Valentina had to admit to an atom or two of envy.

"Your reputation precedes you, Miss Vittorio," Anita said with a smile. "JM Wen Limited needs your expertise. We are expecting great things from you."

She ushered Valentina to the elevators, playing tour guide with relish. "We are housed in one of the few buildings in the world to have double-deck elevators. We have eighty-eight stories and twenty-two high-ceiling trading floors—in Cantonese culture we believe those numbers bring luck and prosperity."

Valentina nodded and did her best to soak it all in. She was accustomed to the grand trappings of high-end business and money to burn, but this really was something else—the luck and prosperity thing was clearly working a charm. The offices of JM Wen International occupied most of the fifty-second floor of 2IFC—not quite as impressive as the Hong Kong Monetary Authority, which had the entire fifty-fifth and fifty-sixty floors, along with the seventy-seventh to eighty-eighth, all to themselves—but impressive, all the same.

With a French-manicured thumbnail, Anita pressed the call button by the elevator doors. The elevator arrived in the blink of an eye, and they stepped in. With them came half a dozen businessmen, none of whom so much as acknowledged their presence, or even one another's. Anita selected their floor and stood in silence as the elevator began to move.

A small TV screen in the corner held the attention of the elevator's inhabitants, including Anita Kwok. Whether because the business news and accompanying stock prices scrolling across the bottom were especially captivating or the screen made for a good excuse to not interact with fellow passengers was difficult to tell. Valentina guessed both, from what she'd researched about Hong Kong culture.

The top right corner of the screen showed rapidly ascending numbers as the elevator made its way smoothly upward—so smoothly, in fact, that if not for those numbers, it would have been virtually impossible to tell the elevator was moving at all.

The doors slid open at the thirteenth floor. A pleasantly polite feminine voice informed the occupants of the fact in English and Cantonese, and a handful of the silent businessmen got out. They were immediately replaced by four similarly dressed, equally stern-faced men; they didn't appear too big on gender equality at 2IFC, Valentina noted, as she'd only seen a handful of women so far. Moments later, the elevator stopped again, one floor up. The screen and the voice let the occupants know they'd arrived at the fifteenth floor. No one got out. Three young men stepped in. As they did so, the conversation died on their lips.

"There's no fourteenth floor?" Valentina asked as the doors closed and the elevator commenced its upward journey.

Anita shot her a withering look and made a soft noise that was barely audible enough for Valentina to get the message. Had she just been *shushed* by an office assistant? First impressions being what they were, Valentina didn't press the point.

"It is not polite to speak in the elevator," Anita explained the moment they alighted on the fifty-second floor. "It is not only out of respect for our fellow passengers, but on a more practical level, it is to maintain the privacy of the companies they work for—the walls have *ears*, Miss Vittorio."

Valentina didn't appreciate the scolding, schoolmarmish tone to her voice, but the old wartime cliché and the harsh sound of her surname had her stifling a laugh. She could be irked by the delightfully impish Miss Kwok or she could be amused. She chose to be amused.

"There is no fourteenth floor"—Anita slipped with ease back into tour guide mode with a smile—"just as there is no fourth, twenty-fourth, and so on."

Valentina smiled wryly. "I get it. In the US there are still hotels and offices without a thirteenth floor. I imagine it's the same deal. Superstition." Her mother had been an incredibly superstitious woman even before her breakdown. After, she'd obsessively covered the mirrors in her room and avoided stepping on cracks in the sidewalk to protect against demonic intrusion. Crossing herself amounted to a nervous tic.

"I imagine it is," Anita agreed, and scooted off down the broad, carpeted hallway with a speed that barely seemed possible in such a tight skirt. Valentina, although the taller of the two by a good five inches or so and with considerably longer legs, found herself struggling to keep up.

"In Cantonese," added Anita, "we pronounce the number four in a similar way to how we say *death*."

Ah. And she'd said the no-no out loud in the elevator. Hence the discourteous shushing; Valentina had broken a whole shopping list of taboos in that one, single sentence.

Learn to read the room, Tina, she told herself, and apologized with a modicum of sincerity.

"And here we are." Anita came to a sudden halt in front of a wide frosted glass door. At eye level, in gold leaf, was the company name: JM Wen International Asset Management Limited. Next to it, also in gold leaf, was a stylized golden lion.

Valentina's perky guide pushed open the doors, allowing a cacophony of voices and ringing telephones to pour out—JM Wen's working day had already begun. She escorted Valentina down a long hallway with red granite floors lined with offices and meeting rooms. More hallways abutted this one and went off in directions unknown. Mercifully, there were frequent directional signs for the uninitiated.

Anita stopped before another thick frosted glass door with a handle of anodized metal. Meeting Room 3, an etched, anodized steel plaque proclaimed.

"You'll be waiting in here with the others," she explained as she opened the door. "I'll introduce you, and you can get yourself something to eat. I'm sure you're quite hungry, Miss Vittorio. You couldn't have had much time for breakfast."

"Others?" Valentina paused on the threshold. She tried her best not to sound put out; she'd gotten the impression from Mai Lin that her summoning to Hong Kong was unique.

"That's right."

Without further explanation, Anita ushered Valentina into the meeting room. A long teak table surrounded by two dozen high-backed chairs with padded red seats dominated the room. The table was filled at one end with urns of coffee and milk tea, a variety of fruit juices, mineral water, and a breakfast buffet that seemed excessive given that there were only six other people in the meeting room—all in power suits, all looking incredibly young, dynamic, and ambitious. All six turned in eerie unison to assess the newcomer.

Yeah, that's right. Take a good look at the competition.

Faced with the openly appraising gazes, Valentina clamped her teeth together, set her smile, straightened her back, and strode across the room with confidence oozing from every pore.

CHAPTER TWO

"This is Miss Vittorio. She's from the Wall Street office." Anita Kwok handled the introduction with an efficiency of words that Valentina was certain was a hallmark.

"Valentina, please." She had the distinct feeling she'd be getting tired of repeating that before the day was out. Smiling, she held out her hand for the shaking.

"Oliver Michaels, London office." The Brit's handshake was firm. His clipped accent had a trace of the northern parts of his home country, which gave him an ever-so-slightly Scottish lilt. He was tall, an easy six-two/six-three, with broad shoulders, neat blond hair, and bright blue eyes that sparkled in the full-spectrum fluorescent light.

"Pleased to meet you, Oliver." Polite, professional.

Anita extricated Valentina from the strong, handsome hand of Mr. Michaels and introduced her in turn to Anthony Li from the Shanghai office, Nadim Singh from Bangkok, Daylen Ng from Singapore, Sofia Reller from Geneva, and Chun Yeung Lam who had, apparently, traveled all the way from the main sales floor along JM Wen Limited's central hallway. That admission on his part was met with polite chuckles from the others.

Valentina smiled, nodded, and asked everyone to please call her by her first name, and repeated theirs to help lodge them in her memory as hands were shaken, new associates weighed up, and snap judgments made.

Her task of escorting Valentina completed, Anita smiled and looked over the group like a beneficent mother duck. "You have each been appointed one of the corporate partners, who will familiarize you with everything," she told them. "They will be along to collect you after you've had time to eat something." With that, the ever-efficient Anita Kwok bid a curt but professional goodbye to everyone in the room and disappeared into the hallway.

"So . . . New York?" Oliver Michaels smiled at Valentina and gave her an obvious once-over. "It's always nice to meet people from our former colonies."

Lam pretended to take offense. "Hey! He's said that about every-body except Sofia. You'd think the Brits would keep mum about losing their entire empire in just over a century. But no, they insist on pointing it out to all and sundry like it was some badge of honor. A guy goes to Oxford and he thinks he's something special!" He winked at Valentina and gave Oliver a hearty clap on the shoulder.

"Cambridge, actually." Oliver wrinkled his nose as if the very notion of attending Oxford University offended him. "Peterhouse College—the oldest and the best. I graduated with first class honors in finance and economics; then I cut my teeth with Brevan Howard."

"Impressive," Valentina admitted. Brevan Howard was the biggest hedge fund manager in Europe and had ridiculously high recruitment standards—it appeared she was not the only overachieving high roller in the room . . . and, although she was reluctant to acknowledge it, that irked Valentina Vittorio more than a little. It irked her that it irked her. If these people were her competition for a slot at JM Wen, she needed to possess enough self-confidence that their stellar pedigrees didn't annoy her. She had to be stronger than that. *Better* than that.

A consistent overachiever throughout her whole life, Valentina had grown accustomed to being the top dog in absolutely everything she ever turned her hand to, and the best among every group she found herself in, be it at school or work. She'd juggled two jobs to put herself through school and gone on to graduate summa cum laude in finance and business from New York University's Stern School of Business.

Then, with her mind ever focused on her ultimate objective of getting close to Jimmy Wen, she'd hustled her bachelor's degree around Wall Street to land the base-level job that would provide her first step into the financial sector. She'd worked her way up from stockbroker to ultra-high-net-worth private banking and on to institutional sales—all within an almost unprecedented two years. From there, she'd climbed the corporate ladder with equal ferocity, and didn't think twice about switching companies if opportunities for advancement hadn't presented themselves soon enough where she was. Valentina had learned quickly that there was no room for sentimentality or loyalty in the fast-moving world of high finance.

That had taken some getting used to. Initially, in Valentina's mind there were two kinds of people in the financial realm: honest players who were above reproach and responsible, and bad actors who scammed and connived and ruined people's lives. It hadn't taken her long to realize how naive that was and that there were no ones and zeroes, only fractions of honesty or dishonesty. No black or white, only varying shades of gray. Not a problem. She could work with that, and she had.

Consequently, Valentina Vittorio had become one of the youngest investment banking associate directors in New York, and one of an embarrassingly low number of women in that position. Never one to let the grass grow beneath her feet, she'd landed a post with Goldman Sachs at junior director level, and had stayed there as one of the top earners until she made a not-quite-lateral move to JM Wen Limited's Wall Street office.

She did not, she told herself, have to feel out of her depth in Hong Kong—even among such obviously accomplished people as the ones she shared this room with.

Valentina fixed herself a milk tea and made an effort to make small talk with her new colleagues. They were all engaged in the same dance: sizing each other up, wondering if they were to be colleagues or competition. She learned the other six had also been summoned to

Hong Kong by a phone call from Mai Lin in HR less than a week ago. All had been sworn to secrecy. Clearly, it was their ability to reel in lucrative new clients that had earned them such a prestigious opportunity. Every one of them had dropped everything to be here; when one's presence was requested by Mr. Wen himself, it was an offer impossible to refuse.

As Daylen Ng strove unsuccessfully to impress Nadim Singh with having made over twenty mil in the past year, and Nadim riposted with having landed the biggest client in the Singapore office's entire history, Sofia Reller sidled up to Valentina and purred in her rich European accent, "So . . . how about you, Valentina? You must have done something *really* impressive in New York to land yourself among such a gifted group."

Valentina caught the satirical gleam in the other woman's eye, and read her struggle in every elegant line of her face. Sofia, too, had forged her way, sans dick, through a world in which having the biggest dick was the whole point. Valentina gave her a knowing smile.

"I've had more than my fair share of success," she said. "I'm just very good at this. Apparently, you are too."

"Let's be honest," said Sofia, tilting a glance toward the men, who'd clustered near the coffee urn. "We've had to be extraordinarily good at our jobs in order to be here." She offered Valentina a wink, then turned to the group of males and asked, "So, Lam, are the rumors true?"

"Rumors?" Chun Yeung Lam continued constructing a sandwich with toast and a goodly amount of scrambled eggs.

Sofia gave a throaty chuckle. "Don't play coy with me. You know what I mean."

"She means the rumors about Jimmy Wen," Anthony Li chipped in. "They're all over the Shanghai office."

Sofia gave Anthony a high-five smile, then turned her attention back to Lam. "You've worked here how many years now? Three, four?"

"Three and a half."

"Then you *must* know. The rumors about this place and Jimmy Wen. It's not just Shanghai. They're all over the Geneva office too."

Valentina was fascinated. Which rumors was the Swiss talking about? She hadn't heard any particular rumors about Jimmy Wen in New York. She moved to where she could see the expression on Lam's face better and plucked a small white bowl from the stack at the end of the table, making business out of filling it with scrambled eggs.

Lam shook his head. "Frivolous gossip is not something that is encouraged at JM Wen." He sounded as if he were reading lines directly from the corporate manual.

"Frivolous? Is that what you call it? Since when is doing business with the Triads merely frivolous? It could certainly account for JM Wen's staggering success."

Valentina leaned a hip against the table and considered the tableau. Sofia's smile might have softened her pointed questions, but Lam still looked as if he were taken aback by the woman's bluntness. Sofia was demonstrating the point they'd briefly discussed: how to succeed without a dick in a world that was full of them. It would certainly not be unheard of for a business man of Jimmy Wen's ilk to have some dealings with the Chinese gangs. In fact, Valentina would have been surprised if he *hadn't* been involved with them in some way. Still, she gave the conversation her full attention; any knowledge that might provide an edge for her own agenda would be welcome. With knowledge came power—another one of her father's favorite sayings.

"I'm sorry, but I can't help you." Lam raised the meticulously assembled sandwich to his mouth in a clear indication that he was checking out of the conversation. "Gossip is—"

"Not encouraged here, yes, I heard you the first time." Sofia shrugged, gave Valentina a wry glance, and moved to freshen her milk tea. "It's not as if anyone can *hear* us."

Lam bit into his sandwich and chewed, seemingly at ease, but Valentina caught the furtive shift of his eyes, a subtle twitch as they darted to the corners of the room. As if he were looking for something.

"Do you think the room is bugged?" she asked him. "Really? Would Jimmy Wen do that?"

Daylen Ng voiced what they were all thinking. "Wouldn't you?"

Valentina nibbled at her eggs and studied Lam, wondering if Wen really did bug his offices or if that was one of those rumors intended to keep loose lips from sinking morale, solidarity, and important business deals. If it were true—if the offices were bugged—Valentina was going to have to be more careful than she already tended to be.

The door to Meeting Room 3 opened, making everyone jump. The atmosphere, heightened by Sofia's ignition of Big Brother paranoia, seemed to have jangled their collective nerves. Valentina took a bit of comfort in the idea that she wasn't the only one who now had the yips.

"Jeez! Who died? I'd have expected a room filled with the company's *crème de la crème* to be a hell of a lot livelier than this!"

The words were delivered in a broad Australian accent; the obviously Asian guy who'd uttered them stormed into the room like he owned it. In an instant, the attention of the new recruits was his, and his alone. He pushed his rolled-up shirtsleeves over his elbows and straightened the burgundy silk tie that was the perfect complement to his pale blue shirt. He smiled at the seven gathered before him, but his eyes settled on Valentina.

"Ms. Vittorio." His tone suggested that if her name had *not* been Ms. Vittorio, she would be expected to change it on the spot. He strode over, his taut, muscular arm outstretched, grasped Valentina's offered hand, and pumped it with enthusiasm. "Lucas Vaughn. Please call me Lucas. It's good to finally get to meet you. Seems like you drew the short straw—you're stuck with me as your allocated mentor for the duration. If you would come with me, please."

Smiling, Lucas led her toward the open door.

CHAPTER THREE

"Chinese Australian, in case you're wondering," Lucas said as they made their way along the gleaming hallway.

Valentina noticed something she hadn't before, that every tile on the floor was inlaid with the company logo—the initials JMW with a tiny lion resting on top of the W.

"I went to high school and Uni in Oz—my mum was originally from the Jiangsu Province, and the old man grew up in the Northern Territory. He's your typical corks 'round the slouch hat, wifebeater-wearing, croc-wrestling, sheep farmer type—the whole fuckin' Aussie cliché in one beer-swilling package!" Lucas cracked a self-conscious smile, which showed off perfect pearly whites. "Jeez, if Mum heard me swearing like that, she'd have my guts for garters! It's the Australian genes, I just can't help myself. Hell, if she heard half of what came out of my mouth, she'd fucking kill me! Mum always told me that Chinese don't swear for fear of offending or losing face. Imagine my surprise to discover my mum had led a sheltered life out in the Province." He let out a low, rumbling laugh.

"I'll be sure to watch my Yankee potty mouth anyway," Valentina said with a conspiratorial smile. "And please, it's Valentina."

Lucas paused at a frosted glass door—there seemed to be a hell of a lot of those about the place. "You may just find me calling you Val, then. I hope that doesn't cause offense—you'll find me one of the less reserved ones around here; being from Oz gives me the perfect excuse." He opened the door and made a big show of doing the whole ladies-first thing.

The noise hit Valentina first. It was followed by a warm wave of nostalgia. She recognized the trading floor immediately—that riotous cacophony of phones and voices and movement. The room was vast, with not a supporting pillar to be seen, and was furnished with row upon row of gleaming white desks. There were a hundred or so traders crammed into the place, each with their own workspace, a phone, and a bank of twelve monitors stacked in columns of three—each one logged into business sites, industry blogs, streaming news channels, and active stock market feeds from around the world.

There was a distinct lack of paper; this was a modern trading floor, after all. The far wall of the room was home to a vast bank of giant TV screens. Each one showed the same feeds as those on the desks, plus global news—the sales guys and girls at JM Wen Limited were kept incredibly well informed.

As if sensing her nostalgia, Lucas grinned a cheesy grin as he led Valentina across the trading floor. "Yeah, I miss it a bit too. I put my time in over in Singapore's sales floors—a long time before Mr. Wen moved me out here."

Valentina nodded. She'd put in more than her own fair share of time in Wall Street's trading pits—far more, in fact, than any of the male counterparts she'd consistently outperformed day in, day out. She'd fought every single hour of every single day in that segregated, testosterone-fueled world—fought goddamned hard to be recognized as more than the cute Guidette in the expensive heels that everyone from the weed-addicted janitor to the CEO wanted to slip it to.

. "We were quite surprised when you first approached us," Lucas said as they slipped unnoticed from the trading floor. "You had a glittering career ahead of you with Goldman."

There was a question in the man's statement, and it put Valentina's guard up. "I like to move around," she told him.

"There's more opportunities if you don't let the grass grow?"

"Exactly."

"Mr. Wen was most impressed with how you handled the Kalso-Moore deal," Vaughn said as they left the hubbub of the trading floor well behind them. "Very few could have pulled that whole cluster-fuck together as well as you did."

Taken aback, Valentina opted to play it cool. She'd brokered the Kalso-Moore deal during her time at Apollo Global Management; only a select handful of people in the private equity firm had known, and—so far as Valentina knew—absolutely no one outside of it. It had been a hostile takeover of epic proportions, with involvement from South Africa and the UAE, both of which had come with their own catalog of issues, compounded by the fact that more than one arm of Kalso-Moore was heavily involved in the arms trade.

The deal had earned Apollo hundreds of millions in commissions and fees, along with ongoing residuals that were still being reaped, and would be for decades to come. It had also sealed Valentina's reputation as a rainmaker, and afforded her an almost legendary status. She was offered the keys to the kingdom by Leon Black himself—she could have literally written her own paycheck. Instead, Valentina had chosen to jump ship and start all over again at Goldman Sachs; she had a long-term plan that she was hell-bent on sticking to.

While it was impressive that Wen had discovered her involvement in the deal, it made her uneasy all over again. What else might he know about her?

"How do you know about Kalso-Moore?" she asked.

Lucas stopped, turned, and fixed her with his intelligent, dark brown eyes. His brow furrowed. "Mr. Wen makes it his business to know everything about the people he finds of interest. And being part of a deal of that magnitude made you of interest."

They walked on.

Valentina weighed the advisability of asking if Wen had continued to watch her *after* the Kalso-Moore deal was done, if he'd followed her career with similar interest, and hadn't been too surprised when she'd approached their New York office for a position *below* the one she'd held at Goldman Sachs.

She asked.

Lucas gave little away. "Mr. Wen thinks you made a wise decision. You made your name as one of the top closers in the business, and have more than proven yourself within our New York office. Believe me, with the type of clients you can bring in, the money you stand to earn in the Hong Kong office is going to make your old take-home pay look like chump change."

"You reckon? I was making pretty good money in New York."

"If you call two hundred and fifty grand a year good, then yeah, I guess you were."

"Plus bonuses," Valentina threw in. She was suddenly playing defense. "I was on target to make one and a half million in my first year, before . . ."

Before she'd received the call from one Mai Lin from HR.

"We have closers here who can make more than that in one month, Valentina. And not one of them could even come close to what you can do."

She relaxed back into her skin. That was it. Jimmy Wen hadn't sensed her agenda, he'd just admired her work. This wasn't about keeping your friends close and your enemies closer. This was just about business.

And greed. Let's not forget greed. It's what makes the world go round.

They turned a corner; some yards ahead lay another of the ubiquitous frosted glass doors. It swung open, and three men in finely cut suits strode up the hallway toward Valentina and Lucas, who stopped so suddenly that she almost took a header trying to put on her own brakes. She glanced sideways at him, then followed the direction of his eyes to the tall Chinese man in the center of the trio, even now buttoning up his perfectly tailored suit coat.

"Who is he?" she murmured.

"Zhang Bo," said Lucas in a voice devoid of color.

Zhang Bo was a name Valentina had come across on the internet when she'd done her research on Hong Kong. There were rumors about him, too, but whatever the truth of those rumors, the man went to great lengths to portray himself as a legitimate businessman and philanthropist. In his expensive suit and stylish jet-black hair, he certainly looked legit. Only his companions—a matched pair of large men dressed in black slacks, turtlenecks, and jackets—gave some credence to the rumors.

Driven by some perverse imp, Valentina put on her most dazzling smile. Before Lucas could stop her, she strode up the hallway toward Zhang and his bodyguards, who, in perfect synch, slipped a hand inside their respective jackets.

She ignored them and held out her hand. "Mr. Zhang. Valentina Vittorio. It's so good to meet you."

Eyeing Valentina with suspicion, Zhang shook her hand. He gave a barely perceptible nod that caused both bodyguards to stand down in perfect unison, hands back by their sides.

"You're American," he said, as if that explained her brashness. His English was perfect, his accent delicate and musical. "I have enjoyed New York on many occasions. How are you enjoying our city?"

Valentina broke the handshake. "I haven't had the chance to see any of it so far. I only flew in this morning."

"You must be sure to take in the sights. I'm sure there will be no shortage of volunteers willing to be your tour guide. And if not . . ." He gave Valentina an approving up and down.

"I'm so sorry, Mr. Zhang." Lucas appeared by Valentina's side to apologize for the intrusion. "Today is Miss Vittorio's first day at JM Wen. She's one of our brightest new analysts."

Zhang waved away Lucas's concern. "It is always good to have the opportunity to meet Jimmy's moneymakers."

"Mr. Zhang is one of our most respected and important clients," said Lucas. "And one of Mr. Wen's dearest friends."

"Now you see, Mr. Vaughn, how is it *you* remember this important fact," Zhang asked mildly, "when your boss seems to have forgotten it? I tried to remind him just now and he seems to understand, but then I leave his office and his memory grows dim."

"I can assure you, Mr. Zhang," said Lucas, in a voice far too small for his personality, "Jimmy never forgets—"

Zhang took a step closer to the Australian, tilting his head to look down at him through eyes so dark they seemed uniformly black. "Don't patronize me, please, Lucas. I need you to remind Jimmy of what you obviously know so well. I'm growing tired of visiting this office only to be given the same vague report about my stock portfolio. I have more important things to do with my time. *You don't.*" Zhang's voice went from silk to steel in two words.

Valentina watched as Lucas shrank from the other man, fear in his eyes. She caught the subtle menace of the two bodyguards as they, too, stepped marginally closer to flank Zhang. Lucas Vaughn was literally up against the wall of JM Wen's posh offices. She stood frozen to one side, her own body flexing and tensing, obeying fight-or-flight instincts schooled by hours upon hours in a Manhattan dojo.

Jesus! Did I just walk onto a movie set? Were they really going to resort to violence *here*, in broad daylight, in front of a stranger?

Lucas seemed incapable of shutting up. "Jimmy can explain the situation much better—"

Zhang cut him off with a tiny shake of his head. "Jimmy has explained nothing new. And I have once more had to reiterate my position—and that of my associates."

The last word was spoken as if in title case; Valentina tossed her speculations about Zhang Bo being Triad onto the stupid question pile.

A nearby office door opened, and a young executive stepped into the hallway. Zhang and his men relaxed back in unison, Zhang adjusting his suit coat. He put a smile on his lips and turned his head slightly toward the young man now hesitating in mid-corridor, his eyes flickering toward Jimmy Wen's executive office.

Following a moment of complete stillness, during which Zhang tilted his head ever so slightly toward Wen's office doors, the exec bobbed his head, murmured, "Mr. Zhang," and scooted past the group and into Wen's inner sanctum.

Zhang turned the gimlet smile back to Lucas Vaughn. "How much does Jimmy Wen mean to you, Lucas? Or should I ask, how much does his money mean to you? Is it worth life and limb, do you think?"

Zhang then turned to Valentina, his smile reaching his black eyes. "Have a good day, Miss Vittorio," he said politely, "and welcome to Hong Kong."

Valentina watched as Zhang and his bodyguards strode off down the hallway and out through the doors that gave onto the elevator core. Beside her, Lucas straightened his tie and quietly composed himself. She said nothing, only watched him from the corner of her eye as he pieced his dignity back together.

"So," he said after a moment. The affable smile was back—as if being menaced by a most respected and important client was an everyday occurrence. "Let's go see where the magic happens." He gestured broadly toward a double frosted glass door across the hall and kitty-corner to the door of Wen's executive office.

The doors opened up into a large sales room that was somewhat more sedate than the frenzy of the trading floor. It held a couple dozen dove-gray desks, each with the company's standard issue phone, a laptop, and a single but ample flat-screen monitor arranged on the tempered glass work surface. Each of the other new arrivals was already seated in his or her designated spot; only one desk stood empty. Evidently, their corporate mentors hadn't taken them through the sales floor . . . or into a confrontation with a suave gangster.

Lucas laughed at the expression on her face and said, "As much as I love the chaos of the trading floor, I have to say it's much more civilized in here. Welcome to the big leagues, Val."

His seeming ability to read her mind was annoying . . . and potentially dangerous.

"Mine, I take it?" She pointed at the vacant desk. It sat with its left edge against a thick, tinted floor-to-ceiling window that afforded a spectacular view of the city, and faced a glass wall with a view to another office beyond.

Lucas nodded. "This is where the real money is made. Sure, the guys and girls on the trading floor bring it in, but in comparison with what's generated here, they're mere penny stock hustlers."

"Penny stock hustlers? You can't make me believe your trading floor staff don't deal in shares over five dollars."

"Adjust your horizon, Val. To Mr. Wen, a penny stock is any business his closers do that's under five *million*. The big fish are already on the hook; all you have to do is reel them in." Looking across the office, Lucas called over to one of the traders. "Say, Chrissy, what did you earn last year?"

The girl responded without looking up from her computer screen. "Six point three million US dollars in bonuses alone; with salary and commission it was—" She glanced up now, her face lighting up when she saw Valentina. "Valentina Vittorio? Is that you?" Chrissy got up from her desk and made her way across the office.

"You two know each other?" Lucas asked.

Valentina eyed Chrissy Huang as she approached; she was a young woman of startling beauty who wore wide, black-rimmed glasses that accentuated her sparkling eyes, and had her raven-black hair tied back in a long, iridescent ponytail that followed the contour of her spine all the way down to her ass. Her skin was the color of old gold.

Valentina nodded. "Chrissy spent some time in New York last year."

Chrissy threw her arms around Valentina in a sisterly hug, though God knew, they'd never been *that* close. Valentina wasn't that close to anyone. She had found Chrissy's knowledge of Wen's Hong Kong office useful, though.

"Why didn't you tell me you were coming to Hong Kong?" Chrissy demanded.

"Because I only found out myself days ago," Valentina offered as they broke the hug; the truth was she hadn't given the girl a second thought after she'd finished her brief temporary assignment in Wen's Wall Street office and returned to Hong Kong.

"We had a few wild adventures on the Lower East Side," Chrissy told Lucas. "Valentina really knows how to party. Now I hope she'll let me return the favor—I know *all* the best nightclubs on the island."

Valentina smiled her warmest smile. "I'll certainly think about it."

"You'll be in the thick of it next week," Lucas chipped in. "I'd take Chrissy up on her offer, if I were you. Maybe I'll join you."

Valentina raised her eyebrows at the suggestion; Chrissy ignored it and leaned over Valentina's desk to scribble something on a stickie.

"Here's my cell number. I'm out of the office this afternoon—give me a call later and we'll hook up. It'll be just like old times." She pressed the note into Valentina's hand, prolonging the touch a hair longer than necessary.

"Sounds good," Valentina said. "I'll call you when I'm done here—I promise. It'll be good to catch up, Chrissy." She placed the stickie on the desk next to her new computer.

Chrissy laughed. "Catch up? I'm going to show you the time of your life!" She swung around and returned to her desk, her ponytail swaying as she walked.

"Small world, isn't it?" Lucas said as he watched Chrissy sashay across the office.

"I guess it is." Valentina thought Lucas seemed a little put out—either by Chrissy's intrusion into his tour guiding, or by her obvious snub of his self-invite to their night out. She wasn't sure how she felt about that. There were obvious benefits to socializing with someone as close to Jimmy Wen as Lucas Vaughn seemed to be.

Valentina slid into her chair. It was sleek, utilitarian, and comfortable, if less stylish than she'd expect for such a prestigious office.

Lucas perched one hip on the corner of the desk. "You won't actually be spending too much time behind that desk. We want you out meeting clients and building your book of business from the get-go. Most of your business will be done in one of our many, many private meeting rooms or out of the office—often on the prospective client's home turf where they think they're safe from our ruthless, high-pressure sales techniques." He chuckled at that. "The more you bring in, and the *faster* you bring 'em in, the quicker you'll earn the big bucks—and Mr. Wen's approval."

He turned his head to shoot a glance at the expansive executive office that shared a gleaming glass wall with the closers' room. Intrigued, Valentina looked up over her computer monitor to follow his gaze. There, behind a wide desk sat Mr. Jimmy Wen himself. He was slight, thin, and balding. Completely unimpressive from this distance. But if there were other people in the room, Valentina didn't notice them. She felt the air leave her lungs in reflexive reaction to the moment, and gave herself leave to take it in.

This was what she had been working toward since her dad's death. Every career move she'd made to this moment had been meticulously calculated to put her precisely where she was—within reach of the man who'd shattered her family beyond repair.

"I'm very much looking forward to meeting Mr. Wen," she told Lucas, smiling up at him. "I'd like to get to know him." *Before I destroy him.*

Lucas's cell phone buzzed. He fished it from his pocket and jabbed a finger at the touch screen. "I'm being summoned. Make yourself at home—but don't get too comfortable."

With a flash smile and a whiff of expensive cologne, Lucas Vaughn strode off to meet with Jimmy Wen.

CHAPTER FOUR

Lucas knocked on the thick glass door of Wen's office and waited. For as many years as he'd known and worked with Jimmy Wen, and for as much as they'd been through together as they'd built up Wen's empire, he always knocked. Always waited. There were some social barriers no amount of familiarity could breach.

Once Wen beckoned him with an absent wave, Lucas opened the door. He knew Jimmy trusted him implicitly—not only with his business, but with his life, should it ever come to that—but notwithstanding their history together, and his involvement in the company, Lucas Vaughn knew there would be consequences if he were to ever barge in and hear something he wasn't supposed to.

The office was spacious, elegant, yet Spartan. It was a statement by Jimmy Wen about Jimmy Wen. Its clean lines and uncluttered surfaces said that *this* man was all business and had no time for trivial affectations. It was intended to suggest a humility that Jimmy Wen did not, in fact, possess. It more truthfully sent a message about what was dear to its owner: The 1,500-square-foot office was constructed of thick safety glass on all but one side so that, from his desk, Wen could see out across the entire expanse of the pillarless, open-plan sales office beyond.

If he turned his head to the right, he could take in impressive views of Hong Kong. He'd chosen that specific floor in 2IFC tower, along with the location of his office, for its views of the Bank of China Tower and the Arch. The latter, one of the tallest residential buildings in Hong Kong, towered high above the city and was an ultramodern homage to Napoleon's Arc de Triomphe in Paris.

If he turned his head to the left, his eyes rested on a bank of a dozen fifty-inch flat-screen TVs. Each one was tuned into stock markets and news feeds from around the globe, and was a direct emulation of the layout of the screens on the sales floor—Wen liked to know precisely what information his people were being exposed to. Wen had two computers on his desk: an ultra-thin MacBook and a wide-screen desktop with a mini tower tucked beneath his desk next to a brown leather briefcase. The computers ran constantly and fed Wen the endless stream of financial data that was essential to the management of his empire. If that weren't enough, Wen constantly fiddled with his cell phone in his persistent search for yet more information that would keep him ahead of the game.

What Wen's office did not have were personal trappings. He had not one photograph of the beloved wife and daughter purported to live with him in his pricey four-bedroom flat on Conduit Road—which he would casually mention had cost him $HK200 mil. Nor were there certificates of higher education, nor treasured memorabilia, nor pictures of Jimmy Wen smiling and shaking hands with the rich, famous, and influential. Those moments existed, of course—Wen was one hell of a networker—but they had not been memorialized here. Here, Jimmy Wen was nothing but business.

Wen contemplated Lucas and ran a hand over the smooth dome of his head. "Zhang Bo paid us a visit."

Lucas's smiled wryly. "I knew that, actually."

"You spoke to him?" Wen's expression was impenetrable.

"He said to remind you that he's our biggest client and that he's tired of waiting. Or words to that effect." Lucas decided against elaborating further. He wasn't about to be taken for a whiner.

He paused, expecting Wen to say something. Instead, the man just snorted and turned back to his computer screen. Lucas continued across the white Berber carpet and stopped a few feet short of the desk to offer Wen's matched set of bodyguards a perfunctory nod. Stationed on either side of his desk in executive chairs, they stood whenever someone entered his office and watched any visitors without seeming to watch them. They were dressed in identical and immaculately tailored navy-blue suits, beneath which they wore identical Glock G43s in identical shoulder holsters. Their names were Lau and Pang, but somehow Lucas couldn't stop from thinking of them as Tweedledee and Tweedledum—not something he'd ever call them to their faces.

Wen loved to have the Tweedle twins by his side at all times, and especially enjoyed having them flank him as he sat at his desk. Lucas thought it made him look like a corrupt third-world dictator of some tin-pot banana republic. The guards were on rotation from the small army Wen employed to take care of himself and his business interests, all recruited from the China Ministry of State Security by Wen's Security Chief, Shum Kuo, who in his former life had been very high up in the MSS Beijing HQ. The MSS had a particularly fearsome reputation, both in Hong Kong and the mainland, and its former employees were considered to be among the best in the world.

"The new arrivals are settling in well," Lucas told Wen.

"I saw." Wen pulled his eyes from his laptop screen with obvious impatience. "So? When will they begin selling?"

"It all depends on how much rein the other partners have given, but I reckon the newbies will be all ready to hit the ground running on Monday. As per your brief, they all brought active client leads with them, and I know for a fact that Vittorio—"

"The girl from New York."

"Yeah. She has a couple of live ones straining at the leash to sign on the dotted line just as quickly as she can get to them."

"That's good to hear, Lucas," Wen spoke distractedly, his eyes still on his laptop. "I don't need to remind you just how much we need to land new business right now."

Lucas didn't need reminding; it was pretty much all Wen had

talked about for the past month or so. The man was a genius when it came to spinning straw into gold, but along with that genius came a dark, reckless, and sometimes self-destructive tendency. The new tiger team of closers was a bulwark against that tendency.

"It's imperative they bring in the big money, Lucas, and bring it in fast," Wen said for the millionth time. "Nothing less than—oh, for *fuck's* sake!"

It was so rare for Wen to use expletives that even Lau and Pang flinched.

"Leave." Without taking his eyes off the computer screen, Wen dismissed the bodyguards with a cursory flick of the wrist.

With a grave nod to Wen, and then to Lucas, the pair buttoned their elegantly tailored jackets and made their way out of the office. Lucas watched them go, grudgingly admiring how each two-thousand-dollar Canali suit was custom tailored to show off the slight bulge under the left shoulder. They were neither open nor concealed carry; more like *obvious* carry. After all, what would be the point of having armed guards if no one knew they were armed?

Jimmy's suit today was a gray sharkskin Tom Ford, with which he had paired wine-colored crocodile loafers from the same design house. His shirt was silk of a shade of rose that few men would even try to pull off. Jimmy could get away with that because he was Jimmy. Jimmy got away with a lot of things because he was Jimmy. He had gotten used to getting away with things, so he took situations like this one as a personal affront.

"What the *hell* is going on with the Golden Six? The prices should all have gone down by now, and yet"—Wen spun the MacBook around on his desk for Lucas to see—"every one of those share prices is going *up!*"

Lucas leaned forward in his chair, squinting at the too-bright screen. He could see for himself that the stocks Wen was questioning were, indeed, climbing in value. Climbing was an understatement; they were skyrocketing, moving so fast, it looked like time-lapse photography. Wen had christened them the Golden Six back in the days before they had become a source of concern. He scanned the screen and mentally checked off each one: New Horizon Credit Card Company Hong Kong Limited, Golden Harvest Group Limited, New World Entertainment Group Limited, Emperor Holdings Limited, JLM Asset Holdings, and Asia Lion Entertainment Limited. The share price of each and every one had shown a significant increase over the past seven days, with Asia Lion hitting HK$60.18. That was eighteen dollars higher than it had been two weeks ago when the client had transferred the collateral, and just ten dollars short of their highest ever value.

He felt a lump forming in the pit of his stomach. They were trading far too briskly, too, which didn't make sense.

Wen echoed Lucas's thoughts. "It doesn't make sense, Lucas. They should all be tanking by now, *especially* Asia Lion. What is going on here?" A hint of sour exasperation in his voice exacerbated the faint hint of a US East Coast accent.

Lucas leaned back in his chair and started to fiddle with his tie, although he knew before his fingers reached the knot it would be perfectly straight. He adjusted the nervous tic and ran a hand through his thick hair instead. Jimmy Wen's annoyance was comparable to most other men shouting down the rafters. Lucas recalled the last time he'd seen that stymied look on his boss's face or heard the accents of the American eastern seaboard in his voice. It had been four years ago when the Securities and Futures Commission had stormed the building in their virtual jackboots and crawled over every square inch of JM Wen Limited. They'd found nothing, of course—Jimmy Wen may have been reckless, but he sure as all hell wasn't stupid—the company accounts, records, paperwork, even the health and safety procedures had been so squeaky clean, it had actually been embarrassing for the SFC.

Besides, Wen had known about the unannounced visit almost a month in advance—low friends in high places were a staple of the Hong Kong financial community, and especially for the likes of Jimmy Wen. It had still put the guy in a weird, hyped-up mood for the entire month and a half of the investigation. This was different; in this case, they'd gone by their standard operating procedure and things were going fine—until suddenly they weren't.

Lucas said the words he knew his boss wanted to hear: "Give 'em time, Jimmy. You know they'll drop again. They always do. This is just a little wrinkle."

"Certainly, they'll drop in *time*, Lucas, but we don't have a lot of time. The client is expecting their collateral back *yesterday*. If they don't have it in their hands soon, things are going to get nasty." He paused for a beat, his gaze scanning the bank of screens to his right, then sweeping the room in which his closers were bringing new clients aboard. He made a dismissive gesture. "Eh. They need us. They need *me*. We'll stall them. Like we always do."

Like we always do.

"Jimmy." Lucas hesitated, not entirely sure what to say. That didn't happen to him often. "Jimmy, why did you trade out the Golden Six? We knew—*you* knew—how dangerous it was. And it wasn't as if we needed a Hail Mary."

In fact, they'd been atop the financial world. Doing stellar business, even without the international hotshots. Lucas knew his boss liked to shake things up when he felt they were going too smoothly. Maybe he got bored. He wondered if Jimmy Wen even knew why he did shit like this.

Wen didn't answer. Instead, he turned to the laptop again and stabbed intermittently at the keys with both index fingers. "We can't afford to leave any of this to chance, Lucas. I'm gonna put a call into the market makers. We need to drive those share prices down, and we need to drive them down *now*."

Lucas sighed. Bad idea. Panic measures rarely paid off in the financial business. Lucas knew it, and he knew Jimmy knew it too. To instigate a sudden and aggressive buying and selling of the Golden Six shares would cause big, fat red flags to start flying all around the SFC. No matter how many Securities agents Jimmy Wen had in his pocket, it wouldn't be enough to keep him out of the agency's sights.

Increased trading activity would also have Hong Kong's market makers and manipulators twitching, and it wouldn't take too much digging in the Central Clearing and Settlement System to see where the shares were being moved from and to. Which meant that curious, accusatory fingers would begin pointing in JM Wen Limited's direction. One thing Wen really couldn't risk at such a time was finger-pointing involving the Golden Six, most especially involving Asia Lion Entertainment Limited.

Lucas knew arguing with Wen would be a fruitless exercise. The Man had made up his mind, and no one—not even his ever-loyal associate and confidante, Lucas Vaughn—was going to change that; Jimmy Wen hadn't gotten to be one of the most influential people in Hong Kong by having his mind changed by subordinates. Jimmy would get out of this situation the way he always got out of these situations—with uncanny skill and unflappable poise. The frustration he'd shown Lucas just now in the privacy of his office would never make an appearance anywhere else. If it did, Lucas thought, the sky would fall, and Chicken Little and the devil would ice-skate to work.

Wen snatched his cell phone from the desk and stabbed at the touch screen with his finger. It rang out precisely one and a half times before it was picked up at the other end.

"Freddy?" Wen barked. "The Golden Six share prices are rising, not falling. I need you to put pressure on those prices. I need you to bring them down. Now."

Lucas was sure he'd heard Freddy Tseng's sharp intake of breath over the phone from all the way across Wen's desk; he knew the guy would be thinking along the same lines as he was at this knee-jerk countermeasure, but Freddy Tseng would also know better than to contradict his boss. There were a million other managers out there who'd be all too willing to step into his highly paid shoes at the drop of Jimmy Wen's hat.

CHAPTER FIVE

J M Wen Limited's Kam Wa Street office was a million miles removed from the grandiose opulence of Finance Street. Located in an old, run-down tenement building just a short stroll from the Shau Kei Wan MTR station, it was home to the seedy underbelly of the company, a part of Wen's empire hidden away in the grubby part of Hong Kong like it was some kind of embarrassment and not the secret to the company's success. The building stood only five stories high and had been constructed of bland, gray concrete back when the Beatles were still a band. It looked out onto one of the poorest parts of Hong Kong through grimy, cracked windows. The first and upper floors were abandoned except for pigeons and the occasional squatter, and the second floor had been gutted to create a single, large room for JM Wen's market makers and an office for its manager.

It was in this office that Freddy Tseng sat with his phone pressed tightly to his ear, his heart sinking as he listened intently to the man on the other end of the call. The cacophony of busy voices coming from the large main room faded into a gray haze as he grasped Jimmy Wen's instructions. They were more than enough to send a nervous prickle running from the base of Freddy's skull down the full length of his spine.

"Perhaps in a week or two—" he began, but Wen cut him off.

"We don't have a week or two. We have days. Do whatever you need to do to get those share prices down." Wen's voice was demanding, certain. "We need to get them *all* below their yearly low points, Freddy."

"Yes, Mr. Wen, sir," he said quietly, and listened as Wen reiterated for the third time just how important this was, and that the Kam Wa office was to drop absolutely everything and prioritize the Golden Six. Wen then asked him for the fourth time if he understood, and Freddy Tseng cleared his tight throat and assured his boss in his most confident voice that yes, he did understand, and the instructions would be carried out to the letter.

Wen terminated the call abruptly, leaving Freddy Tseng to stare at the receiver. It felt hot and heavy in his hand as he placed it gently back on its cradle. If he slammed it down like he wanted to, he'd have smashed it to dust. He had heard his brother—a successful writer—complain that the phone was an instrument of torture. He really had no idea. He'd never received instructions like these. It would be as if his publisher had demanded he write six novels in as many days.

Jimmy Wen was reckless, yes. He enjoyed risk, yes. But this . . . Did he not grasp how dangerous this was? How provocative?

Freddy shook himself. Surely this was some gambit that Wen was making, based on knowledge only he had. He had made such mysterious calls before—though none that would be so tantalizing to the SFC. If that was not the case, Freddy Tseng knew it could only mean one thing: JM Wen Limited was in trouble.

Or, more to the point, Jimmy Wen was in trouble . . . again.

Freddy had witnessed the type of difficulty Wen could get himself into at other companies he'd worked for on the island, and it was precisely the kind of trouble that got other people killed, though Wen always seemed to escape with minor damage. He moved on, he started fresh, he thrived. So far, Freddy Tseng had moved on too, and told himself that this time would be no different.

He stared out through the door of his cramped office at the sea of oblivious, busy faces beyond the glass. Mostly it was young men, although there was a sprinkling of women. All were young, and all had families to feed and bills to pay with the handsome salaries JM Wen Limited paid them. That made them hungry, reliant, incredibly loyal, and not prone to asking too many questions. Freddy Tseng marveled at how diligently each one of them tapped away on their keyboards, all entirely unaware of the profound effect their actions were having on stock markets, businesses, and lives across the globe. He wished he had the comfort of their level of ignorance.

Stock walkers, Jimmy Wen liked to call them. They were little more than glorified market manipulators, glued to their Ikea desks and their computers—laptops to facilitate a quick relocation to another site—and traded stocks back and forth between each other for eight hours a day, every day. That way, they effectively *walked* the stock price up or down—depending upon which direction best suited JM Wen Limited—by buying or disposing of them over a stipulated period of time, and increasing the activity on them a thousandfold. Which, of course, also made them attractive investments to others.

It was not so much the fact of walking the stock that bothered Freddy Tseng—that was the sole purpose of the Kan Wa Street office, after all—it was the impossibly tight period of time Wen had insisted upon. Walking stock prices in either direction usually took place over weeks, sometimes months, but his crew was to drive them down in a matter of days.

Freddy Tseng considered, not for the first time in their long relationship, that Jimmy Wen was crazy.

CHAPTER SIX

The meeting with Jimmy Wen had left Zhang Bo feeling disrespected. Wen's bland assurances that "these things always work out" and "we are waiting for maximum yield" were frustrating. Their contract did not stipulate that JM Wen should wait for maximum yield to return the "collateral" but to return it in two weeks.

Zhang's inability to get the laundered money back or to be given a financial reason that made sense to him made him feel . . . watched. Others in the gang were beginning to question his ability to manage Jimmy Wen. They would not say this directly, of course, but they hinted at it, which only added to his annoyance. If such questioning of his authority became widespread, it would wreak havoc with the cohesion of his organization, weaken him before his peers, and result in more of the same sort of problem he was forced to deal with today.

This pair of thieves had expected a meeting in his offices; he'd had them brought to the Dragon Lodge, a derelict and crumbling mansion on the edge of the Peak, where they now sat side by side in matching white plastic lawn chairs restrained with cable ties—naked, to maximize both humiliation and a sense of vulnerability. The youngest, a handsome kid with metal-rimmed glasses and a thick mop of black hair, was shivering so badly, his teeth were chattering.

His reaction was out of fear, not cold, for the temperature in this dank hole of a room was mild enough. The reason for his fear was in Zhang's hands: a gleaming meat cleaver, which the Triad leader handled with studied unconcern, shifting it from hand to hand, tilting it so that the wan light in the room rippled along its honed edge.

The older thief sat stoically, staring straight ahead. While his young accomplice had begun whimpering at the first sight of the cleaver and pissed himself, his elder had done little more than set his jaw and grip the arms of his chair more tightly.

Zhang tapped the back of the cleaver gently on the palm of his hand and faced the younger man. "I ask again, what made you think you could get away with such a scheme?"

"I did what *he* told me!" Shaking in his own acrid stink, urine dripping from the chair, the younger man forced the words from between clenched teeth. "I did what Simon told me. He said no one would notice."

The elder man gave him a sideways glance and cursed beneath his breath.

Zhang raised his jet brows in a look of exaggerated bemusement. "Really? You didn't think we'd notice the absence of ten million dollars? Do you have any idea how many men those girls need to fuck to make that kind of money?"

He pointed the meat cleaver at the young man as he asked the question, saw the kid's jaw flex in abject fear. Yet, he met Zhang's gaze and shook his head. There was something admirable about that. There was rage in those eyes, too, and Zhang Bo knew it was not directed at him. In the boy's mind, his partner in crime had brought him to this.

Zhang wiggled the cleaver inches from his eyes. "The Wo Hop Yee entrusted you with five of our most profitable houses, and you spent the last twelve months skimming off the top to line your own pockets."

"I only found out about their scam a month ago," the young man protested.

"Liar," the older man growled; it was the first thing he'd said since

Zhang's bodyguards had dragged him up the rotting stairs and into the old bedroom.

The kid shook his head. "A couple months at most. I *swear*. Simon brought me in to help launder the credit card money—"

Zhang cut him off. "With Bitcoin—I know. You are the technical wizard of the team."

"I was following instructions," he repeated, shooting his older partner a dark, frightened glance. "He said if I didn't, I'd never need to work again."

Suggesting that he'd be dead. There was no protest of this claim from Simon. It was likely true.

"And I'm sure the money they paid you to steal from the Family had nothing to do with it? *Where* did our money go?" Zhang tapped the young man's nose gently with the blade of the cleaver; it left a crimson line of fresh blood.

The young man yipped and shrank back as far as he could, staring at the blade as if it had mesmerized him. A drop of blood rose from the cut to perch on the tip of his nose.

"After I p-purchased Bitcoin," he stammered, "it was all transferred into an account under Simon's name."

Zhang turned his attention to the older man, moving to stand before his chair. "Simon Yunfeng—a man stupid enough to use his own name on the account. In the future, the Family should refrain from hiring idiots. Did you honestly believe we would not discover what you had done? Personally, I find that insulting. Did you mean to insult me, Simon?" Zhang drew the cleaver's blade down the line of the man's sternum, tracing a thin, red line.

Yunfeng's jaw bunched and he looked daggers at the Triad boss, but he did not speak.

His young partner was not so stoic. "We can get the money back, Mr. Zhang. Well . . . most of it. Bitcoin value has taken a downturn—"

"I am well aware of the value of Bitcoin," Zhang snapped.

The boy wizard flinched as if he'd been slapped.

"While I would appreciate the return of the money you stole from the Wo Hop Yee, there is more to this . . . *situation* than that, as I'm sure both of you can appreciate. There is the honor of the Family at stake. *My* honor."

"The value will rise again," said the young man. "It will go even higher. You might even turn a profit."

That sounded enough like Jimmy Wen's reasoning for withholding the money he was owed that it irked the Triad even more. He looked at Simon Yunfeng.

"Do you believe that? That the Family will *make* money on your thievery?"

Defiantly, Yunfeng stared the Triad down and said nothing.

"You have both worked for the Clan long enough to understand restitution has to be made. This first requires the return of the money you stole."

Still Yunfeng said nothing.

The man's insolent silence was offensive, grating. Zhang bit back his anger. He disliked losing his temper. To lose one's temper was to lose control, which was to lose face. But it seemed Simon Yunfeng had neither remorse nor respect for the Family he had stolen from. The young wizard at least showed Zhang the respect of fear.

Zhang flicked a narrow glance at the kid. "You can retrieve the money for me?" he asked, his voice thin and tight with the effort it took not to snarl the words.

The young man swallowed, nodded.

Zhang echoed the nod, then spun and brought the cleaver down onto Simon Yunfeng's leg; its keen blade sliced the soft meat of the thigh and bit into the thick bone beneath. The man screamed in pain and struggled against the ties that held him fast to the chair. The sudden outburst of violence had Zhang's bodyguards reaching into their jackets and the Bitcoin wizard cowering away from his wounded collaborator, adding his own shrill screams to the cacophony.

Zhang's rage was a bowl of flame with him at its center. He saw the world through it, and the heat of it choked him, made his skin burn and his eyes water. He ground his teeth against the urge to roar incoherently, wrenched the cleaver from Yunfeng's thigh, and brought it down through the crown of the man's head. It split the skull all the way down to the bridge of the nose and released a cascade of blood that covered his face and poured down his chest.

Rage ebbing, Zhang released the cleaver, stepped back, and straightened his jacket. "*Now*, you may be silent," he said.

He turned his attention to the younger man, who had pissed himself again and begun to cry. Zhang needed him alive to get his money back, although his days would likely be numbered after that—but there was no reason for him to know that.

Zhang gestured at Bitcoin Boy. "Clean him up and find him clothing," he told his body men. "He has work to do."

CHAPTER SEVEN

"You are the best of the best. The *Top Guns* of JM Wen International Asset Management Limited." Jimmy Wen addressed the seven eager young faces gathered around the oval table in the company boardroom. He sat at the head of the table looking relaxed and pleased with himself. He was flanked by two of the biggest Chinese men Valentina had ever seen, dressed in identical navy-blue suits.

Top Gun. She had to smile; it was rumored the guy loved that movie so much he'd tried to buy one of the MIG jets they'd used in the dogfight scenes; the Soviets had sold them off shortly after the USSR had crumbled in such spectacular fashion. They were still circulating on the collectors' markets along with weapons-grade uranium. Sadly, Wen had been outbid for the MIG by a Bahraini oil sheik, and had been forced to console himself with Tom Cruise's bomber jacket—autographed to him, of course.

"And because you are the best of the best, you work for me." Wen's self-aggrandizement was met by a subdued ripple of appreciative laughter.

Up close, Wen looked smaller than he had behind his desk. Of course, he was seated and his goons dwarfed him . . . which they'd do to pretty much anybody but an NFL lineman. He was also dressed unassumingly in a dusty rose silk shirt and a silver-gray tie held in place with a gold tie pin in the shape of the company logo. His head was smooth-shaven, and his round, tanned face had tiny laugh lines and faint hints of crow's feet, but was otherwise smooth.

Asian men, Valentina thought, *sure age well.*

She studied Wen's eyes closely as he addressed them. They flicked and darted between the closers, making swift but solid eye contact, as if he could read their thoughts in their eyes. She'd make damn sure he couldn't read hers. When he glanced at her, she looked the legendary Jimmy Wen straight in the face, daring him to read her, daring to try to read him. What she read, behind the smile, was a chilling, detached coldness in eyes that were so light a brown they were almost hazel.

To Wen's right sat Lucas Vaughn. He was the only one of the seven partners assigned to Valentina and her fellow salespeople who'd been invited into what was turning out to be little more than a sizing up masquerading as a pep rally. That, and other clues she'd picked up, caused her to tag him as Wen's right-hand man. She felt a combination of pleasure and uneasiness that he'd been assigned as her mentor.

Seeming to pay close attention to the proceedings, Vaughn sat quietly, hands resting on the polished wood of the boardroom table, fingers knitted together and still. He watched intently as Wen spoke, his expression admiring. Valentina couldn't decide if that spoke of devotion or something more mercenary. It was important to know which.

After that, Wen once again emphasized to the seven how special they were because of their ability to close the most lucrative contracts. Rainmakers, he called them, and threw in a few key sales stats to show how closely he'd been studying them. Did they know, for example, that Sofia Reller had brought in four brand-new clients in the three weeks prior to flying out to Hong Kong? The combined funding amount had been close to two hundred and fifty million dollars—US, not Hong Kong—and had earned her a seat at the table. At this, the Swiss smiled her perfect smile and puffed out her considerable chest, both of which Valentina guessed had most likely been instrumental in bringing in all that new money. Wen went on to share a tidbit about each of them, then settled into a lecture on client care.

"New clients and their collateral are the lifeblood of this company," Wen told them, eyeing each one of the seven. "Without the constant flow of new business, JM Wen Limited would simply stagnate and become just one more midlevel lender languishing in mediocrity among the business leaders who dominate the global markets. As you are all aware, we take great pride in not only courting the wealthiest and most influential of the world's moneymakers, but in providing them with an exceptional service and second-to-none return on their assets. We trade in only the very best stocks internationally, and have the best financial and legal experts to back up every sales decision and every client contract. Our clients' shares *literally* could not be in better hands."

The man was as full of superlatives as a walking, talking brochure. Valentina had researched Wen and his business thoroughly before signing on the dotted line six months ago, and knew nothing Wen was prepared to say in the meeting would come as a surprise. She tuned out Wen's corporate speak, instead applying her mind to what Wen was pointedly *not* saying, that behind all the rah-rah bullshit and talk of looking after all clients big and small as if they were family, was the badly concealed fact that some of JM Wen's clients were more equal than others and paid for more than just the management of their stock portfolio.

Everyone did a bit of money laundering. It took place on some scale at many asset management companies, it was an open secret around the financial markets, and it was virtually impossible to police. Hong Kong was a prime example of an environment in which it had become common to the point of legitimacy. The clients for these not-quite-respectable services were traditionally fat cat businessmen, politicians, and movie stars who were looking for ways to protect their hard-earned money from the taxman, and who were not interested in the fine print. High-earning sports and music stars had more recently joined the elite group—all looking to hold on to every penny possible, legitimately or otherwise.

Laundering was one thing, but was he laundering for the Triad? That seemed to Valentina a matter of an entirely different magnitude. She'd look into that if it didn't distract from her original objective: finding Jimmy Wen's dirty bank.

There was *always* a dirty bank at the heart of a money laundering operation, since it simply wouldn't work without one, and Valentina wondered which among the multitude of banks used by JM Wen was the muddiest one. Finding that bank was at the top of Valentina's to-do list—and, if possible, discovering whence some of the laundered money had come and what it might have funded. Could be anything from prostitution to illegal arms sales to drugs, human trafficking, even international terrorism.

Money from these businesses would be moved around dozens—sometimes hundreds—of times until its origins were buried deep in the murk; that boutique hotel in the British Virgin Islands where you spent your last vacation could have been bought with money generated among the drug cartels in Columbia via stocks traded in Kuala Lumpur, and liquidized by one of a half dozen or so banks in London's Canary Wharf. A terrorist detonating a suicide vest in an East Pakistan market could just as easily have been bankrolled in exactly the same way. Dirty money was traded on the international money and stock markets, punted around the world under countless company names—real and bogus—and moved so often and so swiftly that not even the best forensic accountants on the planet could follow its trail. It was easy, attractive *big* money, and seemingly liability free . . . until the SFC or one of its equivalent financial regulators decided to earn their keep and the launderers got caught and jailed.

That was the least dire fate Valentina hoped to engineer for Jimmy Wen. If there was something more ruinous to be done, she'd find a way to do it. But first, she had to find that dirty bank.

Wen had moved on to how aggressively his "magnificent seven" must hit the leads generated for them by the Hong Kong office when the boardroom door opened. Stopping midsentence, he glared at the neat young lady who'd stepped into the boardroom. The spitting image of Anita Kwok, she wore the company uniform—black pencil skirt and starched white shirt. She stopped just inside the door.

"I am so sorry to interrupt, Mr. Wen." Her voice was firm yet respectful. "But Mr. Surtees is here for his ten o'clock meeting."

Wen frowned and made a show of looking at his watch, a modest Timex. Jimmy Wen was famous for not displaying his wealth about his person; he much preferred to save such ostentations for the penthouse suites, yachts, limited-edition luxury motor vehicles, and expensive women with which he plied prospective clients.

"It's nine," he informed the neat young lady, who no doubt knew precisely what time it was. "Can't he tell time?"

"I'm sorry, Mr. Wen, but he's here *now* and insists on seeing you."

Instead of roaring at the woman, the Lion of Finance Street turned to Lucas Vaughn and said, "It would seem he couldn't wait an hour to discuss his funding requirements."

Vaughn seemed unsurprised. "It would seem not."

Wen made a face and stood, straightening his tie. One of his bodyguards pulled the chair away with a smooth, well-rehearsed action.

"I guess we should grant the esteemed Mr. Surtees his wish." He glanced at the assistant. "I'll see him in my office."

The young woman nodded and disappeared from whence she'd come.

Lucas Vaughn looked down the table at the closers and smiled crookedly. "Lesson for today, kids: Never keep an important client waiting. Although, when we give him the news, he's really going to wish he'd waited that extra hour." He stood and echoed Wen's tie-straightening, though there was no oversized bodyguard to pull out his chair.

Wen gave his right-hand man a sage nod and shot a glance at his rainmakers. "I'm sorry about this, ladies and gentlemen, but, as I was saying, our clients must *always* take priority—even if it is to give them bad news. I suggest you all make the most of your weekend, relax, see the sights, because you'll be working to the wire beginning Monday." He started for the door, his bodyguards falling in behind him, then turned and added, "There will be a few briefing meetings over the weekend—to bring you up to speed with legal affairs, company policies, and whatnot. So, don't go too crazy."

Valentina murmured her "Yes, sir," then sat in silence with the other six as Wen, Vaughn, and Wen's bodyguards strode from the boardroom. It was Sofia Reller who broke the awkward silence.

"So," she said as she stood up and pushed her chair away with the backs of her knees, "who the hell do I have to sleep with around here to get a goddamn coffee?"

CHAPTER EIGHT

R oger J. Surtees, Esquire, looked decidedly uncomfortable in his gray three-piece suit. The knot of his paisley tie dug into the pasty roll of fat that bulged over the collar of his white button-down shirt. He ran a nervous finger around the inside of the collar, as if attempting to restore blood flow to his reddened, sweating face. Lucas wondered why he didn't just undo the top button. Maybe the blue blood running in his veins prevented such a blatant lack of decorum.

The guy was a throwback to the island's colonial days, when Great Britain was a force of nature with considerable influence—even as it dismantled its vast empire piece by piece. He'd made his money in construction back when there had been a seemingly endless amount of it in sticking buildings up on every available square inch of Hong Kong; property was bought and sold for astronomical sums, and the rich—like Roger Surtees—had just kept on getting richer.

Things were different now. With the Chinese controlling Hong Kong, money was no longer as free-flowing as it had been, which was why a once respectable Hong Kong businessman was sitting in Jimmy Wen's office looking like a coronary waiting to happen.

The part Lucas played in these scenarios varied, depending on the behavior of the client. He was seated unobtrusively to Surtees's right on a cream-colored leather sofa, outside the triangle formed by Surtees and Wen's two bodyguards. Wen himself sat behind his magnificent desk in the center of the pyramid. Probably some symbology there, but Lucas wasn't big on symbology.

"I bought that company for my retirement," Surtees complained. "All I wanted to do was raise some capital on the stock, and now look what you've done!"

Wen gave Surtees his somber yet empathetic look, though Lucas knew he was hiding a smile. Roger J. Surtees had an unparalleled inability to hold onto money, which Jimmy Wen knew because he had a crack research team. They had revealed that Mr. Surtees's problems had more to do with his repeated bad luck in the Macau casinos than poor investment decisions.

"The stock was trading high at a hundred and nine dollars when we made the loan against your shares," Wen explained patiently what Surtees already knew. "And looking at the market trends, we had no reason to believe it would do anything other than increase, especially given the remarkable research Glaber was doing with their nanobot delivery system for cancer drugs."

"I don't understand it," Surtees growled. "You *personally* assured me that stock was watertight."

Wen leaned forward in his chair and bridged his fingers. He cast a glance in Lucas's direction, which was a cue that put him on stand-by. "I assured you as much as I can assure any client. But remember I *also* explained when you signed the collateral over to JM Wen that there is *always* a risk."

Surtees huffed and tugged at his damp collar some more. "I know, I know. But there's risks and there's *bloody* risks!"

"Must you swear, Mr. Surtees?" Wen played the offended card with injured innocence and, for a moment, the man looked more sheepish than angry. "The share value has declined to below the default floor level, which means the loan you took out with us against your shares is now, unfortunately, in potential of default. This is the risk one takes with a repo loan."

No shit. Surtees's shares were now worth less than half of what they had been valued at when he'd taken out the loan against them.

"Yes, I bloody well know that!" he barked. "And you just sitting there and repeating it isn't going to change the fact that I'm out of pocket by twenty million!"

With the mention of a money amount, the atmosphere felt as if someone had goosed it with a cattle prod; the tension between Wen and Surtees assumed a presence in the room. Lucas glanced reflexively at the bodyguards, then laughed to himself. As often as he watched this scene play out, that Moment when the abstract became suddenly Real jolted him. At that moment, tempers were apt to explode, hence Tweedledee and Tweedledum, who stood watchful sentry no more than a single, long stride from their charge, their eyes on Roger Surtees without seeming to be.

Jimmy Wen wagged his head empathetically and made a broad gesture with his hands. "We had no way of knowing Glaber Nanotech was going to be the subject of such negative and very public speculation about that report. How could we?"

"It wasn't even an actual report, damn it! It was a *rumor* of a report —one that Glaber has emphatically denied!"

Wen sat back in his chair with that damnable air of innocence that Lucas had come to admire. Let Surtees rant and rave 'til the sheep came over the hill, but the end result would be the same.

"Your shares were taken as collateral in good faith," Wen said. "You received eighty percent loan-to-value against them, Mr. Surtees, which was far more than any of the banks were offering . . . if indeed, they would have offered you anything."

Which they hadn't, which was what had driven poor, dear Roger to a lender of last resort like Jimmy Wen.

"I'm going to sue that damn Shing Hai," Surtees grumbled. "If he hadn't spread rumors of that report . . ."

Wen sympathized. "People listen to him, I'm afraid, even when they shouldn't. The man's nothing more than a talentless hack, but . . ."

The "but" was that Shing Hai was one of the most renowned market influencers in Hong Kong; he ran online blogs and financial advice columns across every conceivable social media platform, and broadcast a biweekly podcast to over a million listeners. So, when he went public with the rumor of a report he'd heard had been leaked from Glaber Nanotech that a human trial of their groundbreaking drug delivery system had gone horribly awry, people listened. Rumors and speculation were what drove the stock markets; fortunes were won and lost based on a casual conversation at the nineteenth hole of the country club or a half-overheard phone conversation . . . or an internet influencer running his mouth off.

Shing Hai wasn't talentless, but his talent could be bought; there was no such report, nor any horrific side effects. He need have no fear of being sued. Not only was his ass covered with plausible deniability, but there'd be no Glaber Nanotech left to sue anyone once everything was over and done. Liquidators were already waiting in the wings for the company's inevitable collapse, even as Surtees sat sweating and complaining in Jimmy Wen's office. The moment the story had hit social media, it shook confidence in Glaber. People panicked and began offloading their stock, which was exactly what Wen had banked on. Still, such sensationalist stories usually petered out after a few days, as soon as the next one came along. Even Glaber's stock value would have crept slowly back up . . . were it not for Lyn Song.

Lyn Song was the hottest new movie star in China. Already a veteran of over a dozen Chinese action and action/romance films, Song was on the verge of signing a lucrative three-picture deal with Universal Studios that would make her a name in Hollywood. This would give the company that managed her, Asia Lion Entertainment Limited, a firm foothold in the Western film markets. So, when the much-adored and universally trusted Lyn Song tweeted in horror about the horrific (and fictitious) fate of those poor Glaber Nanotech test subjects, the company's shares went into an irreversibly steep downward free fall.

Right on cue, Jimmy Wen threw his client a flimsy lifebelt, a thin glimmer of hope. "Our agreements have provisions that protect both JM Wen Limited and our borrowers against such unpredictable events.

There are remedies we can put into place to see you through this . . . unfortunate situation."

Surtees snorted. "And just what might they be, Mr. Wen?"

Wen frowned, looking uncomfortable. He leaned forward in his chair and fiddled with the Montblanc Mystery Masterpiece that sat between his MacBook and desktop display. The fountain pen, an industry appreciation for his business success, was little more than a gem-encrusted stress toy, but it made for great stage business.

Turning the pen in his hands, Wen spoke with slow deliberation. "Well, according to our agreement, you have five days to remedy the potential default, Mr. Surtees."

"Just how the hell am I supposed to do that?" Surtees grunted and refolded his arms across the broad expanse of his chest.

"You can pay us the difference between the current price and the default floor price. Or you can sign over more shares to us to make up that difference."

"I can't give up the shares I already signed to you."

"Then you will have to give us more shares to make up the short-fall." Wen's voice was calm, calculated, inexorable. "Or cash. Cash works just as well, and you won't have to give up any more of your shares."

"I don't have any more shares to give up! I've already stuck my neck out in borrowing against the ones you have now; if the board finds out I've borrowed against even more, I'll be for the bloody high jump. I'll be ousted from my own company and lucky if they don't sue me for every penny I have left." He slumped back in the chair; it complained of the imposition.

"Then, unless you can give us cash to cover that shortfall, I'm sorry to say the loan will go into default next Friday."

Silence. From his side view, Lucas watched as Surtees pondered the imponderable.

"There is a third option." Surtees's voice had regained a bit of his usual swagger. He leaned forward and rested one meaty hand on each knee. "I had my lawyers take a good look through the contract and brief me on the laws surrounding your particular type of dealing, Mr.

Wen. They told me I can always cut my losses, give up my collateral, and simply walk away from the loan obligation."

Wen's head came up sharply, his eyes moving from the Montblanc monstrosity to Roger Surtees's face. "Wait . . . you're expecting us to take all the risk *and* liability of your worthless shares?"

Surtees's nod was one of self-satisfaction, and at that point, Lucas knew the guy had been planning to pull this ace out of the hat right from the off. Roger Surtees hadn't come here to beg; he'd come here to gloat, so he could play Jimmy Wen like a Stradivarius.

"I have been advised I can turn my back on the whole damn deal without any legal repercussions," the fat man said with a cold *gotcha!* smile.

Wen looked at Lucas, with an impenetrable expression on his face. Time to step in.

"Now, hold on, Roger," Lucas objected. "We gave you that loan in good faith when no one else would touch you."

Surtees turned his head to give Lucas an arrogant half smile, half grimace. "Fuck good faith up the arse. This is business, and you know it. You'd have me pouring in more cash and shares like a fool to prop up the failing shares when you know bloody well how badly they're tanking."

Wen put the fountain pen down and stood. "Rest assured, they'll go back up, Mr. Surtees; they always do. This alleged report leak is nothing more than a storm in a teacup; the media will be all over something else in a few days, people will be bored with gossip about rogue nanobots, and your stocks will climb." He offered his client what was meant to be a reassuring smile, which presented instead as a curled-lip snarl.

"They'll be back up in a few weeks," Lucas added. "A couple of months at the most. Glaber Nanotech is hot property right now."

"Oh, yes. Right up until the unsubstantiated rumor that their trials *killed* people. They're hot, all right. Too hot to handle. Moreover, I don't have a couple of months! I don't even have a few weeks! You greedy bastards are going to default me on the loan in four fucking days!"

Wen looked for all the world as if he was prepping to leap over the desk and grab Surtees firmly by his blubbery throat. "You cannot be serious about defaulting on this—"

Surtees huffed and stood, causing his chair's seat cushion to give up an audible sigh of relief. "I think you'll find that I can, Mr. Wen. You see, my lawyers picked up on a clause you no doubt thought you'd hidden—the one that states any shortfall or loss *may* have to be paid by the client. But, I am advised I have the option to leave my collateral with you to satisfy that clause and forget about the whole sorry business."

Lucas, too, got to his feet; this was beginning to feel like an elementary school playground standoff. "You will still be liable for the shortfall, Mr. Surtees."

Surtees actually puffed out his chest, all but laughing in Lucas's face. "And what do you think you are going to do about that? Drag me through the courts to get it? It would tie you up for years, and if it ever got through the courts, it would raise a million red flags with the SFC . . . and maybe even the police. I'm sure a reputable company like JM Wen Limited wouldn't want to attract the attention of the regulators and law enforcement . . . not that you'd have anything to hide, of course."

Lucas moved to meet Surtees eye to eye. "We helped you out when you were desperate, and this is how you repay us? You're just going to walk away and leave us with fifteen million in worthless stock? You ungrateful—"

"Lucas!" Wen walked around his desk; Lau and Pang took a step away from the wall, maintaining their exact distance from their boss.

With a nervous tic twitching the corner of his eye, Surtees backed away from Lucas and took a step toward the door. "You need to keep your damn attack dog on a leash, Wen."

"Mr. Surtees, we can talk about this," Wen all but pleaded. "Maybe we can delay the default by a few days?"

"No. I'm done with this, and I'm done with you. You really ought to take more care with your contracts, Jimmy. I'd fire every one of my bloody barristers if I were you!"

He turned and beetled to the office door, giving Pang a wide berth.

"Roger, wait!" Lucas spread his arms in entreaty.

At the office door, Surtees turned to crack a grim smile. "You know what? Fuck you both. Fuck you and your dodgy deals and your asinine inflated lending rates. You're welcome to the damn stocks. Keep the bloody things. And good luck with them going back up. After this whole fake news fiasco, you'll be lucky if trading on them isn't frozen before my default time is up!"

Pang took a step toward the Brit, sliding a hand inside his jacket. Surtees paled and bailed, leaving a wide, greasy smear on the polished glass of the door as he barged through it. Roger J. Surtees waddled his fat ass down the hall, still wearing a smug, shit-eating grin.

Wen scratched his chin and wandered back around his desk. He sat down in his chair and contemplated his ridiculously expensive pen. Lau and Pang sauntered after him to resume their places. Lucas let out a long, wheezing sigh, watching until Surtees was out of sight. He heard Wen chuckling and turned.

Wen was shaking his head, his thin lips curled in a smile. "I thought we were going to be here all day. I was afraid the old fool would never realize he could walk away from the debt!"

"He knew damn well," Lucas said wryly. "He thought he was pulling a fast one on us, the poor old sap. Can't blame him for wanting to rub it in. He thought he'd scored a coup."

The coup, of course was Jimmy Wen's. What Roger Surtees didn't know was that Jimmy Wen had sold his collateral shares in Glaber Tech at a high, virtually the moment they were in his hands. That left JM Wen to capture the difference—the spread—between the money he'd lent and the price he'd sold the shares for. That is, if Surtees defaulted on the loan. In default, Wen would keep the difference—a 100% pure profit for JM Wen Limited. Good old Roger had just handed Jimmy Wen his best-case scenario.

"Don't you just love it when these morons walk away and hand us an easy two hundred mil American before lunch? Ah, today is going to be a good day, Lucas." Jimmy shook his head. "And Surtees had the nerve to suggest we should fire *our* lawyers!"

He opened his desk drawer and pulled out four Gurkah Black Dragon cigars, prodding the intercom with his pinkie. "Anita, put three magnums of Boerl and Kroff 2002 on ice—no, make that *four;* I think we can afford to give our new high rollers a taste of the good life!"

Anita told him yes, she would do that, and she would have it ready before lunch.

"Gonna share the wealth with the new recruits, eh?" Lucas slapped a hand on Wen's shoulder as he plucked a cigar from his hand. "That's very generous of you, Jimmy."

Jimmy tipped him a wink and then turned to Lau and Pang. "Will you two cheer up? It's not every day we get a client to walk away from two hundred million dollars!" He handed each of them one of the cigars. "Although we are working on that."

The bodyguards allowed themselves to smile a little as they pocketed their cigars.

Wen eased back into his chair, clipped his cigar, and lit up; in an instant, a thick cloud of pungent blue-white smoke circled his head. It had been a good morning's work. Roger J. Surtees had signed over his Glaber stock to Wen at $109 per share; JM Wen Limited had dumped it all, right before it sank like the Titanic. That had magnified the sell-off and turned it into a market free-for-all when the investing public shareholders rushed to sell. It was a gamble—stock shorting always was, unless you knew how to manipulate the markets in your favor.

Like Jimmy Wen did.

CHAPTER NINE

Valentina had not been too motivated to fish the stickie from her purse and call Chrissy; the busy day on top of the travel, along with the promise of time in the office over the weekend had put her more in the mood for relaxing and taking time to process what needed to be done. Still, she had to admit it was good to see Chrissy Huang again—the only familiar face in Hong Kong. Chrissy was the closest thing Valentina had to a friend—possibly the closest thing she'd ever had to a friend since the day she'd begun her upward climb through the ranks of big finance. Trust was a rare commodity here, and Valentina Vittorio was less inclined to trust than most people in her business.

Now, as the two women made their way into one of the pricier and more exclusive clubs in Hong Kong, she was pleased she'd given in, slipped on her Gucci little black dress—which turned out to be the perfect complement to Chrissy's thigh-skimming Versace LBD—and headed out into the bright lights of Hong Kong. She and Chrissy had enjoyed a number of wild Friday nights in New York; it might feel good to relive those good times, though she'd have to be far more guarded than she'd been back then.

"What do you think?" Chrissy had to lean in close and raise her voice just to be heard above the thumping music in the glitzy club.

"What?" Valentina all but shouted as she followed Chrissy toward the bar.

"I said, what do you think of the club?"

Valentina smiled; Methuselah was one of the most exclusive clubs in the Lan Kwai Fong district, and had cost HK$500 each just to get in; Chrissy had *insisted* on paying for both of them. It seemed to Valentina to be pretty much the same as the expensive clubs back home.

No big woo. "It's . . . nice," she said aloud.

Nice wasn't at all the right adjective. The place was loud—too loud for any meaningful conversation. Normally that would be annoying. Tonight it suited Valentina; it meant she could use the cacophony to cover her thoughts, and since Chrissy was of no use in getting her close to Jimmy Wen, she had no reason to subject her to sly interrogation.

Chrissy was leading the way toward the bar. She stopped suddenly when a large, suited figure blocked her way. Valentina's highly developed fight-or-flight instincts came on line; she stepped up to stand shoulder to shoulder with the other woman.

The bouncer, a broad, shiny-headed giant of a man with a tidy goatee, leaned into Chrissy's personal space and said something loudly in Cantonese.

"We're not VIPs," Chrissy responded in English. She gestured at the bar. "We're just getting a drink."

The bouncer shifted to English as well, and included Valentina in his regard. "Courtesy of the management," he told them. "If you'd come with me."

Chrissy shrugged at Valentina, who shrugged back; the two followed the bouncer through milling patrons to a semisecluded area at the back of the club. There, the guy unhooked a red velvet cordon from a stanchion and pointed to a table in the corner. A semicircle of red distressed leather couches bracketed the low table, while at its center sat a silver ice bucket with a bottle of champagne nestled inside.

The two women seated themselves on the butter-soft upholstery and surveyed the area. It was quieter here and sparsely populated by beautiful people dressed in designer clothing and glittering with jewelry. The air was subtly infused with expensive perfume and colognes.

"You must have made an impression," Chrissy said as she watched Valentina pour out two flutes of their complimentary champagne; it was Armand de Brignac Brut Gold, which had set someone back HK$46,000m—six grand in New York money.

"I've never been here before and I only just walked in, how could I have? The bouncer spoke to you, not me." Valentina chinked glasses with her friend and took the tiniest of sips.

"Zhang Bo owns the club," Chrissy said, as if that explained everything. "In fact, he owns most of the high-end clubs in the district—we'd have been hard pressed to find one that wasn't one of his. You most likely caught his interest with your performance earlier today." She tossed back her drink and reached for a top up.

"My performance?"

Chrissy gave her a *look*. "Phillip Eu has an office near Mr. Wen's. He saw everything."

Valentina recalled the thin, narrow-faced young man who'd ducked down the hall during Lucas's tense confrontation with Zhang. She nodded. "Yeah, I met Mr. Zhang. It wasn't what I'd call an impressive or auspicious introduction, though."

"Well, it was enough for him to treat us to this. Unless it's his way of letting Mr. Wen know he's watching his staff like seagulls watch sunbathers with french fries." Chrissy helped herself to yet another glass, giggling a little at her own turn of phrase.

Two-glass giggles? Damn, but you're a lightweight. "Meaning?"

"Meaning he's been in the office a hell of a lot over the last several weeks—there's no wonder the rumor mill is working overtime. No one but Wen's inner circle knows for certain, but I'd say it was fairly obvious Wen's doing serious business with him. Which means he's doing serious business with the Clans." She took a hearty swig of her champagne.

"You're okay with that?"

"The gangs're a way of life in Hong Kong," Chrissy replied. "If it wasn't Zhang, it'd be one of the others."

Valentina scanned the room; there was no sign of Zhang Bo, of course, but just the thought that he knew she was there put her on alert. She waved over one of the attentive waitresses and reached for her purse. "Two bottles of Perrier please."

The waitress smiled sweetly, held up a tiny slender hand, and said, "Everything is on the house, Miss Vittorio." She turned on her stiletto heels and headed off to the bar.

Chrissy beamed. "This is *awesome*. I should bring you out with me every night."

"Yeah." Valentina was distracted; was all of this some kind of message? Should she report back to Wen that she'd been given the full-on VIP treatment by Zhang Bo? Was she expected to? Was this Zhang letting Wen know he knew where his key employees were at any given time? Whatever it was, it rested uneasily in Valentina's gut.

Chrissy stood up. Already she was unsteady on her feet—the Armand had gone straight to her head. "I need the restroom," she mouthed.

Taking a moment to ensure she was balanced, she shuffled around the table. Valentina got to her feet and emptied her champagne flute into the ice bucket. Following Chrissy, she figured she might as well take the opportunity to have a look around Zhang's club. She wondered if his clientele included other denizens of the financial sector.

The VIP restroom was as spacious and opulent as Valentina had expected for a club as lavish as Methuselah. The floors were Italian marble, the countertops polished granite, and the faucets and lavatory handles gold. The complimentary tissues and liquid hand soaps were in ornate, green onyx dispensers—the VIPs in Hong Kong were clearly more trustworthy than those back home; in New York, the dispensers would have been stolen in a heartbeat. Two girls, exquisitely dressed in gold latex minidresses, were busy washing their hands and inspecting their makeup in the gilt-edged mirrors above the gleaming white porcelain sinks; they giggled and chatted excitedly in Cantonese as they went about their ablutions. Falling silent when Valentina and Chrissy walked in, they watched them select a stall each before picking up their conversation.

Chrissy was done and at the basins when Valentina heard the restroom door open. A gruff male voice barked in Chinese, and the pair of giggling girls scurried out.

"Where is your *gweilo* friend?" one of the voices asked in English.

Chrissy said nothing; there was just the trickling sound of water.

"Are you not listening?" a second voice demanded. "My friend asked you a question."

"Is there a problem here?" Valentina stepped out of her stall. She studied the two young men so out of place in the women's restroom; dressed head to toe in black, they were tall, lean, and quite handsome. Had they not had trouble written all over them, she might even have flirted with them.

"No problem at all," one of the young men replied. Turning his back on Chrissy, he stepped toward Valentina, the heels of his dark blue ostrich-skin boots clacking on the floor. "We were looking for you."

"Well, here I am. How can I help you boys?"

Valentina had seen more than her fair share of testosterone-fueled young bucks who fancied their chances with her, but there was something about these two that made her suspect different motives.

"You must forgive my friend," the other young man said. "He is still learning how to talk to women—especially beautiful American women." He smiled and held out a hand for Valentina to shake. "I'm Joe, my friend is Daniel. We would like to buy you both a drink."

Valentina did not take the proffered hand. In fact, she didn't even look at it but kept her gaze up, watching their eyes. "Perhaps if you hadn't followed us into the *women's* restroom, we would have taken you up on your offer. As it is . . ." She shrugged one bare shoulder.

Joe's expression changed as if someone had flipped a switch. Gone was the friendly Lothario; this was a young man who was obviously unaccustomed to being told no. "Don't you know who we are?" he demanded.

"Actually, we don't *care* who you are," Chrissy threw in; the champagne had slurred her judgment as well as her voice.

"We are Dark Society—Sun Yee On," Daniel of the blue ostrich boots informed her. He loomed over Chrissy with menace in his eyes. "Bitches like you don't say no to us."

"If you guys will excuse us. We're going back to our table now." Valentina sidestepped Joe, took hold of Chrissy's elbow, and made ready to usher her from the restroom.

"I said, no one says no to us." Maneuvering himself into their path, Daniel folded his arms across his chest.

Valentina made eye contact; the little peacock meant business, and his dilated pupils told her he was also high on cocaine. She pitched her voice low, calm, almost seductive. "Let's not have any trouble, boys. We're having a girls' night out—not looking to hook up."

Joe struck like a snake, grabbing Valentina's arm just above the elbow. "You're not going anywhere, bitch."

On cue, Daniel pulled a switchblade from a back pocket; a harsh, metallic click and the blade's tip was pressed tight against Chrissy's neck. She uttered a strangled chirp and froze.

"Say no again and your friend gets her throat cut," Joe snarled, yanking on Valentina's arm.

She caught the flash of hesitation that crossed his friend's face and took the moment. Spinning toward Joe, she wrenched her arm out of his grasp, seized his wrist, and twisted it counterclockwise, forcing him off balance. One hard kick to his knee and he went down hard, yelping in surprise and pain. The instant his knees cracked against the marble floor, Valentina delivered a second kick—this time to the arm she was still holding. His elbow dislocated—if not outright broke; Joe let out a shrill cry and collapsed to the floor.

She'd read Daniel's hesitation clearly. As he waffled, glancing between her and Chrissy, Valentina rounded on him. In one fluid movement, she grabbed the hand clutching the knife, shouldered Chrissy out of the way, and pushed the wannabe gangster against the restroom wall. With her free hand, she snatched one of the onyx soap dispensers from the counter and aimed three sharp blows at Daniel's face, giving him no time to defend himself, let alone retaliate. Blood from Daniel's broken nose exploded across his face, and several broken teeth spilled from his slack mouth.

The restroom door swung open and the sounds of the club beyond flooded in. Valentina turned toward the door, the soap dispenser still in her hand, her arm cocked. Of course there was a third man—someone to ensure his buddies weren't disturbed. As he stepped into the restroom and caught sight of Joe slumped on the floor and Daniel's ruined face, he reached behind his back and pulled a handgun from under his short jacket.

Valentina jerked Daniel upright and shoved him in front of her toward the door. She followed his stumbling path in a half crouch, then darted around him to seize the startled gunman's hand. She twisted it as hard as she could and smashed the soap dispenser sideways up into his nose. The guy's head snapped back, his nose shattered. He let go of the gun. Valentina finished him with a hard kick to his balls with the four-inch heel of her pumps.

He'd no more than collapsed to the restroom floor when two more shapes appeared in the doorway. Tensing, more than ready to continue the fight, Valentina raised the gun.

"Hold your fire!" one of the shapes said. "We're the good guys!" As he stepped into the restroom with his hands held out, Valentina recognized the bouncer who had escorted them to the VIP area.

"What the fuck happened here? You do all this?" The second bouncer eyed the three downed young men, then looked at Valentina with open admiration.

"They said they were Sun Yee On," Chrissy offered, as if she felt the need to explain the carnage.

The bald bouncer shook his head. "I don't think so. They wouldn't dare. More likely rich young punks *playing* at being gangsters—I guess they thought it would impress you. Okay, you ladies enjoy the rest of your evening. We'll clean this up." He nudged Joe's misshapen arm with the toe of his shoe, making the young man groan.

Valentina thanked the bouncers, retrieved her purse from the stall, casually strolled to the sink to wash her hands, then escorted a shell-shocked Chrissy out of the restroom. The poor girl was trembling and the terror was still in her eyes.

"I need a drink," she said numbly as they walked back to the VIP area.

Scanning the bar as they made their way across the club, Valentina was pleased to see that a couple of the single men she'd noticed earlier were still there—after the fight she was running high on adrenaline, and she was horny as hell. She let her libido carry her along at first, joining with Chrissy in a flirtatious encounter with the young studs from the bar, whom they'd impressed to pieces by inviting them to their table in the VIP section.

It was absurdly easy; two hot women in skintight dresses with money to burn was more than either could refuse. Valentina and Chrissy made small talk with them over a couple rounds of HK$225 tequila before Chrissy suggested they take the party outside the club. She'd not even asked the men their names, and when they were offered, she silenced them with a seductive finger to the lips.

Valentina wanted to know their names. She wanted to know where they worked, who they knew. Specifically, if they knew Jimmy Wen or Zhang Bo. As Chrissy rose unsteadily to ask Valentina if she wanted to take the boys back to her hotel or to Chrissy's apartment, the full impact of the situation hit Valentina like a dash of icy water. She looked up from the red sofa at the three faces turned toward her and felt her sexual tension unravel like a cheap sweater.

She knew Chrissy somewhat, but neither of them knew these men. Or knew what might be divulged in an unguarded moment. Valentina Vittorio could not have unguarded moments. Not now. Not after spending ten years to get here.

"You know what, Chrissy?" she said giving the other woman a lopsided smile. "I'm suddenly not feeling so well. I think the bathroom brawl is finally taking its toll. I was already a little jet-lagged. I'm gonna turn in, but you go ahead and have fun. Okay?"

Chrissy's disappointed frown gave way to obvious concern. "Oh, wow, Valentina. I didn't think . . . I mean, you took those guys on all by yourself and—are you okay?"

"Fine. Just . . . a little worn out."

"Oh, well then . . . more for me, I guess." She glanced back and forth between her two new friends.

"If you'd like," said one of them, "we'll have our cab drop you at your hotel."

Valentina smiled. "I'll take you up on that, thanks."

They dropped her off under the portico of the Four Seasons' front entrance. As she alit onto the walkway, Chrissy leaned over one guy's lap to poke her head out.

"Sure you won't change your mind?"

Was there a little unease in the Chinese girl's eyes? Was she having second thoughts about taking two complete strangers into her home—into her bed? Valentina didn't see any. She suspected Chrissy was a bit too drunk to feel unease. She'd managed to extract from one of the guys that they worked for the Hang Seng Bank with offices just down the block from JM Wen and doubted that any repercussions would be no more dire than possibly awkward encounters at the Starbucks between the two buildings.

"Nah," she told Chrissy. "I'm done. Enjoy. You can give me a full report on Monday morning."

Chrissy laughed and all but collapsed into the hookup's lap. He reeled her in, waved at Valentina, and shut the door of the cab. Valentina watched the cab go, wondering if she was missing an opportunity to find out if the Hang Seng did business with JM Wen.

CHAPTER TEN

Suitably revitalized following a night of unbroken sleep, mind sharply focused on her objective, Valentina left the hotel and made her way to the office; her aim was to arrive well ahead of the ten a.m. briefing and spend some time at her desk—she had some preparation of her own to take care of.

Although Valentina was by no means the first one into JM Wen Limited that Saturday morning, the sales office was empty, and the peace and quiet was exquisite. Sitting herself down at her desk, Valentina fired up the computer. While she waited for it to whir to life, she fished her cell phone and wallet from her purse. A quick scan of the room, with particular emphasis on Wen's office at the far end, confirmed she was entirely alone. Valentina poked a manicured thumbnail into the groove on the side of her cell and popped out the tiny plastic tray. Carefully, she plucked the miniature SD card from the tray and inserted it into the card adapter she had secreted in a small compartment within her wallet.

The moment the laptop was fully booted, Valentina slipped the card into one of its SD slots and crossed her fingers until the icon appeared on the screen to inform her the card had been detected.

Another glance around.

Deftly, Valentina set her two displays so that the larger display did not mirror the laptop screen. She opened a stock ticker app to display on the big screen, along with a business contacts app, then she shifted her focus to the laptop display and clicked the SD card's icon. A list of the SD card's contents were displayed on the laptop while the larger display continued to show the stock ticker and contacts app.

She selected an application from the SD card which, once installed, would provide her with the safe anonymity of a virtual private network. She began the install and waited. There were three other VPN apps, each of which would need to be installed, along with the proxy files she'd copied onto the card back in New York. The proxies would add yet another layer of anonymity by bouncing her internet activity between countless servers in the Netherlands, Canada, Korea, and France; she'd also written a neat piece of misdirection code herself that would allow her to bounce activity records to selected IP addresses.

Valentina's diligence at covering her virtual tracks meant she would be free to dig through JM Wen's company records and trawl the World Wide Web in complete secrecy—barring anybody staring over her shoulder as she worked. She was entirely free—and secure—to gather any information she needed. The software she'd purchased from the murkier parts of the Deep Web was designed to hide itself from the computer's activity monitors and lay buried within the operating system where it would remain undetectable to all but the most expert eye, and an encryption-cracking application would render anything Wen attempted to hide readable.

Ten minutes later Valentina was done. Once her laptop rebooted, she logged into the *Hong Kong Economic Times* website. She then minimized that before checking through the system files and clearing out the cache a second time. It was entirely unnecessary, but only then would she be satisfied her tracks were well and truly covered. Valentina knew there was absolutely no margin for error at this stage— the stakes were high, and she couldn't allow her single-mindedness to blind her to potential pitfalls.

An old, terribly familiar memory leapt to Valentina's mind; it had been a long time since she'd allowed herself to entertain the unwelcome thoughts, but being there in Hong Kong, and so close to Jimmy Wen after so many years of planning, they served well to remind her why she was taking such risks.

* * *

A loud, persistent knock on the door in the middle of the night had awoken her. Bright blue and red lights flickered gaily on the ceiling above her bed, as if to announce Christmas, but in the moment she awoke with a start, Valentina instinctively knew something was terribly wrong.

It was cold in the house that night; their power had been shut off earlier in the day, and Valentina's parents had fought over not having enough money to get it reconnected and having to light the place with candles like poor people. She dragged the comforter from the bed to keep herself warm as she padded across her bedroom, the floor icy beneath her bare feet, to peer out between the curtains.

A pair of black and white police cruisers were parked directly outside their house. Valentina could just make out two dark shapes in one, while the other sat empty. She heard the muted squawk of the police radio filtering out through the car's half-open window. Curtains twitched all along the street. She knew she wasn't the only one who'd been woken up by the police. Whatever the cops' purpose, the Parisi family would be the subject of rumors and speculation for at least the next day or so, or until some other petty local scandal gave the gossips something to wag their tongues about.

"What's going on, Tina?" She jumped a little at the sound of her sister's drowsy voice.

"Nothing. Go back to bed, Syl."

"Is Papa all right?"

Valentina turned to face the girl. Framed there in the dark doorway and illuminated by the police cars' dancing lights, Sylvia looked so much younger than her eleven years—she was petite, skinny, and still insisted on wearing her favorite My Little Pony pajamas even though they were a couple sizes too small.

"Everything's okay. There's nothing for you to worry about. You should still be asleep—you have school in the morning."

"So do you." Defiantly, Sylvia took a single, tentative step into her big sister's bedroom and gazed up at the lights on the ceiling. "Can I see?" She pointed at the thin gap Valentina had made in the curtains.

Valentina pulled the two thick panels of together to shut out the cop cars and the street. "No. Go back to bed."

Her tone was harsher than she'd intended it to be, but she was acting in the little girl's best interests; whatever was going on out there, Valentina knew it couldn't possibly bode well. She wanted nothing more than to hold Sylvia tight and assure her everything was going to be okay.

Sylvia huffed and allowed Valentina to usher her back to her own bedroom; just one more year and Big Sister would be off to college. Then Valentina's big-girl bedroom would be all hers.

With Sylvia safely ensconced in her own room, Valentina crept silently to the top of the stairs and strained to hear the soft voices that drifted up from the kitchen. Yellow, flickering candlelight glowed through the door to light up the lower half of the staircase.

The cops—a squat, burly guy and a young Hispanic female officer—were talking to Valentina's mother in calm, hushed tones, and although she couldn't actually make out everything that was being said, Valentina couldn't fail to catch the gist.

They'd found what they believed to be her father's body floating somewhere off Governor's Island—they still needed to make a formal identification, so couldn't officially state for certain it was him, but since he'd had his driver's license in his pants pocket, it was the most probable conclusion to draw. They also told her mother they had every reason to believe it had been suicide; it was somehow supposed to be a comfort to her that he'd not been murdered. They'd have to wait for the coroner's report to make an official statement. Did Mrs. Parisi know of any reason why her husband would want to kill himself?

For Valentina, the question was straight out of some horrendous nightmare. Things had been especially bad of late in the Parisi home, mostly due to her father's constant money worries—the electric company cutting them off had only been the last in a long line of problems—but, of course, Valentina had no idea just how bad things had become. Like any caring parents, her mother and father had shielded their daughters from the harsh reality of their dire financial situation, even though it had been impossible to keep them away from the all-pervading, unbearably strained atmosphere in the house.

Valentina's father had confided in her only a few weeks before his death that his latest get-rich-quick scheme was in real danger of going belly-up. If—when—it did, it was going to take all of the family's savings along with it. Valentina had reckoned at the time her father had confessed to her because he hadn't been able to face telling his wife, and because he'd not only taken out loans, he'd also gambled his daughters' college funds on the deal that was supposed to have been unequivocally guaranteed to double his money at the very least. There was no doubt about it—that was one hell of a burden to dump on a seventeen-year-old.

Mom was crying quietly. As broken as the poor woman was inside, Valentina knew she was doing her best to keep her grief to herself so as not to disturb her sleeping daughters. There came the faint chink of china and the shrill whistle of the teakettle—at least the gas was still connected, even if they couldn't afford to run the heating. Valentina had seen enough cop shows on TV to know one of the officers would be preparing steaming mugs of coffee that none of them really wanted just to maintain some semblance of normalcy for poor Mrs. Parisi.

Taking another deep breath, Valentina finally plucked up enough courage to venture downstairs. As reluctant as she was to face the brutal reality of her father's sudden death, she knew her mother needed someone strong by her side.

When the nice lady cop asked if Valentina's mother would be able to accompany them to the morgue to make a formal identification of the body, she collapsed into her daughter's arms and sobbed uncontrollably. Valentina told them she would arrange for one of the neighbors to watch over Sylvia and that she would go along as support. Then she held her heartbroken mother in her arms as they both sobbed.

One night. One night that would never be followed by day.

* * *

Reliving that night always left Valentina feeling empty and hateful, and neither were emotions she could afford to entertain if she was to destroy Wen. Her father had always told her she must keep a clear head if she was to be successful, and for the majority of the time, she was able to do so. But, once in a while, memories of her father's death and its tragic aftermath would bubble to the surface, and Valentina was forced to push them back into her interior vault and slam the door. Making her plans against Wen would help her keep that door locked.

The first of the weekend's briefings would be kicking off in five minutes, so Valentina made ready to head off to the meeting room. She gave her computer another once-over and, satisfied she had removed all traces of her furtive activity, retrieved the SD card and closed the laptop down. Returning her phone and wallet to her bag, she stepped away from her desk.

CHAPTER ELEVEN

As if Monday morning had revitalized the antigovernment movement, there were yet more protesters on Finance Street. At least they were less belligerent than they'd been on Friday. Valentina had spent much of the weekend between briefing meetings resting up and focusing her mind on what she knew was going to be one hell of a week. Chrissy had not been in touch to report on her night of fun and games, and although Valentina was vaguely concerned, she told herself she'd see Chrissy today and get as much of a report as her friend was willing to give—or able to remember.

Once in sight of the front of the mall entrance, Valentina shouldered her way through the protestors to the front doors. They were jostling anyone attempting to get by them and had begun singing their new anthem, "Glory to Hong Kong," in almost perfect harmony. As she stepped through the doors, someone on their way out barged through and almost knocked her off her feet.

"Hey!" Valentina objected, and for a split second she was back in New York. Acting on instinct, her hand slipped down to her side; a bump like that back home usually meant her bag would have been long gone; Manhattan muggers were not above slicing through a leather shoulder strap with a switchblade, no matter how expensive the bag.

Thankfully, the bag was still there on her hip and all seemed to be in order. Spinning around to take a look at who'd dared to be so rude, Valentina's gut instinct was to shout admonishment after the culprit. She had a fiery temper that had taken years to repress. It was never too far below the surface of her cool, professional facade. Fortunately for whomever had crashed into her with such gusto, they'd been rendered anonymous by the sea of determined, shiny young faces. Beneath her breath, Valentina let the guy—she thought it had been a guy, anyway—know he was one *cazzo di merda*—a real shit head.

Valentina used the stroll down the mall to 2IFC to cool her annoyance before she had to face the inevitable line of security guards. She immediately recognized the chubby young man with the fuzz mustache she'd seen on Friday and elected to join his line; if he recognized her, he might simply wave her through and not subject her to the time sink of checking her bag.

As it turned out, Valentina's logic was flawed. When she arrived at the security guard's table, he seemed *delighted* to see her and eager to finally have the opportunity to go through her bag. Valentina donned a flirty smile, unzipped the little purse, and placed it on the table. The guard went about his job with professional precision. Barely affording her a glance, he pulled her bag open and peered inside. He jostled it slightly, then looked up at her with a quizzical expression on his face, quirking an eyebrow.

Valentina was a bit taken aback. What could he have seen that might have puzzled him? Granted, she had a few tampons in the bag, but nothing really out of the ordinary.

"Miss Vittorio!" Anita Kwok's voice was most welcome.

Valentina looked up to see Wen's ever-efficient assistant scurrying across the elevator lobby toward her.

"She's with me," Anita said, snatched the Gucci bag from under the guard's nose, handed it to Valentina, and led her through the security check.

The young guard glowered at them as they made their way to the elevators.

"Tan Fen has taken a shine to you," Anita huffed. "He will find any excuse to prolong his time checking you in . . . or checking you out. It really is unacceptable behavior; I will have someone speak with his superiors."

Valentina zipped up her purse and followed Anita; a few minutes more and they were squashed into one of the elevators and on their way up to the office. This time she kept her mouth shut. When she entered the closer's sales office three minutes later, Chrissy was at her desk looking none the worse for wear. That was a relief, but when Valentina asked her if she'd enjoyed her "boy toys" Friday night, she was a bit vague on the details.

"They were great," she said brightly. "You know . . . fun. We drank some more and smoked some weed." She frowned. "I'll probably hear about it from my apartment manager. I don't remember their names, though. Too bad, really. I'd like to see them again."

Valentina crossed her arms and looked down on the other woman with a wry smile. "You refused to let them *tell* you their names."

"Oh . . . yes. I did, didn't I?" She giggled and gave an eloquent shrug.

"Sorrow not, Chrissy," Valentina told her. "You can always go hang out in Hang Seng's lobby until they turn up."

Chrissy snorted. "What, and look desperate? No, thank you. I might drop by the Starbucks a bit more often, though."

Shaking her head, Valentina crossed to her desk, sat down, and got to work. She had a breakfast meeting with a client she'd first contacted before she left New York and was eager to bring into the JM Wen fold. He'd called for the meeting, saying only that he wished to discuss a loan. She'd spoken to him by phone and dealt with the US arm of his company—Green Dynamics Construction Partners—during her time at the New York office, managing their investment portfolio. She knew Green Dynamics was expanding its business to mainland China and suspected their meeting would be to discuss how best to fund that expansion. She already had ideas that she was certain would make Jimmy Wen a very happy man.

* * *

Wen's chief of security, Shum Kuo, had an uncanny knack for sucking the fun out of a room simply by walking into it. He was a short, stocky man with a buzz cut and soft, brown eyes that belied his brusque, no-nonsense persona and legendary mean streak. He wore expensive suits, imported Salvatore Ferragamo shoes, and was known for taking pleasure in the finer things in a life he outwardly didn't seem to find all that pleasurable.

He barged into Wen's glass-fronted office without knocking, and the Monday morning energy Lucas had been enjoying fizzled in an instant.

"Cigar?"

Jimmy Wen thrust a Black Dragon toward Shum as he marched up to the desk with a disapproving stare at Lau and Pang, who were preoccupied with enjoying their own cigars; smoking and drinking on duty was strictly forbidden, even though Wen always started his week off with a fat cigar. Judging by the sour expression on Shum's face, there would be reprimands for the two bodyguards once they were off duty.

"Thank you." Shum took the offering—it would have been incredibly rude of him not to accept the gift from the company CEO—and slipped it into the inside pocket of his immaculately tailored jacket.

Lucas knew for a fact he'd ditch the thing in the trash on the way back to his own office. He'd seen him do it. He'd also seen the night maintenance guys smoking Black Dragons on occasion and was glad they hadn't gone to waste. Lucas wasn't sure if it was the opulence of the habit or the cigars themselves that Shum took objection to. The security chief had a fearsome reputation, one he'd begun to craft at the Chinese Ministry of State Security. He'd crafted it so well, his superiors had kept him a safe number of rungs down the ladder instead of elevating him to the position he probably deserved based on his service record.

Lucas understood that precaution. To give that much power to a man like Shum Kuo could have catastrophic consequences. He also got how much Jimmy liked having Shum around. As much as the man spooked everyone in the building—Wen included—he was a valuable and comforting asset. He was paid to spend his days looking over their corporate shoulder so his boss didn't have to.

"I have come to talk about the other matter, Mr. Wen." Shum shot Lucas a look that demanded he leave the office. There was little love lost between the two, especially after Lucas had overheard Shum tell their boss he was uncomfortable with the "half-breed" knowing his business.

"Fine by me," Lucas said. He got to his feet, clamped the fat cigar between his teeth, and buttoned his suit coat.

"He stays," Wen said in a voice that brooked no dissent.

Lucas smiled and sat his ass back down on the cream-colored sofa in a swirling cloud of smoke.

Wen favored his security chief with an impatient glance. "Is this going to take long? I have a meeting with the new arrivals this morning."

Shum smoothed his jacket as if that might also smooth his pride. "No, sir, it won't take long at all. I have concluded the investigation."

"And?" Wen's voice was sharp.

Lucas smiled behind his cigar. Jimmy had little patience for Shum's poor communication skills; he merely pretended to be monosyllabic. Hey, it suited the role and added drama to the job. He never seemed to get the idea that what intimidated his old MSS colleagues only pissed Wen off.

Shum cleared his throat. "I have confirmed the individual who has been talking to the regulators."

"Beyond all reasonable doubt?"

"Beyond *all* doubt whatsoever. The mole has done an especially good job of covering their tracks—too good, in fact. It looks like they were well-schooled in industrial espionage. They used proxy servers, virtual machines, and disposable phones, took clandestine off-site meetings . . . hence the time it has taken my department to verify the individual's identity."

Oh, that wasn't at all defensive. Lucas suspected that Shum more than enjoyed the cat-and-mouse involved in searching out suspected moles within the organization. He'd be bloody sad the game was over and rattling round at loose ends until the next time an employee decided to roll over on Jimmy Wen. Maybe he'd even invent one just to give himself something to do.

"I'm disappointed." Ever the master of understatement, Wen sighed. He looked out through the glass wall of his office, his eyes finding and fixing on Chrissy Huang, now immersed in a client call on her desk phone. As she spoke, she tapped notes into her computer and fiddled with her cell.

His eyes still on Chrissy, Wen said, "Miss Huang will be leaving our employ today, Mr. Shum. But before we let her go, I'd like you to take her out and buy her brunch. Anything she wants, anything at all. My treat. And then . . ." He shrugged and stubbed out his cigar in the gilt-edged ashtray that sat precariously at the edge of his desk.

"Yes, sir."

Lucas frowned. He liked Chrissy. She was bright, funny, and good in bed. He'd be sorry to see her go.

"Anything she wants, Shum," Wen said as the man got up to leave. "Anything at all."

Shum gave a solemn nod and looked out at Chrissy who was deep into her phone call, her fingers a veritable blur as they darted across her computer keyboard. Lucas followed his gaze. Chrissy had that hungry look on her face, the one that was universal across all successful closers when they were about to bring in a big client and were smelling the money. Contemplating her, Lucas's eyes were drawn to the long, iridescent black ponytail that followed the contour of her spine all the way down to her shapely ass.

He glanced at Shum and saw hunger of a different sort. Deep unease fluttered behind his sternum. What had he just heard? Was there a subtext to the conversation that he'd missed?

"And Kuo . . ." Wen's use of the man's given name was a rare occurrence. "Thank you for all your hard work and diligence. It's of great comfort to me to know there are people I can truly trust in this organization. By the way, how are you enjoying the Aston Martin? You must take us out for a spin in her sometime soon."

"I'm enjoying her very much, thank you. And yes, we must definitely do that."

Shum pulled his eyes from Chrissy Huang and crossed to the door. Jimmy had surprised him with the black Volante soft-top he'd received as a bonus for his loyal service. Shum nodded a cursory, begrudging goodbye to Lucas and left Wen's office.

"I hate to lose her," Wen declared once Shum was out of earshot. Lucas thought he detected a trace of genuine remorse. "Especially right now; she's an excellent salesperson—one of the best we have."

Lucas hid his cynical smile. Of course, Wen's genuine regret was for the potential loss of sales, not the girl herself; there would be a thousand other Chrissy Huangs waiting to fill her seat, and hopefully the next incumbent would be less apt to shoot her mouth off at the regulatory bodies.

"You should already have all her passwords," Jimmy said, his eyes already drawn back to his screens. "Shum will have sent them to you. You can access her database and pull her sales leads the moment she's off the premises. Spread those around the new people. They can pick them up with their own marks. Make it an incentive for good performance. You know how much we need that right now."

Lucas nodded and got to his feet. "Yeah, sure. I—uh—I have to go take the meetings now, so if you'll excuse me. I'm already ten minutes late."

"I'm sure it won't kill them."

Lucas gave his boss a sharp look. "Jimmy . . . ," he began, and stalled. He wanted to ask what, exactly, Wen had just ordered Shum to do, but he had no idea how to ask. His mind produced, "So, you're giving Chrissy anything she wants for brunch . . . Jimmy, you're not going to give her a severance package, are you? I mean, that's gotta be off the table because, y'know, mole."

Wen's mouth tugged into an almost smile. "Severance, yes. She will be given that. I am not unreasonable."

Lucas let himself out. On his way back through the sales office, he was forced to walk by Shum, who stood patiently by Chrissy Huang's desk waiting for her to finish up her client call.

CHAPTER TWELVE

Shum Kuo was patient to a fault. Back in the day, he'd work weeklong stakeouts, sometimes alongside an MSS partner, more often than not, alone. He'd eat very little, pee in the plastic water bottles he'd drink dry, and crap in one-gallon plastic baggies. So, waiting for Chrissy Huang to close her sale was nothing.

It wouldn't be much longer. Huang was telling her client she'd have all the contracts drawn up and dispatched by close of market, which he could take to be six p.m. at the latest. Following that, she would arrange to get the bought-sold notes signed and the stamp duties paid for the transaction. The operations manager would then arrange for delivery of the collateral from the borrower brokerage account to JM Wen Limited's account. Done and dusted.

Huang told her client she would inform him as soon as they received the collateral, and the initial good faith deposit on the loan was transferred to his account. She thanked him again for his business. All the while, her fingers darted to and fro across the pristine, white keyboard on her desk with astonishing speed. Mesmerized, Shum watched as the corresponding words appeared on the girl's screen; she made not one single mistake.

Finally, Huang hung up and turned to acknowledge Shum. "Can I help you, Mr. Shum?"

The faint tremor in her voice gave away the fact she knew all too well she *would* be able to help JM Wen's security chief; Shum Kuo didn't stand by your desk unless something was very wrong indeed. Her cheeks flushed and her eyes darted about the room to seek out her colleagues.

Eyes were lowered, phones picked up, and computer screens studied. Of the people on the so-called tiger team, only the American woman looked over with curiosity or concern.

"You need to come with me. Now." Shum kept his voice low and level.

"Am I being fired?" Tears welled in the wide eyes. Her lower lip trembled.

"Now, please."

Huang sniffled and slid open her desk drawer. She reached inside and began to pull out her few personal items: a hairbrush, a tangle of hair ties, an old-school Dictaphone, and a blue ballpoint pen engraved with *Congratulations, Chrissy!*

"Your personal effects will be sent on to you. There are papers you must sign before you leave."

Shum was a little more insistent this time. People were starting to look their way, and the sales office was growing too quiet as the girl's distress became more apparent.

As Huang got to her feet, her legs wobbled and Shum thought he'd have to catch her. His short, solid body tensed beneath his suit. She wore heels, of course, and stood a good four, maybe five inches above him, but there could be no doubt whatsoever as who dominated whom.

"Why?" Her eyes sought Shum's for a hint of clarification, for empathy he did not possess.

He placed a hand—gentle but firm—upon the woman's elbow and said quietly, "I think you know why. Come along, Miss Huang."

He guided her away from the desk and out of the office with dozens of eyes burning into his back.

"I think I know what this is about," Chrissy babbled. "And I can explain . . ."

Shum ignored her. They all babbled once they got caught. Desperate to make amends before they were shown the door, terrified at kissing goodbye to their nice, fat salaries, eye-watering bonuses, and the myriad perks that went along with working for Jimmy Wen. Yes, they'd talk all right. When it was too late—when they'd made their choice to betray the source of all their good fortune.

Chrissy Huang had but one more choice to make.

She was still maintaining she could explain away her misdemeanors when they arrived at Shum's office. He jabbed at the keypad to open the door and ushered her inside. There, he led her by the vast bank of CCTV screens that covered an entire wall—each one showing a different scene from within the maze of JM Wen's offices and meeting rooms. On a trio of black desks, below the screens were a dozen or so laptops, along with keyboards, mice, and thick black cables that snaked off through the wall. The space beneath the desks was crammed with computer towers, their green LEDs flickering.

"Where are we going?" Huang's voice wavered. "Can I speak to Mai Lin or someone else in HR?"

Shum ignored that too.

The door at the far end of the security office opened out into yet another hallway, a short dead end that housed only a single elevator. Shum pressed a button and was rewarded with the immediate opening of the doors.

"Please," he said, gesturing for Huang to precede him into the elevator car.

"If we're going down to the parking garage, I don't have a car here. I came to work by cab this morning."

"Please," he said again, and she finally moved.

They didn't speak in the elevator, and when they exited on a lower floor, they stepped into yet another corridor identical to the others. Only two doors punctuated the tastefully decorated wall. They stood side by side, and one, in gold lettering, declared itself to be Human Resources.

The young woman stopped. "I thought HR was on the fifty-second floor with the rest of our offices."

Politely, Shum moved around her and swung the door open for her. He waited patiently for her to make her way inside the room. It looked like every JM Wen meeting room.

"Please, take a seat."

He watched as Huang relaxed a little and made herself comfortable in one of the low-backed chairs pulled up to the teak conference table. Spread atop the table were contracts, letters, and a whole host of legal documents. The woman scanned them all, one by one.

Shum broke the loaded silence. "It's all standard procedure. Nondisclosure, severance, closure contracts, all the usual paperwork—please sign everywhere that is highlighted in yellow."

Huang turned around in the chair to look back at Shum. "Please, is there someone in HR I can speak to? In fact, isn't someone from HR coming to give me an exit interview? I'd like to talk to Mai Lin."

"What would make you think you would merit an exit interview under the circumstances? There is no question about why you are to be let go. Sign the papers, please, Miss Huang."

Resigned, Huang snatched up the pen that had been left among the meticulously arranged paperwork and began scribbling her signature everywhere she saw a smear of yellow highlighter. Then she began to babble again, the words spilling from her mouth without a single pause for breath.

"Look, I know what this is about, and I only agreed to speak to them to find out what they knew, to help the company. I can tell you *everything*. There's so much I can give you—valuable information I've collected that I know Mr. Wen would be *very* interested in having."

Shum let the girl jabber. As long as she was signing the paperwork, he could put up with her noise. It was always the same old routine with her type—they thought they could go behind the company's back, tattle out of school, cause all manner of trouble, and then negotiate their way out of their duplicity to keep their precious jobs. But Shum Kuo was so thorough, his attention to detail so scrupulous, he knew everything about Chrissy Huang's out-of-office escapades. There was absolutely nothing else she could add that would have been of the slightest interest or surprise to him.

More than that, in her ass-covering barrage of unrepentant words, she had made her choice. Had she groveled, admitted her guilt, seemed at all contrite, she might have saved herself. As it was . . .

Grabbing the tip of Huang's ponytail, Shum wound the long rope of hair around her neck and pulled with the full strength of his short, powerful arms. The girl's smooth, slender legs kicked out as she fought desperately to get out of the chair and away from the man who held her down. Her shoes flew off beneath the table; bare feet—with dainty toes painted a shiny, exquisite red—scrabbled around on the carpet, and her arms flapped impotently by her sides as Shum Kuo throttled her with her own hair. She belatedly reached up and tried to pull the strangling coil from her throat, but there was no way for her to gain purchase and no hope that the delicate fingers could break Shum's hold. No hope her voice would utter a sound urgent enough to be heard beyond this room.

There'd be no brunch. No shame-faced exit with a lesson learned. This one, like so many of the others, had chosen negotiation and bluster over contrition. What was that phrase that absurd British comic had produced in imagining an Anglican Inquisition: *Cake or death?*

Chrissy Huang had chosen death.

Jimmy Wen could be a sentimental fool at times, and Shum knew that was going to get him killed one day; there'd come a time when the man's clouded judgment would get in his way, and any one of the dubious characters he did business with would be quick to take advantage. When that day came, not even the ruthlessly efficient Shum Kuo would be able to save him.

Chrissy Huang stopped struggling within thirty seconds, forty at the most. Her slender body fell flaccid as she slipped into unconsciousness and would have slumped from the chair had Shum not been holding her up. He kept the girl's hair wrapped tightly around her windpipe for three full minutes—plenty of time for the brain to switch itself off and begin the process of dying. Huang's bladder had let go as she'd died, and she'd peed all over the padded conference chair; it would have to be disposed of. He scowled at the girl and made a mental note to replace one of the chairs in the room with something that had a removable pad.

Next, he'd place the body in the chest freezer that was the sole occupant of the cramped copier room next door. From there, Chrissy Huang would be removed from 2IFC in the small hours of the following morning and disposed of.

CHAPTER THIRTEEN

Lucas's Monday morning meetings had been part of his routine since the company was in its infancy and he'd been a wet-behind-the-ears PA. Jimmy Wen didn't believe in long-winded, drawn-out board meetings. He much preferred to deal with issues as they arose rather than allowing them to fester. He also didn't feel the need to rehash the previous week's business; what was gone was gone, and they learned from it and moved on. It was that style of modern, progressive thinking that had put JM Wen Limited so far ahead of the game in such a short space of time.

The new recruits weren't invited—although Lucas had briefly considered bringing Valentina Vittorio along; this was not part of their grand tour. Sure, they'd get to visit with the market analysts and bank liaison managers at some point, but that would be under careful supervision. Left to their own devices in the sales office, Lucas knew Wen's little rainmakers would quickly revert to type and be hustling clients and fixing meetings, so he had no worries there.

Lucas took his time walking the hallways. He needed time to think. To process. He'd known Chrissy Huang since her days as a fresh-faced, eager new recruit. He'd mentored her through those manic first months it always took the new ones to settle themselves in, and had been impressed with how quickly she had found her feet. She'd been pulling in new clients and their nice, new money almost from the start, and that had earned her Wen's attention. She'd been his star pupil for a while, right up until the next star pupil came along, and her stunning looks and effervescent personality had been a constant presence at Wen's renowned soirees at which he entertained the rich, the famous, and the influential.

The suspicions had begun to creep in around the beginning of the year. Wen had received information from one of his many inside sources that the regulators were starting to sniff around JM Wen Limited once again. No names were mentioned, but the source informed Wen there was someone within his company who had been more than keen to play whistleblower. Wen had eight possible suspects —Chrissy Huang among them—placed under the clandestine and ever-watchful eye of Shum Kuo and his team. Soon after that, the eight were whittled down to three. At that point, Chrissy was sidelined. No longer invited to schmooze the big clients and celebrities at the karaoke bars and Wen's famous yacht parties, Chrissy's work was confined strictly to the office and meetings with clients at their place of business.

She should have known, then, something was amiss. If she'd been innocent of Shum's suspicions, she'd have spoken up or gotten herself a new job. Hell, she should've bailed anyway.

But she didn't, Lucas told himself. She deserved the humiliation of being escorted off the premises. She probably deserved whatever demoralizing interrogation Shum had subjected her to. The man was a fucking sadist. The joke around the company was that he'd rip out your fingernails just to get directions to the nearest coffee shop . . . and get a hard-on doing it. He hoped her exit interview hadn't been . . .

He realized he'd turned down a side corridor in his inattention to where he was going and was facing a dead end. A clerk peered out at him through the open door of a copier room, his hands full of paper. Lucas turned around, intending to head back toward the main hallway, but found it hard to move. Somewhere deep in his hindbrain, a question niggled. He wasn't sure he wanted an answer to it.

"Excuse me, sir?" The clerk had come out into the corridor, his arms full of collated copies. "Are you lost?"

Lucas stared at the man for a full two seconds, then managed to pump some words as far as his lips. "No, I'm good. Just, um, getting some exercise. I'm good," he repeated, and put himself in motion.

He ended up outside the HR office, which was in a corridor just off the reception area. He was just making sure there hadn't been a hang-up in getting Chrissy's termination processed—that she'd signed her paperwork and didn't intend to sue for wrongful termination or something. It was a legitimate concern.

Inside the office, he asked for someone who processed terminations and was directed to the desk of a young man with a fresh round face and a trendy haircut.

"A member of our select sales team was terminated this morning and I just wanted to make sure everything was handled. There was, uh, some concern that her case might be . . . difficult."

"Name?"

"Chrissy—uh—Christina Huang."

The young man turned to his computer, tapped a few keys, clicked his mouse, then typed some more. He clicked a few more times, then nodded. "Yes, sir, Mr. Vaughn. It looks as if her paperwork has all been processed as of about half an hour ago. Everything seems to be in order."

"No problem with her exit interview? She was quite upset, as you might imagine."

"Yes, sir. I don't have any notes suggesting there was a problem." He looked up at Lucas.

"Do you know who gave her exit interview?"

The admin looked at his screen again, then frowned. "No sir, I don't see anyone listed as having done that, but her paperwork is all signed. If you like, I can ask around the office—"

"No. No, that's fine. I just wanted to . . . follow up. Thanks."

Lucas gave the guy a half-assed smile and went back out into the main hallway. In the back of his mind was an uneasy feeling that Shum Kuo had given Chrissy her exit interview. He'd seen the way the guy had gawped at the woman's hair as he'd waited by her desk, and couldn't bear to imagine what was going through that sick, twisted little mind of his.

He shook himself. *You're going barmy, Vaughn. Everything's fine. Everything's dotted and crossed. You're just imagining things 'cause the guy makes you squirm.*

He'd set off on this meander intending to visit the company's chief analyst, Jason Woo. It was something Wen used to do, but nowadays his ability to scare the shit out of people meant he'd only rub Woo up the wrong way. They sure as hell couldn't afford to lose any more good people—not now.

"Hey, Lucas," Woo greeted him with a broad grin as he walked through the already open door. "How's things in the executive suite?"

"Everything's just peachy, Jase," Lucas lied. "Everything good in here?" He offered a smile to each of Woo's five underlings who sat all but motionless with eyes glued to their computer screens. Not one of them noticed or looked up to acknowledge his presence.

"Couldn't be better," Woo replied. Vaughn couldn't tell if he was bluffing or sincere. "We've identified three likely candidates on the Growth Enterprise Market board of the Hong Kong Stock Exchange—"

"Verified through Bloomberg?"

"Of course." Woo feigned offense at the suggestion; no one at JM Wen Limited knew the job better than he, not even Lucas Vaughn. "The sexiest of the three is Dragon Wing Holdings Limited—they operate a small group of casinos in Macau, plus a couple in Vietnam and Saipan."

"Same as Emperor Holdings?" Vaughn remembered well the day Woo's team had identified Emperor Holdings Limited as a mark; they'd been low-hanging fruit ripe for the picking, and Wen had increased his Golden Five to the Golden Six.

"Smaller scale, but yeah, in principle," Woo replied. "Dragon Wing only has six locations in Macau, though—and they don't deal with the hospitality side of the business. Strictly casino development and gaming operations—VIP, tables, and slots only."

"Do they have Triad connections?" It was the next obvious question, but one that Lucas had to ask.

"Don't they all?" Woo laughed. "You know how difficult it is to tell just how much involvement the gangs have. So many of their dealings are hidden behind shell corporations and legitimate businesses. From what we can see, the Sun Yee On clan has fingers in this particular pie, so we're going to have to tread *really* carefully."

Lucas curled his lip in a lopsided half smile. Treading carefully wasn't in Jimmy Wen's repertoire right now, and it was virtually impossible to avoid the Triads in Hong Kong, since they practically ran the place.

Woo continued, "They're currently trading at $16.50, and downward movement is steady. It's going to be easy to catch this falling knife, and a walk in the park for Freddy Tseng and his team to manipulate the shares up, and then . . ." His hand made a diving bombing gesture. "It's almost *too* easy."

"You think they're that likely to default?"

"They're overspending on a new casino—quietly, of course—and their CEO is already shifting big chunks of his stock out to proxies. It's obvious he's getting ready to raise capital against them; we ran a dark web check on the guy, and he's mortgaged and remortgaged to the hilt —plus his old family money is tied up in property back home in the Philippines—*and* he doesn't want to sell. If we don't give Relucio Pineda a stock loan, somebody else will, and it won't be the banks."

It all sounded perfect to Lucas, almost *too* damn perfect. Jimmy would be delighted to see Woo's report on his desk, and within the day, the dossier on Dragon Wing Holdings Limited would be passed along to Freddy Tseng and his market makers to arrest the sinking value of Pineda's stock and kickstart the cautious process of building the price up from that modest $16.50. All in anticipation of Mr. Pineda receiving a call and a polite, yet irresistible, request to refinance some of his personal debt and raise capital through JM Wen International Asset Management Limited. All would be done using his Dragon Wing shares, naturally, and all at a lending rate he simply wouldn't be able to turn down.

Catch a falling knife, indeed, Lucas thought. Grab control of the stocks as close to the bottom as possible and build them up for a nice, fat sale.

"Want to see the other two?" Woo asked.

"Huh?"

"The other two marks we've identified?"

"Love to, mate. But I gotta catch Jeff before he leaves."

Lucas was being honest; there was nothing he'd like to have done more than hang around in Jason Woo's office and blow water all morning. Jeff Murphy, bank liaison executive, had a penchant for client brunches (a word that now held unpleasant connotations in Lucas's mind), and he was not likely to wait on Lucas, who was already running late for their Monday morning meeting.

"Email me the info and stats," he told Jason. "We'll talk later this afternoon. I have a batch of newbies to babysit."

Woo bristled. "I heard about that," he said. "I also heard they're more than just new recruits—they're a tiger team Jimmy's assembled to ramp things up."

"News sure travels fast around here."

"What's going on, Lucas?"

"Nothing for you to worry about, Jase. You just keep on digging out those marks—that's some good work right there, mate." Lucas gave the guy a friendly slap on the arm, playing on his Oz accent, which never failed to raise a smile and disarm the suspicious.

He sidestepped through Woo's office door and was gone.

* * *

"You're late," Jeff Murphy greeted Lucas with his customary curtness. He twisted his wrist around to make a big show of checking the chunky watch that hung loose there.

"I'm sorry, Jeff. I've been dealing with the new input since seven." A half-truth.

"I know."

Lucas sat himself down opposite Murphy. The guy was ridiculously dour, early fifties, had an advanced case of male-pattern baldness, grayish skin, and little sense of humor. All the banks loved him. He'd worked previously for Wells Fargo at their San Francisco head office, until Wen enticed him away with a fat salary, pension, and benefits he'd only ever dreamed of and flew him out to Hong Kong. Wen wanted an American to liaise with the private banks because, apparently, the banks on the island still revered and respected the Americans.

"I don't have long; I have to go out." This time, a lingering look at the wide face of the station-style clock on the office wall.

"Brunch. I totally get it, Jeff."

"So, what's with the new people?" As always, Murphy got straight to the point. "I'm told Wen's shipped them in from within the company. He never does that."

"He shipped *me* in from Singapore."

"That was too long ago to count for shit."

"It's all part of the Thing, Jeff. The big push. Don't go reading anything into it that's not there."

"It all seems weird to me," Murphy grumbled. "Are we in some kind of trouble? Is Jimmy?"

Lucas let out a light laugh. "No more than he ever is; you know how it goes with Jimmy."

Murphy allowed a smile to flicker across his thin lips. "Fair enough."

"So, how's things at LCSSC?"

"As you'd expect." Murphy was noncommittal. "I was just about to call Jiang, have him send the *kid* over."

"I thought you said you were on your way out?"

"Don't try to be smart with me, Lucas."

The 'kid' in question, Gao Yanlin, was thirty-two and a client support manager at LCSSC Wealth Management, just one of the multitude of private banks Hong Kong had to offer. His one and only client was JM Wen Limited, which put him at the demanding beck and call of Jeff Murphy. Jeff had Yan over at 2IFC just about every day. He claimed he liked to have the bank close at hand, and he was damned if he'd be the one trailing halfway across the island, given all the money LCSSC and Li Jiang were making off of JM Wen.

Murphy controlled the bank on Wen's behalf. It was as simple as that. He was responsible for what went in and out of the place so far as JM Wen Limited was concerned. He was also the gatekeeper for all of the dirty money that funneled through that ostensibly respectable establishment, and managed it at ground level via trusted intermediaries. Those, in turn, coordinated a network of people who filtered illegally generated money through their own bank accounts and into countless accounts set up by LCSSC. They called it *smurfing* because of the small, virtually unnoticeable amounts involved; by extension, the people who did it were *smurfs*. This had garnered Jeff Murphy the moniker Gargamel at JM Wen, although no one would dare call him that to his face.

Both the bank and JM Wen creamed a fat commission right off the top just for handling the money, plus handsome fees once it was invested into securities. Wen would also claim another fee once the securities were sold for cash or transferred—spotlessly clean—to the client. Jimmy Wen could then make stock loans against the collateral he'd purchased on a client's behalf, which earned yet more fees and yet another layer of respectability for the dirty money.

Sure, Jimmy Wen made the final decisions and hit the buttons on which stocks to trade, but it was Jeff Murphy who kept the cogs turning by keeping Li Jiang and his bank in line. Without Murphy, there'd be no money coming in and no stocks to trade.

"Are you having problems with the bank?" Lucas hoped to hell the answer was going to be a resounding no.

Murphy fixed him with an icy gaze. "Don't you think you'd be the first to know if I was?"

Lucas shrugged. "So why are you dragging Yan over on a Monday morning?"

"There's a few figures I want to go over with him; I'm concerned about their handling of the JLM Asset Holdings securities, and I need to keep a close eye on what they're doing with the latest influx of

Zhang money—it's accumulating a little too quickly for my liking, and some of the numbers don't quite add up."

"You think Mr. Li could be siphoning some off for himself?" Lucas couldn't think of a worse time for their dirty bank to start getting greedy—or careless. That would end very badly for everyone concerned, most of all Li Jiang.

"I think he *could*," Murphy said dryly. "Whether he *is* remains to be seen. You know how thorough Mr. Wen likes to be with his accusations."

Lucas's mind clicked over to Chrissy Huang and her beautiful ponytail. "Be sure to keep me posted, Jeff."

"Like I said, you'll be the first to know, Lucas. Now, if you don't mind seeing yourself out . . ." He snatched his cell phone from the desk, swiped at the touch screen, and held it to his ear. He indicated the door with his chin, then dismissed Lucas without another glance. "Yes, get me Li Jiang . . . I don't give a crap what he's doing. Tell him it's Jeff Murphy from JM Wen, and tell him it's urgent."

Lucas saw himself out.

CHAPTER FOURTEEN

Li Jiang fidgeted uneasily in his maroon leather, high-backed chair. "Mr. Murphy, it is always a pleasure to hear from you," he lied into his phone and shot a look across the desk at Gao Yanlin, who sat in silence. Jiang mentally cursed Mabel, his antiquated secretary, for putting the man's call through—although she had been conditioned to put through any call from JM Wen Limited, no matter what.

The banker listened with forced patience and gritted teeth as Murphy spoke at him. Jiang didn't like Jeff Murphy one iota—he found the man's gruff American voice grating and his Western manner most coarse. He knew the nickname they'd given Murphy over at the JM Wen offices—Jiang had to look it up since he had no children and little exposure to cartoons. He thought it was a funny, fitting caricature for the awful, gray man. But, Murphy was the bank's contact at JM Wen and, for all his abrasiveness, Jiang still found dealing with him preferable to dealing directly with Jimmy Wen.

As Murphy talked, Jiang ran a manicured hand over his short-cropped salt and pepper hair. He looked—and felt—every single one of his sixty-two years. His wife always reassured him that his aging face showed great wisdom, but sometimes he wondered. Five years almost to the day, he'd allowed himself to be seduced by Jimmy Wen and his slick talk of wealth beyond his wildest dreams. It was synchronicity, Wen had told him, that Jiang was nicely settling in after his surprise move over from Deutsche Bank at the same time as JM Wen Limited was in the process of moving away from BNP Paribas and was looking for a smaller, more discreet private bank through which to conduct certain aspects of their business. A veteran of the financial industry, Jiang had been in no doubt even back then what those *certain aspects* would be.

Wholly owned by LCS International Financial Holdings Limited, LCSSC Wealth Management was a relatively modest private bank. It was situated in the Wah Hei building on Jervois Street, just a short cab ride from 2IFC—not "all the way across the island" from JM Wen as Murphy liked to say. Worldwide, it held 56 billion US dollars in assets, and had an unusually high minimum asset per client threshold. It was as near perfect as Jimmy Wen could have hoped.

Li Jiang was no fool. He'd been around the financial industry long enough to comprehend the meaning of Wen's carefully parsed words, but the talk of hefty paydays and lifelong security had been a siren call to a man already squirreling money away for a more than comfortable retirement. In the course of their initial meeting on Wen's magnificently vulgar yacht, Jiang had shifted his sights from a modest home in West Kowloon to a nice beachfront property in the Philippines—Luzon Island was the current frontrunner—or maybe he'd buy a big boat so he and his wife could drift around the Bahamas before they decided which island to settle upon.

Once the decision had been made to exploit the opportunities presented by his becoming president of the small private bank, Jiang had negotiated ostensibly all of JM Wen Limited's *confidential* business in return for the high risks involved in handling the dirty money. He was not naive enough to believe they were receiving *all* of Jimmy Wen's under-the-table business, since the man wasn't the type to put all of his eggs in one basket.

It was an arrangement Jiang was happy to turn a blind eye to, and he knew he could hardly sue Wen for breach of contract. Plus, he'd learned quickly that with the amounts Wen was channeling through the bank, it was easy—*too* easy—to cream a little extra off the top for the retirement fund. Getting caught posed no threat, as Jiang knew he'd be long gone before the whole thing came crashing down.

The money available was, indeed, beyond Li Jiang's wildest dreams, but he knew it was a poisoned chalice. Along with all the wealth came the burden of knowledge of what he'd dragged LCSSC Wealth Management into, and the potential for disaster should it all unravel one day to expose how deep a hole Li Jiang had dug for them; Wen had made it clear he considered he now owned LCSSC.

Finally, Murphy quit talking at him.

"I'm not sure it would be such a good idea to open another account right now. Especially one so far below the bank's ten-million-dollar threshold." Jiang cursed the hesitation in his voice and the way the receiver wobbled slightly in a trembling hand; he was never comfortable saying no to Murphy, even when he knew he was in the right and the man was asking far too much. He looked across at Yan, who raised a quizzical eyebrow. "Yes, I am well aware of who the client is, but with things the way they are with Asia Lion, New Horizon, and JLM, I honestly think we should wait another week or so."

It wasn't just those three; the share value of a whole bunch of companies Wen had gotten LCSSC involved in had begun to rise alarmingly and against all predictions. It gave Jiang an uneasy feeling, and he wanted to avoid anything that might have the bigwigs at headquarters sitting up in their executive suites and taking notice.

Murphy spoke at him some more.

Jiang slumped down in his chair, feeling as if the life was being drained out of him through the connection. The man was a bloody vampire.

"Yes, I understand the importance of the client, and yes, he understands this is Mr. Wen's wish and . . . Yes, Mr. Murphy, he's here with me right now. . . Yes, I will, of course." His eyes met Yan's, and he felt embarrassed kowtowing to the man in front of a subordinate, even one who knew how deep into JM Wen's pocket they all were.

Jiang hung up the call with a heavy sigh. He steepled his fingers and rested his elbows on the desk. "They want you at their offices this afternoon."

Yan looked nonplussed. "It's Monday."

"I know what day it is, Yan, and so do Jeff Murphy and Jimmy Wen. And they want you at their offices this afternoon."

"Problems?"

"Honestly?"

Jiang knew he could trust Yan implicitly; he was the only one in the entire organization who knew the bank's full involvement with Jimmy Wen, his shady associates, and his less than aboveboard dealings. Li Jiang even suspected Yan knew more about his skimming than he was prepared to admit. The two had a dynamic of mutually assured destruction going on between them, so implicit trust was a given.

"Honestly," Jiang continued, "I'd say that given that Jimmy Wen is trying to raise capital on such a large scale, that he's opening up new accounts and pulling in his top earners, yes, there are problems. I think Mr. Wen has holes to plug—holes of his own making."

Now Yan looked uncomfortable. He was the man in the hot seat, painfully aware of the consequences for himself should JM Wen Limited experience any *real* problems. "How bad do you think things are going to get?"

"I'm sure it's a storm we can weather," Jiang told him, hoping his eyes didn't betray his fragment of doubt. "But that's what you're going there to find out."

CHAPTER FIFTEEN

I t was nine o'clock, and Valentina was hungry. She usually ate breakfast first thing, but with a breakfast meeting scheduled, she'd had nothing but a latte before she started work. Her stomach growled audibly as she smilingly seated herself in The Lounge at the Four Seasons; she hoped the client, Kim Yun-Fat, hadn't been able to hear it.

The Lounge had a cozy dining area decorated in muted browns and grays with one long burnished metal wall that reflected the light of lamps and candles. It was a place that witnessed a lot of business deals. Valentina wagered theirs was not the only client meeting taking place over breakfast.

The two exchanged pleasantries, ordered breakfast and coffee, then moved into a discussion of Mr. Kim's business with Wen Limited. Kim's company—Green Dynamics Construction Partners—had offices in the US, South America, Australia, and, of course, Hong Kong. Valentina had first spoken to him about his company's plans a couple of weeks before she'd left New York. Kim, the CEO of the Hong Kong office, had been most receptive to Valentina's exploratory calls, especially after he'd checked her out with his counterpart in Manhattan.

"You said you wished to discuss a loan," Valentina prompted as she accepted her second latte of the day from their smiling waiter. Caffeine helped her "read the room" with greater clarity. If she weren't fully awake, she might miss a tell—a glance, a tightening of the lips, a shifting of the shoulders.

Kim nodded. "I do. As I've mentioned in our phone conversations, Green Dynamics Construction is expanding to the mainland, and I wish to infuse the expansion with, em, greater resources than we have currently allocated. However, capital is tight." He poured cream into his coffee and stirred it, watching the curl of cream fan out from the spoon. "I have been considering pursuing a margin loan to increase the financial resources available for the expansion."

Valentina sat back in her chair and frowned thoughtfully at a splash of light on the anodized metal of the wall that flanked their table. She knew from her conversations with Lucas Vaughn that Jimmy preferred to work with straight stock loans. They were cleaner, quicker, and with less potential for getting hung up in the approval and funding processes.

"A margin loan," she repeated. "What sort of resources are we talking about?"

He looked up at her. "I was thinking something in the nature of eight hundred million, Hong Kong."

Valentina knew her face betrayed nothing of the gleeful dance taking place behind her eyes. "A substantial amount," she said smoothly. "Does Green Dynamics have a margin account with a brokerage?"

"This is . . . a personal loan. And no, I do not have such an account."

"How soon would you need the loan funded?"

"As soon as possible. The first phase of expansion is already underway."

She nodded. "Then I think the first drawback with a margin loan is the time it will take to process. You'd have to open a margin account with a brokerage or bank, and when you do, it will be subject to a great deal of scrutiny."

Kim frowned. "What type of scrutiny?"

"Disclosures, oversight of the source of funds, identification requirements—any information necessary to get the account approved. Obviously, it takes time to complete the process. After all the documentation is gathered and the application—usually thirty pages or so—is signed, then the account is approved and funded with cash or stock. That's only the first step, of course. The collateral used to obtain a margin loan must be evaluated to see if the stock is stable enough to qualify."

"I'm well aware that lenders can be demanding when it comes to the quality of collateral, but I doubt qualification would be a problem in this case," Kim said. "Green Dynamics stock has shown stable growth."

Valentina smiled. "Of course, but I simply want you to understand that JM Wen respects your privacy, Mr. Kim, so if you take out a stock loan from us, there is far less scrutiny of such things as your source of funding." She clasped her hands around her latte and leaned forward slightly. "That's one of the main reasons I would recommend that, instead of a margin loan, you pursue a stock loan."

"One of the reasons? What other reasons might there be?"

Was he being coy, testing her knowledge, or did he really not know? Maybe all of the above? Fine, she'd show off a little.

"Well, for one thing, a stock loan requires you jump through fewer hoops. Nor would you have to deal with disclosures, which means approval and funding are faster. Your loan can be approved in twenty-four hours, and funding can take place in as little as one week."

Kim's eyebrows rose slightly. "So soon?"

Valentina rocked back in her chair, making a broad gesture with her hands. "We want to make the process as easy and painless as possible for our clients. Most people don't want to fill out endless applications only to have to wait for weeks for approval and funding. And, frankly, some aren't comfortable disclosing the source of their money or where it's held."

"These would be company shares."

"Your personal company shares?"

He hesitated. "In part."

She suspected there was more to that story. It was likely he did not have the full approval of his board to borrow against company-held shares; a delicate situation. Clearly, she'd have to do more to convince him.

"You should be aware that margin loans have 'fine print.' Little details that can surprise you if you're not aware of them."

"What sort of details?" Kim glanced up as the waiter placed their plates before them and poured him a second cup of coffee.

Valentina smiled at the server and waited until he had moved away to another table to go on. "Margin loans allow for the 're-hypothecation' of the collateral or the stock in your account."

He raised an eyebrow.

"Meaning that even if a loan is not taken out against the shares in that account, the brokerage can lend out the shares for a short period, without you being aware of the fact."

Valentina would not have suspected that Kim Yun-Fat's cherubic face could form an expression as grim as the one now displayed there. She didn't think it was an act.

"This is legal?" he asked.

"Yes, because the margin documents you've signed allow the brokerage to do this. It's how the firm makes additional money from these financial products." She hesitated a beat then added, "The lender can go even further than that; they can sell your stocks."

He met her gaze. "I find that outrageous, don't you?"

She shrugged. "Personally, yes. But it's part of the loan contract. That contract allows the brokerage to invoke their rights to your collateral to use it in their own transactions. Ultimately, they have to return the stock to your account, and they have a lot of risk management in place to avoid a negative outcome, but still . . ." She let that hang.

"This would not happen with a stock loan?"

"No."

Kim nodded, returning his attention to his breakfast. "Still, as I said, the stock I would use for collateral is exceptionally stable and, given the announcement of our expansion, trending upward. The time factor is, of course, important, but I am not convinced there are enough mitigating factors to make a stock loan more attractive."

Valentina considered her next step in this dance, then set down her fork and clasped her hands on the table behind her plate. "Let me be very frank with you, Mr. Kim. I believe that you would not find it in your best interests to raise capital through a margin loan. First, because of the factors I've already mentioned, but also because of the high interest rates. Margin loan interest rates are significantly higher than what JM Wen can offer on a stock loan. Margin rates are also adjustable—the starting rate is usually between seven and nine percent, depending on the firm, and can go up from there. In fact, some lenders charge anywhere from twenty-four to thirty-six percent. Those high interest rates can eat into any profits you might make from the stock when you pay off the loan. Then, too, the up-front capital required for a margin loan can be prohibitive."

Mr. Kim's dark eyes had kindled during this recitation, belying his neutral expression. "Thirty-six percent. Extraordinary. I doubt I would go to a lender who charged such absurd interest, so let us suppose that my interest rate would be roughly eight percent. What rate does JM Wen offer?"

"Three-point-five percent, fixed rate."

Kim set down his fork and picked up his coffee cup. "Three point five. Really? What, as they say, is the catch?"

Valentina spread her hands in a gesture of openness. "No catch, Mr. Kim. JM Wen extends good deals because Mr. Wen knows that exemplary client care begets client loyalty. It's one of the reasons the company is so successful. I should add that you pay only interest, no principal. You repay the principal at the end of the loan term, when you want to get the collateral stocks back. And, you don't pay principal if you default. Most brokerage firms will take legal action if you don't pay the borrowed amount back. Jimmy Wen lets you just walk away. You'd lose your shares, of course, but nothing beyond that."

"So . . . no carrying costs, then."

"Virtually none."

Kim gave her a wry look over the rim of his coffee cup. "This is, indeed, what you Americans would call a sweet deal."

"It gets even sweeter, Mr. Kim. A margin loan's loan-to-value is capped. That means you can only get a fixed percentage of the market value of your stock when you apply for the loan. The cap is typically fifty percent in the US"—she made a rueful face—"and it's even lower in Hong Kong—thirty-five percent, though you might be able to push it to fifty with some lenders. With our deal, you can get as high as seventy-five percent loan-to-value."

She watched him digest that information for a moment, then leaned even farther forward in her chair, projecting her earnestness across the table. "But the most important thing," she added, "is that a margin loan can increase your risk for loss. If the market loses value, you stand to lose a large chunk of your capital. You might be called on to deposit more cash to cover those losses. You could end up owing more money than you originally invested. In fact, you could lose your entire invest-ment and *still* owe the brokerage money. Moreover, if you defaulted on a loan payment in a margin situation, *any* of your assets could be at risk of seizure. To be honest, Mr. Kim, if your goal is to maximize the capital you have to trade with, to fund the loan in the least amount of time, and to avoid risk, a stock loan is your best option."

Kim nodded at his coffee cup. His face was as serene as ever, but she saw hesitation in his eyes.

"I see," he said. "Seventy-five percent of the value of my company shares, you said."

"Yes, Mr. Kim. Seventy-five percent. As I said, most brokerages are only prepared to offer fifty at most."

Now, he looked up and met her gaze. "You can assure me that my shares would be safe. I will get them back at market value upon repay-ment of the loan. They will not be lended or sold?" He hesitated then added, "If that were to happen, it would be disastrous."

Bingo. Her poking and prodding had revealed his chief concern—losing ownership of his shares. "I assure you, Mr. Kim, your shares are completely safe. And looking at their market performance to date, it's likely they'll rise in value before you have to repay the loan."

"Very good," he said. "I believe I am ready to explore the particulars of such a deal." He smiled for the first time since they'd been seated, and relaxed over his meal. Valentina relaxed as well. She liked Mr. Kim. He reminded her of a smiling Buddha. He was nice and therefore easy to be nice to.

Certain she'd put his reservations to rest, she left their breakfast meeting and walked the sky bridge back to Wen's offices feeling a heady sense of achievement. She had no doubt Jimmy Wen would be pleased; Kim Yun-Fat was looking to take out a substantial loan against shares of Green Dynamics stock—HK$800m worth of substantial.

"Bagged one already?" Nadim Singh looked up at her as she strode back into the closer's office with a serene smile on her lips. "Mr. Wen will be so proud of you."

There was a hint of jealous rivalry there that Valentina couldn't help but relish. Her fellow rainmakers looked up from their respective desks. She shrugged. "It's no big deal really. I had Green Dynamics all warmed up before I left home, so it's kinda cheating."

"I never imagined self-deprecation to be part of a New Yorker's psyche," Oliver Michaels joined in with a chuckle. "I thought you guys were all in your face and *fuggedaboutit!*" The impersonation was uncannily accurate.

Valentina laughed along with everyone; the Brit could be an ass, but he had a smart, funny streak she found quite charming. "The deal's not closed 'til it's closed—you all know that. But I think he's ready to sign."

Oliver jumped right onto that one, fluttering his hands over his heart. "Now that he's met you face-to-face, Val, I'm sure he was hot to sign his life away before you'd finished your first cocktail."

"Thank you, Oliver. But it was over eggs Benedict and coffee. By the way, do those corny British pickup lines actually work on anyone?" She smiled and wheeled around to head off to the ladies room. "If you'd all excuse me, I . . . I'll be right back."

Valentina reminded herself at the last minute she wasn't in the New York office any more, and stopped short of telling them all she badly needed to go pee. Passing by Chrissy's desk on her way out of the office gave her a moment of unease. After she'd gone off with that surly looking guy this morning, she hadn't been back. She'd looked upset at whatever Mr. Frowny-Face had told her—almost tearful. It occurred to Valentina that it looked like a firing, though she couldn't imagine why Jimmy Wen would fire one of his best. Maybe Frowny-Face had brought her some bad news. Did she have family in Hong Kong? Valentina made a mental note to give Chrissy a call over lunch just to make sure she was okay.

The restrooms were at the end of one of the long, impeccably straight hallways. The door to the ladies' swung open before Valentina had the time to so much as touch the handle. An immaculately dressed young woman strode out and almost straight into her. She had hair trimmed into a shiny black bob and wore her dark blue Dior suit incredibly well; her pale, slender legs were on show from a little way above the knee.

"Pardon me," the woman said as she brushed by Valentina.

She left in her wake a faint whiff of Jean Paul Gaultier Eau Fraiche and delicately perfumed hand soap. Valentina watched as she walked away; given the young lady wore four-inch heels instead of the standard flats, she was obviously a step or two above assistant level.

Inside the restroom, another young woman—one of Anita Kwok's clones—preened in the huge expanse of mirror that filled the wall from the row of porcelain sinks all the way up to the high ceiling. She paused from smoothing her already perfect hair and double-checking her equally perfect face for lipstick on her teeth to offer Valentina a cursory smile.

"Hi," Valentina said. She held out a hand. "I'm—"

The Kwok clone's attention returned to her reflection and she fiddled with the collar of her crisp, white shirt.

"Pleased to meet you," Valentina mumbled as she made her way over to the row of five vacant stalls.

Yet another important cultural lesson: In Hong Kong, the elevator no-talk rule also applies to restrooms.

Soft music played through hidden speakers; the lighting was subdued, indirect, and gentle on the eyes, and the whole restroom smelled of jasmine and lavender. It was a veritable haven from the maniacal hubbub of the sales floors and meeting rooms that lay mere yards away. Out of habit, Valentina picked the farthest stall from the door. Easing open the door, she was pleasantly surprised by how clean it was. The New York office, in a fit of political correctness, had gone the route of unisex bathrooms, and they had turned disgusting in a short space of time. It had become habit to spend a moment wiping splashed pee off the seat before sitting down. Here, it was unnecessary.

Valentina clicked the door closed behind her, hung her bag on the gold hook on the back of the door, and settled herself down. It was a pleasure to have a little alone time. She was used to working alone, and while she thrived on the cut and thrust of competition between sales-people, there was an air of distrust surrounding the other six that had her hackles up. They were supposed to function as a team, yet there was still a deep undercurrent of competition. That could be as dangerous as it was wearing.

She heard the preening woman making her way out, her flats padding quietly on the polished chessboard tile floor, and as the door eased open there came a brief, unwelcome blast of the cacophony beyond.

A phone rang.

Valentina cursed beneath her breath as the tranquil moment was so rudely shattered. She was positive the other four stalls were empty, and she'd definitely heard the preening assistant leave, so someone must have come in as she had gone out. Whoever it was, she wished she'd pick up her goddamn cell phone so Valentina could enjoy some peace and quiet.

Again, with the ringing. Where the hell is it coming from?

Tilting her head to listen, Valentina realized the tinny, generic ring tone was coming from somewhere close. Her first thought was someone must have dropped theirs in one of the cubicles or left it by the sinks, but then she realized it was coming from the door in front of her. *From her purse.*

Heart in her mouth, Valentina froze.

It wasn't the usual sound her phone made; she'd set her ring tone to emulate those old-school telephone bells, as it was reminiscent of the ancient black Bakelite phone her grandmother kept in her parlor.

Gingerly, Valentina took her purse down from the hook. The moment she unzipped it, she was greeted by the blue-white glow of a cell phone that was most definitely not her iPhone. It was a small, simple Nokia—little more than a bunch of rubberized buttons and a tiny LCD screen. Perplexed, Valentina stared at the thing as it nestled at the bottom of her purse and buzzed along to its insistent tone. The incoming number flashing on the small screen was not one she recognized.

Valentina snatched the phone out of her purse and stabbed at the end call button. Once more, the soft peaceful music was the only sound in the restroom. Valentina turned the cell phone over in her hands, although she wasn't exactly sure what she should be looking for. There were no stickers or markings on the back to indicate ownership, and no network insignia on the front or on the white screen. It was clearly a burner phone, one that could be bought in any grocery store practically anywhere. As to how the hell it had come to be in her purse, Valentina had no idea.

The thing rang again, lighting up, and vibrating her hands. She dropped it on the tiled floor.

"Shit!" Her loud whisper bounced around the tight confines of the stall. Spooked now, and desperate to shut the cell phone up, Valentina picked it up from where it lay ringing and buzzing by her feet and pressed the little green Talk button. Wary, she lifted the phone to her ear like it was about to bite her and asked quietly, "Hello?"

Silence.

"Is this some kind of joke . . . ?"

"Miss Vittorio?" The voice was male, softly spoken, with the slightest hint of a Cantonese accent.

Valentina almost dropped the damn thing back on the floor. "Who is this?"

"Don't be alarmed. I need you to listen."

"Who—?"

"I need you to *listen*, Valentina. May I call you Valentina?"

Valentina chose to say nothing.

"My name is David. I'm an agent for the Securities and Futures Commission. We have been watching you for some time."

Valentina's heart rate shot up a notch. The SFC were the last people she'd expected—or wanted—to hear from. Especially here, and especially like this—unprepared and vulnerable. Recalling the half-serious chatter Friday about the offices being bugged, she stood and awkwardly pulled up her panties and trousers, then flushed the toilet. It was mercifully loud.

"What do you want from me? How—?"

"I asked you to *listen*." There was now a sharp edge to the man's tone, one that let her know in no uncertain terms that whoever David was, he meant business. "We had the phone planted in your purse before you entered the building, if that answers your question."

In her head, Valentina replayed her contact with the *cazzo di merda* who had almost sent her sprawling ass-over-head at the front doors of 2IFC. The whole incident had happened so quickly that it remained blurred in her mind.

David continued inexorably. "You're going to just have to take my word for it that I am who I say I am, although I'd be more than happy to have my superior and his associate from Interpol pop in and pay you a visit at that swanky new desk of yours." He paused there a second or two, no doubt for dramatic effect.

It worked.

"Okay. Talk," Valentina growled, hyperaware of the growing quiet in the restroom. She slung her purse over her shoulder and exited the stall.

"We have been monitoring you since New York, Valentina. We know who you are, and suspect we know what your motives are here in Hong Kong."

That revelation shook Valentina to the soles of her Louboutin booties; she had been so confident she'd done a thorough job at covering her tracks.

So, you called me on a fucking burner phone? Here?

She was at the sinks now and turned on one of the taps full blast. "You could have called me in the middle of a goddamned meeting!" she growled.

"Relax, Valentina. We can track the phone to within three feet. We knew you were in the restroom when we called. I assume you're not having meetings there."

Oh, you're so funny. "Apparently, I am now."

Was the revelation that they knew precisely where she was and what she was doing meant to reassure her or put the fear of God into her? And his repeated use of her first name . . . she wasn't dumb and knew what he was trying to do; he was trying to make her feel part of the team through familiarity. Basic Psych 101.

"What do you want?" She fought to keep her voice low. Someone could walk in at any moment. Surely the SFC couldn't monitor ladies room traffic.

"What I want is for you to—"

"Listen. Yeah, you said. So cut to the chase."

David took a long, deep breath as if she were trying his patience, then continued. "We know you're looking for something at JM Wen to topple Jimmy Wen, Valentina. And we suspect that you will find it quickly enough. It's not something that Mr. Wen hides too well within his organization. Maybe he's being careless in his confidence, or maybe he knows it's not enough to bring him down."

"You seem to think you know a lot about me," Valentina interrupted. "What makes you think I'm looking for anything other than a fat paycheck?"

He had the gall to chuckle. She decided if she ever met him face-to-face, she'd call him that: Chuckles.

"I'd be more than happy to go through the information we have compiled on you and your life and career to date, Valentina. Although, since it covers pretty much everything from your early childhood, your mother, sister, your outstanding college career . . . and, of course, the death of your poor father—"

Damn it all to hell. "Okay, okay, I get it." It bothered Valentina that the SFC so obviously knew enough to have paid attention to her plans; exactly how long had they been digging?

"As you can imagine, it's a nice, thick dossier, and it gets especially interesting around the time you surprised everyone when you left Goldman Sachs at the peak of your performance." David paused there, as if allowing Valentina time to process.

She took that time, pacing a little near the still-flowing sink. Unless David was bluffing with top-line detail, it was obvious the SFC did, indeed, know a hell of a lot about her. The regulator was well known for being ruthlessly thorough in its investigations.

David's voice broke into her thoughts. "As I said, Valentina, you *will* find what you are looking for, eventually. Maybe you'll unearth something even more devastating purely by chance, who knows? But we have intelligence that points to JM Wen Limited being involved in something far bigger than even you could imagine."

Valentina grudgingly admitted that he'd captured her interest; she wished she was anywhere other than in JM Wen's plush restroom; she felt exposed, defenseless, and all she wanted to do was get the hell out of here before someone listening somewhere wondered why it took American women so fucking long to wash their hands.

"I would like to discuss all of this with you in person, someplace a little more comfortable for us both, Valentina. I'm quite sure you would too."

So now he's a mind-reader. "Go on."

"There's a small, discreet restaurant where we can meet. It's a little off the beaten track, but it's nicely anonymous and we'll be able to talk in confidence."

"I can't just leave—"

"Surely even Mr. Wen allows his big-hitters to take lunch? Get yourself out of the office around eleven thirty, let's say. You've only been here a few days. You want to take in the sights, grab yourself some authentic Chinese food—you know."

There was an adamant edge to the guy's light tone that told Valentina this was an offer she was not in a position to refuse. She allowed herself a wry smile. At least he hadn't been cliché enough to tell her to come alone and make sure she wasn't followed—that much was a given, and she'd have most likely laughed in his ear.

"I had breakfast out with a client. I meant to stay here and take a working lunch."

"I appreciate that you're incredibly busy, Valentina, and that Mr. Wen has high expectations of you and your colleagues. But please remember: We could end your personal quest and your career with just one telephone call to Mr. Wen."

Valentina swallowed hard. She had no choice—that much was evident. The best she could do was go along with David's demands until she could figure a way out of it.

"Okay, where would you like to meet, and what time?"

David told her, adding, "Don't write any of this down."

"Really? I thought I'd run right back to my hotel and put it in my goddamn diary."

Was that a cough or another chuckle? "Then you probably already know that I'm going to tell you to destroy the phone. We'll get another to you when the time is right. Leave your personal phone in the office when you step out for lunch."

She was going to ask why, then realized it could be used to track her. "So, what—I flush it?"

"Not quite that simple. Take out the SIM card—it's under the battery—snap it in half, then flush everything. And don't worry, Valentina, those toilets are pretty badass; it'll all go down, believe me. I'll see you later." He hung up.

You'll see me later.

Chuckles of the SFC made it sound like she had a good ol' fashioned lunch date instead of a clandestine meeting with a man she'd never met, who could undo everything she'd worked so hard for with just one phone call. That left Valentina wondering how many other JM Wen employees David had spoken to while they were sitting in the ladies restroom, and how many other cheap Nokia phones had been disposed of down Jimmy Wen's luxury lavatories.

She ducked into the first stall, dismantled the phone, and disposed of it as instructed. Then she washed her hands, dried them in the Dyson air dryer, and made her way out of the restroom, trailing the scent of sweet jasmine, her stomach tied in so many knots she wasn't sure she'd ever eat again.

CHAPTER SIXTEEN

alentina's lunch plans were complicated by Sofia and Oliver offering to tag along to see the sights with her, while Lam gallantly offered to play tour guide. She politely turned down their kind offers and told them she'd prefer to have some time alone after such a hectic morning. When she poked her head into Lucas's office to let him know she was off for lunch and asked if an hour was acceptable, he told her to take as long as she needed. She walked out into the bright sunshine on Finance Street a few minutes after eleven thirty.

Once out of sight of the International Finance Center, she picked up a small, folded tourist map from a newsstand. She felt lost venturing out into an unknown city without the trusty GPS app on her cell phone, but as David had instructed, she'd left that switched off and in the drawer of her new desk. Glancing over both shoulders as she left the newsstand, Valentina cursed David for making her so damned paranoid and for upending everything she'd so meticulously planned out. She'd had everything down to the fine detail, and in the course of just one call from someone claiming to be an SFC agent, that had all suddenly been thrown up in the air.

She knew she was taking a giant leap of faith that the mysterious

David was really with the SFC, but he'd sounded convincing, and even if he wasn't, he was still someone who had gone to an enormous amount of time and trouble to catch her attention. Given what he knew, he had to be part of some sort of powerful intelligence organization.

She had to admit, his strategy had worked, and worked well. She was already processing what possible synergy could be derived from an association with the Commission. If they could help her, all well and good. It was worth taking the risk to at least meet and talk with their agent. If he turned out to be something other than who he claimed to be and meant her harm, then Valentina Vittorio could take care of herself.

Her map informed her that the restaurant at which she was to meet David was just under a mile away, a bit of a hike. She joined a group of tourists and caught a tram on Lung Wo Road, which carried her toward the Wan Chai district. She got off the tram near the Hong Kong Arts Center, electing to walk the rest of the way, the easier to lose herself in a crowd. The red soles of her Louboutin booties were made for comfort and put it within easy walking distance. On any other day, she might have visited the art center. Today, she turned inland and worked her way to Lockhart Road, on the fringes of the Wan Chai district.

The deeper Valentina got into Wan Chai, the more crowded and less affluent the streets became. The area itself was populated by stores displaying fruits, vegetables, freshly cooked rolls, books, pots, pans, and myriad other wares on rickety wooden racks. These were interspersed with dive bars, seedy strip clubs, and tiny restaurants that appeared to have no more than half a dozen tables at best. The restaurants were all but empty, which Valentina guessed would change quickly in a relatively short period of time. She tried her best to look like just what she was—a businesswoman taking a midday break to ramble—but even this short distance from the financial district, there was not a single office worker or tourist, and not one Caucasian face but her own. Valentina stood out like an ostrich at a flamingo convention.

Her foldout map directed her toward Wah Yan Court. It sat off the narrow street opposite a seafood market, where she caught the unmistakably piscine aroma of fish beginning to turn in the late morning heat. The street itself was a gaudy mix of store fronts decorated with handwritten and cheaply printed signs—mostly black or bright red—some all in Cantonese, some in English, and others in both. Weathered canvas banners stretched out above the street, and old, overladen trucks eased their way below them between the illegally parked cars that cluttered either side. A narrow alleyway by the Sun Luen Tai Food Market brought Valentina out onto Wah Yan Court. There, less than a few strides along the sidewalk, was the Cha Lau Yu Palace.

A palace it was not.

The restaurant was larger than most of those she'd seen on her way through Wan Chai, but no less down-market. Its windows were almost entirely obscured with small posters, gaudy pictures of menu items, the ubiquitous red lettering that Valentina surmised advertised the restaurant's specials, and a row of plucked dead geese that hung by their limp webbed feet. The Palace's long facade was shaded by a grubby canvas awning that hung over the bustling sidewalk; it had once been pristine white but now was rendered an unpleasant smudgy gray by smog and years of dirty rain.

Valentina shook her head—her colleagues back in New York had warned her about patronizing eateries like the Palace, no matter how much she might want to experience authentic Hong Kong. They'd told her that such places were pretty much guaranteed to serve up *E. coli* and *Listeria* with every meal; it was hardly the kind of establishment in which she'd planned to enjoy her first authentically Chinese meal in Hong Kong.

Valentina folded her map and tucked it into her purse. At precisely ten after twelve, she pushed open the grimy door to the Cha Lau Yu Palace and stepped inside. She was greeted by the metallic tinkle of the tiny bell above the door and a fake smile from the dour middle-aged lady behind the counter to her left. Evidently, her hospitality didn't extend to a hello or even to showing patrons to a table, so Valentina made her own way in. There was a wide metal door with a small porthole window behind the counter—the kitchen, she presumed, judging by the sounds emanating from it. From there, a hallway ran toward the back of the restaurant.

Only four diners were occupying the place. They were scattered among the twenty or so tables, and all but one of them openly looked up from their newspapers and half-eaten food at the Caucasian woman in the expensive suit who had just wandered in off the street. Valentina strode with purpose toward that one disinterested patron, sliding into the chair opposite him.

"David, I presume?"

He looked embarrassed. "That obvious, huh?"

"I'm afraid so. Maybe next time you should stare at the white chick more like the other guys?" She glanced pointedly at the two diners who were *still* staring. Other than that *faux pas*—and his polite manners— David blended in perfectly. He wore the down-market uniform of shabby denim jacket, burgundy polo shirt, faded black jeans, and matching canvas slip-ons. He had kind eyes, a handsome, lined, lived-in face, and jet black, short-cropped hair that Valentina suspected came from a bottle. She put the guy in his late forties, maybe even well-preserved early fifties.

"You want a drink?" The dour lady from the cashier's counter apparently doubled as the Palace's one and only waitress. She stood over Valentina and tapped a chewed stub of a pencil on her shabby yellow order pad.

Valentina tensed. The woman had appeared unnoticed and with an uncanny silence, which had done nothing to sooth her jangled nerves. "Tea, please."

The waitress gave an impatient sigh and actually rolled her eyes. "What tea?"

"I'd go for the milk tea," David suggested in much the same tone he'd used when he'd *suggested* Valentina meet him for lunch. "Although the chrysanthemum is excellent."

"Milk tea it is." Valentina smiled at the waitress.

"Bubble or regular?"

"Regular milk tea will be just fine, thank you."

The waitress stomped off as if serving customers ruined her

entire day.

"I hope you don't mind. I ordered food." David watched the waitress-cum greeter disappear through the kitchen door. "The roast goose here is exceptional. And quite fresh." He nodded toward the row of sorry-looking geese that hung in a row across the front window.

"I'm not here to eat. Not much appetite."

"Why *are* you here, Valentina?"

"Well, Chuckles, it's because you gave me no choice."

"Chuckles?"

"You seemed to find our earlier conversation amusing."

David smiled. "I like your . . . straightforward manner. 'Cut to the chase.' Very New York." He leaned back in his plastic chair. "I am actually surprised. You've taken quite the leap of faith meeting me, especially since you don't know for certain I am who I say I am."

The waitress reappeared with Valentina's drink. She plopped it down on the table with a huff. "You want food?"

Valentina told her, "No, thank you" and was treated to a frown and a snort for her trouble.

"I could show you my badge, if you wanted," David said once the waitress was out of earshot. He reached into the inside pocket of his old jacket.

"No. I mean—that won't be necessary. Thank you."

The tinny bell rang out once more, and a young backpacker wandered in off the busy street. Checking his watch, he looked around, shrugged off his backpack, and sat himself down at the table nearest the door. The waitress left her counter to grump at her new customer.

"Nice place." Valentina smirked.

"It's as anonymous as it gets in Hong Kong," David told her. "There's almost no CCTV coverage, and the Triads have the whole district under tight control—they practically *are* the police here, which, ironically, makes it probably one of the safest areas on this side of the island."

Valentina didn't find that comforting. She'd grown up in the gang-run areas of downtown New York and had never once felt completely safe.

David leaned forward in his seat and took a quick sip of his tea. "So. Jimmy Wen is running a stock loan scam. He's dishing out fat percentage loans against securities to desperate clients, and then selling them the minute they sign over control." Apparently, the pleasantries and preamble were over and done with and it was down to business.

"I know what a stock loan scam is." As used as she was to being spoken down to because she was a woman, Valentina still didn't care much for it, but David's condescension wasn't what put a lead weight in the pit of her stomach.

"I'm sorry. I don't mean to . . . *mansplain*, I think you Americans call it?" David appeared genuine enough in his apology. "Here's what I'm getting at: Wen has whole teams of market makers that deliberately drive the share values down in order to push those loans into negative equity. He moves them around so often it's impossible to track them down. We believe it's the same people he uses for his pump-and-dump scheme."

"Pump and dump" was artificially inflating stock prices to make them seem attractive before pulling the rug out from under investors. She suspected that might be the sort of scam her dad fell for. Her mind went to the man she'd had breakfast with this morning—the man she'd assured, barely two hours ago, that his company shares would be safe. Was the same thing about to happen to him?

Beyond that disturbing thought was the sheer balls-to-the-wall insanity of pulling such a scam on businessmen with the stature of the CEO of Green Dynamics. If Wen was caught at it, he'd go to jail . . . along with anyone who'd lured the chubby little sacrificial lambs into the fold.

Valentina pushed fear for her own future aside. She couldn't think about that now. She needed to focus. So, instead of grinding her teeth, she took a sip of her milk tea. It tasted delicious, and a world apart from the lukewarm, insipid stuff they'd dished out at JM Wen.

"That seems like small ball for a company like JM Wen," she said blandly.

David shook his head. "Not so small, when you consider the size of the players. Wen does everything he can to get those clients to default on their loans and just walk away. That way, he either screws them out of more shares, or cash to plug the hole. Or . . . they default and he never has to give back the shares he sold. Even if the client makes good and the loan is paid, Wen can ensure he buys them back for a song and hands them over with a smile and a handshake like nothing ever happened."

David paused to look up at her. "All of it works perfectly, providing the price goes down and not up. We know he's laundering money, too, but he's way more cautious about that part of his operation. And we know he's handling money for a faction of the Wo Hop Yee clan—although we've dug deep and still can't find cast-iron proof of how, or which bank he's using."

Valentina felt a frisson of excitement—or maybe it was dread—course up her spine. That was exactly what she was seeking: the dirty bank or banks Wen was using as a laundromat. If she could prove that Wen was a Triad launderer . . .

"So, you think Wen's laundering money for the gangs?"

"Yeah, but he has so many shell companies—mostly offshore—and banks in his back pocket that it's an all but impenetrable maze to navigate. We have our suspicions, of course, but without proof . . ." David shrugged and took a hearty slurp of tea.

"If you know all this, how come you don't just march in and close him down pending an investigation? Why did you see fit to call me when I was using the goddamned restroom?" She caught the agent's eye and gave him a look she'd been told could incinerate the target in their tracks.

He remained annoyingly intact. "Because, Miss Vittorio, what we don't have is hard evidence. What we need to make all this stick are client names, plus the names, addresses, and inside leg measurements of Wen's associates, the banks he's in cahoots with, dates, numbers— you know how it goes."

Of course Valentina knew. And David knew that she knew.

"I feel your pain," she said dryly. "He's smart enough to have a legitimate front to his businesses, and enough bona fide clients to maintain respectability and divert suspicion."

"Sure. But there's always going to be speculation around someone like Jimmy Wen. He's a man who loves all the trappings of wealth. At times it seems like he's flaunting it to taunt the regulators with what he's up to—like he's operating his business dealings under the premise of hey, it's only illegal if you get caught!"

"So, you want me to dig out all of Wen's secrets and just hand them over to you?"

David nodded and sipped at his tea. "We need someone on the inside who has access to Wen's systems and people. And, considering your motivation to destroy Jimmy Wen, we figured you were someone the SFC could do business with. I believe we can help one another toward our common goal."

An uneasy silence settled between them. David finished up his tea, and Valentina worked on hers. She'd done nothing even remotely illegal or morally reprehensible at this pass, yet the guy was extorting her into whistle-blowing. Either she played ball and fed them what they wanted on Wen, or they'd make that well-placed phone call and it would be game over for Valentina Vittorio.

"Here's the big news," David said, staring into his empty cup. "We have intelligence that Wen is in some kind of trouble. That he's nervous about something—a particular deal maybe, or maybe it's a deal with people he has reason to fear. We hope that if Wen's starting to panic, he'll make a mistake or two we can nail him on. There has to be a good reason for him to pull in his best international salespeople—do you have any idea as to what that reason might be?"

Guarded, Valentina raised one eyebrow. "It's my first morning at real work, Chuck. We've barely gotten through the corporate flag-waving." She wasn't about to mention that she'd already gotten into JM Wen's network and established a virtual machine to operate from inside.

"Wen is trying to pull in big money—*billions* according to our sources—but what we don't know is *why*."

"Where's the mystery? The man loves his money."

"There's got to be more to it than that."

"Look," Valentina told him, "if you're already getting this level of intel on Wen, why do you need me? You're asking me to take some big risks here, which I'm thinking I don't really need to be taking right now."

David studied her face. "May I remind you that if—*when*—Jimmy Wen goes down, everyone involved in his illegal ventures will go down as accessories, innocent or not? You'll all be thrown out on the street and suspended from any kind of trading while the authorities sort the whole sorry mess out—and you know how long those things can go on; we regulators are not known for our urgency when it comes to investigations. Even if you manage to skate by prison, you'll most likely never work in the financial industry again, Valentina."

Valentina processed what David was telling her, feeling her stomach begin to form a slipknot. She hadn't thought any further than finishing Wen, and she knew that even if the SFC didn't tip Wen off about her, David had her pretty much over the barrel anyway.

The waitress materialized with a sizzling plate of greasy roasted goose that smelled of sesame oil and pepper. She plopped it down in front of David who looked over at Valentina as if he felt like he ought to apologize again for eating. He looked up at the waitress and asked, "Could I have another—"

Ignoring him, the waitress turned to Valentina. "Phone call for you."

"Me?"

"You're the only white lady in here. Phone call for white lady."

David's face paled as he fought to conceal his panic. "Who knows you're here?"

Valentina shook her head. "I didn't tell a soul. And I made damn sure I wasn't followed." Her stomach twisted into an even tighter knot. She just wanted to be out of this God-awful place.

David reached out and tapped the back of her hand, making her look back at him. "You should take it."

"Seriously?"

"If it's Wen's people, they obviously know you're here, so there'd be no point lying—but at least you'd know if you should go back to the office or not."

"And if it's not Wen?"

"Then we find out who's following you—besides me."

Valentina stood up and followed the waitress toward the front of the restaurant.

"Phone back there."

The waitress pointed through the gap at the end of the counter and down the long hallway that ran past the kitchen to the rear of the building. Then, done with the "white lady," she plucked a glass of green tea from the counter and took it across to the young backpacker by the door. Standing up, he checked his watch again. He smiled at the waitress, threw a few dollars down on the table, and left.

Valentina didn't catch the waitress's reaction. She turned to peer down the hallway. At the far end was a pair of doors. One, Valentina saw, was the staff restroom, and kitty-corner to that, the rear exit. On the wall next to the exit was an old, yellowed push-button telephone. Its receiver dangled close to the linoleum-covered floor by its curly cord.

Valentina took a deep breath, clutched the strap of her purse, and made her way along the hallway, her heart pounding, her soles sticking to the floor. Bending over, Valentina picked up the telephone receiver, tucked her hair behind one ear, and held the phone to it. "Hello?"

In the loaded silence that followed, Valentina heard the waitress's harsh, grating voice raised in annoyance as she shouted something in Cantonese over the faint tinkle of the small bell above the door.

The explosion shook the air and made the floor buck beneath Valentina's feet. She was tossed against the rear wall of the building like a well-dressed rag doll, hitting the solid surface so hard her teeth clattered together and bright stars danced behind her eyes. Like an earthquake's aftershock came a rush of heated, dusty air and the choking stink of melted plastic and scorched flesh.

Dazed, her limbs trembling with shock, Valentina sat with her back against the wall next to the exit door in an awful, ringing silence. She tried to shake herself back to reality, puzzled by the fact that the telephone receiver was still in her hand.

CHAPTER SEVENTEEN

The first of the screams began.

Muffled at first, they rose in volume as Valentina's hearing began to return; as it faded in, it brought along a piercing, high-pitched ringing that almost hurt.

People were badly hurt out there, on the other side of the wall—the wall that had saved her life. She'd been unbelievably lucky; had she not been called to the phone, had the hallway been any shorter, she would have been caught in the blast. She ran a quick mental check of her body—nothing hurt except her right shoulder and her hip, which she'd jarred when she'd bounced from the wall to the floor. As far as she could tell, nothing was missing, and there was no blood. She even stretched out her legs and wriggled her bare toes just to be sure; everything seemed to be working perfectly fine. Her purse, too, was still tethered to her by its cross-body strap.

David.

He was out there, and it was possible his voice was among those she'd heard screaming. Desperate to be out of the place but needing to know, Valentina struggled to her hands and knees. Her entire body jolted and trembled as she crawled the length of the hallway to where she could peek out into what remained of the Cha Lau Yu Palace.

It was a scene of total devastation. A fog of fine dust and black, curling smoke hung thick in the air, eddying in the breeze from the collapsed front wall of the building. The tables and chairs were all gone, along with the diners who had occupied them—all reduced to shattered fragments by the blast. The front of the restaurant had been blown out into the street, along with the hanging geese and the poor, miserable waitress. Beyond, the handful of bystanders who had not fled wandered aimlessly along the sidewalk. Some bled profusely from cuts to their faces and held their heads in disbelief as they stared open-mouthed at the destruction inside the restaurant, while others just stared vacantly as shock overwhelmed them.

Valentina looked around at the vivid splashes of blood and dripping gore smeared across the scorched floor near where each of the restaurant's patrons had been sitting, and saw the ragged lumps of raw, oozing flesh and randomly scattered body parts: arms, fingers, a foot, part of an old man's face . . .

Above the table she'd shared with David of the SFC only a few moments before was a bright crimson spray that spread all the way up to the charred ceiling. It looked as if someone had thrown a can of red paint at the wall. Valentina choked back the acid tang of bile that crept up from her stomach; the agent was dead, quite decidedly so, and she'd only been spared thanks to an anonymous phone call and the restaurant's long hallway.

Why? How?

Valentina backed up behind the wall and eyed the muted telephone. No one had answered when she'd picked it up, and Valentina had a gut feeling whoever had been there had hung up the moment she'd said hello. Whoever it had been, they had wanted to make sure she was there before . . .

The distant wail of sirens told Valentina it was high time she wasn't anywhere near the restaurant. She had no intention of waiting around for the police, since the last thing she needed was to have an official report tying her name to that of the SFC agent who'd died in a restaurant bombing. She hauled herself to her feet and headed back down the hall, barely catching a glimpse of a terrified face peering through the porthole window of the kitchen. Dust and smoke was thickening in the hallway like an errant fog. Valentina hoped it would cover her from the eyes of the kitchen staff as she made her way to the rear of the building. Once there, she pushed hard on the bar of the exit door and prayed to a God she hadn't entirely believed in until that moment that the damn thing would open.

It did. The stale, fishy miasma in the dark, dank alleyway beyond was a welcome relief from the hellfire stench of death and destruction she'd left behind in the restaurant. Valentina gulped it down and eased the heavy door closed behind her.

Then she ran.

The alleyway was long and gloomy and existed permanently in the shadows of the buildings on either side. Valentina was as grateful for those shadows as she had been for the back door of the Cha Lau Yu Palace; they afforded her an anonymous escape. Gasping for fresh air, Valentina ran toward the sunlight that glinted brightly at the end of the alley; the low heels of her ankle boots clattered unevenly on the cracked, broken, dank concrete. The sound bounced loudly between the grubby buildings, and she feared it might give her away.

Reaching the end of the alley, many yards from the sirens, screams, and reek of smoke and burned bodies, Valentina allowed herself a moment to calm her nerves. She'd been running high on adrenaline since even before the blast (hell, since that burner phone had gone off in her purse) and was beginning to crash.

In the shelter of a stack of orange crates, she leaned her back against the cool damp of the grimy wall to give her heart time to quit pounding. The harsh, high-pitched ringing in her ears merged with the background hubbub of sirens, while vivid images of the devastation inside the restaurant flashed behind her eyes. She wondered about David, the SFC agent who, moments before he was reduced to a wet stain on the restaurant wall, had been busy contemplating roast duck and discussing the downfall of Jimmy Wen with her. Did he have a family who would miss him? Daughters, maybe, and a wife to receive a visit from the police?

No time for this, Tina. Get moving.

Valentina ground her teeth and pushed herself away from the wall. She made another check of her person. Her once pristine, absurdly expensive suit was covered with a layer of dust, the knees were soiled from her crawl down the hall, as were the toes of her boots, and her hair—she put a hand up to it—was a fright wig. Using both hands, she brushed as much of the dust and tiny fragments of debris from her clothes and out of her hair as she could; she couldn't afford to draw unwanted attention to herself by looking like she'd just survived a bomb blast. She pulled a little hairbrush out of her purse and gave her hair several quick strokes, before digging out a palm-sized mirror to check her face for cuts or smudges. Seeing none, she put the mirror away and dared to poke her head out of the alley to cast a quick glance around.

She was relieved to see that the attention of the people near the intersection to her right seemed to be focused on the smoldering remains of the Cha Lau Yu Palace and the injured on the street beyond. While she doubted too many people ventured into the gloomy alleys behind Hong Kong's garishly decorated streets even on a regular day, Valentina knew she couldn't loiter for too long in the sanctuary of the cool shadows. Sooner or later someone would poke their nose into the alley and see her.

How many people, she wondered, had seen the white lady go into the restaurant?

Checking her watch, Valentina made a quick calculation—if she hurried, she'd have just about enough time to get to the Four Seasons, clean up, change out of her suit, and get back to the office before anyone wondered where the hell she'd gone. She thanked her rediscovered God that Lucas had told her to take all the time she needed.

Another deep breath and Valentina stepped out of the shadows and into the bright Hong Kong sunshine.

CHAPTER EIGHTEEN

Valentina caught a cab several blocks southwest of Lockhart. Time was of the essence, and she didn't want to run the risk of getting caught up in another one of the noisy protests. Nor did she want to be walking through the streets in her dusty pantsuit and scuffed boots. Once in the cab on her way back to the Four Seasons, Valentina felt a little more secure. She worked to quiet her still squirming brain and get her breathing back to deep, composed, normalcy. Still her mind spewed out questions and raced after answers she realized she might never have.

Who was responsible for the bombing? And why? Was the bombing part of the eternal Triad wars that marred the underbelly of the island? Or had it something to do with her meeting with David? Had she been the target of the bomb, or had he? Or had it been meant to end their possible collaboration?

The questions made her already pounding head hurt more. All she knew—*all*—was that it had to be more than pure coincidence or simple bad luck. Which meant that someone had been watching the restaurant and her clandestine meeting, and they wanted her alive.

Lucky, lucky me.

The cab dropped Valentina off in front of the Four Seasons. Once through the hotel's expansive glass front doors, she bustled through the vast foyer as quickly as she could without drawing too much attention, and thumbed one of the fat brass buttons by the elevator doors. After what seemed an age, Valentina was safely ensconced in one of the luxurious cars, blessedly alone.

Finally reaching the sanctuary of her hotel suite, she allowed herself to breathe. She piled her hair atop her head in a clip, took a quick shower, redid her makeup at light-speed, then dressed in a suit similar in cut and color to the one she'd stuffed into the dry-cleaning bag and left for housekeeping. That done, she slipped her feet into a pair of Chloé booties the same shade of charcoal gray as the Louboutins. Most men wouldn't notice the difference, and if Sofia did, she might or might not say anything.

Finally, she gave her hair another fifty strokes, sprayed a light mist of Shalimar in the air and walked through it, and grabbed her purse from the foot of the bed. As she was wiping the dust from it, she realized there was a scuff along one side toward the bottom and a smudge of something grimy. Probably happened when she'd been blown against the wall or crawled down the hallway or . . .

Stop it. It's fine. Just keep it against your body.

She offered up a silent prayer of thanks to the ever-efficient Ms. Kwok and her genius foresight to book the new recruits into a hotel literally adjoining the Finance Center. There was no need to run the full length of the glass walkway that connected the Four Seasons with 2IFC. She did, however, pop a granola bar into her mouth to silence her growling stomach.

At precisely two p.m., Valentina Vittorio stepped out of the elevator on the fifty-second floor of the International Finance Center and made her way through the glass doors that took her back into the heart of Jimmy Wen's murky empire.

"There you are, Val!"

Valentina's heart sank as Lucas Vaughn's voice greeted her. He was standing just inside the office's opulent entry as if he'd been waiting to meet her. She offered him her best smile and made ready with the excuses, but quickly discovered he wasn't in the least part interested in where she'd spent her lunchtime.

"I see you've already met Yanlin," Lucas observed.

"Who?" Confused, Valentina suppressed her guilty conscience; had *Yanlin* been the SFC guy's real name? She swallowed the creeping panic rising from the pit of her stomach.

"Hey, Lucas, how are you doing?"

The voice behind her was friendly, yet entirely unfamiliar. Valentina stopped dead in her tracks and spun around. She recognized one of the half-dozen men with whom she'd just shared the elevator ride.

"I'm all good, mate." Lucas pumped the guy's hand with vigor, and the two slapped backs like old, long-lost drinking buddies. "What the hell are you doing here on a Monday? You do *know* it's Monday, right?"

Yanlin laughed awkwardly as he reclaimed his hand. "Yeah, I'm all too aware of what day it is, thank you very much. Jiang works me hard, but not quite *that* hard. Murphy asked me to come in. Well, *asked* is probably not the right word."

Lucas snorted. "No doubt about it. My condolences." He returned his attention to Valentina, who, unsure as to whether she should stick around or head on to her desk, opted to stay put. "Gao Yanlin, meet Valentina Vittorio. Valentina Vittorio, meet Gao Yanlin. He's our bank liaison manager. Works for LCSSC."

"Very pleased to meet you." Valentina gave the guy a firm, professional handshake and a quick once-over. He was good-looking and tall —an easy six-one, wore his pitch-black hair side parted and a bit long on top, and was dressed in an expensive dark gray three-piece suit that accentuated his old gold complexion. She figured he was in his thirties.

"Likewise," he replied. "And please, everyone calls me Yan."

"Yan doesn't care much for the Westernized names the Hongkongers like to give themselves," Lucas cut in. "Reckons it's too common. Although I could definitely see you as a Bruce, mate. What do you think, Val? Is he a Bruce?"

"Oh, most definitely." Valentina thought it prudent not to correct

Lucas on either his incongruent renaming of Yan or his continued contraction of her name—she'd always absolutely hated *Val.*

"Please, don't call me *Bruce!*" Yan smiled.

"Yan it is." Valentina cast a quick glance across at Lucas, who suddenly appeared antsy and eager to be on his way. He gave her a barely imperceptible nod and began to walk.

"May I call you Val too?" Yan finally let go of her hand and the two followed on behind Lucas as he strolled along the hallway.

"No. I prefer Valentina. Lucas is set in his ways."

Yan returned her wry smile. He had a very nice smile. It was warm and made it all the way up into his eyes.

Lucas glanced back over his shoulder as the three made their way toward the sales office to give Valentina a belated once-over. "You changed."

"I'm a klutz," she said offhandedly. "Spilled all over myself at lunch."

"Huh. Never have figured you for a klutz. Where'd you go?"

Quick. Where'd you go? "Some street vendor a couple blocks from here."

Lucas came to a sudden stop by one of the office's cafeterias—JM Wen Limited had four, and this one had been especially designed to emulate a cozy, street-corner coffee shop. Vaughn pushed open the door, and the delicious, creamy scent of fresh-ground beans wafted out to welcome them.

"Mr. Wen can't see you for a few hours," he told Yan before turning to Valentina. "The next orientation meeting is not for another hour yet, so why don't you grab a coffee with Yan? You can consider it part of your executive training. Schmoozing with the Bankers 101."

Valentina nodded. She welcomed the opportunity for some quiet time before being thrust back into the midst of her new colleagues and the high expectations and pressure to begin selling; her day had been an almost literal hell so far, and she definitely needed a little breathing space.

"Sounds good to me. A double latte might just get me through the afternoon."

And fill the empty pit that is my stomach.

"I'll catch up with you later, Yan." Lucas slapped the guy's shoulder. "Maybe we can hit a bar or two after you're done with Murphy? Christ knows you'll need it!"

"Works for me. I always need a beer or three to take the edge off after spending a day here. I really don't know how you do it, my friend."

Lucas pulled a face and turned to go. "You get used to it after awhile. And I'll see *you* at three," he told Valentina. "Mr. Wen's holding the session, so I wouldn't be late if I were you."

Before Valentina could tell him she had absolutely no intention of being late, Lucas Vaughn was gone.

"Double latte?" Yan ushered Valentina into the coffee bar and over to one of the dozen small, round, black-topped tables and, proving chivalry wasn't dead, he pulled out a chair for her to sit.

"Yes. Please."

Valentina sat herself down and watched as Yan made his way across to the solitary barista who stood at the pristine counter. Behind her, a huge stainless steel industrial coffee machine gurgled and steamed. The place was all but deserted. There were just two others—a middle-aged man and a younger woman, the latter dressed in the ubiquitous office assistant's garb. They sat in a corner having what could have been either an intense business meeting or a quiet lovers' tiff.

Valentina allowed herself to relax. This was indeed a welcome distraction, and she had a feeling she was going to enjoy the young banker's company.

Yan ordered up the complimentary coffees—free drinks were just one of the myriad perks of working with JM Wen Limited—and made his way back over to the table. He took his seat, placed his hands on the table, and interlaced his fingers as if he was about to give Valentina a formal interview.

"I'm guessing you're part of Wen's new tiger team? You must be quite the hot shot for Wen to drag you halfway across the world to this godforsaken rock." He cracked an ironic smile.

"New York office. And yeah, I guess I am one of Wen's tigers.

Grrr." Valentina eased back in her seat. The look on Yan's flushed face hinted that she was making him nervous. Attraction, or something else?

Yan gave an exaggerated huff. "Great. Another *lo fan*—just what we need in Hong Kong."

Valentina raised a quizzical eyebrow. "*Lo fan*? That doesn't sound good."

"It's one of our words for you Americans. The literal translation is *barbarian*—because we consider you guys to be very much lacking when it comes to patience and discipline." He grinned, letting Valentina know he was joking.

Valentina shrugged her shoulders and returned the smile. "Fair enough. I really can't argue with that—I've driven in rush hour Manhattan; neither patience nor discipline are in the average New Yorker's vocabulary. I think I'll pass on any other words you might have for us." Feeling the warmth of his gaze, she absently brushed her bangs out of her face.

"I imagine you're finding Hong Kong a little more polite than you're used to?" Yan probed. "We pride ourselves very much on having the patience you Americans lack."

She thought of the young studs in the ladies room at Methuselah, ducked away from that memory and collided into the one in which someone had hip-checked her and left an unwelcome gift in her purse. "Mm. Not too sure you've got grounds for pride. I've gotten caught up in your protests more than once."

Not to mention nearly blown up. Hardly a sterling recommendation for Hong Kong's politeness.

"Ah, yes. The *da lu zi* have certainly stirred up a lot of passion on the island."

"The Chinese?"

"I'm impressed."

"Don't be. I had a bunch of people yelling that in my ear—I kinda got the idea it's not a term of affection."

Yan snorted. "Not in the least; it's used here pretty much how you might use the word 'Chinks.'"

"I *wouldn't* use the word 'Chinks.' Ever."

The barista appeared over Valentina's shoulder and plonked the two large white cups on the table. Caught unawares by the young woman's sudden appearance at the table, Valentina coiled like a spring. In a heartbeat, her fists balled and she snapped her head around; had she not caught herself in time, she might well have lashed out with truly embarrassing consequences.

Visibly shocked by the sudden murderous look in Valentina's eyes, the terrified barista recoiled and took a step backward. "Your latte, ma'am," she stammered, then turned tail and bustled back to the safety of her counter.

Valentina managed to say an embarrassed "thank you" to the retreating barista's back before turning around to offer Yan an apologetic smile.

"Jeez, remind me never to bring you coffee." Yan laughed. "Are you always this wound up, Valentina?"

"It's been an eventful morning." Valentina shook her head to try to clear the mental image of the bored waitress's face at the Chinese restaurant as she delivered the last meal she'd ever deliver to the SFC agent who didn't live to eat it. "I guess I'm just your typical *lo fan*, after all."

The banker raised an eyebrow, as if he was expecting further elaboration.

"So, the protests?" Deftly, Valentina changed the subject.

"They're nothing new, I'm afraid," Yan told her, taking a delicate sip of his coffee. "Hong Kong has been protesting on and off since the British handover back in 1997. It's like anything, I guess. You get used to it after awhile, life goes on, and it all becomes little more than background noise. Which it probably shouldn't. And it's been getting steadily worse since 2014—once it became blatantly obvious the Chinese had no intention whatsoever of honoring their promise to allow Hong Kong's continued autonomy."

Valentina took a tentative sip of her drink, savoring the espresso through the foam atop it. "I don't know too much about the Chinese, but given their stance with Tibet and Taiwan, wasn't it a little naive of you to believe they'd not interfere in Hong Kong's affairs once the British left?"

Yan rested his elbows on the table's smooth surface. "You're right, of course, but what could we do? The handover was always going to happen, and the Chinese are always going to be *da lu zi*. It began in earnest when they put a stop to us having free elections—you should consider yourself lucky you have that, *and* a two-party system."

Valentina's laugh was a sardonic one. "Yeah, I wouldn't go getting all overexcited about that. Partisan politics isn't all it's cracked up to be."

"Yeah, but imagine going from entirely free elections to having to choose from twelve hundred candidates who have all been vetted by Beijing." There was a distinct air of sadness to Yan's voice, as if he were mourning the loss of a loved one. He ran a hand through his dark hair and sighed. "Even though they rescinded the extradition treaty in what I think was nothing more than a hollow gesture, we can feel the *da lu zi* tentacles reaching into every facet of the island's politics and economy. I'm afraid they're not going to stop until Hong Kong is completely absorbed into China. I'm just about old enough to remember the good ol' colonial days." His attempt at levity was less than convincing. "Hong Kong was never this . . ."

"Repressed?"

"Paranoid. These days, people are too scared to speak up, even in their own homes, and especially anywhere public." Yan's eyes flickered around the sparsely populated cafeteria as if to hammer home his point.

Valentina thought back to the silent elevator rides—perhaps the lack of conversation had less to do with politeness and business secrecy and more to do with Big Brother–level paranoia? Not for the first time since arriving in Hong Kong, Valentina longed to be back in the midst of Manhattan's woefully impolite society.

"China has always seen Hong Kong as a cash cow," Yan continued, "especially so since '97. That makes the finance industry subject to an extra special level of scrutiny, which is making it increasingly difficult for companies like JM Wen to function."

"Because the Chinese are interfering in the markets?" Valentina had read online about the mainland's alleged manipulation of the Hong Kong stock exchange and key players in the market. The Chinese were a particularly guarded and secretive nation, and it was difficult to gauge the extent of their meddling.

Yan shook his head. "It's more the fact that Mr. Wen and his contemporaries sometimes skirt the fringes of what's strictly *legal*."

Valentina was surprised at the banker's candor. *Don't look a gift horse in the mouth*, she told herself, and wondered how much her new friend knew about Jimmy Wen's operations. She suspected that, given his privileged position, it would be a hell of a lot. Valentina was more than happy to let the guy spill his guts and was fully prepared to use her feminine wiles to her advantage. If she had to bed Yan to get out of him what he knew about the bank's involvement with Wen's illegal activities, she would. It didn't hurt that the guy was more than easy on the eyes.

"That doesn't sound good," she said, frowning slightly. "Is there something I should know about my situation here that might put me in harm's way, legally speaking?"

"I really can't say. You understand."

"Of course." Valentina leaned forward ever so slightly and made eye contact. "But, Yan, I really don't want to get caught up in anything . . . suspect. I promise, anything you do tell me stays between us." She put just a hint of trepidation in her voice and injected her gaze with worry.

Yan gave her a long, level look, then appeared to come to some internal decision. He leaned toward her, pitched his voice low, and said, "You have to understand that the Asian culture is a world apart from anything you're used to. To us, appearances are paramount, so it's a common practice here for wealth to be built using leverage."

"Leverage? Like fixed assets or borrowing, you mean."

"Mostly borrowing." Yan shot another glance over at the barista. She looked up from her phone, caught his signal, and set to preparing another two drinks.

"Actually, it happens more than you may think back in the States," Valentina countered.

Yan smiled wryly. "Indeed. A large number of businesses in Hong Kong borrow money from banks to magnify their profit potential and increase their return on assets. The banks can't always—or won't always—give them what they're looking for. When that happens, they turn to companies like JM Wen."

He fell silent when the barista appeared with a pair of fresh beverages. This time, the girl made sure to approach within full view of Valentina and announce her arrival at the table with a polite cough. She eyed the American warily as she placed the cups gently on the table before scurrying back to the counter and her cell phone.

Valentina nodded. "Yeah. That's fairly simple math." She'd brokered enough deals on Wall Street for companies wishing to overinflate their net worth to know how that particular ball rolled. She took a sip of her fresh latte; it was perfect.

"As you know, while the practice isn't *strictly* illegal, it's frowned upon by regulators in every market." Yan hesitated and shot a furtive glance around the coffee bar. When he spoke again, his voice was even softer. "I suppose you've heard the rumors?"

I'm sure as hell going to pretend that I have. "I've collected an entire catalog of rumors, Yan. Did you have a particular one in mind?"

He laughed and looked down at his cup—was he afraid he'd said too much? "Well, I'm sure you're aware that there are practices meant to . . . manipulate the stock markets that have been around for almost as long as the markets themselves."

Valentina deepened her look of concern, hoping to keep him talking. "Are you suggesting JM Wen is involved in *making* the markets?"

Yan shook his head. "Even if he was, he wouldn't be the only one playing the pump-and-dump game; the practice is rife throughout Hong Kong. We prefer to do things a little differently over here. So what if a broker trades to artificially inflate share prices before dumping them? It's only illegal if you get caught, right?"

Hey, that wasn't condescending at all, Mr. Gao.

Valentina took a moment to sip her latte as if pondering this information. "So where does LCSSC Wealth Management fit into the JM Wen Limited equation? There're a hell of a lot of banks out there; why would Jimmy Wen choose a small, private one?"

"We're not JM Wen's *only* bank." Yan sounded defensive. "But we are one of the few who are a wholly owned subsidiary, which means fewer people to stick their noses into the business we choose to do. Remember, though, we only handle a very small, very specific part of Mr. Wen's business."

Valentina shifted in her seat as she read Yan's eyes; the guy knew he'd said too much. "How *specific* is specific? Is it something you can let me in on so I can steer clear of it? *Can* I steer clear of it?"

Suddenly, Yan looked uncomfortable. His eyes flicked back toward the couple in the corner as if he feared they may be eavesdropping. Then he lowered his gaze and pretended to study his coffee. Finally, he said, "Just particular clients and transactions; nothing I can talk about —certainly not here. We move money around and facilitate the buying and selling of shares—pretty much everything you'd expect from a private bank. We also refer clients to JM Wen whom we can't deal with for whatever reason."

"High risk?" Valentina prompted.

He shrugged. "Or they're looking for a loan rate against their shares that we are not permitted to give. I mean, as a private bank we're able to offer better rates than the mainstream, but even *we* have a limit."

"So you send them here. To Wen."

He flashed a thousand-watt smile. "For a modest fee, of course."

She responded in kind. "No such thing as a free lunch, eh?"

"Precisely."

The door opened and, in an instant, the intrusion of the office beyond ruined the cozy ambience of the fake bistro. Heads turned as Jeff Murphy strode in like he owned the place; Valentina couldn't tell whether Yan was bummed or relieved to see him.

Murphy made his way across to Yan and Valentina. "Gao Yanlin. I figured I'd find you in here." He shook the banker's hand with his usual aplomb, duly ignored Valentina, and hovered over the table.

Yan pushed his cup to the center of the table; his off-the-record chat with Valentina was officially over. "Lucas tells me Mr. Wen is not available for our meeting until later this afternoon."

"Yeah, he's too busy mollycoddling the new guys to take care of real business," Murphy groused. "But you and I can make a start without Jimmy. We need to talk about JLM Asset Holdings." He fixed Valentina with an icy stare that said "GET LOST" in all caps.

Taken by surprise by the pompous man's sudden acknowledgement of her presence, Valentina offered her hand. "Valentina Vittorio, I'm—"

Murphy declined the customary handshake. "I know damn well who you are, young lady. Shouldn't you be out selling with all the other *wunderkinds* Jimmy brought in—or is this just an exotic vacation for you?" His face crinkled into what passed as a smile, and his stooped shoulders shook as he chuckled at his own joke.

"I guess this is my cue to get to work." Valentina's chair scraped on the tiled floor as she got to her feet.

"Yeah. Me too." Yan followed suit. He shook Valentina's hand goodbye and ventured, "Maybe we could continue our conversation sometime later?"

Valentina gave her warmest smile and tilted her head. "I'll be around for the foreseeable, so yeah, maybe we should do just that." Valentina watched Yan as he followed the tall American out of the cafeteria.

The banker obviously knew far more than he'd dared to divulge in their all too brief exchange—a lot more, if she'd read him right. Valentina reckoned if she stayed close, played seductress as necessary, she might get a much better idea of what to look for in JM Wen's internal records and where to look for it. The sooner she left the realm of rumor for the domain of evidence, the happier she'd be.

CHAPTER NINETEEN

The head of the company stood at the head of the conference room table with his hands by his sides and his jacket draped neatly over the back of his chair. Lucas Vaughn was by his side, of course, and in either corner behind them, like gruff statues, stood Wen's ever-present pair of bodyguards. He looked like he was posing for a spread in *GQ*.

He greeted Valentina and her fellow rainmakers with a firm, dry handshake and rote greeting. Welcoming each one of the seven in their native tongue, he flashed a charismatic smile as he politely invited everyone to take their seat. With a nod and a smile, Valentina took her place at the table—gilt-edged name cards indicated where each of the seven were to sit—and she was surprised, if a little unnerved, to find herself sitting closest to Wen, on his right-hand side. Her paranoia reared its ugly little head, and she wondered, again, about bugs in bathrooms.

From her place across the table, Sofia flashed Valentina a sly grin. "Is that a new suit, Valentina? If I'd known you were hitting the stores over lunch, I'd have invited myself along." Her less-than-discreet voice drew curious glances from around the table.

Valentina returned the grin. "This old thing? Had it since high school."

Sofia was not about to let it go. "I have to say, I'm quite impressed with the costume change halfway through the day. That's more Hong Kong diva than Lyn Song!" She glanced around the table at her colleagues to garner their approval, seeming to revel in the subdued, awkward male laughter.

Give the little lady props for the cultural reference, thought Valentina. Lyn Song was currently the biggest name in Chinese cinema and was notorious for playing the part of the soon-to-be Hollywood diva to the hilt. Valentina didn't particularly feel the need to explain herself to the Swiss girl, but wanted it to be clear she wasn't ruffled by cattiness.

"As much as I'd love to claim diva-hood, I have to blame it all on a badly constructed pork mushu. My own darn fault. As I told Lucas earlier, I'm a bit of a klutz."

Sofia seemed to lose interest in the game at that point. That someone else had already noticed the quick-change apparently took all the fun out of it. Valentina tried to relax into her seat. She could really have done without Sofia pointing out her lunchtime change of clothes. It reminded her what she'd really, really like to forget. Secrets—she'd come here carrying a suitcase full and had acquired even more in the handful of days she'd been here.

How'm I ever gonna get them all into my suitcase for the trip home?

"Why don't we get started?" Lucas took his seat to Wen's left. A respectful hush settled over the room. Only Wen and his bodyguards remained standing.

Jimmy Wen placed his hands on the table and leaned forward. "Okay, people," he said, his voice resonant and commanding. "I hope you've enjoyed the pep talk, the guided tours, and the ego strokes, and I hope you have all taken the time to immerse yourselves in our office culture— I'm well aware it's considerably different than what you are all used to. I'm gratified to see that you've already begun pulling strings and closing deals. But, it's come to my attention—and been demonstrated"—here, his eyes moved to Sofia Reller—"that there is a dynamic we must exorcise if we are to have a coherent, effective *team*. We have already established that you are the best my company has to offer—if you were not, then someone else would be sitting in your seat today. It is important—no, it is *crucial*—that you understand *you are not in competition with each other*."

He paused to let the words sink in, and looked from one to the other of them, making eye contact with all but Sofia, who was inspecting her fingernails.

"Miss Reller, do I have your attention?"

She looked up, her pale cheeks flushing. "Yes, sir. You do."

"Good." He straightened and looked away, letting the woman off the hook. "I do appreciate some rivalry is always going to be inevitable whenever salespeople of your caliber are brought together. But it is *imperative* that each one of you remember that you are part of a team with the same goal: to compete *for* the company that pays your outrageous salaries, not to compete *against* one another."

Grim. That was the word Valentina had been looking for as she watched Jimmy Wen deliver his admittedly needful speech. Her impression of the man so far, underscored by their Friday "pep talk," was that he was a schmoozer and a gadfly. Sobriety did not sit on his shoulders naturally. Perhaps it was feigned? Or perhaps it had something to do with the reason for the Big Push.

"I have brought you all together at a particularly critical time in the company's history. The financial industry in Hong Kong has been hit hard with fear, with anti-China protests and with trade wars." Wen's critical eyes met Valentina's, as if her government's trade tariffs against China were entirely her fault. "Five of our biggest competitors have been forced into bankruptcy this year alone—including one of the biggest independent brokers on the island. It is your job, ladies and gentlemen, to ensure JM Wen Limited does not follow in their wake. Do bear in mind that if you're not up to the challenge, we have plenty others who will gladly replace you. Any questions so far?"

He made eye contact with everyone around the table—Lucas Vaughn included—as if the very question had been a challenge. No one spoke up, though Valentina did have a question: Was it the demise of successful competitors that had necessitated the Big Push? David hadn't thought so. It was not a question she was ever going to ask.

Once more, Wen leaned forward on the table. "Okay, so now I want you to forget how it was in our provincial offices. You are now closers in the World Series of trading." Wen looked over at Valentina as if he'd made the baseball reference especially for her benefit.

She raised an eyebrow; it was amusing to discover Wen considered Wall Street to be one of his provinces . . . and that he'd come up with yet another analogy for his Magnificent Seven Rainmakers and Top Gun Closers on the Wen Tiger Team. The man loved to mix his metaphors.

"So from now on, you will be handling only deals above ten million US dollars. I like to think of them as whales. You must chase only the whales and make real money, not the nickels and dimes you make dealing with pikers. They're a waste of your time. You want clients that can change your life in one shot." He jabbed a finger at the ceiling. "Deals that will pay you for every ounce of hard work and every second of your valuable time. We give the small deals to the newbies, let them deal with the pikers. You are too important and too busy to sweat any deal that doesn't pay a premium. There'll be no more playing small ball like you did back in your home offices. We have people out on the floor to deal with the penny stocks." He said the last two words with a sneer. "They're good people and they're paid well, but considerably less than those around this table."

Valentina glanced at Lucas, recalling his words to her on her first day in the office, though Wen had just raised the bar by five mil. She was surprised to see Michaels, Singh, and Ng furrow their brows almost in unison. Had their assigned mentors neglected to mention Jimmy Wen's creative interpretation of penny stocks?

"We have major, qualified leads for you, and each one is red hot," Wen continued. "You are my closers, people, and your job is to bring them all in—and bring them in fast."

The leads, he went on to explain, had been generated by the company's market analysis department—the new recruits would no doubt meet Jason Woo and his crack team of analysts over the course of the next week. Woo's job was to routinely scrutinize the publicly listed companies on the Hong Kong stock exchange and focus specifically upon those trading over HK$1 million per day, combing their typically expensive websites for growth ventures they might be entertaining. Then they would ferret out contact info for the key players in the company's management team, pull it, and pass it along to JM Wen's tiger team.

"You will then put in a call to a corporate contact," said Wen. "Mr. Michaels, who would you call?"

"I'd call the head whale—the CEO." If the Brit expected kudos for applying one of his boss's pet metaphors, he was rudely surprised.

"*No.*" Wen's voice was sharp. "You would call the whale's *personal assistant*. I know that's not the way you've done it back home, but here you must play Hong Kong's game. That means you must always go in through the PA identified by Jason Woo's team or you will be roundly ignored. The PA is the gatekeeper. The PA is whom you will schmooze and cultivate until you receive an introduction to the corporate CEO or CFO. The PA is whom you will request to have his or her boss set up an appointment to discuss projects their company may have that require funding. The ball is then firmly in their court, and what PA wants to be the one to have passed on an opportunity for his or her boss to acquire a substantial amount of cash money for their company?" Wen at last smiled again, holding out his hands, palms up. "Why, that would be the financial equivalent of some Decca functionary deciding not to bother Dick Rowe about the Beatles."

"And while you're waiting for that callback," Lucas added, "move on to the next lead."

Wen nodded emphatically. "With the promise of JM Wen showing interest in investing in their company's shares, the executive will almost invariably have his people make that phone call within the next day or two—never too soon to appear desperate, of course. All part of playing the game. Jason Woo and his analysts are ruthlessly precise and thorough. They have an almost supernatural ability to pick out the very ripest of the low-hanging fruit. The rest is up to you."

Well, ta-da, thought Valentina sarcastically. *How hard could that be?*

She dared to speak, keeping her manner studiously nonchalant. "You're saying we should get them hooked on this 'easy money.' Build up their dependence, like any good pusher."

"Yes!" Wen's eyes kindled as they met hers, and the grimness vanished in the static wash of his sudden fervor. He stabbed at the air with a finger. "Money *is* the drug! BUT . . . but, the game is not about the money. Not really. It's about what the money *does*. Your wealthy clients are addicted to the most powerful drug of them all—the power that comes with cold, hard cash."

Valentina was fascinated. Here was Jimmy Wen the Evangelist, Minister of the Almighty Dollar, Acolyte of the Capitalist Machine. This was what made him tick, what put breath in his lungs and pumped through his veins. This must have been the side of Jimmy Wen her father had seen.

And it had brought him to ruin.

"Show them the money," Wen said, "and they can't resist; they won't *want* to resist." A smile flitted across the thin lips.

Valentina understood what she suspected every single person around that table understood. Back in the New York office they called it *The Dance*; the salesperson would focus upon the borrower's true objective, the *real* reason they wanted the seemingly limitless amounts of money on offer: what that money could buy. Then they would encourage their clients to visualize how the money would help them obtain their objective, whether it was a palatial yacht or a foundation to end world hunger.

Either way, it could be achieved through JM Wen Limited. It was as easy as that.

"Remember," Wen told them, still smiling, "if they've contacted us and we have them hooked, they're *mine*!" He pounded both fists on the table, and everyone, Lucas included, jumped.

Valentina saw the startled side-eye Lucas gave his boss; Jimmy Wen was not known for his theatrics, but she'd somehow excited a virtual floor show.

"These people need our money, we need their shares, and *you* need to get paid—the rewards are there for you, people, along with a taste of the high life that will make you never want to go home. But, I expect each of you to reel in HK$2 billion in new business by the end of this week—and the same again for every week you're in Hong Kong—with absolutely *no* exceptions or excuses."

Valentina's brain made the quick conversion to US dollars. That was over 250 million in US dollars in just four days. That was a larger number than she'd done in New York. She read the room for reactions. Judging by the expression on Anthony Li's and Sofia Reller's faces, they were wondering if they were out of their depth. Everyone else was wearing their best poker face.

Wen seemed to have read the room as well. He afforded Li and the Swiss girl stabbing glances. "You have all proven your worth on the phones. And I understand that Valentina has had her first one-on-one with a client she brought in." He nodded in her direction. "Now the rest of you get to show what you can do face-to-face with our clients. Step up or step out, people." With that, Wen stood up ramrod straight, clasped his hands behind his back, and looked across at Lucas Vaughn.

Lucas nodded. "Right. I'm sending your allocated leads to your PCs and cell phones now." He tapped his phone's screen.

Valentina's phone vibrated in her purse as it received the information, triggering an unwelcome memory. She reached down, plucked the thing out of her bag, and took a good, long look at the red-hot leads Wen had given her.

Wen had been deadly serious in his reference to Major League Baseball. Each one of the leads represented serious money; there was nothing under HK$700m in the dozen or so she'd been allocated. That was in the ballpark of US$100m per client and, had she been in Hong Kong to make big money, Valentina would have been salivating at the massive earning potential. As it was, her single-minded objective was to take down JM Wen Limited long before she'd have the opportunity to make any commission on the leads.

CHAPTER TWENTY

T he meeting over, Jimmy Wen dismissed the closers with a nod, a half smile, and a polite yet commanding "thank you." Lucas stood. Everyone took that as their cue to follow suit and make their way back to their desks to begin the task of reeling in the big fish who were going to provide the company with so much money. Wen's rousing performance could have left no doubt as to the importance of the job at hand, though he'd nimbly papered over the real reasons for the big push. His talk of trade wars, anti-Chinese protests, and the worsening financial climate in Hong Kong all had the legitimate ring of truth, and were perfectly valid reasons for any company in the same boat as JM Wen Limited to scramble the fighter jets and pull in every dollar it possibly could.

The reality of the situation, of course, was not something Wen would ever have discussed with the new recruits. Only Lucas and Shum Kuo, and the bankers to some extent, knew just how dire a situation Wen's underhanded dealings had gotten him and the company into. Jimmy Wen was feared and respected throughout Hong Kong and beyond—as much for his wealth and powerful clout as for the connections he fostered. But he was also afraid, and Lucas was afraid for him. Somewhere deep inside, Lucas Vaughn was afraid that Jimmy Wen had underestimated the trouble he was in, despite his "I'm a believer" speeches.

Lucas had learned quickly upon arriving in Hong Kong that every finance-based company on the island functioned in a morass of ambiguity. That included dealings with the Triads at some level, whether willingly and wittingly or otherwise. Wen had advised his protégé that if he couldn't get comfortable with that ambiguity, a plane ticket back to Singapore was waiting for him. Faced with that choice, Lucas had stuck around. This was the chance of a lifetime: tutelage under a master of the markets, the promise of wealth and prestige. It had been one hell of a hook.

He'd known from the start that ambiguity came with high stakes and even higher risks and had convinced himself the risks were worth taking. Whether or not he'd had a qualm when he realized that he had swum into the deeps beyond ambiguity, Lucas couldn't recall. He'd gone on to help Jimmy make JM Wen Limited an even more formidable presence in Hong Kong by bending the law where necessary and outright flouting it if bending it was impossible. They had done it all to build the company: stock manipulation, bribery, market influencing, pump and dump, stock loan scams. Maybe more. Almost certainly more. Lucas had more than one colleague who'd unexpectedly left the company that he had tried to contact after the fact and been unable to locate.

Now, he no longer tried.

He supposed it had been a natural progression for Jimmy Wen to welcome Zhang Bo and the Wo Hop Yee clan with open arms when he heard they were shopping around for someone new to manage their assets. Lucas had taken the news with little surprise. He knew Wen coveted Triad money, at least in the abstract, but it wasn't protocol for a business like Wen's to openly approach the gangs. The massive cash injection Zhang brought into the company had been a welcome one, as was the formidable increase in Lucas's salary. Although the deal had meant them having to hook up with a less than reputable bank, and contend with increased scrutiny from the SFC, Jimmy Wen and Zhang

Bo had made great bedfellows. Zhang had dirty money; Wen owned a top-notch Laundromat.

And then . . . and then Jimmy did something more boneheaded than Lucas had thought possible. Did it against Lucas's most strenuous objections. He'd screwed around with Triad money, trading Zhang's shares, intending to sell high, have Freddy Tseng's market makers tank them, and then buy them back low, turning a healthy profit before Zhang was expecting to have them handed back.

He'd done it before successfully, time after time. But this time, something weird had happened. This time, the stocks went up. And because they went up, there simply wasn't enough cash to buy them back—not without a serious influx of new money.

He glanced at Jimmy now, as the closers were heading back to their market shrine, and wondered if he finally got it. Finally realized down to his bones that he was in deeper water than he'd ever been in before. Realized that Zhang Bo was reaching the end of his patience and his civilized veneer . . . and that JM Wen didn't have the money to make up the deficit.

Did he have any idea at all that the company was unraveling because of his carelessness? Did he care that, unlike Roger Surtees and so many others like him who'd fallen prey to Wen's stock lending scams over the years, the Triads were not the kind of people to walk away from what was rightfully theirs?

As he watched the new closers leave the meeting room with eager eyes glued to the hot leads on their phones, Lucas figured that had any of them known how quickly JM Wen Limited was coming undone, and why, they'd be writing out their resignations and scrambling for the next plane home.

"Miss Vittorio." Wen called to the American just as she reached the conference room door. "Do you have a moment?"

She hung back as the others left, a puzzled look on her face.

"Don't look so worried, Valentina." Lucas read the wariness in her eyes and gave her a broad smile. "You're not in trouble. You had a breakfast meeting with Mr. Kim. How did it go?"

Valentina brightened. "It went well. He asked me about margin loans, and I assured him that for his purposes, a stock loan was the best option."

"Ah, and he was reassured, was he?" asked Wen.

"Yes, sir, he was. We're talking about eight hundred million in Hong Kong dollars."

Wen clapped his hands together in boyish glee. "Bravo, Miss Vittorio. This is exactly why we brought you here to the home office. You are a tiger among tigers." He paused a beat, then observed, "I was surprised that you left the office for lunch, Miss Vittorio."

She flashed him a brilliant smile. "After my morning meeting, I had a lot of energy to burn off. I suspect you understand."

"Indeed. Did you find somewhere nice to eat?"

"Well, nice isn't exactly the word I'd use," she replied wryly. "I grabbed some street food and wandered around a little—took in a few of the sights. I was told you can see the Observation Wheel from here."

Wen's eyes sought hers. "On a good day, yes you can. I hope your wanderings didn't take you anywhere near the Wan Chai district, Miss Vittorio."

Valentina smiled crookedly and shook her head, looking a bit bewildered. "Mr. Wen, I wouldn't know the Wan Chai district if it jumped up and down and whistled at me. Is there some reason I should avoid the Wan Chai district?" She glanced at Lucas, as if to say *What's he on about?*

"It's, uh, just not a particularly savory area," Lucas explained. "Not for tourists or anyone likely to be identified as an outsider. Not to mention that an attractive young woman on her own . . ." He let that hang.

"Now, Lucas, I think we should be honest with Miss Vittorio," said Jimmy mildly. He met her eyes. "The district is run by the Triads. It's a dangerous place. There was an explosion there today. Perhaps you heard about it."

Valentina's frown deepened. "An explosion? No. I haven't seen or heard any news since I got back to the office."

Wen folded his arms across his chest and gave the appearance of being most distressed. "They say an entire restaurant went up in smoke. Three dead, according to the early reports, but they are likely to announce more once they get around to clearing the place out. They're saying it was a gas leak, but this is Hong Kong, and a great many things are not what they seem to be. The Triads practically run that district, and while they purport to keep it safe, the different factions are in a constant state of warfare. And when they make war, there is some-times . . . collateral damage."

"They're only *supposed* to kill each other," Lucas chipped in with a wry smile.

Valentina apparently got the Bugsy Siegel reference and smiled back, although she looked a little queasy.

"We would very much hate for something untoward to happen to you, Miss Vittorio," Jimmy told her. "Hong Kong is a beautiful place, but also a potentially deadly one—especially for those who acciden-tally stray onto the wrong paths."

"In that case, I think I will keep my wanderings close to home. Thanks for the warning."

"We are expecting great things from you," Wen reminded her. "I have personally been following your career with great interest. You have been quite the rising star over the past few years."

She actually hung her head a little at the compliment, her hair falling over one eye as she smiled at Jimmy. "Thank you, Mr. Wen. I will try to live up to your expectations."

She sounded most humble. Lucas wasn't sure if it was art or honesty. Either way, he admired it.

* * *

Wen began walking toward the door of the conference room, inviting Valentina to fall into step with him. Lucas and the two bodyguards followed suit.

"I am pleased you were able to connect with Kim Yun-Fat," Wen told her. "I've known his family for a great many years, you see. We are executive members of the same spa. Green Dynamics Construction is one of the most highly regarded companies in Hong Kong, although

I do understand the current political climate is causing them more than a few fiscal problems. Like most businesses here in Hong Kong, they are bracing themselves against the somewhat inevitable Chinese invasion."

They exited the meeting room and made their way along the hall.

"As in *political* invasion?" Valentina asked. Surely Wen didn't mean China intended to take the island by force?

A barely perceptible shake of Wen's head told her otherwise. "We're all safe until October, but after that . . . who knows?"

"The first of October is the seventy-year anniversary of the Chinese Communist party," Lucas chipped in. "It's a big day for the president, so we can be confident nothing too controversial is gonna happen until after then."

"In the meantime, the *da lu zi* are mobilizing along the Chang Jiang —there's little surprise the entire island is so nervous." Wen paused and turned to look at Valentina. "I am more than confident you will take good care of Mr. Kim and that he will prosper in your capable hands, Miss Vittorio."

I certainly hope so. "Thank you," Valentina said aloud. "As I said, he's looking to secure financing against eight hundred million in shares —at seventy-five percent."

Lucas whistled through his teeth. "Impressive," he said.

"I'll be fixing up a meeting with his PA this afternoon—we're tentatively looking at tomorrow for the signing."

"I think Lucas and I should be included in that meeting—since it's your first in Hong Kong, and Mr. Kim and I are such old friends." Wen nodded toward Vaughn. "It will give us the opportunity to show you how to seal the deal the Hong Kong way."

That raised Valentina's eyebrows. They brought her here ostensibly because she already knew how to seal a deal, and now they were going to reeducate her? What was up with that?

"It's not that we don't think you're capable." Lucas picked up on Valentina's reticence at Wen's intrusion on her territory. "But, it's an excellent excuse to have a big night out around the karaoke bars. The KTV bars here are kinda like the golf courses over in the US—a hell of a lot of business is done between singing bad karaoke and downing expensive shots."

Oh, joy.

"Speak directly with Anita; she will book our regular bar for you," Wen told her. "It's one of the better ones in the Tsim Sha Tsui district, and somewhere quite fitting for such a lucrative business meeting."

"We own the place," Lucas explained. "It's one of a chain of six we acquired five years ago. They're all incredibly profitable. We never have an issue with booking private rooms on short notice, and the hostesses are ridiculously hot."

Valentina couldn't help but flash a smile; Lucas Vaughn exhibited the ability to switch between corporate hard man and giddy school kid at the drop of a hat. "Thank you, Mr. Wen. I'll get everything organized with Anita this afternoon."

"Make sure it happens," Wen addressed Lucas. "You know whom to invite."

"Of course." Lucas nodded at Wen and then tipped Valentina a conspiratorial wink. "It looks like your first week in Hong Kong is going to be quite an eventful one. Beats the hell out of all those stuffy meetings you had back in New York."

Lucas's misconception of how business was done on Wall Street struck Valentina as rather quaint. The fact was, along with the majority of traders there, she'd put in more than her fair share of time around New York's dive bars and seedy strip joints. There had never been any concessions for her being a woman; if anything, she was expected to party harder (or at least seem to be doing so) than her male counterparts. Valentina had managed to swing deals her colleagues had deemed impossible just because she was a woman by paying for strippers and drinking clients under the table—she'd been surprised how many of them actually got off on that.

As for the ubiquitous cocaine and myriad other party drugs—ketamine and molly were the current flavors of the month—Valentina had learned to keep well away. Not that she ever balked at making sure her hard-partying clients were well-supplied, of course, and many times she'd even gone as far as pretending to snort lines for appearances' sake, but Valentina Vittorio always made sure her head was clear and she was in full control of every situation she found herself in.

Wen set to walking again with his bodyguards hovering on either side of him like tall, burly shadows, then turned his head to glance back at her. "Miss Vittorio, I think you should go buy yourself something suitable to wear for tomorrow night. Something expensive but cheap—if you know what I mean? Respectable clients such as Kim don't get a hard-on eye-humping a chick that looks like a presidential candidate." He eyed Valentina's Chanel outfit with disdain, as if she were wearing tattered sackcloth and not a three-thousand-dollar suit, before going on his way.

While she stood staring after him with her mouth half open on a retort that she couldn't utter, Lucas produced an Amex Black Card seemingly out of nowhere. He pressed the card into Valentina's hand with an apologetic look. She shrugged to let him know there really was no need for him to apologize for his boss's crass attitude, and pocketed the card. It wouldn't be the first time she'd been asked to flash a little T and A to persuade a horny, gullible client to sign over his hard-earned shares.

Problem was, instinct, research, and experience told her that Mr. Kim was more likely to be rattled by such a display of hedonism, not encouraged by it. These theatrics were a distraction and a barrier to completing deals with men like Kim Yun-Fat, which meant she was going to have to work harder to close the deal.

CHAPTER TWENTY-ONE

Valentina had known full well she was letting herself into the lion's den the moment she'd hung up the phone call from Mai Lin back in her cozy Manhattan apartment what seemed like a lifetime ago. She'd studied Jimmy Wen for years—in the pages of the *Wall Street Journal*, on the internet, and through sucking up rumors and drunken stories about him from colleagues and acquaintances who claimed to have had direct dealings with the man.

She'd entertained one of these not long after she'd accepted the job offer with Wen's New York office. Dominic Hooper, stinking rich but addicted to sleazy dive bars and strip clubs, had claimed to have recently returned from the "Chink Colonies," as he'd affectionately called Hong Kong. Naturally, he'd been flattered by the attentions of the hot, young female broker and had spilled his guts in his vain attempts to impress her out of her panties. Over badly cooked wings and strippers sporting crusted track marks, Hooper had regaled Valentina with tales of the ruthless, legendary Jimmy Wen, and how he'd fought hard to claw his way to the top of the food chain in Hong Kong's financial district. That the guy had seemingly appeared from out of the ether had only served to add to his mystique. Hooper had shared his speculations about how so many of the businesses that stood in Jimmy Wen's way had wound up being absorbed by the mighty JM Wen Limited or driven into the quiet oblivion of bankruptcy, but Valentina was far more interested in the details of how Wen had supposedly built his empire from scratch.

She and Hooper had parted company suddenly after he'd slithered his hands up her skirt in the parking lot of a seedy strip club. She had bid him goodnight with four broken fingers and a badly bruised ego. But his drunken rambles had given her a more complete picture of Jimmy Wen than the dry, lifeless information she'd sucked from the internet or read in *WSJ* accounts of his prowess.

He'd begun by trading penny stocks—in the *true* meaning of the term, not his own overinflated interpretation. He'd graduated to simple stock manipulation and the age-old pump-and-dump schemes that had become his trademark. Those were of particular interest to Valentina; that was ostensibly how he'd gotten her father. That Wen still traded at those lower levels at all was puzzling, until she factored in that the guy was a narcissistic egomaniac. Here he was, regularly cutting deals for tens or hundreds of millions of dollars, yet he maintained the part of his business that hooked the small investor in the street—the Federico Parisis of the world who just wanted to do a little better for himself and his family, and for whom dabbling on the stock exchanges was just one step up from hitting the crap tables and slots on the Vegas Strip.

Valentina remembered her father as a man who had wanted nothing more than to make a better life for his wife and two daughters than his job at the docks would provide. He'd drifted from one sure-thing moneymaking scheme to another; from being part owner of a hot dog stand to breeding Greyhounds to counterfeit rock band merch and everything in between. He'd been introduced to the seemingly lucrative, heady world of stocks and shares by one of his drinking buddies and, although much of the language and concepts surrounding the money markets may as well have been Greek to him, Federico had seen one hell of an opportunity. Since they would be dealing only with shares in legitimate companies, all bought and sold by legitimate brokers, what could possibly go wrong?

What had gone wrong, of course, was the seemingly legitimate broker had been the man who would much later resurface in Hong Kong as Jimmy Wen.

The old drinking buddy who'd introduced Federico to Wen had enticed him with talk of earning more money than he'd ever dreamed of, and of early retirement, a new car, a nice house in the 'burbs, fancy colleges for Valentina and Sylvia, and even that small fishing boat he'd always wanted.

It had taken less than six months for the shares Federico had been persuaded to sink his life savings and remortgage into to drop so low that trading was suspended. He didn't even get back a few cents on the dollar; the broker had vanished into thin air, and there was no government safety net or underwriting by a reputable bank. There was no comfort in knowing he was not the only one who'd lost money to the swindlers. It would take years before the repercussions would fade.

Federico Parisi, unable to face those repercussions, had jumped from the Staten Island Ferry the day after he received the news all of his money was gone. No one had noticed until the ferry reached Manhattan that his car was the only one left on the boat. The drinking buddy who'd introduced him to Wen and the dubious get-rich-quick scheme was one of the pallbearers, and after the funeral, the remaining Parisi family never set eyes on the man again.

Valentina's mother suffered her first breakdown of many shortly after they'd put her husband in the ground. As much as she tried to hold things together, once the meager insurance money ran out, the family wound up in a cramped two-room apartment courtesy of the Staten Island Housing Authority. Valentina had only been able to look on helplessly as her mother's mental health deteriorated rapidly and Sylvia succumbed to the rampant drug culture that held the projects in its deathly grip. Her family had been totally destroyed by her father's desperation to give them a better life, and by those who had seen fit to exploit something he'd done out of misguided love.

It was the thought of her father, and the thousands of honest, hard-working family men just like him that haunted Valentina the most. If she were to follow through with her plan of bringing down Jimmy

Wen, then a lot of people like Federico Parisi would be hurt alongside the unscrupulous businessmen and gangsters who deserved to go down with the sinking ship.

Would it be worth it to have that on her conscience, especially knowing how dangerous it could be to cross Wen? She doubted there was a chance in hell that she could save JM Wen's innocent victims. She thought of Kim Yun-Fat, whom she'd personally brought into Wen's financial abattoir. Realistically, there might not be a damn thing she could do if Wen pulled his stock loan scam on his "old friend." Maybe for the sake of that friendship, he wouldn't.

There is a special hell for you, Jimmy Wen.

This wasn't New York. Valentina had learned that in ways both hard and painful and in a blisteringly short period of time. Hong Kong wasn't Manhattan with paper lanterns, and as much as she'd prepared herself through meticulous research, nothing could have prepared her for . . . any of this. She'd been confident she possessed the skills to find *something* on the man, but was beginning to second-guess her own diligence. The SFC agent—David—had known details about her life the people she called friends didn't even know, which meant the agency had been as thorough in their research as she had been in hers. He also knew something about her motives, and she wondered what the hell he'd intended to do with that information?

It may have been Hong Kong's innate culture of mistrust rubbing off on her, but Valentina couldn't quite shake the sensation of being watched; each time she glanced into her purse, she half expected to find an unfamiliar cell phone lurking within, and she harbored a gut feeling the SFC wouldn't simply fade away and leave her be because of one bombed-out restaurant and a dead agent.

Back at her desk, Valentina pecked away at her computer keyboard; there were particular files she really wanted to dig into, but she stuck to reading up on JM Wen Limited's history and background-checking the clients she'd been allocated as hot leads—all the usual stuff the company would expect a new recruit with a bunch of such leads to be looking at. She was guarded enough to presume they'd be monitoring computer activity, since it was common practice among all the financial companies she had experienced. As distasteful as it was, it was seen as a necessity to ward off client theft, head hunting, and industrial espionage. Valentina figured someone like Jimmy Wen would make knowing every move his people made a priority—especially so with the ever-present, looming specter of the mainland and his own dealings with the Triads.

Valentina would wait; there were far too many people around, even though it was now after five thirty p.m. Warning against competition notwithstanding, her fellow rainmakers seemed to be vying for the title of Last to Leave the Office. As she churned over her plans and the myriad risks—some of which she'd played out on a loop in her head and others she'd only just realized lurked in the fabric of Hong Kong— she knew there was no turning back. This was something she *had* to do; it was a commitment she'd made that, come what may, she was going to see through to the very end.

Oliver, Sofia, and the others left shortly after six. They informed Valentina they'd be hitting a few bars before going back to the hotel for dinner, and they invited her along. She made her excuses that she had tomorrow's Green Dynamics Construction meeting to prepare for, even though Anita Kwok had already organized everything with the KTV club, booked the chauffeur-driven limousines, and made all the necessary arrangements with Mr. Kim's PA. Valentina politely promised she would join them later for dinner, even though she didn't particularly relish the idea—she needed some time alone to gather her thoughts . . . and armor-plate them.

Yes, she knew that the social aspects of the job were just as important as reeling in the clients' much-coveted money and that being seen as part of the team was vital. She'd watched enough promising careers go down the drain over a purported lack of team spirit to know she had no other choice than to play Jimmy Wen's game—for now.

For tonight at least, Valentina did have the cast-iron excuse of having some clothes shopping to do. After all, Mr. Wen himself had insisted she look the part for the Kim meeting—and no one in their right mind was going to argue with that.

The sudden quiet in the room brought her suddenly out of her head.

She realized she was clutching her hands in her lap and that they were shaking.

CHAPTER TWENTY-TWO

It was a little after six thirty when Valentina finally left JM Wen's offices. It was still hot and humid outside, but thankfully the street was finally free of protesters. A pressing crowd at this point in a horrific day would have been one more straw than this camel's back could bear.

She hailed a cab on Finance Street and asked to be taken to the famous SOGO department store in Causeway Bay. Anita Kwok had advised her that this would be a more than suitable place to take the shopping trip mandated by Wen. As Valentina was an employee of JM Wen Limited, and hence an ambassador, there were certain standards she was expected to adhere to. Designer labels were *de rigueur* because appearances were everything in Hong Kong business. One more jarring difference between HK and NYC, where high-earners and high rollers dressed down and attitude was the whole Megillah.

The sprawling SOGO store dominated Jaffe Road in Causeway Bay and was world-renowned as much for its staggering range of exclusive designer labels as its fat price tags. Still, with an unlimited amount of Jimmy Wen's money in her wallet, Valentina figured she may as well make an effort to enjoy herself.

The cab pulled up outside the store, and she clambered out onto the hot, bustling street. She made sure to tip the driver well, and turned to gaze up at the huge blue logo above the immaculate stone eaves that sheltered the main entrance. It reminded Valentina of an oversized hourglass. *Tempis fugit.*

Inside, the place felt much like any other big department store. Had it not been for the abundance of Chinese characters, accompanied by their English translation, Valentina could have imagined herself in Bloomingdales. Gripping the strap of her securely zipped purse, Valentina battled her way through the crowded sales floors as she searched for something suitable for the Kim meeting. Or, at least, what Jimmy Wen thought suitable. She wondered how Wen could claim to be "old friends" with Kim and not know that "expensive but cheap" would prove as uncomfortable for him as it was for her.

While Valentina had a fairly good idea what the boss had in mind, finding the right dress proved more difficult than she'd imagined. Absolutely everything looked sumptuous to Valentina, and knowing money was no object, she was beginning to feel like a little kid in a candy store who'd been given *carte blanche*. Swallowing her frustration, Valentina rode the escalator up to the second floor. There, the likes of Gucci, Louis Vuitton, Chanel, Dior, Hermès, and Prada vied for shoppers' attention alongside local designer brands such as Phvlo, Aayna, Sketcharound, and Kay Li. Confident that at least one of the designer boutiques would have the perfect outfit for her, Valentina went from one evening wear boutique to another.

After an hour or so of fruitless browsing, Valentina was delighted and relieved when she stumbled across the store's Dolce & Gabbana boutique. She had a couple of D&G outfits in her closet back home, which she wore only for the most special occasions; the designer brand had a reputation for being classy, daring, and ridiculously expensive.

Perfect.

Valentina went into hunter-gatherer mode and picked out a handful of likely suspects—some red, some black, one blue—all short, clingy, and revealing. More than confident she had the legs and figure to carry any one of them off, she made her way over to the fitting rooms. The cute Chinese girl behind the counter handed Valentina a hanging door tag and ushered her behind the counter and into the luxurious fitting area. There, the girl pointed out one of the vacant cubicles. Behind the mahogany door, Valentina was pleased to see a generous room with a small red velvet divan and a matching chair. A table had been placed between them as if the occupants might request tea while trying on clothing. Perhaps some did.

Before she left, the sales associate told Valentina to please ask if she needed any of the dresses in a different size or color.

"I will. Thank you." With a dismissive smile, Valentina eased the door to the spacious cubicle closed, hung up the dresses, kicked off her shoes, and removed her suit.

The first dress was a definite no. It was black with short sleeves, a low-scooped neckline, and a hem that stopped midthigh. Too demure in the skirt, not enough in the neckline. She wanted to show off leg and less cleavage.

The blue dress was equally unsuitable. It had a slash that ran along the thigh all the way up to her hip and large cut-out panels on the sides and midriff, which were covered over with fine blue mesh. She felt like a Kardashian in the thing—it screamed cheap without uttering a peep about affluence. Though she'd spoken to Kim Yun-Fat by phone a number of times, this would still be his first impression of her. The phrase *cheap tart* leapt to mind.

Losing patience, Valentina slipped on the first of the two red dresses she'd picked out. It felt good. The thin, slinky material clung to her body like a second skin and accentuated her every curve. The neckline sat high to circle her throat, and the back was scooped so low it skimmed the upper curve of her ass. The hem of the dress rode high on Valentina's thighs and showcased her toned legs to perfection, which pleased her. Checking out her ass in the cubicle's full-length mirror, she made a mental note to purchase a suitably discreet, seamless thong in order to avoid the all-too-obvious panty line the thin, clingy material was creating. There was absolutely nowhere to hide straps, so she would definitely have to ditch her bra if she were to wear that red dress.

Valentina thought she looked hot as hell and had every confidence

Jimmy Wen would approve. And, with the HK$25,000 price tag, the dress would definitely fit all expectations expense-wise. While the dress didn't show off any cleavage, it did a magnificent job of emphasizing the curve of her breasts. As far as Valentina was concerned, too much cleavage screamed *bimbo*; she was hopeful her long, bare legs would give out a strong message of power and control, not sexual availability. As for the vast expanse of bare back the dress exposed, that should appease Jimmy Wen while not distracting the prospective client.

As long as I keep him in front of me.

She was chuckling over the comic image of her trying to face Mr. Kim at all costs, when someone knocked on the door of the cubicle.

"I'm okay, thank you," Valentina huffed. "I'm still trying things on in here. I promise I'll shout if I need anything." She hated to be hurried, especially when making important decisions, and especially by some young shop girl who was overkeen to make her commission and go home.

"Miss Vittorio?" A voice, not quite a whisper, came from the other side of the door.

Valentina froze. She hadn't given the shop girl her name.

"Valentina Vittorio?" The voice, a little louder this time, was female, older, and had a decidedly British accent.

A more insistent knock.

"Hello?" Valentina ventured; there was no point staying silent and hoping whoever it was would go away. Instinctively, she searched the cubicle for a quick way out. She even checked the ceiling for hanging tiles or a convenient air vent, but she was trapped. She eyed the Chanel suit hanging from a hook on the back of the door; wearing nothing but the skimpy red dress and panties, she felt impossibly vulnerable.

"May I come in, Miss Vittorio?" The voice was polite but persistent.

"Um, no." Valentina wondered if she had time to slip out of the dress and change back into her suit.

Time before what? Surely whoever was out there wasn't about to kick the door in?

"We need to talk, Miss Vittorio. I'm an associate of David's."

Hearing the name hit Valentina like a gut punch. Fighting a sudden wave of vertigo, she sat down heavily on the little red velvet chaise. What the hell was she supposed to do? Had Wen seen something in her eyes when he'd quizzed her about the lunchtime foray away from Hong Kong's well-beaten tourist path? Had she given herself away, despite playing it cool and giving her best poker face? Had Wen had her followed? He'd know where she was, of course, because his PA had made the strong suggestion Valentina shop there.

"His real name was Chung-Sun Fan," the voice persevered. "He had a wife and three children. You were the last person to see him alive."

The tired technique of using her name to build familiarity grated on Valentina; it was the same one David had used in the phone call she'd taken in the ladies' restroom that morning.

"Who are you?" Valentina's voice shook slightly as a cold wave of panic swept through her.

Silence.

A movement at the bottom of the cubicle door caught Valentina's attention; suddenly she was assessing the gap beneath it to see if it was wide enough to accommodate an explosive device.

"There's nothing to be afraid of, Miss Vittorio," the voice reassured. "It's nothing dangerous—just my ID."

The thing sliding under the door was just that—a photo ID. Curious now, she picked the thing up off the floor and saw it belonged to one Katherine Bennett, an agent for Interpol. The small, plastic card looked like a driver's license; it had a picture of a handsome woman in the top left corner; she was most likely early forties and had thin lips, a stubborn chin, straight black hair, and hazel eyes that blazed with intelligence.

"Could you open the door now, please?" Bennett's voice was calm and convincing; she obviously had no intention of going away. "We can't talk properly like this, and we *do* need to talk. If you need me to give you a moment to make yourself decent, that's perfectly fine."

Valentina cracked open the cubicle door and peered out. She was relieved to see that the woman standing outside in the waiting area was a dead ringer for the picture on the ID. So, unless it was a fake, Katherine Bennett was exactly who the card claimed her to be.

Valentina swung the door open, noting that the cute shop girl was busily showing another shopper to a cubicle on the other side of the waiting area.

"I told her I was your mother and I was helping you pick out something suitable for your honeymoon," Bennett explained to Valentina as she stepped into the spacious cubicle. She took an admiring look around. "My, I'd heard these places were roomy, but this really is something else. Believe me, Miss Vittorio, you don't get to buy designer frocks like these on an Interpol agent's salary." She cracked a wry smile and glanced at the dresses that hung on the back of the door.

Valentina studied Bennett. The agent could probably still carry off any one of the D&G dresses; she certainly had the body for it, if not the pay, although she didn't quite give off the air of *expensive but cheap*.

Valentina handed the woman her card back, pushed the cubicle door closed, and locked it behind them. "I take it you've been following me, Miss Bennett?" She sat down on one end of the chaise lounge again and eyed the older woman with suspicion.

Bennett sat herself down in the midcentury modern chair. Her ID disappeared into an inside pocket of the stylish jacket she wore over a maroon T-shirt and fashionably faded jeans—as a throwback to Hong Kong's colonial days, the woman fitted in perfectly. Her eyebrows went up and humor glinted in her eyes.

"Call me Kate, please. And of course I've been following you, Miss Vittorio. Surely you don't think I'd just happened upon you purely by chance? I've been following you since you left Finance Street—and halfway around the department store—you certainly take your sweet time making up your mind."

Valentina considered asking the agent to use her first name, but decided against it; she preferred to keep things formal, at least for now. Besides which, she figured the woman would no doubt want to call her Val.

"Too many choices," Valentina said dryly. "I'm sorry if I've taken up too much of your time."

"It comes with the territory. Don't you want to know *why* I've been following you?"

"I figured you'd tell me when you were ready. I guess you didn't follow me halfway across Hong Kong to tell me about David."

"Fan," Bennett corrected. "He was a good man, Miss Vittorio, and one who will be missed."

"How did you know him? You guys were working together?" Valentina pressed. She wanted to find out what Interpol required from her and then get the hell out of the fitting room and department store; drinks with her new colleagues were sounding better by the minute.

Bennett nodded. "He and I were working the same case. We have . . . *had* been for a couple of years now."

"That same case being Jimmy Wen?" Valentina came to the obvious conclusion.

Bennett nodded, and a flicker of sadness flared in her eyes and was gone.

"Which is why you've chased me down in here?"

"You were the last person to see Fan alive, Miss Vittorio," Bennett repeated. "He'd identified you as a possible informant; he was impressed by your skill set."

So far, Bennett hadn't told her anything she didn't already know; the SFC agent had made it quite clear he was expecting to recruit her. "We barely had time to talk; I have no idea why he targeted me."

Bennett eased back in the chair. "Fan had arranged for all of the information he'd gathered on Jimmy Wen and JM Wen International to be sent to me should anything happen to him. I'd received those files before you got back to your office after the explosion." She paused there for a moment, as if struggling to collect her thoughts. She swallowed.

Honest bereavement or cat-and-mouse? "And?"

"And there's an impressively detailed dossier on you, Miss Vittorio. It would seem that, between the SFC here and the SEC in the

States, you've been under scrutiny since before you joined JM Wen in New York."

That long? That was worth a moment of sheer terror. Her all-too-brief conversation with the SFC agent had revealed that he had a lot of information on her, but how much? What were the possible implications for her personal agenda?

"Like I said, we didn't get too much time to talk," she told Bennett. "We were interrupted by a phone call, and then . . ."

"You spoke long enough for Fan to tell you that he knew what you think you know about Wen's involvement in your father's death, your intentions toward Wen in Hong Kong, and how he thought you could help him. He was never one for beating about the bush. Although, ironically, it wasn't Fan's directness that got him killed."

"So the bomb *was* meant for him?" Valentina's suspicions were confirmed.

Bennett raised her eyebrows. "Of course. Did you think it was meant for you?"

"I thought maybe it was a Triad turf war," Valentina said. "Why would I ever think it was for me?"

"Because you have already made inroads into Wen's computer files?"

"You couldn't possibly know that." The woman had to be fishing.

"I don't," the agent replied. "But I know you are a capable hacker, Miss Vittorio. So, I would be more surprised if you had not. There's also the fact that you snuck out of the office to meet with an SFC agent —that would certainly have got me thinking." She smiled.

"Do you know who killed him?"

The sadness returned to Bennett's eyes. "I'm afraid my associate had been playing a very dangerous game for the past year or so. Specifically, playing both sides against each other for his own gain. That was his undoing."

"Both sides?"

"Fan was playing the regulators *and* Wen. All the while he was keeping himself busy, he was lining his own pockets. He was digging up a ton of incriminating information on Wen but turning over just enough to his bosses at the SFC to make himself look virtuous."

Valentina was stunned. "You knew he was corrupt?"

"Eventually," Bennett admitted. "Everything he was giving up to the SFC was all relatively low level, but I suspected he had more. At least, he hinted that he had more, but he was keeping all of that to himself. He was more than happy to bank his SFC paycheck and shake down the bad guys, but he was not prepared to kill the golden goose until it became necessary. I'm afraid it was only a matter of time before he came unstuck—I ought to have seen it coming."

"You *knew* he was double dealing and you did nothing? I get the sense that he was more than just a business associate."

"No romance, if that's what you're hinting at. He was a friend. A *dear* friend. You build that sort of trust bond in our business, which is why it's . . . difficult when trust is violated. As far as his . . . side business goes, I *guessed*. I confronted him some weeks ago, but he denied it all, of course. And, before I could do anything about it . . ."

"Yeah, I was there."

"He had someone on the inside at Wen's—that much I knew for certain," Bennett said. "He never confirmed a name, but I understand that one of your colleagues went AWOL this morning. I never had direct contact with any of Fan's sources, and I had the terrible thought that he might have sold her out to cover his own tracks. Before all this, I'd never have suspected him of something like that, but money changes people, Miss Vittorio."

Valentina cleared her throat. "Chrissy Huang."

"Yes. Were you aware she was . . . terminated this morning?"

"Not really. I knew she had a meeting with one of the functionaries. I didn't think much of it. But I didn't see her again. You're saying she was fired?"

It seemed improbable to her that Chrissy would have gotten herself mixed up in any kind of subterfuge, let alone become a mole for the SFC. If she had, wouldn't she have said something to Valentina? She had had plenty of opportunities Friday night.

"I'm saying," said the agent, "that I suspect Miss Huang is dead."

Valentina could only stare at her with her mouth half open and her eyes watering. By God, if Wen had made her friend disappear, no matter what his reasons, Valentina was determined the son of a bitch would suffer all the more. She fought the surge of grief and anger under control, took a deep breath, and asked, "You think *Wen* had your friend murdered?"

Bennett nodded. "That's a distinct possibility. Then again, given some of Mr. Wen's questionable associations, it could just as easily have been one of the Triad gangs who wanted him silenced—or maybe it was the Triads working under Wen's instruction. You'll learn soon enough how business is done here in Hong Kong, Miss Vittorio, and hopefully not the hard way."

Valentina fixed Bennett with an icy stare. "Too late, *Kate*," she snarled. "I've already learned. So, what the hell do you figure I can do about any of it?"

"To the point, Miss Vittorio—I like that," Bennett said approvingly. "I know you have worked hard for a long time to get yourself into a position where you can ruin Jimmy Wen. You are a smart, accomplished hacker who is entirely capable of covering your tracks, and you are more than capable of taking care of yourself. Add to that your undoubted skills at manipulating people, and I'd say you were a prime candidate for picking up where Fan's contact left off."

"You're making one hell of an assumption," Valentina objected. "Why would I want to be a mole for anyone when, as you say, I'm more than capable of taking care of business alone?"

Bennett spoke slowly, deliberately; the accent Valentina thought endearing at first was beginning to grate. "Your motive of justice for your father is admirable, Miss Vittorio, but if you try to take down Jimmy Wen by yourself, you *will* fail. And I don't intend to watch someone else die because of Mr. Wen."

The comment took Valentina aback. Her mind reeled and she felt her mouth go dry. "You were *there*?"

"I was keeping surveillance from across the street. I knew Fan had arranged a meeting with his contact, and I'd planned to pick her up after their meeting was over—I had a few questions of my own for

Miss Huang, as you can no doubt imagine." Bennett attempted a friendly smile; it came across to Valentina as sinister.

"You didn't know he was meeting with *me*?"

"You were a last-minute change of plan. I think Fan panicked when Huang was uncovered and he didn't have time to let me know. Or didn't want to." She looked up and met Valentina's gaze, her eyes empty. "I saw a young man go into the restaurant with a backpack and leave without it. I knew what was about to go down; I've done this job in Hong Kong long enough to have seen more than my fair share of improvised explosive devices—"

"*You* made the phone call?" Valentina's heart pounded hard in her chest as the words left her lips; it was obvious what the reply was going to be. Tugging gently at the hem of her little red dress, she felt suddenly naked and self-conscious.

"I doubted the bomb was on a timer, Miss Vittorio," Bennett explained. "Which meant the assassins were watching the restaurant. I had time to make only the one phone call—and a tough decision."

"You could've called David's cell phone, though. Told him to get out."

"He wouldn't have picked up. Not during a meet-up. I chose to get you where I was hopeful the impact of the blast would be less. Fan . . . Fan knew what he was in the midst of. You didn't."

An uneasy silence crept between them as Valentina processed the stark realization that the Interpol agent's snap decision could have gone either way; the mysterious phone call that had interrupted her meeting with the SFC agent could just as easily have gone to the guy she knew as David—and she wouldn't be sitting here in a Dolce & Gabbana fitting room in a tiny twenty-thousand-dollar dress.

"When it came down to it," Bennett said, her voice brisk and sure once again, "I figured I would be better off having someone on the inside at JM Wen, and since Miss Huang was nowhere to be found and Fan had seen enough potential in you to reach out, I figured that someone may as well be you."

Valentina's stomach rolled over as she read Bennett's now emotionless face. The woman had stood by and watched her associate die—hell, she'd even played God and decided who was to be sacrificed.

"And the others in the restaurant? The innocent people who had nothing to do with any of this?" The rude waitress popped into Valentina's mind; surly or not, she hadn't deserved to be blown to pieces like that.

Bennett frowned and exhaled loudly. "Collateral damage, they call it. Welcome to Hong Kong, Miss Vittorio; I think we will work well together."

Valentina's eyes felt as if they'd been replaced with live embers. "You allowed people to die; that's hardly a glowing reference if you're looking to recruit me."

"You're here, Miss Vittorio. And Fan is not. We will get to Jimmy Wen in the end, one way or another. All I'm suggesting is that you and I work toward our common goal together. I have access to resources and information that you don't, and I will do everything within my power to shield you from interference from either Wen or the regulators. The SFC is going to be very publicly sticking its nose into Wen's business before too long, and it would be a shame to have you caught up in any of that before you achieve retribution for your father."

Valentina leaned back on the cubicle wall; it felt wonderfully cool against the bare skin of her back. "Justice," she said quietly. "Justice is what I want for my father. I want Jimmy Wen to pay a fair price for what he did." Then, she took a deep breath and asked the question: "What do you want me to do?"

The Interpol agent leaned toward her, elbows on her knees. "I would like you to pick up where Fan and Chrissy Huang left off. I'll be your direct point of contact. I think that's the best way forward, since it's going to take the SFC some time to regroup, and I don't want to lose the momentum."

Valentina sat forward on the small divan, bringing her face close to the other woman's. "I know you're used to this sort of—of life, but I'm a damn stock broker with some computer chops and martial arts training. The danger—"

"You willingly put yourself in the line of fire the second you stepped off that plane on Friday morning, Miss Vittorio." Bennett's tone was stern, almost schoolmarmish, and it set Valentina's nerves on edge. "The way I see it, if you choose to work with Interpol—with *me*—your chances of getting back on that plane at the end of all this will be much higher than if you insist on going it alone. It leaves aside the distinct possibility of you getting caught up in Wen's downfall—collateral damage works both ways in this business."

"Meaning?" Valentina's hackles went up. Was this a legitimate warning or had Bennett stepped beyond manipulation into straight-up blackmail?

"Meaning, if you're still around when the SFC and Interpol finally catch up with Jimmy Wen, then you and your colleagues will be assumed to be complicit in his illicit business practices—which now seem to run to murder. And let's not forget Wen's Triad clients. If they begin to feel exposed . . ." A tight smile played at the corners of Bennett's mouth.

Valentina's mind returned to the wet crimson splash that decorated the charred wall of a ruined restaurant. Perhaps Kate Bennett was the best guarantee she had of not ending her days in Hong Kong the same way as the corrupt SFC agent.

"You want me to feed you inside information on Wen."

"As much as you can gather," Bennett replied. "I understand Fan's source had picked up on something potentially catastrophic that's looming on Wen's immediate horizon—something big enough to make him panic, and Jimmy Wen *never* panics."

Valentina tugged at the hem of the little red dress again as Bennett hit upon the thread of truth; right now Jimmy Wen was a driven man. "Do you have any details?"

"None."

"So, why not just allow Wen to implode on his own and let his bad gangster clients deal with him?"

Valentina was all too aware Bennett was skillfully drawing her—bit by bit—into her investigation. She told herself she was only allowing it to happen, as it suited her purpose. Having said that, she was still determined she wasn't going to lose sight of her own agenda.

Bennett sat upright again, looking poised and authoritative. "Because it's imperative we bring Wen down in a controlled manner. That way we get to pick off as many of his associates and contacts as possible—including his dirty bank and the gangsters—and we can begin to make reparations for the inevitable innocent victims of the fallout."

"Collateral damage?"

"Precisely."

"Very altruistic of you."

Bennett ignored the dig. "What I need you to do is gather as much information as you can about Wen's market manipulation, illegal trading, share collateral lending, and anything else you feel might be appropriate to the investigation."

"The dirty bank?"

"God, yes, the dirty bank. You will feed it all through me, and I'll make things happen."

"So, you're telling me you're pretty much going to be my handler?" Valentina cocked an eyebrow at the agent; this wasn't quite the synergy she'd had in mind.

"I prefer to think of us as *associates*, Miss Vittorio."

"And what do I get out of our . . . *association*?" Valentina was determined to get at least a few of the balls in her own court.

"You get the acceleration of Mr. Wen's demise," Bennett told her, "and I can give you that certain level of protection you wouldn't have if you insist upon working alone."

"Like you did for David?"

Bennett recoiled as if Valentina had slapped her hard in the face. "David had gone rogue, Miss Vittorio. He made a decision to step outside his protection."

And he paid for it. "I guess I don't have too many options right now, do I? But how do I know *you're* not the one playing both sides here?"

"You don't." At least Bennett wasn't attempting to bullshit her. "But I'm all you've got at the moment, Miss Vittorio. And don't forget, I am the one who—"

"Saved my life at the restaurant this afternoon. Yes, I got that. Am I supposed to feel eternally grateful for it?"

A spark of humor lit up the other woman's hazel eyes. "Eternally? Good Lord, woman, it's only been"—she checked her watch—"four and a half hours."

Valentina exhaled loudly. "Okay. So what do we do now?"

Bennett fished around in the front pocket of her small purse, and plucked out a handful of tampons in pretty floral biodegradable wraps. She laid them all out on the little table between herself and Valentina, then produced a cell phone from an inside pocket of her jacket.

Puzzled, Valentina picked up one of the tampons and eyed it with suspicion.

Bennett plucked the thing out of Valentina's hand, tore away the paper, and pulled the tampon out of its cardboard applicator. She tapped the applicator on her palm and a SIM card slipped out.

"Each one contains one of these. The cardboard tubes are lined with a special carbon-fiber foil to conceal their contents from X-ray machines and metal detectors—both unlikely scenarios, but I think it's always best to be prepared for any eventuality." Bennett held up the tiny green SIM. "Use each one in this burner phone once—and *only* once—that's most important, Miss Vittorio."

Valentina nodded. "Very James Bond."

"Emma Peel, actually," quipped Bennett. "After each use, simply remove the SIM from the phone and destroy it. If you can't dispose of the SIM immediately, swallow the damn thing if you have to—for God's sake make sure you destroy it before you flush it in any of Wen's office lavatories." Bennett slipped the SIM into the appropriate slot, then snapped the battery back into place and handed the phone over to Valentina.

Pointing to the remaining half-dozen tampons, she said, "Keep these with you at all times. We hid the SIMs in sanitary products because Wen's security guards do love their spot-checks—and even the meatheads on security detail aren't going to look too closely at these."

Valentina set the phone down next to the tampons and stood up. She needed to put at least a little psychological distance between herself and Bennett. She needed time to think; things were moving too fast. She was feeling distinctly out of control, something she loathed and avoided at all costs.

Bennett remained seated and looked up at Valentina. "I'll contact *you*, not the other way around, unless there's an emergency or you happen across some particularly time-sensitive information. My number is the only one programmed into the phone; *please* try to use it sparingly. I'll arrange when and where we meet up."

Bennett stood up and gave the little red dress an admiring—and wistful—once-over. "Between you and me, Miss Vittorio, I think you should go with that one—it really suits you. I've been working in Hong Kong among men like Jimmy Wen, Lucas Vaughn, and their ilk for a hell of a lot of years now, and I think I know what catches their interest," Bennett said as she slid open the lock and opened the cubicle door.

"Thank you," Valentina replied.

"Welcome. Oh, and if I were you, I'd treat myself to a nice Hermès bag while you're out spending Wen's money—your company Amex card has no spending limit and even offers a personal shopping service in some of the higher-end stores. Make the most of it all while you can. How the other half live, eh?"

The Interpol agent gave Valentina a friendly smile, stepped out of the cubicle, and was gone.

CHAPTER TWENTY-THREE

The sun was barely up over the horizon, and already Sergeant Andy Chen was feeling stressed out. He checked his watch for the thousandth time that morning—it was a touch after six—and ran a hand through his close-cropped hair. The body had been called in well over an hour ago by some fitness freak who'd been out jogging on the beach. The cop could never figure out what the hell possessed people to go running at such an ungodly hour, no matter how beautiful the scenery.

The ever-efficient police constables had already put up yellow crime scene tape around the corpse by the time Chen had arrived. Now they stood around on the sand, smoking and looking bored; this wasn't the first time a body had washed up on that particular beach, and Chen knew it wouldn't be the last.

He glanced around. Other than a sparse collection of inquisitive people held back by a lone constable a hundred yards or so along the sand, the beach was completely empty. In the distance, a fine, ghostly mist rose up from the surrounding mountains to envelop the tower blocks below them, and a solitary crane towered above a construction site where yet more exclusive sea view condos were being built. It was all an unexceptional Hong Kong Tuesday morning with life going on as usual—except for Huang Xinyi, of course, who lay facedown on the beach.

As protocol dictated, the police constables had left it to Sergeant Chen to fish out the girl's ID—she'd carried a small wallet in the inside pocket of her Prada jacket. The wallet's contents were nothing out of the ordinary, but nonetheless gave the cop enough details to at least know who she was. A drivers' license showing a beautiful round face with prominent cheekbones and bright, smiling eyes was accompanied by three twenty-dollar bills, a credit card, and a couple of sodden business cards that gave the dead girl's Westernized name as Christina Huang.

"Looks to me like she got hit by a boat and drowned—most likely drunk or high on something." Station Sergeant Donnie Shih stood next to Chen, contemplating the body. "And I guess at this stage we can't rule out that it was deliberate on her part—we've seen a considerable rise in suicides in the past year or so."

Chen was all too aware of that fact, and hardly needed reminding since he seemed to be the station sergeant's go-to guy for white-collar suicide. Sadly, it was becoming inevitable that the more China exerted its grip on Hong Kong, and the tighter things became within the financial district in particular, more executives would elect to choose death over unemployment and the terrible dishonor of financial ruin.

The increasingly angry protesters congregating in the streets, the airport, the train stations, and the shopping malls with their placards and anti-China chants certainly hadn't made things any easier—Chen had also put in more than enough of his time dealing with them. The beat cops had taken to referring to the protesters as *cockroaches*, such was their disdain for the disruption and increasing level of violence they were bringing to the island. The whole thing was turning into one big mess, and there were some days when Chen could empathize with those who decided to leave Hong Kong under their own terms from the top of an office building, under the wheels of a tram, or over the side of a boat.

Silently, he studied the body that lay at his feet on the sea-soaked sand. Her long hair was fanned out around her head like a dark, macabre halo, and Chen thought she resembled a mermaid. He'd helped drag bodies out of the sea that had been hit by boats, and they were usually a gruesome, ripped-up mess with limbs and chunks of sea-bleached flesh missing. Yet, Chrissy Huang's expensive business suit was barely damaged and her body intact, which made being hit by a boat highly unlikely. In fact, Chen could see no outward signs of trauma at first glance, although her head seemed to be canted at an odd angle. Possibly a broken neck.

Sergeant Chen knew well enough to keep that particular observation to himself. He was, after all, looking at the same dead body as Shih, and the station sergeant hadn't offered any other comments. They had both seen this before. Chen was willing to bet a month's salary that once the coroner opened her up, he'd find the girl's lungs empty of water, which would mean she'd been deceased before she was dumped into the sea.

Still, he'd seen the company name on Chrissy Huang's business cards, and if the station sergeant said she'd been hit by a boat, then she had been hit by a boat.

* * *

At the same time Sergeant Chen was staring down at Chrissy Huang's lifeless, sodden body, Valentina was making her way into 2IFC. She'd received a call from Lucas the evening before as she'd made her way back from SOGO and her unplanned meeting with Kate Bennett, and he'd requested she get into the office early to make herself available for a client breakfast meeting at seven. He hadn't mentioned the name of the client.

Seizing the opportunity, Valentina had set her alarm for five and was standing in line with the other Finance Center early birds at six a.m. sharp. The other closers would be in early as well—each had received a call from their respective mentors to summon them to the same meeting. She was almost certain none would be here this early. That meant she had a little under an hour, uninterrupted, to get done what she needed to get done and carefully lay more groundwork for further digging around in Jimmy Wen's business.

While Oliver, Lam, and the others had complained about the interruption to their planned evening of a celebratory first-night dinner and a ramble through Hong Kong's myriad bars—all courtesy of JM Wen and their generous expense accounts—Valentina had been glad she'd abstained. She'd needed the time to process the stunning events of her day and, as alluring as the thought of getting plastered was, she knew that going out with her work cohort would have been a dodge. She needed to think, to plan, not switch her brain off.

So, thanks to the Tuesday morning meeting, the prearranged night of fun and debauchery had been somewhat subdued for all; cynically, Valentina thought maybe it had been planned that way all along—Wen would want his tiger team sharp and on the ball, not hungover and half-assed.

A security guard waved Valentina forward, and she was pleased to see it wasn't the same fat, creepy guy she'd encountered the day before. This one was short, slim, and actually smiling. He wore his uniform well and looked incredibly smart. However, lurking a step or two over his shoulder was a taller, thickset man—the name tag on his dark jacket gave him away as one of JM Wen's security detail.

"Good morning, miss," the shorter guy greeted Valentina with a broad, friendly smile. "If you would please open your bag."

Valentina placed it gently onto the table in front of the guard and unzipped it. "Please be careful, this is a Hermès," she told him. Yes, she'd taken the Interpol agent's advice and treated herself to a designer purse that had cost about the same as a small apartment in the Bronx.

"Yes, ma'am." The security guard pulled open the bag and peered inside. The taller guard appeared over his shoulder and followed suit. Valentina watched as slowly, deliberately, the guard rummaged through the bag's contents. He picked out her cell phone and gave it a cursory glance. She had the burner phone Bennett had given her in the fitting room in the pocket of her suit coat; while having two phones was not uncommon in the business world, she didn't want to have both in the purse—especially with the burner being a cheaper model; that may well have aroused some unwanted suspicion if it got back to the wrong ears.

The guard placed Valentina's cell phone back into the bag and, upon shuffling around the few things she'd transferred over from her Gucci purse, he came upon the tampons, which she'd ensconced in a clear plastic makeup pouch.

Valentina controlled her breathing to remain calm. They were just feminine hygiene products after all, and even if the guard decided to slide them beneath the X-ray or pass his metal-detecting wand over them, the SIM cards they contained should remain concealed—providing Bennett had been telling her the truth. As much as she tried to suppress it, a niggling grain of doubt presented itself at the back of Valentina's mind that maybe, just maybe, she was being set up.

The guard looked up at her as she concentrated on maintaining her poker face; a guilty conscience could be all too easy to give away.

"Which company?" The burly guard loomed over his counterpart's shoulder like some sinister shadow.

Valentina looked the guard straight in the face. "JM Wen Asset Management."

"I haven't seen you here before." Valentina didn't much appreciate the accusatory tone to his voice.

"I'm new," she said calmly and maintained that eye contact. "I only flew in from New York Friday and started work yesterday."

The guard huffed and eyed Valentina up and down. "I'll need to check—"

"Listen to me." Valentina took a step forward and squared up to both guards, raising her voice just enough to catch the attention of the sparsely populated vestibule. It didn't take much for the New Yorker in her to come through loud and clear. "I have a very important meeting to prepare for—why else do you think I would be in at such an ungodly hour? My meeting is with Jimmy Wen and one of his biggest clients, so if you'd like to call Mr. Wen right now to check my credentials, then please . . . be my guest."

Valentina kept her gaze locked with the big guard's even as he blustered. As was evident by his red-flushed face and flared nostrils, he wasn't used to being spoken to in such a confrontational manner, especially by a woman. He curled his lip and took a step back, mumbling something beneath his breath.

The younger guard closed up Valentina's Hermès and pushed it the short way across his table back to her. "Have a nice day, miss." He flashed her another friendly smile.

"Thank you." Valentina scooped up her bag and made her way past his table. She cast a sideways glance at the burly Wen security guard who made a point of watching her closely as she made her way toward the elevators. Valentina relaxed; the jerk was most likely just checking out her ass. She avoided the urge to wink, but gave her hips a more exaggerated swing.

Take that, meathead.

Once inside the elevator, Valentina breathed a sigh of relief. She had the car all to herself, which was nice, and she made a mental note to get herself into the office at six every morning; it had been too early for even the protesters to be chanting, scuffling, and blocking Finance Street. She could grab a cup of coffee, sit down in the quiet office, and get her head on straight.

The sales office was still empty, although Valentina did hear the sound of distant voices in other parts of the building as the early risers began to go about their day. While she knew she couldn't risk someone having even a casual, inquisitive glance over her shoulder—much of what she needed to do would be best done after hours—she decided a little digging around while she had the place to herself couldn't hurt; she'd be sure to keep one eye on the office door, which she could see clearly in her peripheral vision.

She first set up her displays so the big flat-screen monitor was showing work-related applications, while the smaller laptop screen would show what she was really working on. Even so, she could obscure that with a single keystroke. She knew that if she pulled the screen to the edge of the desk and tilted it slightly, her body would block it from any cameras in the room.

A stick pen gripped between her teeth, Valentina stabbed at the computer keyboard with determined efficiency. It was an old habit, one that went back to her days in elementary school when she'd discovered that chewing on the wooden barrel of a pencil helped her concentrate. At first glance, the company's digital infrastructure appeared to be virtually indistinguishable from the one in New York, so she was more than confident about where she ought to be searching. Valentina offered up a small prayer of thanks to corporate standardization.

The VPN software Valentina had installed over the weekend got her around the network's firewall easily enough, as well as ensuring she would go undetected once she began digging around. Navigating her way through the maze of folders, Valentina came across nothing that shouldn't have been there, nor anything that ought to be and wasn't; a niggle emerged at the back of her mind that Wen possibly had a secondary system where he hid his dirty little secrets. If that was the case or if he was hiding things behind a virtual machine, finding them could be complicated.

She typed a couple of keywords into the search field; Wen was unlikely to be so obvious, but it was worth a try.

Nothing.

Next, she tried a handful of likely file extensions, and still she came up empty. Though the search was frustrating, Valentina had learned that a steady, methodical approach would always pay off in the end.

One step at a time, Tina.

Aloud, she whispered, "Okay, you son of a bitch." She switched her attention to the program directory; if she wasn't seeing Wen's files in the system, he'd likely hidden them from view rather than storing them elsewhere.

After spending quite some time searching and drilling down into the program registry subfolders, Valentina found what she hoped she was looking for. Secreted within a folder named *drpsq* were the program files for Folder Lock, a proprietary software package used for keeping folders and their contents hidden from prying eyes and computer searches; it would render anything Wen didn't want to be seen entirely invisible—and accessible only by using the direct file path.

Finding the file meant both good news and bad for Valentina—good in that it meant Wen's dirty files *were* somewhere on the company's intranet, and bad because accessing the locked files would require a serial key or password, neither of which she had.

Valentina sat back in her chair and contemplated the computer screen; her next move would entail uninstalling the file-hiding program on the mainframe, which would carry the risk of being detected. But, the hour was early and any eagle eyes in IT would unlikely be around to see. And providing she reinstalled the program when she'd gathered what she needed, unless someone was looking for specific activity on Folder Lock, everything she was about to do would go undetected.

She had the SD card out of her phone and in the slot on the laptop in mere seconds. She backed up the Folder Lock subfolder onto her SD card, then turned back to the intranet and double-clicked the Uninstall program icon. A dialog box opened, displaying a green progress bar. Valentina was watching the bar move slowly through the process when she first heard voices out in the hallway.

No fucking way.

The green bar continued its journey, uncaring of Valentina's growing alarm. From the corner of her eye, she saw blurry shapes beyond the frosted glass of the office door just before it swung open, the voices—chatting away in Cantonese—swelling in volume.

Valentina quickly toggled a web page to cover her computer screen, hiding the uninstall dialog, and looked across to see a trio of the office cleaning staff. They quit their chatter and blinked at Valentina. The youngest of the three bowed his head rapidly several times.

"Sorry, miss. Sorry." He turned and shooed the others out into the hall again, and they headed to Wen's office. She saw them again through the glass walls as they went about vacuuming and dusting.

Chastising herself for not being alert to the intrusion sooner, Valentina let out her breath and toggled back to check the progress of the uninstall.

The green bar had vanished, and a message box informed Valentina that the program was uninstalled. Valentina clicked out of the box and then rebooted her computer; this was the moment of truth—if Wen's files were indeed hidden on the system, they'd be exposed now.

The screen froze.

"Shit." Staring at the immobile mouse pointer, Valentina jiggled her mouse; the cursor remained unresponsive. Tapping a fingernail on the escape key, Valentina looked up from her computer; she fully expected to see Wen's security team racing toward her, guns drawn and ready to drag her from the office.

She was still alone.

She hit the power button and the screen went blank. Counting to ten, she pressed the button again; her eyes didn't leave the screen.

The home screen, with its generic landscape picture, appeared as the computer sprang to life. Valentina retraced her steps back to where she had predicted the hidden files to be, and found they were no longer hidden.

Scanning down the list of files, Valentina saw spreadsheets, document files, and a JPEG image file—the thumbnail showed it to be of an expensive yacht. Each filename was made up of a half dozen seemingly random numbers. The file extension indicated they were all spreadsheets. She was hopeful they would contain JM Wen's system of double bookkeeping. It would require her opening up each one to inspect its contents, but she was almost certain what she'd find in at least one of those files.

She paused with the pointer hovering over the first of the spreadsheets, eddying in indecision. The software she'd installed Saturday morning would create a virtual echo of the file, which it would then save directly to the SD card. Since she had not opened the file on Wen's system, there would be no trace of activity—even from an IP address other than her own. Even so, this was a big step for her to take. Once she began copying Wen's secret company files, there would be no going back.

Valentina selected all of the spreadsheet files and copied them to her SD drive. Once they were all safely aboard, Valentina turned her attention to the document files and repeated the process. As they appeared on her SD card, Valentina opened up a handful; they detailed

Wen's pump-and-dump schemes with different clients. Although, as with the double accounting, such schemes were pretty much routine—and not only in Hong Kong—she knew they could be a gateway to Wen's more nefarious activities.

As far as she was concerned, all this intel was preamble. They were teases, making her lust for the big reveals—the particular scam that had Wen so worried, and his dirty bank or banks. She had to acknowledge that Bennett had piqued her interest, and the irony of it appealed to her: The reason that she had been summoned to JM Wen's main office might be the same shady dealing she could use to put him away. She also had to admit that having an Interpol agent at her back made her feel less as if the earth might shrug out from under her feet at any moment.

A glance at her watch proved that less time had passed than she'd thought; she had time to delve into files that related to Wen's stock loans. While there was nothing illegal in handing out loans against a client's shares above bank lending rates, such loans could all too easily step over the thin legal line, depending upon the timing of the sale of the shares. A company as astute as JM Wen was more than capable of fixing the dates on the official accounts, but their original, unofficial counterparts would still show original dates and timelines. Now, if Wen was also manipulating the *value* of the shares, that would be a bigger step across a darker, fatter line. But even that would be doubtful to make the guy as nervous as he appeared to be.

Something far bigger than stock loan scams was eating at Jimmy Wen, and she was damn well going to find it.

"Damn it." Valentina cursed beneath her breath as a dialog box stopped the transfer process, demanding that she type in a password before it would allow her to access a folder labeled Contacts, which resided within another folder labeled *Shing Hai*. She poked around a little—cautiously—but could find no quick way around the password request. The delay was maddening for sure, as the files hidden behind the password most probably contained details of JM Wen's other influencers, along with the inevitable list of media personalities, celebrities, corruptible politicians Wen would have in his deep pockets, and the proxies he used. Still, she had expected to hit firewalls and encryption at some point, and was surprised she'd been able to get as far as she had. At least now she knew where she should focus. The presence of the firewall was actually a Big Red Flag, and Valentina's every instinct told her the real dirt lay beyond it. She needed to find and decrypt Wen's keychain file.

Easier said than done.

Valentina scanned the files in the once-hidden folders, looking for something anomalous—something that hinted in any way that it was unique. God, there were so many files and folders, and the keychain could be concealed within any one of them; where the hell would someone like Jimmy Wen hide that information?

Her eyes lit on the lone JPEG file with its tiny image of a yacht—MCIV.jpeg. What would a JPEG of a boat be doing among all these data files in a business setting?

Hiding something.

Valentina hadn't copied the JPEG over to the SD drive, but decided she would once the last of the document files were saved off. Just for hoots, she tried to open it. It was encrypted, which increased her sense that she was onto something.

Who encrypts a yacht selfie?

Clearly, this required the application of her decryption software. She started with the premise that the encryption key might have been assigned using a random character generator for at least part of the code. Knowing that random code generators used the computer's internal clock for seed values, Valentina fired up the decryption app and dug down into the network to identify when the image file had been encrypted. Once she uncovered the public key, Valentina ran that through the decryption process, which began creating key pairs until it hit upon the one used to encrypt the image.

Valentina took another quick look around the office while the decryption software churned through the millions of potential number combinations. She knew she was pushing her luck now; her colleagues would be making their way in for the meeting in a matter of minutes. Time was running away from Valentina.

When she returned her attention to the computer, a small box in the center of the screen informed her that a match had been made and the encryption key generated. She input the code to the image's decryption dialog and held her breath.

"Well hello, Mr. Wen," Valentina whispered as an image of an impressively large yacht filled the window of her photo editor. It was moored in a marina filled with a spectacular array of similar boats, each one of which screamed money, although none appeared as opulent as the *Morning Cloud IV*. There, leaning upon the polished brass railing at the yacht's side, was a smiling Jimmy Wen with a drink in his hand and surrounded by a handful of bikini-clad beauties.

What Valentina wanted wasn't in the image—exactly—but in encrypting the image file, Jimmy Wen had essentially shouted out loud to anyone who knew what to look for that there was more in the file than a picture of a vain man and his pretty possessions.

Valentina opened up a text editor on her laptop and dragged the image into it. The image itself was reduced to a string of code that included the filename and dimensions. Above that was a long stack of comment lines that each began with /* and ended with */. Between those comment brackets was what Valentina had been seeking.

Valentina smiled, heat fanning her cheeks. "Gotcha, you old-school son of a bitch."

CHAPTER TWENTY-FOUR

From the comfort of his black leather executive chair, Shum Kuo stared at his bank of monitors. Most showed empty hallways, some tracked the movements of the staff who preferred to begin their working days an hour or so before their colleagues, and three kept an eye on computer activity both within the company intranet and on the World Wide Web.

He noticed some early activity on one of the computers in the sales department. That was nothing unusual in itself; salespeople would often arrive early to get a jump on international clients. Shum had watched the American woman's progress through the office with some interest after her tense encounter with a member of his security team. He'd followed her via the network of CCTV cameras through the foyer, into the elevator, and then all the way through JM Wen's offices to her desk. He watched her from one of the five cameras in the sales office as she logged onto her computer, at which point he switched his attention to the activity monitor on his own screen.

He'd seen Vittorio around the office the previous day. She had a sultry attractiveness about her—a smoking hot body, as Lucas Vaughn would say—and was definitely worth a second look. He hadn't pegged her for being particularly diligent, especially after having spotted her ducking out for an early lunch her first day on the job. Shum knew she'd had a client breakfast meeting scheduled at seven that morning, since nothing happened at JM Wen without the security department knowing about it. So he'd been surprised to see her striding in an hour early as if she owned the damn place.

He kept one eye on the crisp, color image of the woman, and the other closely on what she was browsing on her computer; she appeared to be doing nothing more than poring over the Hong Kong news and overseas stock exchange numbers, and typing notes. Shum studied Valentina's face as she pattered away at her keyboard, and suspected her—of what, he couldn't have said. But something about her made him uneasy. She seemed too . . . watchful. Perhaps it was his ingrained distrust of women and dislike of all Americans—a legacy from his days with the Ministry of State Security—but his gut was telling him she was up to something, and Shum Kuo's gut was rarely wrong.

After all, he'd sniffed out the Huang girl's underhanded dealings with the SFC, and though Wen had had a hard time believing his one-time star player to be capable of such disloyalty, Shum had eventually been proven right. Disposing of Chrissy Huang had been most satisfying, though, something private and intimate between the two of them; Wen would never ask what became of the girl, and Shum sure as hell wasn't about to tell him.

Absently, Shum rubbed the top of his head; the skin there was rough with bristles and scratched at his palm. He'd been far too busy to go home and had spent the whole night at the office—as a consequence, he had yet to shave. Snatching his cell phone from the desk, Shum thumbed the thing to life, hit redial on the last number he'd called, and waited to be connected to Jimmy Wen.

* * *

"This had better be good," Jimmy Wen growled as he barged through the door to Shum's office. "I have a meeting in—"

"I know you have a meeting, Jimmy," Shum interrupted. "If you'll recall, I was the one who let the caterers into the executive conference room while it was still dark outside."

Jimmy huffed and checked the time on his wristwatch. "You needed something?"

"I thought I'd give you the debrief on yesterday since you were in early this morning."

He almost said no—he didn't want to know the details of Shum's work. But he might have loose ends to tie up. Those, he should know about. "Okay—you've got five minutes."

"Even with Chrissy Huang out of the picture, the SFC guy went ahead with his scheduled meeting," Shum told him. "We thought he was just having lunch, maybe even meeting a mistress—but he was seen with some blonde *gwai lo* just before . . ."

Jimmy narrowed his eyes; he'd been wrong in the beginning about Huang, and Shum had gone to great lengths to rub his nose in that fact once the truth came out. If he'd had the SFC agent eliminated—well, that would have been beyond overkill; overt theatrics in Hong Kong's current climate were never going to be a good idea—especially in Triad territory. Nor did it pay to attract negative attention with the Chinese scrutinizing the island under their communist microscope. If he'd gone overboard with the agent, what might he have done to Chrissy Huang?

Jimmy batted the thought aside. "The blonde wasn't his mistress?"

Shum shook his head. "For a start, I imagine this woman would be far too old to appeal to Chung-Sun Fan—he was a lover of certain strains of Japanese anime, I've heard. And, according to my informant, they did not seem 'chummy,' I think that's the word. She was dressed for business, not pleasure—a dark suit and expensive shoes—and she stood out. Our man didn't get a good look at her, unfortunately, and there's no CCTV footage from the restaurant or any of the surrounding area."

Jimmy shrugged. "Okay, so he was working on another mole; what's to say she was from JM Wen?"

"Nothing." Shum's eyes twitched toward the bank of monitors.

There, on the middle screen, Valentina Vittorio worked diligently at her computer.

"You've *got* to be kidding me," Jimmy spat. "I had Vittorio thoroughly vetted before we flew her out here—more so than any of the others because—"

"She's American?"

Jimmy managed a smile. "Something like that. She checked out, otherwise she wouldn't be here."

"You said the same about Chrissy Huang."

He flat-out refused to be drawn in to that one. "Keep an eye on the American if you want, but don't get in the way of her bringing in money, Kuo. You know we can't afford to lose momentum."

"So I have heard." Shum's attention switched to his computer screen as the activity monitor lit up as more JM Wen employees booted up their laptops. "You know you can trust me to be discreet, Jimmy."

Jimmy left the man to it. He hated Shum Kuo's dark, cramped office with all the surveillance equipment spying on his staff. He knew the place—and the man—was a necessary evil, but that didn't mean he had to like it.

CHAPTER TWENTY-FIVE

Keenly aware of the cameras peering from the corners of the room, knowing there must be an unseen watcher or watchers monitoring her computer activity, Valentina peered at the files in Jimmy Wen's carefully secreted folders, her pen gripped so tightly in her teeth that her jaw ached. She'd copied the keychain codes from the text file and pasted them into a new file on her SD card, which she named *gotcha*. Now, she scooted the mouse around on her company-branded mouse pad, copying any of the newly exposed files and folders that looked promising. The keychain was proving its worth; Valentina hadn't yet come across something it couldn't open.

Valentina was searching for something specific—or rather, *someone* specific: Zhang Bo.

The *elusive* Zhang Bo.

Despite his visit to JM Wen and the cryptic "conversation" she'd witnessed between Zhang and Lucas, and the suspicions of Kate Bennett, the gangster's name was conspicuous by its absence, which raised more questions in Valentina's mind than it answered; was the man a ghost hidden behind so many pseudonyms and shell companies that tracing him would be virtually impossible?

You're not that good, Jimmy. If the motherfucker's in here, I'm gonna find him. She smiled to herself and continued to dig down into the files JM Wen Limited had gone to great lengths to bury.

A movement caught Valentina's peripheral vision. Her heart tripped a beat and a chill prickled the skin between her shoulder blades. Reflexively, she keyed the laptop screen to the *Hong Kong Economic Times* website and afforded a glance at the door to the hall to see who'd disturbed her at such a critical moment; in the split second she'd swapped the windows on her laptop, she'd caught sight of the letters *ZBo* on a subfolder hidden among a lengthy stack of other such folders with equally terse names.

The new arrivals were Chun Yeung Lam and Nadim Singh. Deep in conversation, they made their way into the sales office and didn't seemed to register Valentina's presence. Something about their body language and the way they maintained constant eye contact had Valentina thinking theirs might just be the first office romance among the new crew.

Frustrated she'd been interrupted on the cusp of discovering what she'd been looking for, Valentina took a moment to shut down the SD card window, then pretended to be immersed in the *Economic Times*. She couldn't be too careful and was ever mindful of one of her father's well-worn mantras—*trust no one*—which, bearing in mind what Jimmy Wen did to him, was grotesquely ironic.

"Oh, hey, Val," Nadim called across when he finally realized she was there.

"Hi." Valentina waved a hand above her head and allowed the pen to drop from her mouth to the desk. It was a wounded warrior, bearing the marks from her teeth and red smears from her lipstick.

"Never had you figured for an early riser," Lam chipped in as the two walked over. "How long have you been here?"

As Valentina shrugged, her eyes flitted to her laptop screen; a touch of paranoia had her double-checking to ensure nothing incriminating remained. "For about an hour, I guess. I figured I'd get a head start on the day and put in a little research before the meeting. Speaking of which, I guess we'd better shift our asses, otherwise Mr. Wen is not going to be happy."

In perfect synchrony, both Nadim and Lam checked their watches.

"If there's one thing the guy hates, it's tardiness," Lam said, as if Wen were a high school homeroom teacher rather than a temperamental billionaire. He smiled at Valentina and added, "If you're not early, you're late, right?"

A shiver ran the length of Valentina's spine.

"After you, ma'am." Smiling down at Valentina, Nadim held out his arm in an exaggerated gesture of chivalry.

Valentina played along. She shut her laptop, grabbed her purse, and got to her feet, batting her eyelashes. "Why thank you, kind sir. We mustn't keep Mr. Wen waiting."

"Especially when he's about to give us a crash course in how an expert reels in the big fish."

Lam laughed as if Nadim had said something hilarious. His eyes flicked to the other man's, and Valentina saw that look pass between them again. As she followed the two out of the office, she cast a fleeting glance back at her computer's blank screen, frustration boiling away below the surface of her cool facade. She'd found what was possibly the first hint of Zhang Bo and a potentially ruinous relationship with JM Wen, but he was going to have to wait for now.

CHAPTER TWENTY-SIX

The corporate conference room was less a meeting room and more a great hall from a palatial estate. It was designed to impress potential clients and inspire them with a glimpse of what JM Wen's money could do for them. Sumptuous works of art hung between hunting trophies on the beautifully papered walls; Valentina recognized a Jackson Pollock and a Warhol among them, and very much doubted either of the paintings were mere prints. She fought the urge to sidle up to one and run her fingertips over it. The floor was adorned with a thick, antique Persian rug, its colors as vivid as if it had been hand-knotted yesterday. Valentina guessed that, too, was authentic.

The room was about the size of the average hotel ballroom, but with none of the same accouterments—vinyl wall coverings, ridiculous light fixtures, mind-numbing patterns in cheap carpeting, or that empty-room air that ballrooms had even when hosting an event. And no giant conference table centered the space. Instead, an array of small, round pedestal tables with marble tops and antique Chinese monk chairs of burnished cherry wood were scattered at one end, bracketed with a row of stainless steel catering carts manned by a half-dozen stunning hostesses. The array of exotic food on the carts filled the room with the most luscious, seductive aromas. Valentina's mouth was watering.

She was used to exquisite—and overly expensive—catering back in New York, but this presentation was on a whole new level; the company had evidently spent tens of thousands of dollars on food, staff, and drinks *to impress one client.* For a man supposedly under outsized pressure, Wen was not cutting back any. Made no sense . . . and made perfect sense. A display like this was a great smoke screen. How could anyone experiencing this extravagance imagine that JM Wen might be floundering?

Valentina had to admire the strategy. This room spoke of taste and sophistication and gave the impression that this cozy, comfortable, yet lavish space had been here for centuries and would endure for several more. All the better to soothe the client (whoever he was) into signing his shares over to Jimmy Wen.

Lucas waved Valentina over the second she stepped into the room with Lam and Nadim. As she made her way across, her two colleagues drifted off to join the rest of Wen's tiger team, who appeared to be deep in conversation by one of the little tables.

Lucas greeted Valentina with a wink and a sly grin. "Nice of you to join us, Val. Mr. Wen will be along with the client shortly."

"Who is this guy . . . or gal?" she asked. "Is it a state secret or something?"

"Not at all. It's just something that came together very quickly. A contact that Chrissy had been working on for a while." His face did something funny at the mention of Chrissy Huang—a sort of grimace/tic. "His name's Pham Ngoc Chi."

Valentina tilted her head. "Vietnamese?"

"Yeah. He's in telecommunications, I think."

"You think?"

Lucas shrugged. "Jimmy's taking lead on this one. He wants to—"

"Show us what's what?" Valentina guessed.

Lucas gave her a loopy grin and nodded. "Nailed it in one."

Valentina looked around at her colleagues and the veritable swarm of hostesses. Unlike the pretty office assistants Wen seeded throughout his company, the hostesses wore vividly colored silk dresses cut in the form-fitting *cheongsam* style with slits up each side that stopped just below the hip. Each one looked as if she'd just stepped off a Milan catwalk and was so delicate and petite that Valentina felt like a damned giraffe.

"Isn't this all a little heavy-handed? In New York, this many people would make a client run screaming from the building."

Lucas snorted, waving over one of the hostesses who was in possession of a tray of drinks. He watched with an appreciative eye as she crossed the room, gliding so gracefully, the drinks barely rippled in their cups and glasses.

"You ain't in *Noo Yohk* any more, Val. In Hong Kong, it's all about putting on a grand show of expertise and quality—staking out your home territory, if you will."

"How much gelt are we talking about?"

Lucas shrugged. "About eight hundred mil, Hong Kong."

"So little?" Valentina couldn't resist the dig.

Lucas gave her a bemused look as if he couldn't tell if she was joking or not. She'd said it with a straight face and thought he was going to clap back, but now, the hostess stood before them with a fixed smile on her immaculately made-up elfin face and the drinks tray expertly balanced on the upturned fingers of her left hand. Lucas plucked a coffee from the tray and Valentina selected a glass of iced water—the thick, black coffee looked far too strong, even for a hardened New Yorker.

"It's kind of like parking all your Rolls-Royces, Teslas, and Mercedes on the front lawn to impress the in-laws, and ostentation be damned." As he spoke, Lucas's eyes remained glued to the pleasantly swaying ass of the hostess as she turned away and made her way over to Valentina's colleagues.

Valentina followed Lucas's gaze and gave him a disapprovingly raised eyebrow.

"Hey, she's pretty. You gawp at pretty guys, too, don't deny it."

"I don't *gawp* at pretty anything. I have a bit more class than that." She smiled to take any sting out of her words. "Do you go all out like this for every client?"

"Only those looking to finance eight hundred million or more—Hong Kong," he added, then gestured at the buffet. "It'd be about a hundred mil US at today's rate. Hungry?"

"Now that you mention it," Valentina admitted. She hadn't been especially hungry, given the rampant case of nerves she was coming off of, but the sight—and delectable aromas—of the *pho* noodles, *bahn xeo* pancakes, *bun cha* meatballs, and whole host of other exquisite traditional Vietnamese dishes actually had her stomach rumbling. She recognized most of the dishes she'd seen in the small backstreet restaurants she liked to frequent in Manhattan's Little Saigon.

"Mr. Pham is flying in from Ho Chi Minh City," Lucas told her as they crossed to the buffet. "Private jet, of course. The guy's big in telecommunications and based mainly in Vietnam, although he does have significant interests in China and Hong Kong."

Valentina nodded along and eyed the food as Lucas spoke. She felt it would be rude to eat before Pham arrived; Wen wouldn't want the artistic display of food to be ruined before he'd had a chance to be suitably impressed by the hostesses, room, priceless art, and exquisite food. Wen's caterers had gone to a tremendous amount of detail in preparing each authentic dish, from the plump frogs' legs sticking out of the curry to what appeared to be *tiet canh*—the traditional Vietnamese soup made from duck's blood.

"How long has Pham been a client?" she asked Lucas as he snuck a pancake from the steaming pile in front of him.

"Just over eight months. We loaned him big when the last of the private banks blew him off. He needed to pay off a couple of pregnant mistresses, apparently, and a failed condo deal on the mainland." He spoke with his mouth full, which Valentina didn't find the least bit endearing.

"LCSSC Wealth Management?"

"As a matter of fact, yes." Lucas seemed impressed that the hot chick from Staten Island was catching on so quickly. "They sent him our way when he was desperate and had pretty much exhausted all avenues. Well, barring a header off Landmark 81, of course." His lips curled up at the corners in a wry smile.

"The perfect referral, then."

"Absolutely. And here he is, now." Lucas nodded toward the door as Wen made his way into the room accompanied by the black-suited, ever-present Lau and Pang—an entirely unnecessary but impressive detail—and his VIP client, the slightly built, gray-haired Pham Ngoc Chi. Close to Pham's side was a petite young lady in a red silk dress who had all the appearances of being rather more than a personal assistant; her surgically enhanced figure and perfectly sculpted face were so incredibly beautiful that she actually put Wen's hostesses to shame. The comparison was unavoidable as four of said hostesses glided smoothly over to the newcomers to offer trays brimming with drinks and hors d'oeuvres.

Pham had no entourage; had it been a regular business meeting, he, too, would have likely brought along an army of assistants, secretaries, and anyone else who could bolster his show of strength—possibly even his own bodyguards. But, since he was looking to raise capital on company shares he had no business using as collateral, the fewer eyes and ears to witness his financial subterfuge, the better.

With barely a glance at Valentina's colleagues, Wen ushered the client over to meet Lucas.

"*Xin chao*, Pham Ngoc Chi." With a barely perceptible bow of the head to show respect, Vaughn shook Pham's hand and introduced him to his protégée.

"New York?" Pham said with a smile as he pumped Valentina's hand with enthusiasm and his assistant eyed her up and down as if she were a potential rival for his affections. "You must be from Queens?"

"Staten Island," Valentina corrected with a warm smile as she extricated her hand from his.

"Of course, of course," Pham said absently; he was already eyeing up either the *pha lau bo*—cow's intestine soup—or the delightful young lady serving it . . . possibly both.

Valentina's lips curled wryly. *Ah, the fickleness of man.*

Wen was quick to pick up on the body language. "I can see you are hungry. Let's eat before we conduct our business—I find it is always better to talk numbers on a full stomach." He led Pham across to the beginning of the buffet and invited him to let the hostesses know what he wanted.

Once Pham had filled a plate and had it deposited at one of the small tables by a tall, ebony-haired hostess who towered over him by an easy eight inches or so, Lucas, Valentina, and her associates all took their pick of the glamorous foods. Eschewing the duck blood and frogs, Valentina opted for the more moderate *bahn xeo* pancakes and other less adventurous fare.

Wen kept close to his client. They ate together, speaking in earnest, then circulated as Wen introduced Pham to each one of the other salespeople in turn. He made a big deal of explaining they had been flown in from JM Wen's many international offices—a fact which clearly impressed the client. It was all part of Wen's peacock act, of course, a big show of power and success designed to complete the process of wooing the man away from his shares. Unsurprisingly, Pham lapped up the attention, especially that of the myriad hostesses who brushed by him, touched his hand gently when they spoke, and dazzled him with secret smiles that hinted there might be more to their presence than serving drinks and fine food.

Finally, the time came for what was essentially a signing ceremony. Wen sat Pham down at one of the small tables and beckoned one of his bodyguards to him. The guard—Valentina thought it was Lau—produced a leather folder with an elegant gold lion reposing on the front cover and handed it to Wen. She wondered if he'd been carrying it around all afternoon and she just hadn't noticed.

"We have everything in place," Wen said, opening the folder on the table top and revealing a neat stack of documents. "We just need your signature and we're good to go—I can have the money transferred within the hour."

Pham frowned for the first time since he'd entered the room and appeared hesitant, as if having second thoughts. Valentina couldn't blame him—not if he'd been maneuvered into a corner by JM Wen over the course of the past eight months. The diminutive Vietnamese businessman nodded slowly and paged through the contract. He would have seen and possibly even signed an electronic copy, though under the circumstances he couldn't have allowed his own legal department to hold it up to scrutiny. The shares he was using for collateral were not his to use in such a way.

Valentina wondered how often that factored into the situation. The fact that a man had reached some pinnacle of success in business didn't mean he personally possessed any legal chops; that's what you hired experts for. Now, though, Pham Ngoc Chi was alone in his decision-making process.

"This will allow me to prepare my company well for the 5G roll-out," he offered by means of an explanation as he picked up the pen Jimmy Wen had placed on the table next to the contract.

Valentina watched Wen's face as he smiled and nodded. He couldn't give a damn what the money was going to pay for, only that those shares were passing into his hands. He knew Pham had gotten himself into a financial mess and he'd be lucky if he could plug enough holes to keep from going under even before he had chance to default on the loan. He *knew* . . .

Valentina realized she was grinding her teeth, and willfully relaxed her jaw. God help her if Jimmy Wen caught her wearing what her little sister had called her Death Star look. She plastered a pleasant smile on her lips and hoped any smolder in her eyes would be taken for something other than disgust.

With a distracted air, Pham Ngoc Chi signed at each of the neon green sticky markers so thoughtfully placed about the document, then closed the folder and pushed it across the table to Wen. Both men stood up, and Jimmy Wen gave Pham a hearty handshake to seal the deal. Someone snapped a photo, which earned another momentary frown from Mr. Pham.

"It has been an absolute pleasure doing business with you," Wen declared. "Please, stay and enjoy our hospitality."

Pham declined. "Thank you, but no. I must get back to the airport —there is much to do, as you can imagine." Shoulders slumped, he seemed to have shrunk since he'd entered the room. Even the accommodating hostesses no longer held his attention.

Wen offered a wide, warm smile. "Of course, I fully understand. Next time, when you can stay longer, we should take in a spa and enjoy an evening together." He took a step away from the table and began to escort Pham toward the door.

Pham gave Wen a thin, pained smile as his young assistant reappeared by his side. "Perhaps. Assuming there is a next time. *Tam biet,* Mr. Wen."

Wen walked with his client as far as the door, and then allowed a pair of the hostess girls to take him the rest of the way out of the office. Apparently, there was no longer a need for excessive niceties.

"And that, ladies and gentlemen, is how we do it in Hong Kong." Wen addressed the assembled sales team, his smug expression suggesting he was expecting kudos for reeling in such a relatively small whale.

Valentina was underwhelmed, but if the boss expected a round of applause . . . A glance at Lucas, who kept his hands firmly by his sides, let her know the correct protocol.

"We have another client to entertain this evening," Wen continued; he was on a roll. "Courtesy of Miss Vittorio, this one has the potential to be a real game-changer for JM Wen Limited. You and you will attend," he said, pointing at Oliver and Sofia. "A car will pick you up at your hotel at seven." He then turned on his heel and left the room. Lau and Pang followed with creepy synchronicity.

"We're not all going?" Valentina asked Lucas. Anthony, Nadim, and Lam looked so put out by their exclusion that she almost felt sorry for them.

Lucas shook his head. "A show of strength here, on our home territory, is essential for a client's confidence in the company. But out there on neutral ground, something like this would scare the living shit out of them. Like we were sending a posse. You all should go back to work. I may be awhile here." He made his way back over to the food carts and the charming young hostesses.

Duly dismissed, Valentina headed for the door; already her mind was fixed upon returning to the exploration of those buried computer files with Zhang Bo's name all over them.

"Miss Vittorio." The voice rose above the hubbub of the office— now a veritable hive of activity—startling Valentina as she stepped out into the hallway.

Valentina turned around. A Chinese man built like a small tank (or a large bulldog) stood with military rigidity several feet from the door. He looked familiar, but she couldn't quite—

"Do you have a moment?" He took two strides toward her and stopped.

Valentina's eyes flicked down to the ID badge that bounced on a gold fabric lanyard against the man's broad chest. Shum Kuo: Chief of Security. Her heart jumped and her mouth felt suddenly dry. Had the head of Wen's famously diligent security department already managed to see through her proxy and VPN software? Did they know she was sticking her nose into company affairs that had nothing whatsoever to do with her job?

She fixed him with a cool, polite gaze. "Is there a problem?"

Shum glanced each way along the hallway before ushering Valentina through the open door of an empty office across the way from the conference room. He closed the door behind them.

"Why would you think there's a problem, Miss Vittorio?" he asked, a film of amusement on the words.

Valentina turned to face him squarely, looking down at him. "Sir, you're the chief of security. So, logically, if you wish to discuss something relevant to security with me, a salesperson, there must be a problem . . . or at least, you *think* there is. So, why do you wish to speak to me?" She could tell by the sudden tension in his face that something she'd said had irritated him.

"I don't trust you, Miss Vittorio. You have aroused my suspicions and, as a consequence, I am keeping a very close eye on you."

"Well, that's blunt and to the point. I appreciate you cutting to the chase, Mr. Shum."

Shum twisted his thin lips into some semblance of a smile and stared at her silently.

Ah, yes. Intimidation 101: silence encourages the guilty to chatter.

Valentina maintained her composure and simply stared back. If the odious little man had anything more tangible than unfounded suspicions, they would be having an altogether different conversation. This was one hell of a shot across the bows, though, and it occurred to her to wonder if he did this to all the new hires. Put the fear of Shum into them.

"Are you suspicious of everybody," she asked, "or have you singled me out for some reason?" She did her best to look offended, not wary.

Shum stroked the smooth, shiny skin of his scalp. "As a general rule, I trust no one. I find that to be the best strategy—don't you?"

Something in the man's smile had Valentina's skin crawling, and she suddenly remembered where she'd seen him before. This was the man who'd hovered over Chrissy Huang yesterday morning. The man who'd escorted Chrissy from her desk. She felt as if a shaft of Arctic ice had lodged in her core, and her ears were filled with the sound of her pulse.

Shum had started talking again. "I also am an advocate of following my gut instincts—and right now they're telling me that you, in particular, require my full attention, Miss Vittorio." He swept her with a look that was equal parts lascivious and disdainful.

She crossed her arms over her breasts as much to block that inspection as to keep herself from shivering. "And why is that, Mr. Shum?" She kept her voice low and purring, but did not bother to expel the Death Star from her gaze.

"I am aware you left the building yesterday just before noon."

Valentina did an attitude crash turn, taking a step back and flinging her arms wide, palms up, and giving the security chief a look of sheer incredulity. "Really? That's it? That's the incriminating behavior? I was feeling brain dead. I took an early lunch. Lucas told me to take as much time as I liked. I admit, I did a little sightseeing. I wasn't aware I was obliged to sacrifice meals for the good of the company."

Shum's face reddened. "Of course not; that would be unreasonable." His voice was low, clipped. "But you would be best advised not to go against the norm. I'm sure you would not wish to court false accusations of any wrongdoing. Rumors and backbiting run rife in this office, and I'm sure you have seen for yourself the unrest that is going on out there. It is not as safe as you may think, Miss Vittorio."

And what the hell does that have to do with anything? Valentina smiled. It had nothing to do with anything. She'd called his bluff and made him uncomfortable, and he was backpedaling.

"I'll bear all that in mind. Thank you, Mr. Shum, for your kind attention to my reputation."

Valentina sidestepped Shum and pulled open the door. Stepping out into the hallway, she was relieved to see it was momentarily deserted—had any one of her colleagues spotted her coming out of a cozy, closed-door chat with Shum Kuo, the gossip would have spread like wildfire.

Gossip was the least of Valentina's concerns, though. Despite the *volte face* he'd pulled at the end there, Shum had her in his sights, and the SFC agent had tracked her down and led Bennett to her. Valentina had been so sure she'd covered her tracks, but it was becoming obvious that all her care had not been enough. Perhaps her mistake had been in not planning any further ahead than catalyzing Wen's downfall? With little regard for her own escape once Wen's empire fell, Valentina had created gaps in her plan that could well lead to its undoing.

She scolded herself for her naivety. She should have assumed the regulators would have been investigating Wen, and she should have assumed that Wen's security team, given the secrets it was intended to protect, would be run with military efficiency . . . and effectiveness. Shum made the heads of New York firms she'd worked in look like rent-a-cops.

None of that mattered to her end game, she told herself. She would remain single-minded in her focus upon her goal; neither the SFC, Interpol, nor Shum Kuo would get in her way.

Her thoughts turned to Agent Kate Bennett. It was time to check in with Ms. Interpol, let her know some progress had been made, and tell her about the chat she'd just endured with Shum. Valentina was going to have to be extra vigilant (read: paranoid) if she was going to see all of this through.

She squared her shoulders and strode off along the hallway, headed for the nearest restroom.

CHAPTER TWENTY-SEVEN

"Yeah, the guy's name is buried pretty deep, but I managed to find it." Valentina spoke softly into the burner phone. The restroom was empty—finally—but her healthy paranoia still kept her voice to a loud whisper and made her wish the piped-in music was louder.

She'd had to wait ten minutes after securing herself in a stall, as one of the Kwok clones had raced in straight after her, locked herself in the end stall, and proceeded to throw up. Along with the loud sobbing that followed the noisy vomiting, the performance screamed morning sickness. Valentina had emerged the moment the girl left and went to the sinks, where she turned a tap on full blast and leaned on the counter next to it.

"You're being careful?"

Valentina thought Bennett sounded uncharacteristically protective —more likely she was concerned about losing another mole than her personal safety. "Of course. Hear that?" She held the phone out toward the stream of water. "White noise."

"Clever girl, but I meant the field work you're doing."

"Completely subterranean. Did I mention that I'm a world-class tracker? Half bloodhound, half ferret, that's me. I'm covered, Katie."

"Well, you're in a rare mood."

"Nah. I just hate bugs."

"Don't get cocky, Vittorio." Bennett's voice switched to that stern schoolmarm tone that grated on Valentina's nerves. "Wen's head of security is ex–Ministry of State Security, and they have quite the brutal reputation. There's nothing that man wouldn't do if he so much as suspected you—"

"I actually had a nice chat with Mr. Shum," Valentina interrupted. "Just now, as it happens. He came right out and said—well, you can probably imagine what he said. I'm not his favorite."

The sound of Bennett sucking air in through her teeth whooshed in Valentina's ear. "Jesus Christ, Vittorio! How the bloody hell did you manage to get on his radar in so little time?"

The bathroom door sighed as it swung open. Valentina straightened and used her free hand to reach for a soap dispenser, watching as one of the saleswomen from her department crossed behind her on her way to the stalls. She was humming and ignored Valentina completely.

"Valentina?"

"So, you remember I took an early lunch yesterday," Valentina said, waving her hand under the faucet to make it sound as if she was washing her hands. "Well, I ended up spilling hoisin sauce or plum sauce or something all over my suit. I mean, there was red sauce *every-where*. I told you about that, right? So naturally I had to go change my clothes, and naturally *somebody* thinks I'm shirking. Me, shirking."

"There's someone in there with you, yes?"

"No shit, Sherlock."

"Right, then I . . . right. Can you tell me what you've found so far? If not, we can try when you're back at your hotel tonight." Bennett's voice softened, and in the background, Valentina heard the unmistakable sounds of street traffic; the Interpol agent could have been sitting outside 2IFC in her car for all she knew.

"Might be too late by then."

"All right. Shoot—you'll pardon the expression."

"So," Valentina continued, "you knew I've been seeing this baker —Tod. Poor guy is totally into *short* bread and he rides the temperature on his oven like a madman. Turning it up and down, up and down. Swears that makes the bread rise faster or something."

There was only a moment's hesitation before Bennett said, "Got it. How?"

"No idea how he does it, but his kitchen is squeaky clean—until you start looking under the stove, that is." Coded chatter notwithstanding, a noise from the stalls made Valentina hold her breath for a moment, before saying, "I'd be happy to let you know if Tod's got any satellite bakeries in your area."

"Did you find the client lists?" Bennett prompted.

The saleswoman came out of the stall then and hurried to the sinks to wash her hands, giving Valentina a polite nod.

"You know, Katie," Valentina said into the phone, "I've been trying to wash my hands this whole time. Can I put you down until I'm done?"

"Sure."

Valentina washed her hands so carefully that the other woman was out of the room before she'd finished rinsing. She turned off the water, picked up the phone, and stuck one hand in the Dyson dryer. The sound of rushing air filled the room.

"Okay, where were we?" she asked Bennett.

"Clients."

"Ingredients? Oh, he keeps those *secret*. I mean, all the usual stuff is on paper—sugar, clotted cream, all that. But off the record, he's got secret ingredients up the yin-yang. I know a few of them." She swapped hands in the dryer.

"Let me know when you get a significant number or someone of particular importance." Bennett sighed. "I wish you didn't have to speak in code. If you could get away from the office—"

"Oh, yes, because that went so well the last time."

There was a long moment of silence, during which Valentina pulled her hand out of the Dyson. It shut off, and the only sound in the restroom was the music oozing through the speakers in the ceiling.

Valentina had moved to stand directly beneath one of them, when

Bennett said, "Point taken. I'm sorry I suggested it. Did you find anything related to Zhang Bo?"

Valentina hesitated. Was this something she should keep to herself like an ace up her sleeve? She decided against it. "That is definitely one of Tod's favorite recipes."

"Can you get it for me?"

"I think so. My little baker is a bit on the sloppy side."

"That's good to hear. Do you think Zhang is a contributor to Tod's . . . sloppiness?"

"I'm thinking yes. Not sure when I'll be free to check it out, though. The boss has got all of us hustling our asses off here. We are bringing some major cash into the company."

"It's all just one big fucking Ponzi scheme," Bennett growled. "Wen needs to bring new money in to plug the leaks he made and keep his old clients happy. The scam has to catch up with him sometime— these things always do."

"We can only hope. Now, I have a shitload of work to do. I'm gonna have to go."

"Keep digging, Valentina," Bennett said. "And good work."

Hanging up the call, Valentina couldn't help but smile; had she just been given a pat on the head by Interpol? She went back into one of the stalls, teased the SIM card out of its slot with steady fingers, and snapped it in half.

"Good work my ass," she growled as she dropped the ruined SIM card into the toilet bowl and hit the handle.

CHAPTER TWENTY-EIGHT

Valentina's run-in that morning with Wen's security chief gnawed at her more with every passing hour; if the guy had eyes on her, one careless move could easily thwart her plans. She hadn't thought herself prone to making mistakes, but if her short time in Hong Kong had taught her anything, it was how singular focus could slide, unnoticed, into tunnel vision. Hong Kong in print and online was one thing; Hong Kong in the real was an unknown quantity. And so, too, was the inevitable Mr. Shum.

She'd not been able to continue her dig into Wen's badly hidden files and look into Zhang's involvement in JM Wen Limited, as the sales office had filled up straight after the morning meeting and her colleagues had hit the phones to fix those all-important meetings for the remainder of the week. She was going to have to take her files back to her hotel and look at them on her personal laptop. As frustrating as that was, she welcomed the enforced normality of her job—it made for a nice change from subterfuge and explosions and sudden death and Kate Bennett.

Lucas had left Valentina very much to her own devices again. He and Wen had spent most of the day schmoozing a client at the luxurious Peninsular Spa. The place was highly exclusive, members only, and overlooked Victoria Harbor. It was the perfect magnet for the kind of money Wen was looking for. The deal for HK$900m had been done over hot stone massages and saunas, the client had been treated to a two-girl happy ending, Wen had come away satisfied with a day well spent, and Vaughn had returned to the office in a jovial mood. The rest of the day passed without incident, and the three closers to be included in the evening's work excused themselves to get ready for the event.

Evening was closing in to paint the dusk sky a gaudy salmon pink when a company limo picked up Valentina, Oliver, and Sofia from their hotel. It drove them a short way across town and deposited them at the door of Mr. K's karaoke bar.

The KTV bar, one of a chain owned by JM Wen Limited, and which occupied a prime spot in the Tsim Sha Tsui district, was a tony joint with door, drink, and food prices designed to keep out all but Hong Kong's most affluent and influential. The loud, rhythmic boom of music thrummed through the door as Valentina and her two colleagues made their way along the short red carpet that had been rolled out especially for Jimmy Wen's party; it wasn't every day the bar's owner and one of Hong Kong's most powerful businessmen paid a visit. The pair of tuxedo-clad, broad-chested doormen opened the bar's doors, and the cool, conditioned air from within slipped straight though the flimsy material of Valentina's dress to spread gooseflesh across her bare back.

Sofia and Oliver walked into the bar beside her. Sofia had clearly received Wen's briefing on the dress code too, as she wore a traditional little black dress, and wore it well; it stopped a good way above midthigh and was scooped so low at the front as to have her formidable breasts all but spilling out. On her feet were a pair of Gucci stiletto-heeled slingback sandals in black and silver in which she somehow contrived to move as if she'd been born in them. Valentina had opted for a departure from stiletto heels with a pair of Manolo Blahnik pumps in black, red, and white that boasted somewhat sturdier geometrically sculpted heels and an ankle strap. If she ended up spending most of the evening on her feet, schmoozing, she might as well be comfortable and less inclined to topple over if the place got rowdy. Oliver looked natty in khaki Armani slacks, a blood-red Lauren polo, and a white jacket—roll up the sleeves and the Brit would have been the spitting image of Don Johnson back in his *Miami Vice* days. Dashing, Valentina thought.

The room they stepped into was huge, high-ceilinged, and multi-leveled. To their right, along the front wall was a raised food bar and a scattering of small square tables, each with a top of deep blue tile. Half of the entire rear wall was taken up by a wet bar, the glasses and bottles on display backlit to great effect. It was fronted by a sunken grotto of seating groups laid out in a series of alcoves, each of which had a kidney-shaped sofa, a low oblong coffee table, and a handful of padded side chairs. Across from the bar in the opposite corner was the karaoke stage, fronted by an immense dance floor, also ringed with tables, some bar height, some standing height.

The cavernous room was dimply, dappled with shifting pools of light in blues and purples, with sprays of tiny white LEDs. Even in the deepest shadows, the decor glistened in a way that suggested diamonds or ice, but was probably just cheap mirror glass and glitter. Places like this felt rich and substantial in the half-light, but were often cheap and gaudy in the full fluorescents discreetly tucked up into the shadows. It amused Valentina to realize that the cleaning crew were probably the only people who saw Mr. K's for what it really was. There was a life lesson in there somewhere.

"Hey, Val, Sofia . . . Ollie!" Lucas Vaughn's inimitable Australian twang greeted Valentina as she and her colleagues stood taking in the room. He hove out of the dappled darkness, glass in hand and, taking Valentina's arm, he escorted them across to the bar. At one end of the long marble counter a HK$56k bottle of Dom Perignon Vintage 1998 sat in a gold ice bucket; the cork had been popped. Beside it sat what Valentina suspected was in Lucas's glass—a bottle of L'Art de Martell cognac. At HK$60k, he was at least going to get drunk in style.

The thought made Valentina uneasy. Surely, with a client of this magnitude who was still only a client in *potential*, Lucas ought to be as clearheaded as possible. Being drunk—or even lightly buzzed—in this situation put the deal (and possibly the company) in jeopardy. Especially with the sort of man she suspected Kim Yun-Fat to be.

"We've got the place to ourselves—for now, at least," Lucas said. "Jimmy booked out the whole bar to make sure our client feels every inch the VIP." He laughed and handed the three closers each a chilled flute of champagne. "Here's to Kim Yun-Fat." He clinked glasses with the others and downed his in one go.

Valentina took a tiny sip of her drink and looked around the sparsely populated bar. There were more hostesses—all scantily clad in minuscule shorts and crop tops that showed off their taut, perfectly tanned bellies—than patrons. Near the low stage, she recognized Lyn Song, who was surrounded by an entourage of a dozen or so.

"Come on over and I'll introduce you," Lucas said, following her gaze. "Lyn Song is quite the big deal over here. She's a personal friend of Jimmy's, and she's gonna make it *really* big in Hollywood."

He ushered Valentina and her colleagues across to where the movie star was immersed in conversation with a young man who was clearly her videographer, judging by the camera that hung from a strap from one shoulder. Song was making a dramatic show of poring over the endless karaoke listings on a large iPad.

Valentina shook hands with the starlet and the two exchanged pleasantries, although the performer appeared a little irritated that Valentina wasn't at all starstruck in her presence. The others fared better, as Lyn Song lapped up Sofia's gushing praise of her movie work, and Oliver charmed her with his refined British accent, exaggerated for her benefit.

Valentina left them all to it. While she was impressed to see that Wen had commandeered a movie star for the purposes of gaining Kim's respect, she was more interested in the presence of Shing Hai, whose name had turned up in Wen's secret files. The guy, seated thigh to thigh at the bar alongside a handsome young man in a tight, teal Armani T-shirt, was Hong Kong's premier financial influencer—one tweet from Shing Hai could easily make or break any one of the island's companies; Valentina would make a point of spending some time with him before the evening was out.

The front doors of the club opened and a flood of people flowed in. Startled by the sudden influx, Valentina studied the array of stunningly attractive young men and women as they made their way into Mr. K's. Each one was more beautiful than the last. They were part of Wen's stage setting to create a glittering, sexy party atmosphere, of course, and all had been lured by the opportunity to rub shoulders with the fabulously rich and influential *and* to party with the famous performer —they were also most likely hired hands. The bar's hostesses swarmed over, carrying trays teetering with champagne-filled flutes, tumblers cradling malt whiskey, and a mind-blowing array of wonderfully elaborate cocktails in glasses that were, themselves, works of art.

Soon the place was buzzing. Joining Valentina at the bar, Lucas noticed she was still nursing her champagne. He touched the side of her glass and made a face.

"Still on your first glass? What's wrong with you, girl? C'mon, that's gone warm and flat. Let's get you a refill."

She agreed but had no intention of doing more than sipping at it; she was still determined to keep a clear head for her meeting with Kim. Lucas, true to form, had the bartender toss the glass and bring another. He had just started in on harassing her to drink up when Lyn Song took to the small stage by the bar, much to the delight of the crowd of carefully selected revelers. The DJ had been the only one singing up to that point, since his job was to warm up the party, but now the stage was all Lyn Song's.

In what Valentina considered to be an obvious, carefully orchestrated PR exercise, Lyn Song launched into a pitch-perfect rendition of Joey Yung's "Pretty Crazy"; the irritatingly catchy Cantopop tune had become popular across Hong Kong, thanks to Ms. Yung being a local girl. Lyn Song's performance—complete with all the appropriate dance moves—was filmed by her videographer for the benefit of Ms. Song's millions of Instagram and Twitter followers, and any record producers who thought Lyn Song was just an actress.

Valentina lifted her champagne slightly in wry salute. *You win the karaoke. More power to you.*

Lucas's phone buzzed and he pulled it from his pocket to glance down at the bright screen before pocketing it again. "Right, you're on," he told Valentina. He nodded toward the doors, which opened once more to admit Jimmy Wen and Kim Yun-Fat.

The latter had a pretty young girl on each arm, neither of whom was his wife. He looked . . . tremendously uncomfortable. Wen, of course, was flanked by his ubiquitous bodyguards and looked every inch the high-powered financier.

"Go on. It's your chance to wow him. Make it count, Val." Lucas all but patted Valentina on the ass as he sent her on her way.

She struck out to where Wen and Kim, in sharp suits that contrasted with the casual-but-expensive garb of the crowd around them, stood looking about at the gleam and glitter of the place. She had to wend her way through the bevy of hostesses who'd scurried over to offer the executive and his guest their pick of beverages. Wen plucked a cognac from one of the trays, while Kim opted for a tall flute of champagne. He had to awkwardly disengage his hangers-on to retrieve it.

Valentina moved to stand in front of Kim and held out her hand. "Mr. Kim . . ."

"Miss Vittorio!" His face lit up in a beatific smile of recognition as he bowed over her hand. "I am delighted to see you again. May I say, you look lovely."

Valentina smiled, making immediate eye contact. "You may. Thank you. Please, call me Valentina."

Kim gave Wen an imploring look; the broker nodded and shooed the simpering escorts away. Valentina thought she saw something like relief in her client's dark eyes.

"I was teasing Valentina yesterday morning at breakfast," said Kim, "that having her fly all the way from New York just to meet with me in person was extraordinary client care. Do you indulge all of your clients with such a personal touch?"

"Only the most important ones, Mr. Kim," Wen flattered.

"I have always valued your company's business in New York," Valentina added, "so I was delighted to have the opportunity to meet with you here."

Kim took a step forward, positioning himself between Valentina and her boss. "May we talk, Valentina? Privately?"

His expression was not in the least flirtatious. Was he having second thoughts? What should she do if he was?

"Of course."

She allowed Kim to lead her away from Wen. Clearly, this was not a clumsy attempt at hitting on her. He seemed sincerely uneasy. She shot a look back at Wen; Lucas had wandered over to stand with his boss. The two were looking after her like the proud but concerned parents of a kindergartner in her first ballet recital. Lucas gave her a thumbs-up.

"I find I am still having reservations," Kim told her once they were out of Wen's earshot, "about signing over the shares."

And I'm sure this display of cheap ostentation doesn't help. Valentina studied the man's face. He was on the brink of bailing—this was hers to lose. A part of her wanted to lose, wanted to tell Kim Yun-Fat to turn tail and get as far away from JM Wen as he could. But she couldn't do that for any number of reasons.

"Are you no longer interested in expanding Green Dynamics Construction to the mainland?"

"I am still interested," Kim replied. "But perhaps this is not the right way."

"You need to raise a substantial amount of money in order to expand, though. A stock loan is an ideal way to do that. Your shares—"

"My company's shares. If the board discovers I have used them in this way, even to further the interests of the company, there will be trouble. And with the political unrest on the island . . ."

"Mr. Kim." Valentina stepped closer to him, putting a hand gently on the cool silk sleeve of his suit. She knew full well what the gesture would look like to her two watchers. "The Chinese are going to exert their authority over Hong Kong sooner or later—there is an inevitability to that. You are not wrong to recognize it."

He met her gaze, his own solemn. "Then you understand my hesitation?"

"I do," Valentina empathized. "But I know you want your mainland projects to be successful, and I know you think they're currently under-funded. What would it mean for your company if the expansion should fail due to a lack of sufficient funding?"

She could see Kim was beginning to question his own indecision; he wasn't truly worried about what the Chinese government thought—there probably wasn't an official he couldn't buy off if he chose to—his main fear was getting caught misappropriating company shares, for any reason.

Valentina stepped a little closer, pitching her voice as low as she could, given the hubbub in the room. "A successful expansion into mainland China will attract more money into your company and increase its standing in both Hong Kong and China. Surely, that can only ever be a good thing, Mr. Kim."

Kim fell silent.

Valentina followed suit—the power of silence was one of the first sales techniques she had been taught: Let the client walk through your arguments. It wasn't lost on her that this was the second cousin of what Shum had tried to do to her earlier in the day. In this case, she didn't want Kim to panic, but to consider her arguments. She watched his face while, in her peripheral vision, Lyn Song continued her energetic performance. It occurred to Valentina to wonder just how much in Wen's pocket the starlet was to be shaking her trim little ass up on stage at a private party. Was there something useful there, perhaps?

Kim broke the standoff. "I could still go to one of the banks."

Valentina gave him her full attention. "You could, Mr. Kim, but no bank will give you the seventy-five percent that JM Wen is offering. Nor will any other lender. The deal you have on the table with us right now is the best you'll find in Hong Kong, and the sooner you have the loan in hand, the sooner you can concentrate on breaking ground on those mainland construction projects. May I ask you one more question, Mr. Kim?"

"Of course." Kim's eyes remained fixed upon hers; most other men would have been staring at her breasts.

She gave his arm a subtle squeeze. "How much money do you

really need? To cover construction, business expenses, and . . . *other* expenditures?"

"I don't understand," he started to say, then hesitated. "You suspect I have expenses of a personal nature that I wish to cover?"

"There are always personal expenses involved in such big undertakings, Mr. Kim," she said. "And it's a common failing that clients ask for less than they actually need. I would hate for you to come back to the table for more money to find we can no longer honor the percentage against collateral on offer."

Kim's head lifted, and a spark of anger glinted in his eye. "You are correct, Miss Vittorio. I am asking for less than I feel we need, but you are wrong about my intent. I would never appropriate the company's assets for my own personal use. Rather, I am concerned that in expanding our facilities to the mainland, my board has accepted the suggestion that we need not build to the safety standards we would adhere to here or in Europe. I refuse to cut corners on materials. Perhaps that stance seems . . . naive or misguided."

Valentina gritted her teeth, cursing her own cynicism. "No, sir. It seems"—she took a deep breath—"let's just say it's the best reason I've heard in some time for taking this step. How much do you think you'll need to make sure Green Dynamics doesn't expand on the cheap?"

After a moment more of silently holding her gaze, Kim nodded almost imperceptibly. "Two billion," he said. "But that is all of the shares I have at my disposal. If the board finds out—"

"They won't," Valentina reassured him. She had no guarantee of that; a deal of this magnitude would be a lifeline to Wen, and he wouldn't let Kim's fear of his board get in the way of a HK$2 billion deal. But she would do her damndest to make sure that Wen didn't pull one of his loan scams on Kim Yun-Fat. "You have my promise that I will personally keep a close eye on your portfolio. Your shares will be safe." She had no guarantee of that either, but she held out a hand and he took it, seeming to unwind slightly.

"Thank you, Miss . . . Valentina."

She had brought herself back from exile in the realm of icy politeness. "Mr. Wen has the contracts for you to sign; he'll be more than happy to increase the loan to meet your requirements."

The deal done, Kim and Valentina moved back to where Wen and Lucas were standing, pretending not to watch.

"So, what do you think of the strife in Hong Kong, Valentina?" Kim's attempt at post-deal small talk seemed inappropriately somber for the environs. "The protestors are petrol-bombing the police now—do people do that in New York?"

Valentina shook her head. "We New Yorkers aren't known for our mild manners, but no, we haven't started throwing Molotov cocktails at the NYPD just yet." She gave Kim a half smile and resisted the urge to tug at the hem of her skimpy dress.

"Speaking of cocktails . . ." Shing Hai leaned into the group over Valentina's shoulder; he'd left his handsome young companion at the bar. "I was promised a Mandarin Oriental—gold flakes in champagne and Remy Martin! I hope it's worth the hundred-fifty-thousand-dollar price tag. It's *so* good to see you again, Mr. Wen." He thrust out a hand in Wen's direction.

Wen shook the influencer's hand as the two played out what Valentina was certain was a carefully scripted, preplanned encounter. "Likewise—and may I introduce you to Kim Yun-Fat?"

"Of course." Shing shook Kim's hand and gave him a reptilian smile. "I'm told Green Dynamics Construction is really going places."

"With help from JM Wen Limited," Wen interjected. "Mr. Kim is seeking investment to develop many properties on the mainland."

"Then you are in exceptionally good hands, Mr. Kim," Shing gushed as he relieved himself of the handshake. "You know JM Wen Limited is one of the largest institutional investors and lenders on the island?" The question was rhetorical; had Wen not already given Kim that impression, he wouldn't be here. "With my reputation at stake, I don't endorse many funding platforms, as you know. I've not only done so for Mr. Wen, but I've also referred people to him. I must tell you that every single one has been more than happy with the outcome."

"You flatter us, Mr. Shing." Wen's faux modesty was most convincing. He turned to Kim. "One post from this guy can have a company's shares skyrocketing practically overnight; social media is so critical in today's marketplace—remember that we live in a time when a second-rate rapper like 50 Cent can grow or destroy a company's shares with a single tweet."

Kim nodded, his smile *pro forma*. The so obviously stage-managed conversation amused Valentina; Kim appeared unimpressed. Tapping a finger rhythmically against the stem of his glass, he turned to look over his shoulder at the movie star who was singing her heart out up on the stage. Valentina smiled. His deal done, he seemed to have tuned Wen and Shing out. Lyn Song was onto the repetitive refrain of her song, and as the music faded away, she jumped down from the stage to rapturous applause from around the bar.

"There'll be time to talk business later," Wen cut into Shing's flattering pitch to grab Kim's attention. "I must introduce you to Lyn Song —are you a fan of hers at all?"

"Our whole family enjoys her performances. Though my daughter is her biggest fan and will tell anyone who asks that this is so. I'm sure I must have mentioned that to you, Mr. Wen."

Of course, he'd mentioned it; that likely was the sole reason the starlet had been invited to Wen's party. Suddenly grinning like some giddy, starstruck teenager, Kim Yun-Fat followed Wen across the room to the stage, where Song's audience and entourage parted to allow them through.

Left to her own devices, Valentina wandered to the bar, procured a tall club soda with lime syrup and a twist, and found a small round table next to the stage from which to watch a succession of people embarrass themselves to a variety of popular tunes. Sofia Reller and Oliver Michaels performed a rendition of "Paradise by the Dashboard Light," even though neither of them could carry a tune in a bucket. Lucas's unique rendition of Neil Diamond's "Cracklin' Rosie" didn't sound half as dreadful as Valentina imagined it would.

Over the next hour or so, the party degenerated into a drunken rabble set to music. The hostesses engaged the revelers in drinking games while others sang—mostly badly. Their creative use of a Yahtzee-style dice game had the crowd slugging back expensive cognac and whiskey shots, champagne, and imported beers. The bar overflowed with raucous laughter and loud music that—in combination with the room's shifting light—was starting to make Valentina's head hurt. The hostesses maintained their decorum as a bunch of hot young couples dirty danced on the polished wood of the dance floor by the stage. She marveled that, in all the chaos, no expensive drinks were toppled from their precariously balanced trays. It was like watching a wild ballet.

Valentina sat at her little table watching the people around her in the dim, glittering room, sipped her way through several more club sodas, and pondered a trip to the ladies room. It seemed to her that only she and the movie star were making any effort to remain sober. Mr. Kim had left earlier, clutching an autographed photo and a Lyn Song EP. Valentina wondered how well she'd be able to keep her promise to him to protect his shares without tipping her hand. She might be able to drop some veiled hints on Lucas.

"Just your typical Hong Kong Tuesday night!"

As if she'd summoned him, Lucas appeared at her side, making her jump, nearly spilling her drink. The guy's eyes were glazed, his speech slurred, and he had one arm around the tiny, exposed waist of a bar hostess. "You having fun, Val?"

"Oh, I'm having a *great* time."

He tried to focus on her tall glass of clear, fizzy club soda. "You're not drinking?"

"I'm pacing myself." Valentina rocked gently to the music as she spoke. "I'm really not a big drinker. Don't much care for the taste of alcohol." A lie. She loved the flavor of good beer and dark rum, but she was still more enamored of being clearheaded and in control of herself and her surroundings.

Lucas laughed. "I guess it'll be good to have one of us not hungover in the morning. Glad it's you and not me, though, Val." He gave the hostess's bare midriff a squeeze and she giggled on his shoulder.

"I take it Mr. Kim signed his paperwork before he left." She doubted Jimmy Wen would be wearing that cat-eat-cream smile if he hadn't. She glanced past Lucas at the plush, sunken seating area of the bar where Jimmy Wen was surrounded by a bevy of young hostesses and a selection of the prettiest patrons. Holding forth on something, glass raised, smile big and bright, the man was in his element.

"Hell, yeah!" Lucas said with feeling. "You did good reeling him in; he's bringing a hell of a lot of shares to the table. Jimmy is impressed."

"I just hope we'll be able to return Mr. Kim's shares with a good profit." She gave him what she hoped was a significant *look*. "Does your little friend speak English?"

Lucas glanced down at the girl. "Not a word. Why?"

"Are Mr. Kim's shares safe?"

Lucas frowned. "Why wouldn't they be? Where's this going?"

"I personally assured him that his shares are safe. I'd hate to be made a liar. I know that sometimes brokerages . . . get itchy trigger fingers when a client's shares are trading high."

His smile suddenly twitchy, Lucas glanced away. "Why would you think Wen would—"

"I've heard rumors."

He shrugged and said, "Well, *fuggedaboutem*. Kim's a friend of Jimmy's." He flashed a smile. "You did good, Val my gal."

Valentina thanked Lucas with a tight smile as Oliver and Sofia made up an absurdist version of "Another Brick in the Wall." Valentina found Lucas's reassurances as hollow as his praise; she'd done little that night but look like a whore, misjudge a client, and come damn close to losing the deal as a result. And unless she could find a way to stop it, it seemed likely that Kim Yun-Fat's shares would be sucked into the big, black hole of Jimmy Wen's Ponzi scheme.

Valentina found herself fighting a sudden, unwelcome surge of hot anger. A rude observation leapt to the tip of her tongue. She bit it back and jumped as her new purse vibrated. She'd kept it close all night for fear of someone stealing it—it *was* a Hermès Verrou, after all—and now she was beginning to wish she'd left the thing at the hotel. She unzipped the bag and peered inside.

Shit. The burner phone was lit up and buzzing.

"You okay, Val?" A flicker of concern crossed Lucas's rugged features.

Valentina fought to compose herself . . . and a decent lie. "Yeah. It's my mom. She doesn't understand the time difference between here and New York." She gave Lucas and his giggling consort a weak smile and excused herself, grabbing her drink.

Despite her situation, Valentina couldn't help but crack a wry smile; she was spending far too much time in public restrooms—at least it was relatively quiet in here, peppy restroom muzak notwithstanding. There were a handful of pretty young things preening in the restroom's mirrors, gossiping excitedly between themselves and sharing long lines of finely cut cocaine. So that's what kept them on their feet.

All but one of the stalls was occupied; Valentina slipped inside, locked the door, and was confident neither of the stalls on either side contained anyone who knew her; Sofia had been immersed in conversation with one of Lyn Song's handsome assistants, who'd had the Cheshire-cat grin of a young man who very much fancied his chances of getting laid.

Kicking the lavatory seat down with her foot, Valentina rested her glass on the cistern, sat herself down, and pulled the buzzing burner phone from her purse.

"What the fuck, Katie?" She struggled to keep her annoyance to a low hiss. "It's after midnight. Do you have any idea where I am?" It was a naive question; of course the Interpol agent knew precisely where she was.

"So, I'm Katie now, am I? An old but annoying friend, apparently. Yes, I'm well aware of the time, Valentina. Obviously, I wouldn't be calling you if it wasn't important."

"Okay. Speak."

"Stay away from Zhang Bo." The agent's tone was grim.

"Seriously?" Valentina growled. "*You* pointed me in his direction, remember, and I've already found where—where he's been hiding."

"It's Wen we're after right now," Bennett reminded her. "I'm confident we can get enough on him—with your help—without you getting involved with the likes of Zhang. We can't afford to risk more lives, Valentina."

Valentina closed her eyes. She sucked in a long, whistling breath and focused her mind on the music that thumped from on high. Bennett had deliberately dangled Zhang's name in front of her when they'd first met, and now she was backpedaling?

"What the hell is going on, Katie?" Valentina kept her voice low, although she was being deliberately vague, and the ambient noise in the restroom was doing a great job of masking her conversation. "Am I in trouble here?"

Bennett took her time to reply. "Nothing immediate," she said. "But you must stay out of Zhang's way; he's a dangerous individual who wouldn't think twice about having you . . . *removed* if he thought you were a threat."

The euphemism made Valentina's skin crawl. "I'm sure I'll be just fine." She terminated the call with a jab of her thumb. "The man isn't even here," she grumbled for her own benefit as she unclipped the battery, slid out the SIM card, and snapped it in half.

Standing up, Valentina lifted the toilet seat and was about to flush the card when she saw the bowl was blocked by thick wads of paper and a used panty liner.

"Fuck!" she said a little too loudly.

"You okay, lady?" A concerned voice spoke in faltering English and sounded far too young.

"Yeah. Fine." Looking around the cramped stall, Valentina could see only one realistic solution to her dilemma. She popped the SIM card—one half at a time—into her mouth, and swilled it down with a hearty swig of room temperature club soda.

Upon exiting the stall, Valentina took a few minutes to compose herself, wash her hands, and check her flawless makeup in the mirror. Then, she straightened her tiny dress and returned to the bar just in time to see Zhang Bo stride into Mr. K's bar like he owned the place.

CHAPTER TWENTY-NINE

Valentina sensed the subtle shift in the energy of the large room. The drunken debauchery, the games, the off-key singing, and ever-accommodating hostesses were still continuing, but now with an underlying hint of tension.

"Where the hell were you?" Lucas appeared by Valentina's side, a worried frown knitting his brow. He'd ditched the hot little hostess and had slipped with ease back into professional mode.

"I was in the restroom."

"You took your time."

"Really, Lucas? You're timing me? I completed my assignment for the evening." She shot a pointed glance at his near-empty whiskey glass. "What is that, your fifth?"

He blushed rose red, his eyes still on Zhang Bo and his quartet of bodyguards as he made his way through the crowd. "Sorry, Val. We didn't need this guy turning up tonight—Jimmy's gonna stress the fuck out over this."

"So, what's his deal with Zhang?" Valentina fished. "I thought the guy was bad news."

Lucas shrugged. "He's that all right—nothing but trouble. We'd better get to Jimmy—make a show of force and all that. Come on, Val, looks like we're on again." He drained his drink in one and sat the glass down on the closest table.

Valentina and Lucas made their way across the bar to the seating area—which was suddenly all but empty—stepping down into the plush grotto just as Zhang Bo shooed away Jimmy's little group of hangers-on. The Triad leader sat himself down in a chair kitty-corner to Wen as if arriving for a dinner date. His bodyguards stayed close by; they exchanged courteous nods with Lau and Pang, who stood behind Wen's alcove up on the bar level.

Lucas halted at the bottom of the carpeted steps, and Valentina saw no reason to venture further. She watched in horrid fascination as Zhang sat back in his chair and fixed Jimmy Wen with an unreadable gaze.

"Lyn Song seems to be enjoying herself very much," Zhang observed, nodding to where Oliver Michaels was deep in conversation with the movie star; he appeared smitten. "You know I have big plans for her in America?"

Wen smiled. "I've heard she's going to be bigger than Ming-Na Wen, Jet Li, and Jackie Chan put together. Especially with your backing, Bo."

Well, that sounded friendly. If it weren't for the slight quiver of apprehension in Wen's voice and the sudden glisten of perspiration on his upper lip, Valentina might have believed that smile.

"Without a doubt. But launching a new star in Hollywood is not cheap." He looked Wen in the eye. "Which is why I need my shares . . . and I need them yesterday."

Wen shifted uneasily in his seat but still managed to maintain an unruffled facade—one arm lying along the back of the kidney-shaped sofa, the other resting on the ankle of a negligently crossed leg; this was obviously a game he'd played countless times before. Valentina had to wonder if he'd ever had an adversary as dangerous as Zhang Bo.

"Your shares are climbing even higher than we'd anticipated, which is why I have been reluctant to trade them right now. In fact, I think it would be foolish to—"

Zhang narrowed his gaze. "I am well aware of their worth, Jimmy.

I would like to take advantage of their high valuation while the market is strong."

Jimmy wagged his head like an old sage. "I can assure you everything is going incredibly well. If you are patient, you can expect another ten points on the price, maybe even fifteen."

"I think I have been more than patient with you, Jimmy, don't you?" Zhang sat forward in his seat and clasped his hands between his knees. "You promised me the shares three weeks ago, and yet here I am, reduced to begging like a child. I find I do not like being treated like a child."

Wen looked over to where Lucas and Valentina stood frozen at the edge of the seating area. He raised a hand to beckon Lucas over.

"Shit," the Aussie mumbled, but he went.

Valentina debated following him but decided against it. She stayed put.

Zhang stood as Lucas approached, honoring him with a handshake. "It is good to see you again, Mr. Vaughn," Zhang said, as if he had not subtly threatened the other man—dear God, was it only days ago?

"Good to see *you* again, Mr. Zhang." Lucas faked a smile and pumped the gangster's hand.

Zhang peered over his shoulder at Valentina. A raised chin was the extent of her reaction, notwithstanding a deep urge to turn and run. Zhang gave her the ghost of a smile before turning back to Wen and Lucas.

"I was just saying how well Bo's shares are doing," Wen prompted, too urgently.

"And then some," Lucas said with a confident smile as he seated himself next to Wen on the sofa.

Zhang retook his chair and scooted it a bit closer to the coffee table, effectively trapping Wen on his end of the sofa. He'd have to slip past the gang lord or crawl over Lucas if he wanted to leave in a hurry. Valentina recognized the tactic. She'd employed it herself from time to time. Make the target feel physically trapped and you don't have to say anything openly threatening. The sense of powerlessness does at least half the work.

Lucas was soldiering on cheerfully: "Golden Harvest and Asia Lion Entertainment are doing especially well in the Hong Kong market. In fact, the performance of these stocks has taken us by surprise."

Lucas's words triggered a thunderclap in Valentina's head. Was that the reason for all the cold sweats and the influx of big-hitters and the panicked recruitment of more clientele like the gullible Mr. Kim? Had Jimmy Wen *sold* Zhang Bo's shares out from under him, expecting to buy them back at a profit to himself? The word that leapt to mind was one Valentina did not often associate with this level of asset management: harebrained. If Zhang was what she knew him to be—hell, if he was *half* that—Jimmy Wen was playing with . . . well, fire didn't even begin to cover it. This wasn't just risky behavior; it was a freaking pathology.

"They are all destined to do much better, of course," Wen was saying. "You can expect a massive payout when you sell them."

"I *expected* my payout three weeks ago," Zhang said tonelessly. "Past tense."

"Bo, it takes time to pull out such large quantities of money and shares," Wen said. "Not only would it tank the share's prices to pull them out precipitously, but it would more than likely attract the attention of the regulators. You will agree, that is attention neither of us can afford."

Zhang eased back into his chair, his expression hooded. "Leave the SFC to me. Whatever happens, and whether you are being transparent or lying through your teeth, you have until the end of the week. This Friday, I shall expect to have my shares—are we clear?"

Wen smiled and made a casual gesture, lifting his hand from the back of the sofa and turning it palm up. "Abundantly. I will return the shares regardless of their value."

In a heartbeat, Wen was all smiles once again. He looked up to where Valentina watched as if mesmerized and beckoned her over. She moved on autopilot, her mind still grappling with her epiphany.

Zhang got gracefully to his feet and greeted Valentina with a firm handshake. "Miss Vittorio, it is a pleasure to see you again."

"Mr. Zhang," Valentina said as the Triad boss scrutinized her. Again she felt the need to tug at the hem of her dress.

"You are wasted in finance, Miss Vittorio." There was something about the way Zhang enunciated her name that had Valentina thinking of Kate Bennett. "You are really quite beautiful."

"I'll try to take that as a compliment. But I must protest that I'm smarter than I am pretty and have what I've been told is a very unfeminine appreciation for numbers. I'm good at everything I do—I believe we should all exploit our talents to the fullest." She shifted one bare shoulder to underscore the play on words.

"I do love American candor," Zhang replied with an appreciative smile. "Are you available for further entertainment this evening?"

Valentina glanced across at Wen, and was more shocked at the expectant look on his face than Zhang's request. This wasn't the first time she'd been propositioned by a client, and Zhang Bo certainly wasn't the only powerful (and attractive) man she'd ever come across who was used to getting absolutely everything he wanted. But the fact that Wen clearly expected her to prostitute herself in the interests of whatever business dealings he had with the gangster had raised her hackles.

Valentina smiled. "This morning, you mean? It's a very kind offer, Mr. Zhang, and tempting. But I think I shall have to decline on this occasion. I do have to find it in me to work tomorrow—or rather, later today."

Wen came to his feet, his face dark with fear or anger or both. "I think what Miss Vittorio means is . . ."

Zhang waved a hand to silence him, and for the first time, Valentina saw the great Jimmy Wen put firmly in his place. Zhang cracked a smile that went all the way to his eyes. "You have some real balls, Valentina. I admire that in a woman." His eyes lingered on her long, bare legs as he spoke.

"Ovaries," she said. "What I have is some real ovaries."

Smile deepening, Zhang held out his hand for the shaking. "Mr. Wen is a lucky man to have such an employee."

"Yes he is." Valentina shook the Triad leader's hand and, studying his face, saw no hint of menace in his dark brown eyes.

"I hope we will meet again soon. And I hope that we will do business together." Zhang let go of Valentina's hand and turned to go.

"I should be honored." Valentina uttered the words, knowing they begged the question of whether she actually was honored. She didn't want to think about what kind of business Zhang Bo might want to do with her.

As Zhang's bodyguards took their places at his sides, he turned his attention once more to Wen. "I shall see *you* on Friday, Jimmy. Do enjoy the rest of your evening."

CHAPTER THIRTY

Zhang Bo's unexpected appearance at the karaoke bar had put a tangible damper on Wen's spirits, and essentially ended their night out. Lyn Song and her entourage had withdrawn unobtrusively during the Triad leader's visit; once Wen realized that, he announced it was time to leave. He had Lucas and Valentina round up Sofia and Oliver and ordered the valet to bring the car to the front of the bar.

Unpleasantness notwithstanding, as soon as Lau was behind the wheel with Pang at his side, Wen had Lucas crack open a bottle of champagne.

Wen proposed a toast as the car pulled away and made its way along the quiet Tsim Sha Tsui streets. "To the conclusion of a good night's business, and to Valentina for bringing Mr. Kim our way."

Glasses chinked as the group knocked back chilled champagne, and, although the sentiment seemed a tad hollow, Valentina thought Wen had perked up considerably in the aftermath of his discussion with Zhang. Jimmy Wen, she surmised, was a cockeyed optimist by dint of the fact that he simply refused to believe that conventional wisdom or other people's rules or reality itself applied to him. She wryly acknowledged that, in that way, he reminded her of someone she'd grown up with: her father. But her father had never displayed such a lack of empathy. He'd cared, desperately, about his family and friends. He'd understood loyalty and practiced it. But like Jimmy Wen, he'd been a risk-taker. Another essential difference between the two men was that Jimmy Wen risked other people's money, not his own.

Lucas refilled his glass. "Mr. Kim left us a very happy man indeed; an unbelievable loan against his company shares *and* the acquaintance of a movie star—what more could a man of his stature ask for?" He downed his drink in one and gave Valentina a sly wink.

Valentina gave Lucas a half smile and nursed her champagne, realizing that—aside from Lau and Pang, she was the only person in the party who was stone-cold sober. She might, she thought wryly, be the only one who showed up at work today before one p.m.

She had turned her head to look out at the quiet streets when the limo bucked like a bronco, sending champagne and glasses into the air. The air was filled with the sounds of breaking glass and rending steel as the left side of the car bowed suddenly inward as if punched by a giant's fist. Hurled out of her seat, Valentina tumbled to the floor atop Oliver and Lucas while Sofia screamed hysterically. The limo continued its sideways slide. Small chunks of safety glass rained on the occupants from the limo's shattered windows.

"What the fuck is happening?" Wen shrieked at his bodyguards as the car slammed to an abrupt stop with its front end half inside a small but swank organic grocery.

"We've been hit! *Everybody get down!*" The agony in Pang's voice was apparent as he stated the obvious: They'd been T-boned.

Beside him, Lau slumped, motionless, over the steering wheel with blood pouring from a long, ragged gash in his temple. The sharp, acrid stink of gasoline filled the car.

The fuel tank. Self-preservation kicked in, and Valentina extricated herself from the flailing arms and legs of the two men beneath her. Escape—that was the first order of business. Ensure a means of escape. She reached for the door handle on the uncrushed side of the car and caught a movement through the shattered window. A dark figure darted around to the front of the car. Valentina followed the movement, aware that Pang, still trying to free himself from his seat belt, had seen it too. He stopped jabbing at the seat belt lock and pulled his gun from its holster. He was too late: A pair of powerful arms reached in through the side window; two huge, gloved hands grasped his head.

"No!" Pang's yelp was silenced by a swift twist of his head; the sharp, wet snap of his neck breaking filled the car.

Adrenaline shot through Valentina in an icy flood. She levered the door handle and heaved a shoulder against the warped door.

Once.

Twice.

On the third shove, the limo's door opened with an ear-splitting screech, and Valentina toppled out onto the cool sidewalk. She pulled herself into a crouch behind the car door and looked around.

To her left, the dark recesses of the upscale bodega were slashed by the flickering light of the wrecked limo's headlights. To her right, about ten feet from the rear of the limo, four black-clad men stood in the glow of the streetlamp and moonlight. All wore ski masks. She saw no drawn guns, but at least two were armed with aluminum baseball bats. Behind them was a huge black Hummer. Its wide, chrome bull bar was dented, scratched, and smattered with paint scraped from the wrecked side of Wen's car.

Valentina sucked in air and swung herself around to the other side of the door, putting it between herself and the sinister quartet. If the thugs had seen her there, quivering in her little black dress, they made no move to harm her. They didn't move at all until Oliver and Lucas clambered out onto the sidewalk and made the mistake of standing.

The gangsters were on them in seconds.

Valentina shot to her feet and was swiftly felled by a hard shot to her back that drove the wind from her lungs. She sprawled on the ground, catching her breath, listening to the chaos around her. Training and reflex kicked in; Valentina knew she had to keep the chaos out of her head.

Think, Tina. You need to act. You need to do something.

But what, and to whom?

She played possum for a moment and centered herself, ignoring the soft, sickening thud of metal against flesh as two of the black-clad thugs set about Oliver and Lucas with a baseball bat and what she thought might be a billy club. She turned her head toward the rear of the car but couldn't see them. What she saw was another of the attackers dragging Wen and Sofia from the car and dumping both roughly to the sidewalk.

Sofia screamed. The sound seemed to have been ripped from her throat, shrill and full of agony. She clutched at her belly with both hands, and Valentina realized the entire front of her dress glistened dark and wet with fresh blood. As if bored with Sofia, the thug turned away from her and swung his bat at Wen's stomach.

In his moment of inattention, Valentina got to her hands and knees and scrambled to Sofia's side.

"Sof, I'm going to get you out of the way," she whispered. She managed to get her hands under Sofia's armpits and pulled her several feet away from the car into the lee of the grocery's broken facade. She heard Jimmy Wen let out an agonized cry as he hit the sidewalk. She shut the sounds out and concentrated on Sofia.

A solid kick to her side bowled her over, forcing her to let go of the other woman. One of the gangsters loomed over her, bat raised to strike. She blinked up at him, struggling to catch her breath again. He hesitated. Astride her legs, he actually paused to give her a once-over as if in appreciation of her scantily clad body. She imagined the wolfish glint in his eyes and let her anger flare.

The best defense . . .

Valentina kicked straight upward with the pointed toes of her Blahnik pumps. She caught him just to the right of his balls. He roared and brought the bat down, more in reflex than intent. She was ready for that. With one swift motion, she grabbed at the bat before it could connect with her flank, cocked her leg, and went straight for his knee. He'd locked it, preparatory for the swing, and she punched it backward with a powerful kick that she meant with every fiber of her being.

The thug bellowed like a mad bull and crumpled to the sidewalk, his knee hyperextended, his leg useless. Valentina was on her feet in a second, in sole possession of the baseball bat. Without a moment's hesitation, she turned the guy's weapon on him and gave his head a sweeping knock worthy of an MLB designated hitter. He'd had no time to shield his head with his hands, and the bat connected with his skull in a wet, resounding crack.

One down.

With a glance at Sofia, Valentina turned her attention to the other three, all of whom were busy raining blows on Lucas and Oliver. She gave a splinter of thought to ditching her shoes, but realized how foolhardy that would be. Her Blahnik pumps easily qualified as a lethal weapon.

Seeing Valentina on her feet and wielding a bat, one of the thugs barked something in Cantonese, and his two colleagues converged on her, swinging. She ducked and thrust her own bat aloft. One weapon whooshed within an inch of her head, while the other crashed into her bat with a reverberating, metallic *clank*. The bat bucked painfully in Valentina's hands. She lost her grip and it spun away to hit the ground, bouncing and clattering into the middle of the street. Undeterred, Valentina jumped, twisted her body midair, and delivered a fiercely accurate roundhouse kick to the face of the nearest thug.

It became a one-two punch as first the toe, and then the sharp heel caught him in the nose and cheek. She felt the warm splatter of his blood against her bare leg, and he went down clutching his broken nose and torn cheek. As Valentina righted herself, the thug's colleague took another swing. This time, the bat connected with her shoulder.

Growling against the sharp pain that spread down her arm and into her chest, Valentina launched herself at the guy. Leaping high, she wrapped her arms and legs around his thick, muscular torso. This took him completely by surprise, and Valentina clung on tight as he staggered backward and crashed full force into the side of Wen's ruined limousine. The baseball bat, useless in a close fight, hit the ground as the thug unleashed a flurry of punches directly at Valentina's ribs to try to dislodge her.

Valentina tensed her muscles to take the punches, but still they hurt like hell. Straining her neck backward, and in the yellow glow of streetlights, for a brief moment, Valentina looked directly into the thug's cold, callous eyes. Then, snapping her head forward, Valentina slammed her forehead into the bridge of his nose. He let out a low, pained grunt, and his fists quit their pounding. Aiming lower, Valentina headbutted the guy again; this time, he let out a gurgling, bubbling groan as blood and shiny white shards of shattered teeth spilled from his mouth.

Someone grabbed her from behind, gloved fingers digging into her throat, jerking her backward, away from the thug. Not finished, she delivered a powerful parting kick, thanking God for the ankle strap that kept her shoes solidly on her feet. She had no idea where the blow landed. Her focus now was on loosing the death grip on her neck. She lashed backward with both feet, the sturdy heels of her pumps coming into sharp contact with her assailant's shins.

He bellowed and let go. She hit the sidewalk hard, head spinning, gulped in a deep breath, and started to roll to her feet when he was back, this time aiming a hard, angry kick at her. He caught her in the thigh, sending her tumbling. She tried to regain her feet, but her legs threatened to betray her. Instead, she rolled over onto her back. Her skimpy dress, torn and dirty now, rode high to flash the matching silk panties that had cost Jimmy Wen a small fortune. The thug came at her again, pausing to retrieve his buddy's abandoned baseball bat, tapping it against the palm of his hand and chuckling like a bad B-movie villain.

"Are you kidding me?" Valentina rasped. "How many cheesy gangster movies have you watched, Jasper?"

"Bitch," he replied and kept coming, slowly, inexorably.

No time to struggle to her feet, one leg all but numb, Valentina scuttled backward until she was pressed up against the rear wheel of the limo with the masked thug towering over her. He snarled something at her in Chinese and lifted the bat high.

"Bastard!" The roar came in Lucas's voice; it was accompanied by the dull, crunch of metal bat on skull. The thug standing over Valentina toppled sideways—bat still clutched in his hand—and hit the road with a stomach-churning smack.

Valentina hauled herself upright, using the limo for support and lurched toward Lucas, mouth open on words of gratitude. What came out was, "Behind you!"

Ignoring Lucas's bewildered look, she shoved him aside and went after the thug whose nose she'd smashed with her forehead. He'd rallied and was crawling on his hands and knees toward a gun that lay in the street just beyond the rear of the limo. She caught him with his hand outstretched, reaching for the weapon, lifted her good leg, and brought her foot down on the back of his neck, leading with the sharp, sturdy heel of her ruined Blahniks.

The thug's arms and legs crumpled beneath him, and he hit the blacktop face-first. He struggled to push himself up, but Valentina threw her weight onto that leg, digging the heel into his neck at the base of his skull, until the bones separated and the body convulsed. Valentina gasped and toppled backward. She landed on her ass next to him as he let out a final, rattling breath.

It took her a moment to grasp it: She'd broken a man's neck. Killed him.

For some reason, the realization conjured the specter of David—no, of Fan Chun-Sung—sitting across from her in a sketchy restaurant. Her lungs felt suddenly too small and she panted, trying to get air.

"We gotta go." Lucas stood next to her, holding out a hand to help her to her feet. "Reller's hurt bad; we need to get her to a hospital." He glanced over to where Sofia lay groaning softly against the broken wall of the grocery in a spreading pool of her own blood. Oliver knelt beside her; he'd stripped off his jacket and was holding it tight against her belly, from which protruded a jagged shard of dark glass from a broken champagne bottle.

The street lit up as two cars rounded the corner at the end farthest away. Valentina tensed and clenched her fists.

"It's backup," Lucas told her. "Jimmy called 'em. It's all right. We're safe."

She stared at him, incredulous. "Are we?"

The first car was identical to the limo that sat bowed and ruined among the spilled contents of the grocer's; black, long, dark windows —it made for an imposing sight as it sped along the empty street. The second, a black Aston Martin Volante, followed closely behind. The limo's harsh LED high beams illuminated the four fallen thugs as it screeched to a halt alongside its broken twin.

Valentina blinked in the glare. *I killed a man.*

Two of Wen's security guards leapt from the new limo the moment it stopped, while one remained behind the wheel. As Valentina followed Wen and Lucas into the back of the vehicle, the guards made their way over to Sofia. Carefully, they scooped her up from the street and carried her to the car. All the while, Oliver kept pressure on the wound with his blood-soaked jacket. Someone had extracted the glass shard and it lay, bloody, on the sidewalk, a dark slash amid the glittering remnants of the limo's windows.

Reaching the car, they laid her gently on the back seat with her head on Valentina's lap, and climbed in. Cradling Sofia's blood-smeared head, Valentina placed a hand on top of Oliver's and pressed hard on the jacket that was failing to stem the pulsing flow of blood from the wound. She stroked the hair away from Sofia's tear-stained face with a trembling hand and watched as the girl faded in and out of consciousness.

"Stay with me, Sofia," she murmured. "We're getting you to the hospital."

"Fucking step on it!" Oliver yelled at the driver. "She's dying back here!"

The limousine lurched, its tires squealed loudly on the blacktop, and it roared up the street.

"Hold on, Sofia!" Valentina urged desperately as the girl's eyes rolled so far back in their sockets that only the whites showed. "Don't you dare die on me—don't you fucking dare."

A bright golden light lit up the back window of the limo, making Valentina jerk her gaze upward to look back at the scene of the attack. The Hummer and the wrecked limo were both engulfed in flame. Against the fiery backdrop, a short, stocky figure stood in silhouette, holstering a handgun. After a beat, the man turned and strode toward the Aston Martin, which proceeded to follow the limo from which Valentina watched. A second later, a thunderous explosion shook the neighborhood as the gas tanks of the two burning vehicles exploded.

Now, finally, Valentina heard the plaintive cry of sirens.

CHAPTER THIRTY-ONE

To say the atmosphere in the sales office was subdued was an understatement. It was nine o'clock in the morning, and Jimmy Wen's little team of rainmakers were in and at their desks. All but one, that is. Wen and Lucas were ensconced in Wen's office and embroiled in a serious discussion that had Wen looking sweaty and frazzled—a state Valentina had never seen him in before. She studied them from across the office and didn't need to hear what they were saying to know they were reviewing the events of the night before.

"I can't believe it." A voice broke in to Valentina's thoughts.

She turned around. Daylen Ng stood in the aisle between their desks; his red-rimmed eyes suggested he'd spent most of the morning crying.

"I was only talking to Sofia yesterday," he said. "I just can't believe she's dead."

"Yeah, it's been a shock." Valentina didn't add that she'd spent most of the night and into the early hours at the hospital and talking to the police. That Sofia had bled to death in her arms. That it had been less than an hour since she'd finally been able to wash the Swiss girl's blood off her hands and discard the ludicrously expensive dress that she'd ruined fighting off the quartet of thugs hell-bent on beating the crap out of them. That she'd killed someone.

Nothing in her life, no years of research or calculation could have prepared her for any of this.

"Are carjackings common here?" Daylen asked Lam. "Are any of us safe?"

"It happens," Lam replied with a glance at Valentina. "Although never in the Tsim Sha Tsui district—at least not to my recollection."

Oliver wandered over from his desk, where he'd been sitting in quiet contemplation. He was limping, and winced with each step. The attack had left him battered and bruised, but thankfully without broken bones or internal damage. He nodded at Valentina, his smile pained. "You guys should have seen her. That was some seriously kick-ass scrapping back there. You saved our lives."

Valentina shrugged. "I was taught well," she replied. "My father insisted I learn how to defend myself when I was a kid, and I've had . . . some martial arts training—I guess it finally came in useful." She offered Oliver and the others a weak smile, wondering if, in designing those badass pumps, Manolo Blahnik had ever considered how they'd perform in a street fight.

Death by stiletto—heel, that is. Death with style. Killer pumps.

She cut off the aimless flow of twisted sarcasm with a will.

"It was amazing," Oliver continued. "She put three of the bad guys flat on their backsides all by herself—those bastards will think twice before attacking a limo again."

The thick glass door of the sales office closed with a hushed sigh behind Lucas Vaughn. With a sidewise glance at Wen, who appeared to have composed himself and was speaking calmly on his cell phone, Lucas beckoned Valentina over.

"If you'll excuse me," Valentina said to her colleagues. She was grateful for the distraction from Oliver's hero worship and didn't feel too much like the heroine of the piece. Nor did she relish perpetuating the carjack story Lucas had insisted she and Oliver stick to even as Sofia Reller gasped for her last breath. Making her way across the office, Valentina walked briskly by Anthony and Nadim; they sat quietly at their desks and didn't so much as lift their heads to acknowl-edge her.

Lucas greeted her with a lopsided smile. Half his face was swollen, bruised, and abraded—scraped raw where he'd come into conflict with the glass-littered asphalt. Both hands were bandaged, and she knew he was wearing protective brace around his rib cage. Even speaking seemed to be painful.

He ushered her to a quiet corner of the office, out of earshot of her colleagues and away from the prying eyes of the cameras. "How you holding up, Val?"

"I'm exhausted and sore here and there, but otherwise I'm okay," Valentina lied. "You took one hell of a beating last night."

"Nothing broken or busted. It could have been a whole fucking lot worse if you hadn't stepped in, though."

"Hey, you rescued my ass."

"You rescued mine first."

Valentina swallowed painfully. "D'you think they'd have *killed* all of us?"

Lucas shook his head. "If they'd wanted us dead, we'd be dead—that's why they weren't carrying guns. Sofia was hit by shrapnel from a broken champagne bottle, if you can wrap your mind around that. They didn't mean for her to die. This was a warning. A really agonizing warning."

"From Zhang Bo?"

Lucas visibly recoiled at the sound of the Triad boss's name. His eyes flicked across to Valentina's colleagues, and then toward Wen's office. "Considering his unexpected appearance at the bar last night, I'd say that was a safe bet. It's important we keep a lid on this, Val. You guys stick to the carjack story we discussed and it'll blow over soon enough."

Valentina's skin prickled at the sheer callousness. "Sofia *died*, Lucas. That's not going to blow over. And how the fuck can you be so blasé about the whole thing? What if the police don't believe our story?"

Lucas shook his head. He looked suddenly years older. "I didn't mean to sound callous. But here's the reality: The police will believe what they are paid to believe."

"Meaning?"

"Meaning . . . the Triads run the island, and when they have business to attend to, law enforcement knows to make themselves scarce."

She stared at him for a moment as the wee morning hour's events tumbled into place. "That's why there were no cops around last night." She'd thought it odd at the time; in New York, a car wreck of that magnitude would have had the street swarming with police cruisers and possibly even FBI agents within minutes. Not to mention a theater's worth of looky-loos.

"Or witnesses," Lucas added. "The street was empty, which is rare, even for that time of night. If I'd been sober, I'd've likely noticed that. It had all the hallmarks of a Triad hit."

That fact hadn't escaped Valentina's notice—it made sense Zhang would instruct the police to clear the area and keep a respectful distance. Maybe now was the time for a little digging, while Lucas was vulnerable.

"I don't understand why Zhang would need to send us a message like that," she said. "If his shares are increasing in value and the stock is doing so well in Wen's hands . . ." She paused to look up and meet his gaze. "Unless, of course, there's something I don't know about Wen's dealings with the Triads?"

Lucas's eyes shifted ever so slightly up and to the left as he lied to Valentina. "We have no idea, Val. Maybe the guy has got his wires crossed—Mr. Wen is doing everything in his power to ensure Zhang Bo gets the biggest possible return on his shares. Some clients just get impatient."

"Last night was more than impatience, Lucas," Valentina pressed. "What the fuck is going on? Does it have anything to do with Wen's push to bring in the big money?"

Lucas's face paled beneath its bruises and abrasions, and all hint of friendliness evaporated from his eyes in an instant. He lowered his voice so it was barely a low grumble. "You need to quit asking so many goddamn questions, Val. You've had a taste of what those people can do, and you'd be best taking something away from that. Keep your nose out of what doesn't concern you and get back to business."

Of course, Valentina couldn't tell Lucas that it did concern her now—very much so, all thanks to Kate Bennett . . . and Sofia Reller. She returned his suddenly icy gaze with one of her own. "Understood."

She started to return to her desk, but he caught at her arm, making her wince. She turned back to fix him with a stony stare.

The grim menace had left his eyes and he tried to smile. "I'm sorry. I'm tired and I hurt and my brains feel like scrambled egg. You look pretty bushed yourself; it was a long night."

"And a deadly one. Don't worry, Lucas, I'll get my second wind after an espresso or two. It's not the first time I've pulled an all-nighter. It was, however, the first time I've been almost murdered in a gangland hit, killed another human being with a pair of designer shoes—or, hell, killed another human being at all—and had someone I worked with die in my arms. It's like Capone's fucking Chicago out there. Hong Kong only looks like a modern, first-world metropolis. Scratch the surface and it's just a bad D-grade gangster movie."

She swung back around and limped back to her desk, her back ramrod straight.

"Hey," he called after her. "Don't mince words, Vittorio. Tell me what you *really* think."

"Fuck off," she told him, but smiled, pretending it was in jest.

As she downed cups of strong black coffee from the cheery little faux café and tried to flog her floundering brain to life, she got a text on her phone from an unknown number.

Take care, it said. That was all. She stared at it. Bennett? Chrissy—was there any hope she was still alive? She shook herself and set the phone aside. Now was the time to focus. Her calendar for the day included a hustle on Jimmy Wen's yacht that afternoon. She'd been looking forward to it, until last night. After last night, Valentina found it difficult to raise any enthusiasm for business as usual.

CHAPTER THIRTY-TWO

By eleven, the tiger team's section of the sales office was deserted, save for Valentina. Each of her colleagues had been summoned for individual meetings with the partners mentoring them, and Valentina got the impression it was more about taking their minds off Sofia than business imperatives. Sofia's partner-mentor was closeted in her office with the door closed.

Lucas was in yet another solemn conference with Wen, so Valentina took a chance on delving into the hidden files—specifically those she thought might have Zhang Bo's name attached. She was taking a hell of a risk, but having met the Triad and being on the receiving end of his brutal business practices, Valentina didn't want to waste any more time in digging up what she could. Bennett would be getting impatient for something more substantial, and Valentina had no illusions about the fact that time was running out for Jimmy Wen.

Valentina pulled up a couple of legit client files and a global stock exchange website, fired up the VPN and proxy software on her laptop, inserted the SD card, and followed the route to the secret directories. Popping her cheap plastic pen into her mouth, she took a fleeting look around the office; the salespeople at the far end were all immersed in their work. She began copying the files from the *ZBo* folder across to the SD card.

As the files appeared one by one on the card, Valentina hovered her mouse pointer over each, eager to open them. Since each file name was a seemingly random sequence of numbers, it was impossible for her to tell what any of them contained; all she could hope for was they contained something—*anything*—that would slip the proverbial noose around Jimmy Wen's neck.

The first file—*0642797*—contained a spreadsheet with a list of companies:

- New Horizon Credit Card Company Hong Kong Limited
- Golden Harvest Group Limited
- New World Entertainment Group Limited
- Emperor Holdings Limited
- JLM Asset Holdings
- Asia Lion Entertainment Limited

The spreadsheet informed her that JM Wen had purchased vast amounts of shares in each of the companies under what she presumed to be a shell company named ZB Ltd—it would appear creativity was not Jimmy Wen's strong suit. Valentina opened up another spreadsheet. This one showed each transaction behind the sale of the shares, and that the money had come through LCSSC Wealth Management.

So far, everything appeared above board—relatively speaking. Other than the fact Wen had obviously gone to some lengths to hide the files, and the fact he was using Zhang's money to purchase shares on the gangster's behalf, nothing leapt out at Valentina's trained eye as being abnormal. JM Wen certainly wasn't the only company on the planet laundering money for the criminal underworld. But she already suspected that Wen was doing more than that. If she found that he was, should she give the intel to Interpol, or to Zhang Bo?

She rebuked herself for the thought. Zhang was a cold-blooded killer. Worse, he was a coward who hid behind his expensive suits and urbane manners and sent minions to do his dirty work. She had the bruises and lacerations to prove it. Not to mention a ruined pair of $1,500 shoes that had just become a sort of twisted keepsake.

Another file showed a recent investment of HK$4bn channeled through LCSSC in Asia Lion Entertainment—somewhere around 500m in US dollars.

"Son of a bitch." Valentina clamped down hard on her pen and took a deep breath through flared nostrils. Another mouse click brought up Asia Lion's company information. The name leapt out at her from the screen: Zhang Bo—majority shareholder and CEO.

There it was: The direct link between Wen and Zhang, and with it, the dirty bank. Here was irrefutable proof that shares in Zhang's company were being purchased using dirty money via LCSSC in order to legitimize it.

All right. Okay. She'd uncovered the money laundering operation, but there had to be more. There had to be a record of the thing she suspected had locked Jimmy Wen and Zhang Bo in battle. The ultimate cause of Sofia Reller's death—and possibly Chrissy Huang's as well. Just how high was Jimmy Wen's body count?

She pulled herself back from the edge of that abyss and focused on the files. What she needed was something to confirm her suspicion about why the Triad boss was less than delighted with Wen's investments on his behalf.

Another click, another file.

Three more to go, and then Valentina knew she'd have to quit pushing her luck. The others had been gone well over an hour, and she knew Wen would want them back at their desks and earning big money —the time for mourning was over. Sofia's family would have been advised of her death by now and arrangements made for her body to be flown home to Geneva—all at JM Wen's expense, of course. Her leads would be divvied up between Valentina and the others, and it would be back to business as usual.

0632896. The penultimate file on the SD card.

With one eye on the office door, Valentina clicked on the file icon and a cluttered spreadsheet flashed up on her laptop screen.

"Sweet mother of God."

As the words left Valentina's lips, the pen slipped from between her teeth and clattered to her keyboard. Flicking quickly through the file, she picked up on a select few of its myriad pages with the dawning realization that Jimmy Wen was in the shit all the way up to his greedy little eyeballs. The file was filled with names of companies, share purchases and sales, names of individuals, and a date stamp for every single transaction made. Jimmy Wen might have been as crooked as they came, but he was most meticulous when it came to his double bookkeeping.

There was an entire worksheet within the file dedicated to Zhang Bo. Here, in his Holy of Holies, Wen had made no effort to disguise the gangster's name. He was egotistical enough to believe he'd hidden the file so cleverly within the intranet that no one could ever find it. There, in one column, were the dates of each sale of every batch of shares JM Wen Limited had done on behalf of Zhang Bo. Valentina compared them to the dates Wen had loaned money against those shares, and the pattern leapt out at her trained eye. There, in black and white, were all the figures proving Wen was pulling his stock loan scam with the Triad gang.

Jimmy Wen, you dumb fuck. You sold the shares almost the minute they took the loan. But why?

This was about more than merely making a buck—or even a lot of bucks. This was risk-taking elevated to an extreme sport. To play the scam on a Triad gang, and to loan them back their own dirty money was beyond comprehension. No wonder Wen was terrified. He'd have bet on the shares tanking, as would be expected once he quit buying huge chunks of them, unnaturally inflating the price. Their value would dwindle and he'd just buy them back at a bargain-basement rate. Now, unless Wen had the extra money to pay out, there was going to be an insurmountable deficit in JM Wen's reserves.

Valentina's hand trembled on her mouse as she closed that file, then all the others on the SD card. She'd seen enough to make her head hurt more than it already did; there was a hell of a lot to process, and decisions to be made as to how much of what she'd discovered she should divulge to Bennett.

And when.

She'd returned the SD card to her phone when her colleagues returned, as if on cue, all appearing more relaxed than when they'd left. She suspected there might have been some liquor or other palliatives involved. Valentina glanced at her coffee mug and decided that a nice glass of Merlot would be more appropriate to her current state of nerves.

Either way, Oliver, Anthony, Nadim, Daylen, and Lam sat themselves down at their respective desks and hit the phones as if their lives depended upon it. Perhaps they did.

CHAPTER THIRTY-THREE

I t was lunchtime before Valentina looked up from her desk again. She'd spent the remainder of the morning doing the job JM Wen limited was paying her so handsomely for—phoning prospective clients and researching the handful she'd inherited from the unfortunate Sofia. They'd all appeared delighted to hear from her—each one had been expertly qualified and set up perfectly by Jason Woo's department—and were more than keen to set up meetings and discuss loans.

With two meetings set up for the next couple of days, and three for the following week, Valentina turned her attention to getting herself out of the office; the client meeting on Wen's yacht was scheduled for two p.m.; a car would be waiting for her in precisely half an hour. All participants from JM Wen would arrive separately by privately contracted drivers. It seemed the boss was at least reluctant to have all of his best closers traveling en posse. Of course, since they were all going to end up at the same party on the same yacht, she had to wonder how big a deterrent that might be to the angry Mr. Zhang.

The yacht meeting had apparently been on the calendar for weeks. The mark was a rich client Jimmy Wen had brought in personally, and Lucas had informed Valentina it would not only be a good experience for her to attend and a welcome distraction from the gloomy atmosphere in the office, but also an opportunity for her to see a whole new level of Hong Kong opulence. As Wen himself liked to say, you had to spend big to win big, and absolutely no expense would be spared to reel in the next desperate industrialist and his myriad low-hanging shares. Plus, Valentina reckoned, every penny counted when you were in the mire up to your deceitful eyeballs with Zhang Bo and the Wo Hop Yee clan.

It bothered her more than a little that she was the only one from her team invited, but she was less spooked after Oliver told her he'd been invited as well but had declined due to his obvious injuries. The evidence of Valentina's brush with the Zhang Gang was artfully hidden beneath clothing and makeup. There was not enough makeup in Hong Kong to disguise his black eye and facial lacerations—both bound to be upsetting to a potential client.

Grabbing her cell phone from her desk, Valentina threw it into her Hermès bag; she was still leery of looking at it too closely, certain if she did she'd see more of Sofia's dried blood on it. Spotting the burner phone at the bottom, Valentina made a mental note to switch her hotline to Bennett back on as soon as she left the office. Having the thing off had been a welcome respite from the jittery feeling at the back of her mind that the Interpol agent might have tried to reach her while she'd had the thing off. She wondered whether that made her more or less nervous than the suspicion that the woman was tracking her every move and could call her at any given moment, no matter how inopportune.

"I'm leaving now," Valentina announced to no one in particular as she flicked off her computer and got to her feet.

Oliver and Anthony looked up from their respective screens; they were the only ones in the office, as Nadim and Daylen were in a client meeting at some swank restaurant.

"Make it a good one," Oliver said with a crooked smile that, with all the cuts on his face, made it look as if he were wearing a fright mask.

"I always do—isn't that the plan?"

Valentina turned to go and found herself facing Sofia Reller's empty desk. Her stomach lurched, and something in her chest hardened and set. The poor Swiss girl had been an innocent victim—collateral damage, as Bennett would call it—of Wen's duplicity, and here she was walking straight into the proverbial lion's den with her eyes wide open.

"Yeah," said Oliver quietly from behind her. "Me too."

She nodded. "I'll see you tomorrow." With nothing else to say, Valentina walked briskly from the sales office with her Hermès clutched tight to her side, as if everyone in 2IFC knew her guilty secrets.

"Miss Vittorio." An unwelcome, all too familiar voice called after her as she strode along the hallway in the direction of the elevators. Every nerve in her body went on high alert.

She stopped, stifling the impulse to scream and plastering on her most obviously fake smile. Turning around, she said, "Mr. Shum. How can I help you?"

"You can't." Shum Kuo looked around and seemed disappointed at the number of people who had a clear view of them and the lack of empty offices he might drag her into. "But you can help yourself."

Valentina was in no mood to put up with Shum's cryptic crap, but she knew she had to keep her guard up and not lose her cool, despite how much she despised the menacing little creep. She made a show of looking at her watch. "If you have something to say, please say it. I have to be on Mr. Wen's yacht in less than an hour."

"I'm watching you, Miss Vittorio. I'm watching you very closely." The sinister threat was back in Shum's tone.

Take a number. "Yes, you told me as much yesterday."

"There are eyewitnesses from the restaurant saying they saw a blonde woman in a dark suit and designer shoes leaving the scene. Shoes with red soles." Shum dropped his gaze pointedly to Valentina's feet. "Do you own a pair of Christian Louboutin shoes, Miss Vittorio?"

Well, wouldn't that be ironic—to be undone by the iconic soles of her footwear. She kept her voice low and even, as if completely unfazed. "I happen to have several pairs of Louboutins, Mr. Shum. So do half the businesswomen in Hong Kong. And I'm not blonde."

He stiffened and stared at her as if she'd sprouted horns. "You are blonde," he insisted.

"I'm brunette. Sofia was blonde."

"I fail to see the difference. Your hair is not black, therefore it is blonde."

She was torn between laughing and raging. Chrissy had made the same observation and by the same logic. "Funny. Chrissy Huang used to say the same thing. You remember Chrissy?" The words popped out of her mouth before she could stop them.

The reaction they elicited in Shum was gratifying. His face reddened, his eyes narrowed, and he speared her with a look intended to freeze her to the carpet.

"I know you're up to something," he spat, then fell silent as a trio of administrative assistants made their way by; they, in turn, dialed their chatter down to a reverent whisper. He watched them disappear into a cross corridor, then turned back to Valentina, his black eyes glittering with cold fury. "And I will find out precisely what. Be assured of that, Miss Vittorio. And when I do . . ."

Last straw, you ill-mannered fireplug. Valentina took a swift step toward him. "You'll do *what*, exactly, Mr. Shum? Have me beaten up in the street? Zhang's guys tried that. How'd that go for them?"

He quivered as if he stood in the middle of a tiny, invisible wind storm. She'd startled him, and it made her feel powerful. As if he saw that in her eyes, he leaned toward her, pitched his voice into a low growl, and said, "I shot them, Ms. Vittorio. That's how it went for them."

She was quivering now too, but refused to let him see it. She gripped her purse strap so tightly, her hand hurt. "I'm sure you did, Mr. Shum. Except, of course, for the one I killed. I crushed his neck with the heel of my designer shoes. Ruined my favorite pair of Blahniks."

She'd caught him off guard again; he blinked like a TV android whose program had been interrupted, then took a half step closer, so that their faces were only inches apart.

Baring his teeth in what was more of a snarl than a smile, he growled, "One word from me to Mr. Wen, Miss Vittorio, and they'll never be able to find all of you. So you should take care."

Refusing to be the first to break eye contact, Valentina flashed her brightest smile. "I will most certainly do that, Mr. Shum. Thank you for the well wishes. Now, if you'll excuse me, I have a meeting to get to."

Shum straightened and removed himself from her personal space. "I think you will be most impressed by Mr. Wen's boat," he said, then added, "I'll see you there."

Well, shit. "Maybe we can have another cozy chat, then?"

"That would be most pleasant." Shum once more cast his eyes downward to Valentina's shoes as if to memorize them.

"They're Ferragamos," she told him, pivoted on her expensive designer heels, and continued on her way to the elevators.

CHAPTER THIRTY-FOUR

The protesters were back outside 2IFC; they were noisy and restless and seemed determined to antagonize anyone attempting to go about their day. The crowd was at least a hundred strong, and they brought a distinct air of menace to Finance Street as they chanted, jostled, and waved their printed placards. At the periphery of the crowd stood the police—at least a dozen or so—with riot shields and tear gas at the ready; the increasingly volatile nature of Hong Kong's protests meant they had to be prepared to fight back.

Shielding her bag, Valentina shouldered her way through the protesters and stood at the outer perimeter of the hotel's circular drive. She'd only just started to scan the curb when a dark blue BMW drew up in front of her and the driver rolled down his window.

"Miss Vittorio?" he asked. "For Gold Coast Marina, yes?"

"Yes." Valentina opened the rear passenger side door. She froze with one foot in the car, and the other still on the sidewalk.

"Get in," Kate Bennett instructed.

With a nervous glance over her shoulder—she fully expected to see Shum Kuo's shiny head bobbing through the crowd after her—Valentina had little choice but to comply.

"What the fuck, Katie?" she growled as she sat down and snapped her seat belt across her lap.

"You switched your phone off, Valentina. What was I supposed to do?" Leaning slightly forward, she tapped the driver's shoulder. "Drive," she said.

"I had one hell of a night," Valentina replied as the car pulled away and 2IFC shrank into the background. "I couldn't risk you calling again, and I figured you could leave a voice mail if something urgent came up."

"Do you really think I'd be that reckless?"

"You just turned up at my fucking office, so yeah, I *do* think you'd be that reckless."

Bennett rested a hand on Valentina's. "Relax. As far as anyone knows, I'm just sharing a car with a friend or coworker."

"What about the car I was supposed to take?"

Bennett made a broad gesture. "As far as he knows, he will pick up Valentina Vittorio and drop her near the marina."

"Then this guy—"

"Is one of ours, yes." She met Valentina's eyes, her gaze solemn and intent. "I heard about the 'accident.'"

"I'm not surprised. A fire guts a neighborhood bodega, leaving a bunch of bodies and a couple of burned-out vehicles, someone's bound to notice."

Bennett's eyes shifted to the view from the window. "I'm sorry you got mixed up in all of that."

"I survived," Valentina said.

"You were supposed to."

"Yeah, they said it was a warning—it's a pity that sentiment didn't extend to Sofia Reller."

Bennett shook her head. "I doubt that was supposed to happen."

"She died in my arms," Valentina said, her voice raw. *What the fuck have I gotten myself into?*

Bennett fixed her with an unreadable expression. "I didn't know that. I'm sorry, I truly am. This is unfortunately what it means to be involved with someone like Jimmy Wen. Please reflect on the fact that, with us on your side, you have more chance of surviving this."

"I could just quit and go home to New York."

"Could you?"

Valentina met the agent's eyes and knew she couldn't. This had started out being about her dad, her family. They'd been her reason for being here, for doing what she was doing. Now she had other reasons: Chrissy Huang, Sofia Reller, the unfortunate Chung-Sun Fan and his bereft family. She didn't want any more reasons to bring down Jimmy Wen. Not one more.

Valentina broke the loaded silence. "Wen's security guy threatened me again."

Bennett sniffed. "Shum Kuo is a nasty little man who enjoys his job far too much. I guess that's only to be expected, considering his background with the State Police. Please try to stay out of his way."

"No, really?"

Bennett's smile was wry. "Well, as much as you can, of course."

"He asked me about the bombing again," Valentina said. "He says there are witnesses who saw someone matching my description at the scene. I think he knows I was meeting David at the restaurant."

"I can assure you there are no records of any eyewitnesses," Bennett assured her. "And certainly no one saying any such thing. Remember, this is Hong Kong, and there is a great deal that goes unseen, especially when the likes of Jimmy Wen are involved. The only person who could possibly have seen you, and survived, was the bomber himself. If he *had* identified you, and Shum knew for certain you were there, you'd be dead by now."

"Well, that's a big comfort—thanks."

"You're quite welcome, my dear."

As the Beemer made its way along the nose-to-tail Shing Tai Road traffic, the offices and stores crawled by. Valentina checked her watch and saw it was already one thirty.

"Don't panic, we'll have you there on time," Bennett said. "We can't keep the illustrious Mr. Wen waiting, can we?"

"He'll be pissed if I'm late. He hates tardiness."

Bennett nodded, a crooked smile twisting her lips. "I'd heard that about Wen; tolerance of any kind really isn't his strong suit. So, tell me about Zhang Bo."

The sudden change of tack threw Valentina a little, which, she guessed, was the point. "He's a memorable guy; I met him on my first day in the office, and again last night." She hesitated then added, "Zhang is one of the clients Jimmy Wen is screwing with."

Bennett whistled through her teeth, a most unladylike affectation. Valentina liked her a bit more for it. "Bloody hell. He's selling the shares he's loaned against?"

"Shares bought with laundered Triad money. The guy must have a death wish."

Bennett let out a long, snorting laugh. "Men like Jimmy Wen are all ego and overweening confidence—they think they're invincible. My, my. This just keeps getting better. We really need to get a move on and corner Wen. Before Zhang does the job for us."

"Would that be such a bad thing?"

Bennett turned to give her a disconcerting look. "If we are to bring down Wen's network of 'associates,' we need him alive and kicking. We also need a complete list of all the companies involved, the shares Wen has loaned against and shorted, how much is owed against them, and, most importantly, the dates of the transactions. We need his red ledger." She reeled off her demands as if it was nothing more than a grocery list. "Nailing Wen to the table is all going to come down to timing. If you can find out who—and *where*—his market makers are, that would be a nice bonus."

For both of us. "You have to give me time to pull all of that together. There are eyes everywhere in that office, and now Shum is breathing down my neck."

"All the more reason to step up," Bennett insisted. "Time is of the essence, Valentina. I'm sure you can see that."

Valentina was all too aware that time was running out, and running out fast. Less than a week in Hong Kong and her meticulous plans were already fraying around the edges. "I'll do my very best, Agent Bennett."

"Ah, here we are." Bennett rolled down her window to let in the salt and ozone fragrance of the sea. "I told you we'd get you here on time."

It was ten 'til two when the BMW drew up a discreet distance from the marina. Valentina gave the Interpol agent a backward glance, then exited the car.

CHAPTER THIRTY-FIVE

As Valentina was ride-sharing with an Interpol agent, Lucas Vaughn sipped on his second cold beer of the day. He stretched out on the lounger and stared out across the sundeck at the vast array of gleaming yachts that bobbed gently about in the Gold Coast Marina. Jimmy Wen had the biggest boat there, of course—the 210-foot *Morning Cloud IV*. He'd bought it outright for HK$390 million less than three years ago, along with a rare ninety-nine-year mooring lease he'd had to bribe his way into because of the usual five-year waiting list. He'd had the yacht completely refitted all the way down to the gold-plated fixtures and fittings and was not averse to chartering it out to his favored clients and bankers at HK$250,000 a day to earn himself a little pocket change.

Bigger even than the famous *Ambrosia III*—moored at the opposite dock—Jimmy's yacht sported a crew of twelve, four sundecks, two helipads, a cinema, Cordon Bleu kitchen, space for five Jet Skis, and a main deck salon with a fully stocked bar.

"I asked you here early to talk about the Zhang situation, not take in the scenery," Wen growled at Lucas, who looked perfectly at home in a loud Hawaiian shirt, khaki shorts, and navy-blue deck shoes; other than Wen wearing a blue shirt to Vaughn's red, the two were dressed identically. "There'll be plenty of time for eye candy later."

He followed the younger man's gaze across the aft deck to a bevy of stunning young ladies clad only in string bikini briefs on the yacht moored next to them. Wen sat himself down on the sun lounger next to Lucas and sipped at his Macallan whiskey. His new bodyguard, Fung—the late Pang's cousin—took up his position behind his boss, which was mercifully in the shade of the stark white awning that extended from the salon to shield the spacious hot tub. By his side stood Lau, sporting a row of neat black stitches across his temple. Lucas thought it made his head look as if it had a zipper. He felt bad about calling the poor guy Tweedledee all these years.

"Did I miss anything?" Shum Kuo's voice startled Lucas; damn guy made everyone jumpy.

Wen gestured his security chief to a deck chair across from Lucas. "We were waiting for you. I take it your trip here was uneventful?"

He glanced up at the two-seater Robinson R22 on the helipad atop the bridge; the rotors were still spinning as the pilot was making ready to depart to pick up the prospective client for the yacht party.

"I prefer to drive," Shum said.

"We need to talk." Wen looked over his shoulder at the hostesses and crew who were preparing for the party; he'd given them all explicit instructions to stay in the salon or below decks until the meeting was over.

"Of course." Shum sat down.

Lucas fought the urge to say something sarcastic about the guy being made of ice; he was still wearing a damned suit and wasn't even sweating.

"Lucas, have you seen the share prices this morning?" There was a tense edge to Wen's voice that Lucas had only heard a handful of times.

He nodded. Of course he'd checked out the Golden Six before the meeting, and he'd been alarmed to see how well they were doing—the gap Wen had to fill to placate Zhang Bo was widening by the day.

"Someone is surely making them perform this way," Shum observed. "If we can find out who—"

Wen cut him off. "This is no time for your thuggery, Shum. We have no choice but to come up with the money. It's as simple as that." He took another sip of his whiskey.

"That's a lot of cash, Jimmy," Lucas threw in. "And we can't keep stalling Zhang, that much is clear. After last night—"

"You think I don't know that? Do you think I didn't get the message?"

Wen's sharply raised voice also raised Shum's eyebrows. Behind Wen, Lau shifted uncomfortably, and the hostesses fled the salon for the safety of the foredeck.

"We could always produce a patsy," Shum said. "Someone we can tell Zhang is creaming off the top and delaying the deal. That would at least throw him off the scent and buy you more time to bring in the money—or get the share prices down."

"I spoke with Freddy Tseng, and he's doing everything he can to tank them," Lucas said. "Our only avenue is to raise enough capital to cover the difference."

"Don't you think that's what we're trying to do here, Lucas?" Wen drained his cut-crystal glass and leaned forward on his lounger to face Shum. "You have a patsy in mind?"

Shum's thin mouth puckered as he considered the idea. "The new girl from the Bronx—or wherever she claims to be from."

"Are you fuckin' serious?" Lucas snapped.

Shum met his gaze, his face devoid of expression. "She's not really proven herself, she's asking far too many questions, and I'm confident she was the one meeting with the SFC agent on Monday."

"What d'you mean she hasn't proven herself?" Lucas made his tone dry and sarcastic, tamping down on his very real anger. He'd clashed with Shum before and knew from bitter experience the minute he lost his cool, he'd lose the battle. "She brought in Kim Yun-Fat last night, which was *huge*. In the end, he increased the size of his loan because of Val. What the fuck do you know about what she's done? That's not your job."

"It *is* my job to know if she has been . . . disloyal."

"Oh, c'mon, Kuo, you have absolutely no proof Val was in that restaurant."

"She was there," Shum all but growled. "You're just trying to get yourself laid, Vaughn. When will you learn to leave the staff alone? Only a fool soils his own bed. Besides which, what would be the point of Miss Vittorio bringing in big money if there's no company left?" A glimmer of a smile played at the corners of his mouth.

Wen agreed. "He's right, Lucas. Surely even you can see that? We have to do everything within our power to buy us the time to get through this. Zhang Bo doesn't fuck around; we all know that."

"Are you ready to throw Miss New York under the bus?" Shum pressed. "You have to make a decision, Jimmy, and make it fast."

CHAPTER THIRTY-SIX

Jimmy Wen was pissed. Valentina could see that before she'd stepped from the gangway onto the yacht. Gordon Yip had committed a mortal sin; he was late to his own party. Now, though the client had yet to arrive, Wen had his captain, Leslie Man, maneuver *Morning Cloud IV* out of the marina and head out toward Victoria Harbor. The great man was brooding over his Macallan, keeping a close eye on the sky, as if he could make the helicopter bearing Gordon Yip appear by sheer will.

The crowd Wen had gathered to impress the prospect included Shing Hai and Lyn Song. The starlet looked especially spectacular in a minuscule, neon yellow bikini that left very little to the imagination. Valentina felt absurdly overdressed. The only other person in business attire was the ubiquitous Mr. Shum. Valentina shed her suit coat, glad she'd worn a relatively sheer silk blouse.

Wen had also invited along Tony Wu, the outspoken Citizen's Party politician; he seemed nicely at home surrounded by exquisite food, limitless drink, and the nubile, swimsuit-clad hostesses. Wen had also insisted Li Jiang and his liaison manager, Gao Yanlin, attend. Having the CEO and assistant of the LCSSC would be seen as a great show of strength and couldn't possibly fail to impress. Lucas had divulged that the tardy party had been directed to them by Li Jiang himself.

Valentina was pleased to see Yan on the yacht; he and his boss had joined the party shortly after she'd arrived, distracting her from the emotional hangover of her unplanned meeting with Kate Bennett. Yan had introduced her to the dour Li Jiang, who had the air of a man with the weight of the entire world upon his shoulders. He appeared quite uncomfortable with the opulent surroundings and ostentatious display of wealth.

Lucas had once more abandoned Valentina in favor of chatting up Lyn Song. Valentina was perfectly fine with that, as it meant she was free to chat with Yan and Li Jiang, who became more and more open as the drinks flowed. She was also pleased to be having a business meeting dressed in something less revealing than the night before, although even in her shirtsleeves she felt overdressed, notwithstanding the blue deck shoes the purser had insisted she change into. At least she wasn't on display like some star prize in a seedy game show.

"How are you finding Hong Kong, Miss Vittorio?" Seated in a deck chair opposite Valentina and Yan, who were relaxing on a padded bench that ran along the rail on the port bow, Li Jiang struggled to make small talk. It clearly wasn't his forte. "I understand our island is one and a half times bigger than New York."

Valentina smiled and sipped at her iced soda water. She had no idea if the banker's snippet of trivia was correct or not, but she nodded politely anyway. "It's much the same as back home. Bad traffic, rude people, too much concrete and glass."

"If you prefer greenery, then you must take a trip up to The Peak. The views from there are most spectacular." As Jiang spoke, his eyes flicked over to where Wen and Shum sat on their sun loungers and within sight of the helipad.

"If you prefer shopping," Yan chipped in, "the best stores are right here in the city or on the Kowloon side." He'd made his way back from the bar, where he'd been caught up in a conversation with Shing Hai; the influencer had seated himself alone at the bar and was getting steadily drunk at Jimmy Wen's expense. "Let me know if you'd like a trip out. I'd be delighted to play tour guide."

Yan was on his third martini, and Valentina couldn't quite make out if he was just being friendly or if he was hitting on her. She settled for a bland, safe answer delivered with a slightly impish smile. "Thank you. If I have the time for shopping, you'll be the first to know."

"Gordon Yip should be here by now." Li Jiang studied his watch with narrowed eyes, as if somehow it was lying to him. "He should not be late, it is very bad manners. Maybe I shall have another drink after all." His soft-soled shoes made loud squeaks on the polished wood of the deck as he rose from his deck chair and headed toward the bar.

"Is he always that talkative?" Valentina asked Yan with a wry smile.

"Only when he's having fun," Yan replied. "Which really doesn't seem to be all that often, now I think about it. In fact, I think the man's only social interaction outside of the bank and family celebrations is coming to business soirees. You should see the old boy hit the karaoke after a few whiskeys and Long Island Iced Teas—you'd not believe it was the same man."

Valentina relaxed a little and laughed along with Yan's playfulness. Her mind still remained focused on Jimmy Wen, though. Something about the way he'd eyed her when she'd arrived at the marina and boarded his precious yacht had made her uneasy. It hadn't helped to see Shum Kuo cozying up to Wen, either. If you could call his scowling cozy. The man left a wake of bad vibes.

Morning Cloud IV sailed all the way around Hong Kong Island twice, and still there was no sign of Gordon Yip. Jimmy Wen's mood grew darker with each passing hour and crystal tumbler of whiskey. By the time the yacht dropped anchor in the quiet, uncrowded waters of Victoria Harbor, even Shum Kuo had excused himself and taken advantage of the chopper (that had returned sans client) to head back to the island.

In the absence of a wealthy client to schmooze, Valentina had spent much of the day with Yan. Not only did she find his company refreshing, she'd also discovered he loved to talk. And, the more booze the banker consumed, and the further away from his boss he got, the looser his lips became. At first, his conversation had been small talk and chitchat about living in Hong Kong, how the Chinese were seen by virtually everyone on the island as the bad guys, and the dissenting political climate. Then Yan had become clumsily flirtatious. Finally, as darkness closed in, he'd begun to let slip small details of the bank's dealings with Wen that had Valentina hanging on his every word.

"We've been buying shares on behalf of JM Wen clients for many years now." Yan gave a guilty look around the empty bar area as if he was divulging some great and terrible secret.

"You're a wealth management bank," Valentina observed disingenuously. "Isn't that what you're supposed to be doing?"

Yan put a finger to his lips and dropped his voice with a conspiratorial wink that looked more like a grimace. "Yeah, but you don't know *what* clients, and what money. The bank has worked with money from the . . . the . . . from powerful people who need special treatment for a long time. Every bank in Hong Kong does, sooner or later—even though we don't care to know where most of it comes from."

"How can you not know where your money comes from?" Valentina propped her chin on one fist and pretended to be a bit buzzed. She hadn't had a drop of alcohol all afternoon.

"It comes in via a whole army of smurfs, mostly in dribs and drabs, sometimes in larger amounts from offshore accounts—that money has usually been through at *least* another couple of banks with tax haven domiciles."

Yan helped himself to another hefty shot from the bottle of Handover gin he'd liberated from the yacht's bar. He dropped in a couple of fat ice cubes from the silver bucket on the tiny round table in front of him; they clinked cheerfully as they bobbed around. "It's all dirty money, of course, and we only buy shares with that money in order to launder it."

Yan paused to watch the ice float around in his glass, then gave Valentina a drunken, lopsided smile. "I think I may have said a little too much, Val . . . *Valentina*—I'm sorry."

"We're supposed to be on the same side, remember?" Valentina reassured him. "We both work for Jimmy Wen, one way or another."

"And we don't mind spending his ill-gotten gains." Yan toasted Valentina's Hermès bag with his gin. "Welcome to conscience-free Hong Kong, Miss Vittorio! Did you know it was us who sent Gordon Yip your way? Or rather, Li Jiang did, which means Mr. Wen is not going to be at all pleased with him—what with Yip being a no-show."

Suddenly, Yan looked stone-cold sober.

Understatement of the year award goes to . . . "Do you know why he didn't come?"

Yan shrugged, leaning back against the ship's rail. "Who knows? It happens from time to time. Sometimes they get last-minute financing from a more traditional source that lets them sleep at night, sometimes they just get cold feet about selling shares they shouldn't be selling, and sometimes . . ." He drew a finger across his throat.

"You think Yip . . . ?"

Yan frowned. "Most likely not. I'd guess he had second thoughts about dealing with JM Wen. Jimmy has quite the fearsome reputation, you know."

Valentina raised an eyebrow but said nothing.

"*I* think Li Jiang deliberately turned the man down, even though the bank could have accommodated his loan. Just so he could refer him to JM Wen Limited."

"For which he was handsomely rewarded?"

An artless shrug.

"How much?"

Yan shook his head. "I'm little more than a bank clerk, Valentina, and not party to such information." He chuckled at the self-deprecation.

Valentina laughed along with him and wondered what his cut of the illicit income was; a dirty bank like LCSSC would definitely be paid handsomely, not only for its referrals and services, but for its silence—silence Gao Yanlin was not doing too well at maintaining.

He raised his wrist and his Apple watch blinked on, displaying a dizzying watch face that swirled with colors like an aurora borealis.

"We should get to the top sundeck. The light show will be starting soon. I'm sure you won't want to miss it."

Valentina took her cue and got to her feet; the Symphony of Lights show was right up there on her Hong Kong bucket list, and since Wen's yacht was anchored in a prime spot in the harbor to witness the spectacle, it would have been remiss of her to miss it. Besides, she got the impression Yan was aware he was talking too much, and it served as a convenient way to break off the conversation. Valentina was comfortable with that; she suspected he wasn't finished divulging his bank's grubby little secrets yet, and she was prepared to give him every opportunity to reveal more.

Side by side, along with Wen's other guests and most of the crew, Valentina and Yan watched the Symphony of Lights as it lit up Hong Kong's magnificent skyline with bright, vibrant colors that danced and shone through the night. From the Convention Center to the CITIC Tower, the Queensway Government offices and City Hall, to Jardine House and the 2IFC building, the city lit up and was accompanied by soaring, uplifting music that filled the harbor.

When Yan, fueled with the gin's Dutch courage, asked if Valentina would invite him back to her hotel room later, she found herself saying yes.

CHAPTER THIRTY-SEVEN

Zhang Bo was waiting dockside along with two of his bodyguards when the *Morning Cloud IV* returned from its excursion. He waited for the guests, crew, and most of the hostesses to disembark before making his way onto the yacht; Tony Wu was still down in one of the cabins with a couple of the hostesses, and as far as Lucas knew, the politician and his playmates were the only ones down there. He was tempted to try to leave the boat himself, but knew Jimmy would see that as cowardice. So he sat at the bar in the main deck salon, sipped coffee, and ate fancy peanuts, hopeful that he'd be sober enough to not say something stupid and make Zhang mad.

He had no direct evidence to support it, but he had a suspicion that the Triad's steel-hand-in-a-velvet-glove demeanor concealed a deep-down capacity for personal violence. Jimmy was convinced the man preferred to keep his gang's violent activities at arm's length—or further. Out of sight and out of mind.

Nonetheless, Jimmy Wen was visibly agitated by the Triad boss's slow advance up the gangway and all the way into the salon's fairy-lit seating area; his eyes twitched between Zhang's bodyguards and his own, as if he was expecting a gunfight to break out any moment.

Zhang took a seat at one of the little tables, casual as you please, crossed his legs, and said nothing.

Jimmy, hovering near the bar, broke the silence with false jocularity. "Bo! Would you like something to drink? Eat?"

"This is not a social occasion, Jimmy," the gang lord said mildly. He gestured for Jimmy to take a seat across from him at the table.

Jimmy bobbed his head, almost bowing, and obeyed. "No, of course not. To be honest, I am surprised to see you this evening. After what happened last night . . ." He blanched, leaving it to Zhang to finish the sentence.

"Yes, last night." The Triad leader ran a finger down the crease in his flawlessly tailored trousers.

Jimmy looked as if he'd just realized he was skating on quicksand. "If this is about what happened to your men . . ."

"They were sloppy and got what was coming to them." The corner of Zhang's mouth twitched. "Your Miss Vittorio put up one hell of a fight, which was unexpected."

A chill trickled down Lucas's spine. He was pretty sure he'd seen Val Vittorio kill a guy with her high heels. Should he mention that? He opened his mouth to say something, but Jimmy had seen an opening and seized it.

"That's not the only thing unexpected about Miss Vittorio."

Lucas made a choking sound and tried to catch his boss's eye. Jimmy's gaze merely grazed his as he plowed on through. "My security chief believes she is siphoning cash from the amount we're cleaning for you and depositing it in offshore bank accounts. She was doing it in New York, and it would seem she's already got her hooks into our Hong Kong clientele."

Lucas squirmed internally. Lies, all of it. Lies that could possibly get another innocent woman killed.

Zhang raised an eyebrow. "So why is she still working for you? Why did I see her leave this boat, unhindered, in the company of a banker of our acquaintance? More to the point, if she was skimming in New York, why would you bring her to work for you in Hong Kong where she would be in reach of my assets? Shouldn't you have fired her . . . at the very least?"

Lucas thought he might throw up. Whatever had possessed Jimmy Wen to make that accusation and then embellish it?

"I can assure you we did not realize what she'd been doing until after she arrived. She's been with us for less than a week, and Shum only informed me of her behavior in the New York office late today. I had high-profile guests aboard—celebrities and politicians. It was neither the time nor the place to deal with employee misconduct."

Listening to Jimmy weave more lies into his narrative was like watching a downhill skier trying to outpace an avalanche.

"Employee misconduct," repeated Zhang. "How very . . . insignificant that sounds."

"Trust me when I say it is not insignificant to me. My chief of security informs me that he's had suspicions about Ms. Vittorio since his department vetted her before she came to Hong Kong," he lied glibly. "He wanted to be certain before he took it any further. We will see to the matter."

"Perhaps *I* should see to the matter," said Zhang. "It is, after all, my money she is stealing . . . if what you're telling me is true."

"Of course it's true," Jimmy assured him. "And if Shum were here I'd have him give you a full report. He had to go back to the city to handle another matter of some importance. But, Bo, if you . . . deal with Ms. Vittorio, she might not survive. She's an American citizen with family in the States. Her death could cause international difficulties."

"Do you doubt that I have the right to deal with her as I see fit?" Zhang's voice was a low purr. Deceptively soft, reasonable, lulling.

Lucas felt as if invisible hands had wrapped about his neck and were beginning to squeeze. He took another swig of coffee and eyed the whiskey behind the bar. He wanted to signal Jimmy somehow that he was getting out over his skis and needed to . . . to what? Did he even have a safe move?

Wen played the only card he had left. "If Vittorio dies, the whereabouts of the money she's taken dies with her. Until we know the precise channels she's using, and where she's hidden the cash, we need her alive. She's been working alone, which means she's the only one who can lead us to it."

Zhang took a deep breath and settled a contemplative look on the older man. "I see. Well, you need to deal with it, Jimmy, and deal with it fast. I am getting tired of repeating myself; I want my money and my shares." Zhang stood, buttoning up his jacket.

"And you'll get them," Jimmy reassured with seeming sincerity. "But until we can sort this situation out, it will be better to keep the shares where they are so we don't raise any red flags with the SFC."

Zhang Bo had the best poker face Lucas had ever seen. His expression gave no indication whether Jimmy's misdirection was a hit or a miss. Zhang and Wen eyed each other in a moment of frozen silence, while Lucas stared, mesmerized, at the two.

"Hey, where's the party?" Tony Wu's drunken voice boomed across the deck as he appeared in the broad forward entry to the salon, his arms draped around the shoulders of two hostesses who were struggling to keep him upright.

Zhang's bodyguards spun and pulled their guns. Jimmy Wen's guards pulled theirs a second later, but seemed unsure whom to point them at.

Wu's unfocused gaze focused with lightning speed. "Whoa, what's going on here?" Terror edged his voice as he froze in place between the bikini-clad girls, a spreading stain darkening the crotch of his jeans. Lucas could smell the piss from where he sat, trying to remain invisible.

"Something that does not concern you," Zhang said, sounding almost amused.

He pulled out his cell phone and took a photograph of the Citizen's Party leader and his 'party favors,' then nodded to his bodyguards. They advanced on the politician, shoved the hostesses aside, grabbed Wu by the arms, and escorted him through the salon to stand before Zhang. The two girls scurried back below decks. Whatever was going to happen, they were not going to be witnesses to it.

Lucas fervently wished he could pull the same disappearing act, but he was stuck where he was—to the damned barstool.

"Hold on a minute!" Wu protested. "Do you know who I am?"

Zhang Bo actually laughed. It wasn't a particularly pleasant sound. He leaned into the other man's face until they were nose to nose. "I know exactly who you are, Mr. Wu. And I know why you are here. Given my recent experience with JM Wen, you would be best advised to choose your company more wisely." The Triad boss turned to Wen. "I want what's mine, Jimmy; deal with your American problem in your own time, and no more excuses."

"What's he talking about, Jimmy?" Wu turned on the bluster. "If you've been involved in illicit—"

Following a nod from Zhang, one of his guards slugged Wu in the solar plexus. As the air left his lungs, Wu doubled over, fighting for breath, and wet his pants some more. Zhang's other guard lifted the politician up by the back of his shirt and dragged him out of the salon and over to the starboard rail.

"No!" Wu screamed and grabbed hold of the guardrail. "You can't do this!"

Ignoring the politician's protests, Zhang's guard pulled out his hand gun and aimed it at Wu's head. Wu stopped screaming and started whimpering. His eyes sought Zhang Bo, begging mutely for mercy.

Lucas's stomach pitched and he swallowed bile.

Zhang made a flipping gesture. "Jump, Mr. Wu. Wang Jun wants you to jump."

Wu looked up at the bodyguard, who tilted his head toward the rail and glanced into the water. His lips curled in a creepy display of enjoyment.

"I suggest you do it while you have a choice," said Zhang, "and can still swim."

Not taking his eyes from the bodyguard, Wu started to clamber over the rail. He was still drunk enough to be clumsy, and Zhang's goon, whether in impatience or twisted playfulness, grabbed him by the waistband of his jeans and heaved him over the side of the yacht. Wu's last yelp of outrage and fear ended in a loud splash.

Zhang Bo straightened his already straight jacket and tilted his head, listening to the sound of the politician splashing his way toward the dock. "You should pray," he told Wen, "that the inestimable Mr. Wu can swim better than he controls his temper. If you should see him before I do, please ask him if he'd like me to send this picture to his wife." He lifted his cell phone before returning it to his jacket pocket, then beckoned his bodyguards, who returned to his side like a pair of sheepdogs. The trio made their way to the gangway.

Just before he stepped onto the ramp, Zhang turned back to give Jimmy Wen another dark, reptilian look. "I regret the death of that woman last night. It was not my intention that anyone die. Good evening, Jimmy, Mr. Vaughn."

Lucas felt that peculiar creeping chill again. He had desperately hoped Zhang hadn't noticed him. He and Jimmy watched the Triad leader and his two goons debark to the tune of Tony Wu's noisy effort to reach the dock.

"Lucas." Jimmy's voice was gravel gray. "Take Fung and make sure Mr. Wu makes it safely back to the yacht."

Lucas swallowed his desire to flee the *Morning Cloud IV* and nodded curtly. He and Fung tracked Wu to where he hung, panting, at the base of a Jet Ski ramp, pulled him out of the drink, and brought him back to the boat, notwithstanding his stated desire never to board the damn thing again. Jimmy Wen offered him a change of clothing and a drink, both of which he refused.

"Damn you, Wen!" the politician raged. "I don't know what kind of shit you're in, but I want no part of it. You hear me?"

Color suffused Jimmy Wen's face, and his jaw set.

Shit, Lucas thought. *Here we go.*

"I can assure you," Jimmy said, in a voice dripping with acid, "that Mr. Zhang wants no part of you either."

Wu's eyes widened. "Zhang? Zhang Bo? That was Zhang Bo? You're on the wrong side of the Wo Hop Yee?"

"Not as much as you will be if you try to turn this to political advantage. Bo made a request of me before he left. He wanted me to ask you if you thought perhaps your wife might enjoy the photograph he took of you with your . . . new friends."

Wu's eyes spat embers, but he said nothing for a long moment, during which Lucas was certain he was combing through a list of things he wanted to say but couldn't.

"No," he said at length. "I am certain Min would not enjoy that photograph."

Jimmy nodded and leaned back in his chair like a benevolent monarch—as if he had not just been scared out of his gourd by Zhang Bo. "So, if anyone sees you in your current state of . . . disarray, you can tell them you suffered an unfortunate accident. You slipped and fell from the dock. Silly, but simple. You failed to watch your step."

Wu all but ground his teeth. "Yes. I will be more careful in the future."

"That would be best . . . for all of us."

Wu turned and strode from the boat with as much aplomb as was possible, given that he was wet and frightened and probably more sober than he wanted to be.

"You think he'll say anything?" Lucas asked, watching the politician's receding figure.

"Tony Wu is many things—an arrogant ass, a buffoon, a grifter— but he is not stupid." Jimmy Wen tossed back the last of his whiskey, then stood unsteadily and went below.

Lucas left the *Morning Cloud IV* as fast as his Nikes would carry him.

CHAPTER THIRTY-EIGHT

Yan was still a bit drunk when they reached the Four Seasons, but less so once he stood in Valentina's room, staring at the view from her bedroom windows. His initial alcohol-fueled bravado seemed to evaporate the moment they got into the room.

Valentina was not above making the first move. She kicked off her shoes, threw off her jacket, and unbuttoned her blouse, pulling it out of the waist of her skirt, which she unzipped and dropped to the floor. Yan seemed mesmerized. Smiling, she moved to stand inches from him, as close as she could get without touching. She met his eyes and savored the wash of sexual electricity that flared between them. Valentina swore she could feel her nipples harden. She held his gaze for a moment before she kissed him, her tongue dancing over the warmth of his full lips.

He moaned and grabbed her, pulling her against him, pushing her back onto the expansive bed. They discarded the remainder of their clothes in a writhing horizontal striptease. With physical barriers gone, Yan returned Valentina's kisses with interest, moving from lips to neck, to breasts, nibbling the taut, soft skin of her belly, teasing her sex. She wanted to howl. So she did. It had been so long since she'd let herself get this close to a man, but somewhere in the back of her mind was regret that this had to be less about trust or desire than it was about hunger for the information he held in his head.

Their coupling was urgent, intense, and satisfying. Valentina gave voice to each spasm, every release of the pressure she'd been building up. Yan laughed the first couple of times she did it, then worked with eager exuberance to elicit more gasps, yips, and cries of pleasure.

The guy was good; Valentina gave him ten out of ten for his technique and expertise. As sweating, panting limbs entwined, they fucked with a hot, fervent passion that Valentina could in no way describe as making love. They devoured each other. She'd read that sort of language in novels from time to time. It seemed perfectly appropriate here. They'd both been starved of *something*. In her own case, she knew what that something was—human intimacy, something she'd had to sacrifice to her cause. She could not afford real friends or real lovers. Not now. Not yet.

After their breathing had returned to normal, Valentina lay entangled in the rumpled bed sheets and stared up at the ceiling. The bed shifted as Yan got up. She watched admiringly as he padded naked across to the mini bar, tossing his condom into the trash on his way. He was quite beautiful, really.

Starved of something. She frowned, reassessing her rationale for this . . . interlude, and admitted that information wasn't all she wanted from Gao Yanlin.

"So, how long has LCSSC been involved with the Triads?" She grimaced, knowing she'd waited until he had his back to her to ask.

Coward.

Yan plucked a couple of chilled bottles of Perrier from the small refrigerator and nudged its door closed with his knee, then side-stepped the question with a wry smile. "We have never been *directly* involved. We have only ever dealt with their indirect accounts and people like Jimmy Wen."

"Sounds very fussy to me. The distinction, I mean." Valentina took a bottle from Yan as he rolled back onto the bed.

"It's being fussy that keeps banks like us one step ahead of the law. It's what sets us apart from the likes of HSBC and Deutsche Bank—the ones who are dumb enough to get caught. Li Jiang has always been careful, although I don't think he fully considered all the implications of getting involved with Jimmy Wen."

He cast an admiring glance at Valentina's exposed breasts, which she was making no attempts to cover up. Smile deepening, he let a couple of drops of condensation from his Perrier fall on one of them, making the nipple contract.

"Sorry," he said, then lowered his head and licked the droplet off.

Valentina clamped down on the flare of sexual static that ran from breast to groin, and sat up. She cracked the cap off her water, took a long swig, and relaxed back into the downy pillows with a will. "Implications?"

Yan nodded then pulled himself up to lean against the headboard. "Wen has a bad reputation for ruthlessness in Hong Kong—there are even rumors he's Italian Mafia."

Valentina let out a genuine peal of laughter. "That's news to me. He hardly looks the part of a Sicilian don."

"True, but he's always been happy enough to mix with dubious company and is not averse to working with business interests that are outside the law—including Zhang Bo."

"The same could be said of Li Jiang and LCSSC. Albeit *indirectly.*"

Yan took a delicate sip of his water. "There are certain . . . *advantages* to dealing with the underworld elements. Since the gangs pretty much run the island, there's not too many who dare to refuse to work with them and survive. And, of course, it can be an absolute minefield deciding which of the gangs to get into bed with. If you'll pardon the terminology."

"So bankers like Jiang use people like Jimmy Wen to play the middleman?"

"Precisely." Yan set his water on the bedside table, then rolled up on one elbow to look down at her. His fingertips danced down the valley between her breasts. "It adds an extra layer of protection if things should ever go wrong. It also gives the banks—and unscrupulous bankers—the opportunity to skim a little more off the top without arousing suspicions, at least not in the bank's direction."

"Jiang is skimming Triad money?" Valentina tried her best to sound surprised.

Yan looked scandalized . . . or maybe defensive. "I didn't say *that*. But if he was, Wen would assume it was the Triads shorting him and say nothing."

Fucking brilliant. "And Zhang would assume Wen was helping himself to a little more off the top and decide not to rock the boat, provided he didn't get too greedy?"

"You catch on very quickly, Miss Vittorio." Yan cupped Valentina's left breast with one hand and nuzzled her neck, nibbling and licking his way along her smooth jawline toward her lips. "Which reminds me, I have a meeting tomorrow at The Peak with a potential client. I think it would be in your best interests to attend."

"You do?" Valentina realized with some surprise that she was ready for more of the very skilled Gao Yanlin.

"He's asking for too high a percentage against his shares, so he's good and ripe for JM Wen." Yan's lips played along Valentina's, each word a warm breath on her mouth. "I have not said anything to Li Jiang or Wen yet, as the guy has only just requested the meeting. I was thinking I'd wait until a deal was requested." He teased Valentina's mouth with the tip of his tongue. "It would be a nice feather in your cap if you managed to bring his shares in for Wen, too."

Valentina's reply was stifled by Yan's mouth on hers and his tongue parting her lips. She figured it couldn't hurt to meet more money and keep up appearances for Wen, plus it would get her out of the office and away from Shum Kuo's scrutiny *and* she'd get to see The Peak and spend some more time with this lovely man, whom she could tell by the pulsing against her thigh, was also ready for more of her. Without breaking the kiss, Valentina reached to her bedside table for another condom.

CHAPTER THIRTY-NINE

Unfortunately for Gordon Yip, being awoken in the small hours of the morning by the police was not an uncommon occurrence. His son, Andy, had fallen in with a drug crowd and was on the verge of ruining his entire life at the tender age of twenty-one.

"I'm coming!" Yip hissed at the door as he knotted his silk robe's tie around the slight bulge of his waist. His bare feet slapped noisily upon the travertine tiles as he scurried across the long hallway, the knocking on the front door becoming ever more insistent.

"Who is it?" His wife, Sue, appeared at the top of the broad, sweeping staircase.

"Who do you think it is?" Yip growled as he reached the door. "Go back to bed and let me deal with this."

Sue was already on her way down the stairs. Andy followed close behind; his eyes were glazed, and the pungent stink of skunk marijuana wafted out from him as he made his way down.

Yip pulled open the door and fixed a placatory smile on his face. "Can I help you, officers?"

Stepping aside from the doorway to invite the two police officers in, Yip peered out onto the street in the hope that none of the neighbors had been disturbed—police visits in the middle of the night were most definitely frowned upon in the respectable Mid-Levels estates.

"Andrew Yip?" the bigger of the two officers asked. He looked decidedly pissed at being out so late, and overweight enough for his uniform to look uncomfortable around his thick midsection.

Yip turned to look at Andy, who was doing his best to not look as stoned as he clearly was. "That's my son. What has he done now, Officer?"

The cop stepped around Yip and made his way across the expansive vestibule. His colleague, a short, slender man who looked to be not much older than Andy, followed with one hand resting upon his holstered gun.

"Andy's been home with us all night," Sue told the cops. She pulled her white, fluffy bathrobe around her shoulders and looked to her husband for support.

"Can you please tell me what this is about?" Yip strode after the cops. "I shall call your superiors. Unless you have a warrant, you can't —" He was the one who had invited them in, so he knew his protests were quite hollow. "What is Andy supposed to have done?"

"Nothing," the big cop growled. He swung a hard punch at Andy's jaw, and the kid hit the tiled floor.

"Hey!" Yip yelled and ran at the cop.

Sue squealed and began to cry as her son lay groaning at her feet; thick, bright blood bubbled from his mouth and pooled on the pale gray tiles by his head, suggesting he'd bitten through his tongue.

"Stop where you are, sir!" The young cop barked at Yip and pulled his gun. "Hands on your head. You too, lady." He pointed his weapon directly at Sue's face; she whimpered and, following her husband's lead, did as instructed and placed her hands on top of her head.

The older cop pulled his thin metal baton from his belt and held it high above his head.

"Please, no," Yip groaned. "Whatever he's done, we can make it right."

The baton swung down fast and hard and connected with Andy Yip's ribs. He screamed in pain and writhed on the cool tiles. The baton found its mark once more, and the wet, splintering crack of snapping ribs echoed around the high ceiling of the mansion's lobby. Andy yelped like a kicked dog and sobbed. He attempted to scramble away on his hands and knees, but the cop lashed out with a heavy boot; it connected with the side of Andy's head, the boy's ear split open, and he crashed, face first, to the floor.

"Stop it!" Yip yelled at the cop. Ignoring the gun pointing at him, he stepped forward with his hands still on his head. "What has he done?"

"Nothing, Mr. Yip," the cop snarled. "It's what *you* have done—or rather what you've failed to do. Mr. Wen says he's very much looking forward to seeing you at his office tomorrow. He asked me to tell you that he anticipates picking up on the meeting you inexplicably postponed this afternoon. He'll have his assistant call you to fix a mutually convenient time. And if you should consider standing him up a second time, we will be forced to pay you another visit." He gave Sue Yip a significant look, then swung around and made his way to the door.

His young partner put away his gun and followed. "Thank you for your time," he said as Sue Yip cradled her son's bloodied head in her arms and cried softly. "Enjoy the rest of your evening, folks."

The cops stepped out into the warm night and closed the door gently behind them.

* * *

"I hope you didn't kill him," Shum Kuo said from the shadows. He sucked on a freshly lit cigarette; its tip glowed cherry red in the black, still air.

The older cop seemed offended by Shum's implied criticism. "It's not like we haven't done this before, sir. You trained us well. The kid'll live."

"And Yip got the message."

"Loud and clear."

"Good," Shum said with a bleak smile. "Then you've earned your money tonight, gentlemen."

CHAPTER FORTY

Valentina met Yan at the Garden Road tram station, where Hong Kong's historic funicular railway began its journey of just under a mile up to the top of The Peak. He'd left her hotel room a little before dawn to go home to shower and change, and was at the station looking smart, wide awake, and daisy fresh by seven thirty. As it was early on a weekday, few tourists were about. In fact, the station was all but empty. Valentina chalked that up to the protests and their violent put-down, which had caused Hong Kong's tourist traffic to fall off drastically.

"I let Lucas know I was heading out to a client meeting," Valentina told Yan. "'It's all good,' he says. I'd swear he was a little buzzed. Sometimes I think that guy is too laid back for his own good."

Yan shook his head, his expression dead serious. "Don't let that charming facade fool you, Valentina. Lucas Vaughn can be a cold bastard when he's doing Wen's bidding. He just shoves his conscience into a hole and carries on. You really ought to be careful around him." He stepped into the tram's front carriage and held out a hand. "Shall we?"

Valentina took Yan's hand and climbed aboard. "Where's your

client?" She looked around the carriage and saw that it was empty, apart from the two of them and the driver in his little cab up front.

"He will be getting on at Kennedy Road; he lives in Mid-Levels and it's closer to home. So, what do you think?" Yan gestured out the window at the surrounding countryside as the tram's doors closed and it set off on its upward journey.

"It's lovely . . . picturesque. Somehow I'd gotten the impression that all Hong Kong business was done in the karaoke bars and spas."

The banker laughed. "Or on absurdly large yachts? KTV is not quite this guy's scene, and women don't do business in the spas—not this kind of business, anyway. The spas are very much a male domain in Hong Kong."

Yan slipped an arm around Valentina's waist; he apparently thought the one-hundred-thirty-year-old Peak Tram was romantic. She couldn't disagree.

As the tram slowly trundled its way up to the higher elevations of Hong Kong Island, the skyscrapers came into view below, along with the glinting backdrop of the harbor where, just the night before, Valentina had watched the light show from Wen's yacht. The city all looked so very different in the light of day, artificial, like one of those artful matte paintings used in science fiction shows. Gazing out across the cityscape, Valentina espied a few tiny curls of black smoke snaking their way up between the concrete and glass buildings; the protesters had made an early start.

She turned her gaze to the verdant treetops that bordered the tram's track; she was surprised at how much she missed greenery. She found it soothing. Even the cold, gray stone of the mountainside on the opposite side of the track was delicately draped and dotted with moss and lichen. After days of deep city canyons, broken up only by her excursion around the island on Wen's yacht, it felt good to be close to nature for a while.

Valentina's body still ached a little from Zhang's "warning," but not as much as yesterday. Her vigorous workout with Yan the night before had ironed out a great many of the kinks and knots Zhang's thugs had given her, and she was anticipating a repeat performance. She dared hope she was healing in more than the purely physical sense.

At several of the stops before Kennedy Road, a handful of people boarded the tram. A couple wore the archetypal bulky backpacks and chatted excitedly to each other, which immediately singled them out as tourists. Valentina's mind snapped back to the Cha Lau Yu Palace, and to the young man who'd left his backpack on the seat by the front door. Unconsciously, she checked out the exit doors and calculated her chances of surviving a drop down into the tree canopy below.

Kennedy Road stop.

All but Valentina, Yan, and the matching pair of chattering tourists alighted, and a diminutive but portly Chinese gentleman in a too-tight, navy-blue, three-piece suit clambered aboard.

"If I had to guess . . ." Valentina whispered.

Yan nodded. "Stephen Yen-Sheh," he said. "CEO of Tech-Radio LLC—radio over the internet."

"A neat idea," Valentina replied, flashing Yan a sassy grin. "Even if it is a technological step backward."

"A backward step worth over five billion Hong Kong dollars." Arm outstretched, Yan stepped forward to greet Yen-Sheh as the door eased shut and the tram began to move again.

The older man's wan smile revealed a mouthful of crooked, yellowed teeth. "It is good to see you, Gao Yanlin. And your beautiful assistant, of course."

He glanced across at Valentina as she studied his prematurely aged, sallow skin and graying hair; she was getting used to seeing Hong Kong's world-weary and desperate by now, and tried to imagine what vice had landed the poor man in the predicament he was about to walk headlong into.

Yan made the introduction. "This is Valentina Vittorio. A colleague."

"Italian?" Yen-Sheh all but had to strain his neck to look Valentina in the eye.

"American. I'm from New York." She gave him a firm handshake, glancing over his shoulder at the pair of tourists. They had stopped talking and removed their backpacks to rest them on the floorboards next to their seat. A cold chill coursed through her veins, raising the hair on the back of her neck. She could still hear the echoes of the explosive destruction of the Palace.

Was this PTSD or . . . ?

Yen-Sheh's small, clammy hand was still in Valentina's when the tourists rose in unison, turned toward the back of the car, and advanced on the trio standing there, each wielding a so-called "zombie-killer" knife—a small, slim machete with a smooth, keen blade on one side and a sharply serrated one on the other. The weapons had been popularized by the movies and TV shows that gave them their horror movie moniker.

The harsh glint of keen, polished steel flashed in the morning sunlight, and Valentina abandoned cogent thought and put her reflexes in control. She tightened her grip on Yen-Sheh's hand, grasped his forearm in a steel grip, and pulled him behind her. The businessman yelped out an indignant protest, which cut off when he saw the two young people moving toward him with silent and deadly purpose. Something deep in Valentina's gut told her this was no ordinary mugging; this was an assassination.

Her instinct was proven correct when the young man attacked with not so much as a demand for money. He lunged at Yan, flailing the zombie-killer and hissing like an oversized serpent. Terrified eyes fixed on the wicked silver blade, Yan leapt backward with a strangled cry.

Valentina grabbed the guy's wrist just as the razor-sharp blade sliced through the sleeve of Yan's jacket. Yan shrieked and grabbed at his wounded arm as the sleeve darkened with a bloom of crimson blood. Valentina twisted the assailant's arm and felt the bones grind beneath her fingers. Still refusing to relinquish his knife, the guy lashed out with his free hand and landed a solid blow to Valentina's already bruised flank.

The wave of sharp pain that filled her body loosened her grip on the would-be assassin's arm, but it also set off a cascade of cold fury. This guy had poked his stick in the wrong damn hornet's nest. Before he could slash at her with the knife, she aimed a powerful kick at his knee. She connected, the knee hyperextended, and with a loud grunt, he teetered on the verge of collapse.

Seeing her companion in distress, the young woman let out a shrill, ear-splitting shriek and launched herself at Yan. Staggering back, the banker pressed himself against the rear wall of the tram carriage and held up his arms to defend his face. Beside him, Yen-Sheh scrambled under the steel frame of the tram's back seat and did his best to disappear.

Valentina spun toward the girl, aiming a fist toward the cute, round face. The girl was fast; Valentina's hand skimmed the ponytail that flew like a silky banner behind the assassin's head. She growled and half turned to go after Ponytail, but the other assassin had stopped himself from collapse and made a limping lunge at Valentina with the zombie-killer. The way he was dragging his right leg, Valentina was sure she'd broken the knee, but he was still fast. She took advantage of his weapon's length, which made it a poor choice for close combat: She sidestepped, grasped his outthrust arm, and pulled, using the guy's momentum to carry him past her. As he drew level, he twisted his wiry body and shot out his free hand to grasp Valentina's throat.

She reflexively bent herself backward, allowing her attacker's weight and impetus to carry her to the floor, where she rolled, carrying the would-be assassin with her. She used the strength of her legs to lift him, intending to fling him over her head. She couldn't. He clung to her throat with the tenacity of a bulldog and enough strength to cut off the air to her lungs. Valentina's brain began to fog, and her lungs heaved painfully in her chest as they fought to draw breath.

Atop her, half suspended by her legs, his knife hand in her grip, he leered down into her face, teeth bared, eyes full of artificial fire, spittle oozing from the corners of his mouth. She couldn't let go of his arm, couldn't allow him to regain his feet, to put enough distance between them to slash at her with the blade. So she simultaneously brought a knee up between his legs and smashed her forehead into the bridge of his nose.

He shrieked in pain and spat a thick wad of blood and snot into

Valentina's face. As his hand loosened from her throat, she gulped down much-needed oxygen and wrenched her mind back into sharp focus. Tightening her grip around her attacker's wrist, Valentina twisted hard. This time she felt—and heard—the bones snap. He roared in pain, but somehow managed to hang on to his damned knife.

Valentina took comfort in the knowledge that his ruined wrist would be unable to lift it. With a broken knee and a broken wrist, both on the same side of his body, any attacks he might attempt now would be slow and weak.

Fine, then. Keep the damn knife. Valentina pushed him off her body and scrambled to her feet. What she saw when she looked toward the rear of the tram felt like a gut punch.

Yan had clearly been doing his damndest to fight off the girl; his hands were cut and bloodied, and blood streamed down his face from a vicious slice across his cheek. The entire lower half of his face was coated with a curtain of blood, and the assassin had him pinned against the rear of the tram. He didn't stand a chance without Valentina's help.

Beneath her feet, the tram jittered as it ground slowly to a halt. Outside the large windows was nothing but woodlands. They were between stops.

She heard the male assassin moving, gathering himself. From the corner of her eye, she saw him transfer the knife from one hand to the other and twist to face her. She shot out a hand, grabbed a fistful of his short black hair, and twisted. He screamed in rage and tried to swing his knife at her legs. Despite the fact that he was off balance, Valentina had to twist her hips and jump back to dodge the keen blade. It caught the crossbody strap of her purse and severed it. The Hermès bag dropped to the floor of the tram. With a pained snarl, Valentina slammed her clenched fist into the guy's throat and, finally, he let go of the blade to clutch at his crushed windpipe.

Taking no time to watch her assailant as he fell gasping and choking to the floor, Valentina picked up the zombie-killer and turned back to face the girl. The tram came to a full stop and the doors slid open. The driver bolted, leaping from the tram and disappearing into the woods below.

No help there.

Panting for breath, her throat on fire, Valentina advanced on the girl. Yan had done an admirable job of fighting her off, but now he lay at her feet with his back propped against the blood-smeared carriage. He was a complete mess; his shirt was cut to ribbons, the flesh behind it sliced and bleeding and raw, and his lacerated face was a mask of sticky, glistening red. His hands were shredded to ribbons and had at least two fingers missing from each as far as Valentina could tell. The girl still stood over him, unconcerned or unaware that her companion lay dying and oozing blood only a few feet away. She had lifted her blade to deliver her *coup de grace.*

"No!" Valentina screeched and slashed at the girl's back with the knife.

Blood splashed out from the cleanly sliced jacket, and as the girl spun around, her slack, emotionless face registered no sign of pain. Her eyes were black holes with dilated pupils. Drugs, Valentina guessed. She swung her blade at Valentina's face. Valentina jumped back—over the body of the assassin she'd just killed—and felt the breeze of the metal as it missed her eyes by a hair's breadth. Before Valentina could gain ground, the girl lunged at her, two-handing the zombie-killer into a slashing arc aimed at Valentina's throat.

Valentina's instinctive parry stopped the assassin's blade dead, with a jarring clang of metal on metal. She fought hard to keep hold of the hilt as the shockwave drummed its way up her arm and threatened to loosen her fingers. The remembered wisdom of a Little League coach after she took a 60-mph pitch too high up the bat made her clamp down, gripping the hilt with both hands. The girl leapt back and lashed out with her foot; it caught Valentina's already bruised thigh. The muscle spasmed, threatening to spill her onto the floor. Propping the opposite hip against a seat to steady herself, Valentina thrust the zombie-killer out, arm's length, toward her attacker. The wicked blade gleamed.

Valentina did not so much as twitch, but the girl's eyes flicked from side to side, as if seeking something. The briefest hesitation caught

Valentina's attention. The assassin was eyeing the backpacks she and her dead colleague had discarded by the tram's door.

Burn the evidence.

Taking advantage of the shift in the other's attention, Valentina feinted at the girl's chest. The assassin was quick enough to not take the blade in the heart, but the honed tip sliced through the thick, padded jacket at her shoulder. The girl shrieked like a banshee and leapt forward with her blade aimed at Valentina's breast. She put everything she had left into the attack, grunting with exertion and pain from the two wounds Valentina had dealt her.

Blocking with her own knife, Valentina jumped backward onto the seat behind her—narrowly escaping the blade as it whisked past her thigh. Tensing, she prepared to drop onto the assassin and use her superior weight and strength to overpower the petite girl. But, instead of turning her weapon back on Valentina, the girl spun away and made a dash for the tram's open doors.

"Fuck you!" Valentina screamed. "Fuck you!" In an uncontrollable outpouring of rage and fear, she hurled her zombie-killer through the doors at the fleeing assassin. As if guided by an invisible hand, the blade found its mark between the girl's shoulder blades at the very base of her neck; she went down like a headshot deer and lay twitching and gurgling up dark blood on the slope below the tram.

For a moment, Valentina could only stare at the other woman and flail mentally. The tram was silent; the only sounds were birds in the hemming trees and the creak of tree branches in the breeze. She'd killed . . . again.

Fuck this. I need to move. I need to do something.

Valentina shrugged off her paralysis and got down from the seat. She stepped over the body of the male assassin and knelt down by Yan.

"Yan?" She pressed her fingers against the banker's neck, slick with coagulating blood.

There was no pulse.

Maybe I'm just too rattled. Maybe . . . .

She tried again, his wrist, then his neck. She put her face close to his, hoping to feel his breath on her cheek. As she had felt it last night.

There was no breath to feel. He was gone.

Valentina groaned aloud as she surveyed the damage the assassin had done to her lover's body. A single thrust of the deadly knife would have sufficed to put Yan down—he was completely unarmed, after all. But *this*—the shredded clothes; bloodied, exposed flesh; and the lacerated hands and face—this was more akin to the fabled Death of a Thousand Cuts that had been the favored method of torture and execution in the China of old. Valentina understood the attack had been more than an assassination of a local banker—it had been a message.

"Police?"

The suddenness and unexpectedness of Yen-Sheh's voice startled Valentina. She was on her feet with her hands raised to strike; she'd forgotten all about Yan's client.

Shaking, Yen-Sheh crawled out from beneath the tram seat. Keeping his eyes fixed firmly on Valentina, he seemed determined to avoid looking at the blood and carnage around him. "We call the police?" He pulled a cell phone from his pants pocket, thumbed it on.

Valentina snatched the phone from the guy's hand and handed it back to him. "No! Do you want everyone on the island to know about this meeting?"

Yen-Sheh shook his head.

Valentina glanced in the direction of the two backpacks that still sat at the front of the tram car. "I thought as much. Look, Mr. Yen-Sheh, we really need to get the fuck out of here."

Grabbing his arm in one hand and her ruined purse in the other, she dragged the old man out of the carriage and down onto the track bed. He gagged as he tripped over the female assassin's arm and she let out a low, liquid moan.

How stubbornly we cling to life. Even the kind of life she must have had.

"Forget about her," Valentina told him. "Forget about Gao Yanlin, his crooked bank—and you have to forget about me too. You never met me, Mr. Yen-Sheh."

She led the shocked businessman away through the woods. Time was ticking, and she knew she had to get them both away from the tram. It tore her up to leave Yan behind like that, but to risk their lives to save a dead man made little sense. Yan might have once been one of the good guys, but he'd gotten caught up in Hong Kong's vicious cycle of greed and corruption. Despite that, he hadn't deserved to die like that.

The tram was a good way behind them, although Valentina could still see it through the trees. She finally let go of the man's arm. "Most of all, Mr. Yen-Sheh, you need to stay the fuck away from Jimmy Wen. Do you understand me? Jimmy Wen is why Gao Yanlin is dead."

Face gray with nausea, silenced by shock, Stephen Yen-Sheh could only nod his reply.

They'd no more than turned to resume their escape when the tram exploded, a fireball blossoming in a deadly bloom taking its three victims with it and blasting shards of wood into the air. Valentina felt the heat of its destruction on her back as she guided Stephen Yen-Sheh down the hill toward the road.

CHAPTER FORTY-ONE

The explosion on the Victoria Peak Tram was all over the news by the time Valentina made it back to 2IFC at a little after two o'clock. Given the increasing unrest in Hong Kong, the incident was swiftly and conveniently attributed to the actions of the antigovernment protesters, and served to ensure all police were green-lit to shoot with more than rubber bullets and water cannons. No mention was made of any victims—just that the search of the tram's wreckage was continuing. Valentina found herself hoping the girl who'd murdered Yan had held on long enough to feel the searing heat of her own bomb blast.

She'd looked a wreck. Her suit coat was in tatters, her hair was in wild disarray, and she had a few new bruises and cuts to show for her close encounter with the assassins. Under other circumstances, she'd have rued the loss of yet another expensive suit, but she was past caring about anything that ephemeral. She'd had to return to her hotel to shower, tend to her wounds, and make herself look presentable. She had chosen her replacement outfit carefully, selecting a purse with a chain for a strap (too little too late) and a high-necked blouse to cover the new bruises on her neck that could not have been passed off as anything other than an attempted strangulation. A coy suggestion that it was the result of an amorous encounter would only reflect on Yan; that was a nonstarter.

On her way back to the office, she'd stopped at a Starbucks for a muffin and some coffee. The food was hard to swallow for reasons both physical and emotional, but she found if she chewed the muffin to a pulp then used the coffee to almost liquefy it, she could manage. She used the careful process as a means of composing herself. She could not return to the office looking hyped up or beaten down.

Things were moving too fast. People were dying all around her. She felt out of control.

Downhill ice-skating.

She realized with a jolt that she'd survived two explosions now. Which aphorism applied: Third time's a charm, or bad luck comes in threes? Did it matter?

She thought of Kate Bennett—a blessing and a curse. Even though the Englishwoman gave her some sort of backstop or ally, she complicated things as well. But she had to admit that Zhang Bo complicated them more. She wished she'd never found his name buried in Wen's secret files, then realized how absurd that was. Whether she knew about his skeevy relationship with JM Wen or not, he'd still have done what he'd done; perhaps her only salvation now was that she was playing mole for Interpol.

Yesterday's absentee client, Gordon Yip, was on his way out of the office as Valentina walked in; she recognized him from the briefing document Lucas had sent to her cell phone prior to the soiree on the yacht. She held open the door for him. Staring directly ahead with worry etched into his haggard face, the man didn't as much acknowledge Valentina's presence, let alone her courtesy.

"Miss Vittorio." Shum Kuo greeted Valentina as the oversized glass doors closed behind Yip. He'd escorted Yip as far as the reception foyer, apparently. "It's nice of you to make an appearance. Better late than never, they say."

"You look surprised to see me, Mr. Shum," Valentina countered with a half smile as she made her way along the hallway. "I had a client meeting, but then again, you probably knew that already."

"There's very little I don't know." Shum walked alongside Valentina as if he, too, had business in the sales office.

"Then you'll also know it went very well—more client shares for Mr. Wen."

Shum shrugged his broad shoulders and twisted his mouth into some semblance of a smile. "I'm sure it did, Miss Vittorio, but separating clients from their shares and money is none of my concern. Why would it be?"

It was Valentina's turn to shrug. She supposed it was possible Shum had nothing to do with the attack on the tram—on Yan. "Well, this is me," she announced with her hand on the sales office door. "Thank you for keeping me company. It's been a pleasure."

Valentina watched as Shum eyed her for a moment before turning on his heels to head off in the direction of his own domain. He had no reaction to her condescension; maybe the guy didn't get sarcasm.

Sitting down at her desk, Valentina noted Anthony and Lam were the only other rainmakers in the sales office, and both were engrossed in their respective phone calls. They'd seen her come in, but neither bothered to acknowledge her presence—they only gave her leery side-eyed glances. It was as if they were instinctively worried about their own self-preservation . . . as if they *knew* something. Or maybe they were scared of her now, having heard Lucas extolling her ninja-like reflexes and killer instincts.

There was an email from Lucas in her inbox, or rather a forwarded email from Jimmy Wen. It was marked *urgent* in bold, capital letters. It came as a welcome distraction from the vivid images that insisted on replaying in her head like a demon slide deck. She had liked Yan. He'd been sweet and fun and engaging, and she'd enjoyed their intimacy. She'd wanted to be able to look back on that with pleasure; now she didn't want to think about it . . . or think about him at all, let alone in the past tense.

Valentina banished the ghost of Gao Yanlin and read through the email.

More of the same: *sell, sell, sell!* Wen was really panicking now. Even without the knowledge she'd unearthed of his double-dealing with the Triads, Valentina would have easily been able to read between the lines of her boss's ostensibly motivational email. She was sick of hearing it.

Naturally, Wen's email skirted around the reasons as to why the company required such large sums of cash in a short period of time, and made no mention of the fact that the share prices of the six key companies pertinent to Zhang Bo's portfolio were still inexplicably rising. It also failed to mention among its ebullient sales speak and motivational call to action that each and every one of the top performers Wen had pulled in from the international offices were unwitting parties to a Ponzi scheme of gargantuan proportions—it was all designed to save Wen's lying, manipulative, duplicitous skin from the wrath of arguably the most ruthless, vicious gangsters on the planet.

Too little, too fucking late, Jimmy. You're on the ropes, Zhang knows it, and his patience has run out.

Valentina clamped down on the plastic pen gripped in her teeth; she'd chewed her way through a half dozen of the things—each one to the point of tasting the sour tang of spilled ink in her mouth. Zhang must have known damn well what was going on with Wen and his shares. If the deal had gone as Zhang expected, his money was not only squeaky clean, it had multiplied like the loaves and fishes. He may not have been entirely aware that Wen had sold the shares before the ink was even dry on the contracts, but he *had* to have known Wen was lying through his teeth about why he wouldn't just hand them over.

Jimmy Wen had sinned against the wrong guy, and Valentina Vittorio Parisi was going to lay those sins bare—with help from Kate Bennett and Interpol. What she'd hoped to do was steer the bastard toward disaster without implicating herself. Was that now out of the question? So far, nothing had gone quite the way she'd planned, and she'd only just come to appreciate how much risk she'd bitten off.

She pushed the implications of being discovered to the back of her mind. If she thought about that—and about every freaking, awful thing that had happened to her or to the people around her, she'd be on the first plane back to Staten Island. She shook her head; how invincible she'd felt as she'd formulated her plans, plotted her upward trajectory, exulted over the phone call from Mai Lin, stepped triumphantly onto the plane to Hong Kong, and breezed through the doors of JM Wen, Limited. She didn't feel invincible now. Not under the watchful eye of Shum Kuo and the Triads.

Valentina sat back in her chair. What if she handed over *everything* she'd unearthed to Bennett, got the hell out of Dodge, and let Interpol and the SFC deal with Wen?

Bennett had made it painfully clear that Valentina still had a pivotal role to play in the Interpol agent's grand scheme, but if she was back home and safely ensconced in New York, she'd be well away from any fallout as Bennett brought Jimmy Wen to justice—even if it did take her another year or so.

Providing Wen didn't do his vanishing act again, that is.

That was the thought that stopped her—that made absconding back to the States a no-op.

Jimmy Wen had used a string of pseudonyms and fake documentation when he'd fled Staten Island a decade ago to leave his two hapless associates to carry the can. He'd been known as Jackie Roberts back in those days, and had built a back story of having been adopted at birth by a nice, working class American couple and given a Western name. The truth was, no one knew where Wen had actually come from. He'd simply popped up in New York with his small, penny-stock trading company and a whole lot of big talk about making people filthy rich. It was the kind of magical thinking that appealed to the desperate, the gullible, and the hopelessly romantic—all of which had applied to Federico Parisi.

Valentina didn't like to think of her father as desperate, but she'd known him well enough to vouch for his gullibility and idealistic romanticism. The elusive Jackie Roberts's high-octane sales spiel had resonated with her father to the point that all he could see were the dollar signs—and lots of them. He'd clung to the hope that the investments he'd sunk all of his family's money into would come good just as Roberts assured him they would, right up until the moment he'd leapt from the ferry.

Jackie Roberts/Jimmy Wen may just as well have pushed Valentina's dad off the ferry with his own two hands.

Valentina shoved all thought of fleeing back to New York out of her head and leaned forward to read Wen's frightened bleat of an email message again. He would not disappear this time. It had taken her far too many years to track him down, to chip away at the countless aliases and dummy companies he'd left in his wake. No fucking way she'd allow him to vanish into thin air again. With Zhang Bo circling like a buzzard over fresh road kill, it was only a matter of time before Wen tried to bolt from Hong Kong—and he'd take with him a large portion of the money she and her colleagues had brought in. She had to bring him down before that happened. For the pain he'd caused her family, Valentina was going to make damned sure the son of a bitch suffered.

She jumped when the burner phone in her purse buzzed, and realized she'd broken yet another pen in two.

CHAPTER FORTY-TWO

"We're meeting here? Why?"

"Why not?" Bennett peered around at the mix of locals and excited tourists who shared the line with them. "A well-populated tourist spot after hours is ideal. And unexpected. You need to learn to relax a little, Valentina—unless you think you were followed?"

Straining her neck to look up, Valentina took in the view of the huge Ferris wheel that towered above them. "I was last out of the sales office and I left through the back door to avoid the protesters," she told Bennett. "I definitely wasn't followed."

"Then all is well and good. It's really quite spectacular, don't you think?" Bennett sounded like Mary Poppins. "They call it the Observation Wheel. One hundred and ninety-seven feet with commanding views of Victoria Harbor. Most impressive . . . though not quite as impressive as the London Eye. That one is three hundred and ninety-four feet. I took my kids when it opened back in 2000."

"You have kids?" Valentina was taken aback; she'd not once considered the lady agent might actually have had a life outside Interpol.

Bennett's nod was wistful. "All grown up and flown the nest now, of course. I like to get back to England to see them when I can."

"A husband?"

"Widowed. Iraq." Bennett kept her eyes on the wheel.

The line shuffled forward and the group in front of Bennett and Valentina made their way into the awaiting gondola. It was a red steel-and-glass pod the size of a small U-Haul van that looked like a gigantic Chinese lantern and boasted utilitarian white plastic seating for eight people. Valentina stepped forward; there was ample room in the pod.

Bennett held out an arm to stop her. "Ours is the next one," she said. "I thought we should have a carriage to ourselves. I know a chap—"

"Of course you do."

The next gondola discharged its passengers, and the amiable young man managing the line waved Bennett and Valentina forward. He held up a hand to the small group behind them to make it quite clear they were to remain in line. It was the VIP gondola, a more luxurious car with a capacity of five, leather seats, and a glass floor.

"I feel like royalty," Valentina said as she followed Bennett into the gondola and the door slid shut behind them. "But I'm guessing you didn't invite me along to show me the sights."

"Of course not." She sat herself down on one of the plush leather seats and stared out across Central Harborfront. "First of all, I'd like to say how very sorry I was to hear about Gao Yanlin. You two were . . . close?"

Valentina settled onto the bench opposite and considered her answer. Clearly, Bennett knew she and Yan had been together the night before . . . and she wanted Valentina to know it. She shrugged to imply it was no big deal. "We had a little fun together. He was actually turning out to be useful. Yan loved to talk, especially when he was—what is it you Brits say—in his cups? He had quite a bit to say about LCSSC and Li Jiang. I think he assumed I was a JM Wen insider."

Bennett was still for a moment, watching Valentina through hooded eyes. The weight of the agent's regard made it hard to maintain her unemotional facade, hard to keep at bay the twist of regret that she'd been unable to save Gao Yanlin.

Something of this must have showed in her face, for the Interpol agent leaned forward in her seat and fixed her with a disconcertingly direct gaze, and said, "There's nothing you might have done, Tina."

Her voice was gentle but firm—Mary Poppins again—and Valentina tried not to react to her jarring use of the pet name. Her sister and father had called her Tina. She thought of herself as Tina. She opened her mouth to protest, but the impulse faded.

Just let it go.

Bennett turned to stare out across the water as the wheel turned soundlessly and the gondola rose high up into the dimming sky. "Doubtless Mr. Gao's chattiness was what got him killed. Running his mouth off about the bank and its dealings with JM Wen and Zhang Bo was always going to make him some dangerous enemies."

"You think Yan was the target, not his client?"

"That's my opinion."

"Who do you think orchestrated the hit on the tram? The Triads?"

"It's fifty-fifty right now as to who ordered the hit, but my money would be on Wen."

Valentina found the idea beyond disturbing. "Not Zhang?"

"I really don't think so. The killers underestimated you, which would have been an unlikely mistake for Zhang to make once, let alone twice."

"But Wen was there when we got carjacked." Valentina countered. "He knows what happened."

Bennett seemed to be intent on the ripples in the water below. "But Jimmy Wen doesn't mastermind his own hits. He relies on the likes of Shum Kuo, who arrived too late on Tuesday night to witness your performance firsthand. Then too, both of them were on the yacht yesterday, and if Mr. Gao said anything to you there . . ."

Valentina nodded. He had. He'd said a lot to her there, and while there'd been no one close enough to overhear him, it was entirely possible that the boat, like the offices of JM Wen, was bugged. It hardly mattered now.

"So, where do we go from here?" She didn't much relish further discussion of Yan's murder with Bennett; it had affected her more deeply than she cared to admit, and she had to keep her head clear to ensure she didn't meet with the same fate.

"Going by the information you've sent me so far—and guessing at what I'm pretty damn certain you're holding back, I'd say we are good to go with the final phase. You do know how to get to Wen's market makers?" The agent raised a quizzical eyebrow.

Valentina gazed out across the cityscape as their giant Chinese lantern neared the top of the wheel's arc. "I don't know where they are, exactly, but I'm sure I can tap into the line of communication Wen has with them."

"Then we continue to pump the prices of Jimmy Wen's Golden Six up as high as we can, as quickly as we can. That's sure to push him over the edge."

Stunned, Valentina stared at the agent. "You? I mean, Interpol has been inflating the stock prices?"

Bennett's smile was teasing. "Surely you don't think my list of helpful friend extends only to people who can get me a private gondola on the Ferris wheel?"

"Market making is illegal," Valentina said. "How the fuck can Interpol justify that?"

"Bend the law to uphold the law—it's kind of our motto in the Hong Kong office."

"Are the SFC involved in market making too?"

Bennett shook her head. "I've already divulged too much, Valentina, so I shall leave that for you to figure out." She returned her attention to the world beyond the window. "What you must remain focused upon is that the bigger the hole Wen gets himself into with Zhang and the Wo Hop Yee clan, the more mistakes he's going to make."

"And the more self-made rope for Interpol and the SFC to hang him with?"

Bennett smiled again. This one had a bit of tooth and venom to it. "From the highest lamppost we can find, my dear. In the mean-time, I will need you to feed fake information to Wen's influencers, celebrity friends, politicians, and the like. For my part, I'll be liaising with the SFC to provide the necessary cover once the red flags start going up. A sudden increase in activity on those company's shares is likely to have the regulators shutting down trading—pending investigation—especially with Asia Lion Entertainment being involved."

"Zhang's company."

"Nail on the head," Bennett replied. "The SFC is just waiting in the wings for an excuse to shut that one down. With the specific stock loan and share sales dates you're feeding me, along with the clients involved—and you do need to be sure to provide me with *all* of those —once Jimmy Wen makes his big, lethal mistake, we can bring him and his whole illicit empire down."

Bennett shifted on the padded seat and craned her neck to watch one of the omnipresent tourist helicopters circling above the wheel.

"I hope you're right," Valentina murmured.

"They all do, you know—make that big, glaring, stupid mistake," Bennett told her. "In the end, and with enough pressure, even the hardest criminals and coolest con men panic and undo themselves. It was client names, dates, and proof of repaid loans that brought down Argyll, Spanier, and McClain. The devil is very much in the details with these things."

Valentina frowned. "But what about the dirty bank? You're not going to let them off the hook."

Bennett met Valentina's gaze again. "I know you have your own motives, and I appreciate your desire to bring Wen down in an inglorious blaze. But, as they say in American baseball, you have to have a deep bench. And if you can't get the home run, you have to be prepared to play small ball." She paused, then added, "Tina, I'm sorry that nothing we can do here will bring your father back . . . or any of those we've lost."

An uneasy quiet settled between the two as the wheel slowed to a gentle stop with their carriage at the top. The sound of chopper rotors created a rhythmic white noise, the gondola rocking slightly in the wash of its blades. Glancing up through the glass canopy, Valentina could see the running lights of the copter above them. She imagined the tourists inside were far more appreciative of the spectacular view of Victoria Harbor than she was.

"Having said all that," Bennett said at length, "I'm thinking we may well have enough incriminating information to go for Wen's dirty bank, too, for money laundering and taking fat kickbacks for illegal client referrals. It would certainly be a feather in the cap to close those bastards down—Li Jiang has been flouting the law for a hell of a long time now, and it's about time that caught up with him."

Valentina leaned forward, elbows on knees. "But what about the small investors—those who have legitimate dealings with LCSSC and JM Wen Limited? For every dirty deal I've uncovered, I've seen three times as many legit clients. There are a hell of a lot of innocent people who will be ruined once Wen and his dirty bank go under; it'll be Enron all over again. Families losing their savings—"

"You're just going to have to trust me on that one. You know that I have resources, and I will use those resources to try to ensure the innocent are protected. I give you my word on that. But that part of this is strictly between you and me."

Despite Bennett's reassuring words, Valentina was reluctant to put her entire trust in the Interpol agent. Bennett was the catcher, the one who could make things happen with the information she dug up, but Valentina still didn't know for sure whom she could trust—after all, Hong Kong was run by Triads and crooks like Jimmy Wen, who had people like Bennett in their pockets as a regular part of their enterprises. It made sense to keep a few secrets to herself, and it made equal sense that doing that might tie Interpol's hands and keep them from the sort of "inglorious blaze" she wanted for Jimmy Wen's reckoning.

"You know," Bennett mused, pulling Valentina from her private thoughts, "I'm even beginning to think you might just have gathered enough intelligence for Interpol to pin something on Zhang Bo. Closing down a Triad gang—now, wouldn't that be something for me to retire on?"

A low, muffled *pop* reverberated through the glass carriage, making it tremble.

"What the fuck?" Valentina stood up and steadied herself on the quaking floor. She stared at the ceiling. "Did something just break?"

"Most likely just the fireworks." Bennett squinted at her watch. "Though they're quite early."

Another pop came, louder this time, and sharper. It reminded Valentina of her childhood days firing bottle rockets from the high school track with her dad and little sister.

A second later, the carriage dropped sharply on the landward side, and the glass ceiling shot through with spiderweb cracks that fractured the sky. Valentina stared upward through the riven glass, barely able to make out the shape of the gimbals that held the gondola to the Ferris wheel's frame. The seaward one was now deformed, and a wispy curl of gray smoke drifted away from it. This was not fireworks.

"That was an explosive charge." She struggled to keep her voice calm. "I think whoever was in that chopper was doing more than taking photos."

They were now at the apex of the Ferris wheel. Buffeted by the evening breeze, the gondola rocked, listing farther to port. The rotating joint groaned as its broken, deformed pieces grated against each other. Valentina took a quick assessment of the situation: the wheel was surrounded by hardscape and positioned away from the water—ironically for safety reasons. That meant that, should their carriage fall, it would hit the frame of the wheel or concrete.

"They're already evacuating people," Bennett said tersely.

They were. Far below, security people were clearing Central Harborfront of tourists. Valentina saw at least one police car making its way along the waterfront. She peered down through the glass floor toward the ground beneath the wheel; people were fleeing from the gondola currently at ground level. They had begun evacuating the ride as well.

Valentina turned to Bennett, her pulse spiking when she saw fear written across the older woman's face. "What the fuck are we supposed to do? There must be someone you can call."

Bennett snorted at her. "I'm not James Bond, Valentina, and there's no Q. We're seventy meters up in a glass coffin—what the hell do you think I can do? Pop a glider out of my shoe and fly us out of here?"

The Ferris wheel began to move, making the carriage lurch dizzyingly again. The broken gimbal complained loudly, and the gondola listed still farther to port. Acting on instinct, Valentina moved across to the seaward side of the carriage and held onto the seat next to Bennett. Perhaps if the thing was counterbalanced, the gimbal would hold?

Whether it would or not became suddenly moot; another explosion went off far below—right where the wheel's steel spokes joined the hub. The entire structure sagged toward the piers.

"Jesus!" Bennett cried. "They're going to bring down the whole thing!"

"We need to get out of here," Valentina growled. "If this thing topples, we're going into the water and we will drown in this damned fish bowl."

Using the seats for support against the erratic sway of the carriage, she inched over to the door, which now faced upward into the pink dusk sky at a near forty-five-degree angle. Reaching them, she glanced back at Bennett, who was staring down at the ruined hub and spokes.

"You gonna help me here, Kate?"

As the agent went into action, Valentina pressed her fingers against the tight rubber weather stripping between the glass doors and, using her fingernails as wedges, began to pull. Bennett added her short, strong fingers to the process, and between them, she and Valentina managed to pry the doors a half inch or so apart. The tiny victory was followed by another sharp rending groan from the mangled gimbal. The gondola jolted yet again, going into a swaying dance. The wheel groaned, shivered, and tilted toward the harbor like a palsied drunk. Valentina fought to keep her balance, refusing to glance at the ground. That was getting closer as the crew evacuated the cars below them, but it might as well have been a million miles away.

The doors gave a little more—this time just enough for Valentina to push her hands between them and pull hard. A hot, sharp pain spiked through her flank as her outraged muscles spasmed. With a loud grunt, she heaved at the doors with every ounce of her strength, wedging one hand through the growing aperture. Bennett added her own efforts and slowly, surely, the doors eased apart.

A sound somewhere between a roar and a moan rose from the tortured hub, and the great wheel tilted sharply by a dozen feet or more, making the carriage rock like a boat on a rough sea. The doors flew open. Caught off balance, Valentina and Bennett fell backward and landed in an ungainly heap together on the opposite side of the carriage; the glass of the harbor-side window cracked and bowed beneath their weight.

They lay there for a heartbeat or two, neither daring to be the first to move lest the glass give way and deposit them both onto the pier below; Valentina didn't need to look down to know they would never survive such a fall.

Hardening her resolve, using the leather seats for leverage, Valentina pulled herself up and made her way back toward the door she and Bennett had just pried open. The cool evening air wafted in to send prickling gooseflesh crawling across her body.

"We have to get out before this falls," Valentina said more for her own benefit than Bennett's.

She dared a glance at the carriage's busted gimbal, which showed scorched metal through its smoke-blackened red paint; might it hold long enough for the Ferris wheel to topple? If it did, there was a slim chance they might end up in the water. A very slim chance.

"You're serious?" Shaky, Bennett struggled to her feet and balanced herself against the thin bench.

"Why else would we open the fucking doors?"

With nothing constructive to say to that, Bennett stared out through the doors at the thick, steel beams of the wheel. It was canted at about a 45-degree angle and threatening to tilt farther.

"If it comes down slowly, we can do this." Valentina did her best to reassure; she knew it was a hell of a gamble, but what other choice did they have? "If we can time it right, we can get to one of those." She pointed at one of the thinner support struts that crisscrossed between the main beams like a metal cargo net.

Bennett shook her head. "No chance. I'm too bloody old for this."

"It's your choice, Kate." Ignoring the pain that flared up in her side and shoulder, Valentina hauled herself up through the doors and perched her ass on the side of the swaying carriage. Looking down, she held a hand out for Bennett.

Fighting hard to keep her feet, Bennett reached up to take Valentina's hand. Hers were slick with sweat. The agent was heavier than she looked. Valentina groaned out loud as she hauled Bennett up through the doors, and the white-hot agony in her side spread out through her entire body. Almost there, Bennett managed to grasp the side of the carriage to help Valentina with the effort of heaving her out.

A sharp, deep thud issued from below them and the wheel dropped dizzyingly another ten or fifteen feet before a jarring halt. As the carriage tilted wildly, Bennett lost her tenuous grip on the doorframe and fell, pulling Valentina down with her. They hit the lower side of the carriage to the sound of shattering glass. On its heels came the death roar of the ruined spokes as the weakened metal gave way.

The Ferris wheel toppled toward the harbor, gaining speed as it went. The gondola plummeted with it. At last breaking free of its broken gimbals, it plunged into the water between two piers, narrowly missing the concrete and stone of the wharf.

Bennett added her screams to those of the other unfortunates trapped in their steel cages. Ears ringing, hands grappled to the seat, Valentina braced herself, hoping the cracked glass would hold long enough to cushion the blow when they hit the water. It did, shattering inward. The dark water of the harbor flooded the carriage—so cold it tore Valentina's breath from her lungs. Craning her neck to keep her head above it, she coughed out salty water and dragged in what fresh air she could before the carriage sank beneath the surface.

All too quickly, they were submerged in the near darkness. Groping blindly around, Valentina located Bennett and grabbed the collar of her jacket; the agent was conscious but dazed from the shock of hitting the water. Small, silvery bubbles of air leaked out through her nostrils and slack mouth, and Valentina knew she had little time to get them both to the surface.

With a tight grip on the older woman, Valentina planted her feet on the seats, aimed herself toward the carriage's open doors (she hoped), and kicked off into the darkness.

CHAPTER FORTY-THREE

I t had been a hell of a long night.

Valentina had somehow gotten them out of the sinking gondola to the surface and used a lifeguard hold to drag Kate Bennett through the dark water into the shelter beneath Pier 9. Once the agent had gulped in air and recovered enough to think strategically, she started calling the shots. Valentina was only too happy to let her. At Bennett's insistence, they did not emerge onto the promenade with its bright lights and frantic activity. Instead, they'd inched their way beneath Pier 9, atop which the authorities were setting up to search, then swam for some yards in the shadow of the harbor wall. Hauling themselves out onto the promenade behind the police cordon and gawping crowds, they'd lost themselves in a noisy protest group, which had provided a more than convenient cover for their escape.

Bennett had steadfastly refused to allow Valentina to take her to a hospital, even though they both knew she'd taken a hard knock to the head and swallowed far more seawater than was good for her. Instead, she'd called her car; the two had hunkered in the lee of the Central Ferry building until it arrived.

Valentina was still soaking wet when she slipped into the Four Seasons through a side entrance. She lucked into finding an elevator with only two occupants and laughingly explained to the couple that she'd fallen into the pool.

"Not watching where I was going," she said, and knew they suspected she'd been drinking. She hardly cared.

It took a hot shower and a room service order of bouillabaisse and hot tea to get her to shop shivering. She'd spent the remainder of her waking hours going through Wen's files on her personal laptop and compiling a list of the key players she needed to manipulate into pushing Wen into a full-fledged panic.

With that done, she allowed herself to wonder about the source of the hit. Bennett had suggested the "accident" could easily have been the work of Jimmy Wen or Zhang Bo, either one of whom could have connected Interpol with the dead SFC agent. But then again, the sabotage of the Observation Wheel could just as well have been perpetrated by a radical faction of one of the antigovernment groups and the two women had simply been in the wrong place at the wrong time. Valentina didn't believe that for a New York minute and was pretty sure Bennett didn't believe it either. They were getting close to unraveling Wen's grubby little empire, and she figured someone was out to stop them.

She fell asleep in the middle of her ruminations and had weird dreams—all involved falling. By the time she woke, she'd learned to fly.

As of the next morning, the police were still searching the harbor for the two women who had been reported as being in the VIP gondola, although once first light flooded the wharfs, the news reported the search and rescue was now a recovery project. The only thing the police released about the two were that they were not Chinese. Several witnesses had said they thought they were British. Witnesses had also noticed the helicopter that seemed to hover too near the Observation Wheel. News analysts theorized that it might have come low enough to collide with the Ferris wheel's superstructure. Valentina suspected they'd only discover the truth once they dredged up the shattered gondola. God only knew what they'd make of it then.

With hard-earned detachment, Valentina pushed the events of

Thursday evening to the back of her mind—absolutely essential if she was to concentrate on the job at hand. She'd seen enough violence and death in the short time she'd been in Hong Kong to last her two lifetimes, and the sooner she was done with what needed to be done, the sooner she could get the hell away from the island and head back to New York to start a new life.

The sales office was peaceful and quiet, as it always was at seven in the morning; the overnight cleaning crews had been packing up when Valentina made her way in. She had the room to herself.

She brought her computer to life and contemplated the list of Wen's pet politicians, media personalities, and influencers. It included Lyn Song and the ubiquitous Shing Hai. She also had a direct email to Freddy Tseng all queued up. Just one choice message to the manager of Wen's stock walkers would prompt the market maker team to trade aggressively. That would send the key stocks through the roof and Jimmy Wen right along with them. In the irrational voodoo that drove the stock market, Valentina's email would be as powerful as a spell.

She'd composed the message in the wee hours of the morning. It was as clear and direct as if Wen had written it himself: Freddy Tseng was to drop everything he and his team were doing and prioritize the Golden Six. The objective, which went against everything Wen had previously dictated in regard to the six companies, was to drive the share prices as high as possible. Along with the note to Freddy Tseng, a corporate email to each of the other key players Valentina had listed would have them all publicizing and promoting the Golden Six, which would push those prices yet further skyward.

The emails would ostensibly be from Jimmy Wen's corporate account, though if anyone traced them, they'd find a different source. Valentina's tracks would remain covered—at least long enough for her to make good her escape.

Ever vigilant, she double-checked her proxy, VPN, and redirect software. Then she checked them all again. Another glance around the early morning office and a final tweak of the redirect software, and Valentina hit Send.

She sat back in her chair and let out a pent-up breath. God, but she wanted a cappuccino.

* * *

"Well, stick a fork in me. I'm done." Valentina's voice echoed in the restroom. "I mean, I am so done. Stayed up last night like a ninny just to finish that assignment. Then I couldn't get my brain to shut off, you know?"

"I'm watching at this end," Bennett said. "Now all we can do is wait."

Valentina took in a deep breath. "Really, Katie? You're sure you got this?"

"I got this," Bennett said, a tracery of wry humor in her tone. "You're becoming very proficient at 'spook speak.' Keep up the good work." She hung up.

Valentina let out her breath in a long, uneasy sigh. She slipped the SIM out of the burner phone, snapped and flushed it, and let herself out of the stall just as a pair of Wen's young office assistants burst in and filled the restroom with their chatter and giggles. Valentina smiled in silent greeting and headed for the company coffee bar.

CHAPTER FORTY-FOUR

"How the hell is this happening?" Jimmy Wen yelled at the bank of screens on his office wall as if they were capable of giving him some kind of answer. "Somebody has to be manipulating the fucking shares!" Leaning over his desk, he slammed his hand down hard and his phone clattered onto the floor. Even his bodyguards flinched.

"I can't see how that could even be possible without us knowing about it," Lucas observed.

He remained in his favored spot on the couch by the desk and studied Wen's reddened face and clenched fists. Those, along with the uncharacteristic obscenities told him Jimmy was so close to the edge there may be no dragging him back—and there was no imagining what the man would be capable of once he was inescapably cornered. And, for as much as he projected an outward countenance of calm, Lucas was terrified; when Zhang Bo lost his last atom of patience with Jimmy Wen, Lucas Vaughn would likely be right there alongside him.

Jimmy slumped down in the chair behind his desk and lifted his laptop's lid. "Why are they trading so high?" he whined. "All six, Lucas, all fucking *six*! They're all so hot now that we have no chance of plugging the hole and paying back Zhang-fucking-Bo."

He studied the screen as it lit up with the morning's trading figures and ground his teeth so hard that Lucas could hear the dull, grating sound from six feet away.

"Fuck it!" In a flash of temper, Wen picked up his laptop and hurled it across the office—it sailed straight over Lucas's head and smashed against the glass wall behind him.

"For fuck sake, Jimmy!" He protested as the laptop's dislodged keys rained down on him.

"Get me Freddy Tseng on the phone!" Wen barked at Lau. "Now!"

The bodyguard flinched and scrambled to pick Wen's desk phone up off the floor. Most undignified for a man of his size. Lucas might have laughed under other circumstances. Lau hit the speed dial number for the remote office and punched the speaker button. Freddy Tseng picked up on the second ring.

"Just what the hell is going on over there, Freddy?" Wen snarled at the phone.

"Pardon me, Mr. Wen? What *is* going on?" Freddy Tseng sounded puzzled and more than a little scared.

"Why are the share prices of the six going up?" Wen snapped. "You were given explicit instructions to tank them!"

There was a noticeable pause before Freddy said, "You told us to *buy* them, Mr. Wen. We received your email first thing this morning."

"Bullshit!" Wen screamed at the phone, and Lucas was positive he heard Freddy Tseng drop his handset.

"I have the email right here," Freddy Tseng said timorously. "It says—"

"Show me, for fuck's sake. Forward it to me."

Again the perplexed pause. "Yes, immediately . . . There. I've sent it, sir."

Jimmy reached for the laptop, his hand halting above the spot it had occupied on his deck. Seeing his confusion, Lucas got to his feet and moved to switch on the desktop PC—he didn't trust Wen not to throw that at him too, if he received yet more bad news.

It took less than thirty seconds for the computer to boot up, but felt like minutes. The second it whirred to life, Lucas opened Wen's email and found the message from Freddy Tseng.

The two men read the forwarded message in unnerving silence; the only sound was Jimmy's teeth grinding. His face was worryingly red, his neck and the top of his head flushed and glinting with fat beads of sweat.

"It's got your email address on it, Jimmy." Lucas stated the obvious.

"No shit, Sherlock. You know damn well I didn't send it. Who the hell did?"

"I'll check. Give me a minute." Lucas opened the IP checker from the mail app's toolbar and had it ping the source address of the suspect email.

"So?" Wen's impatience got the better of him.

"Hold on," Lucas murmured.

He cross-checked the exposed IP address against the company database; whatever the checker was about to reveal was not going to help Wen's foul mood any, nor would it bode well for someone.

"Son of a bitch." Lucas shook his head. *Can this be right?*

"*Who?*" Wen demanded.

Lucas let out a sharp breath and turned the desktop display so Jimmy could see it. "That's the origin of the email Freddy got." He pressed his finger against the information on the screen for emphasis.

Jimmy Wen surged to his feet and, for a split second, Lucas thought he was going to upend the entire desk and throw the computer out the window. Instead, he turned to Lau, twisting the display so the body-guard could see the email address.

"You know who that is?" he demanded.

Lau peered at the screen, eyes narrowing. "Yes, sir."

"Then, bring that goddamned piece of crap to me. *Now!*"

CHAPTER FORTY-FIVE

Faces set with grim determination, Lau and Fung were two men on a mission. The pair didn't exchange so much as a single word as they strode briskly down the hallway, nor did they acknowledge any of the office workers who scurried out of their path with downcast eyes. Other than Jimmy Wen himself, no one was feared more at JM Wen Limited than his security team.

When they reached their target, Lau signaled Fung to open the door. The younger guard complied, and Lau and Fung strode into the room. Lau slipped his right hand inside his jacket to wrap his fingers around the grip of his Glock. He felt Fung behind him, moving to stand in the doorway, blocking their target from escape.

"You will come with us." The menacing growl in Lau's voice was the first indication to their mark that anything was amiss.

"What did you say?" Shum Kuo looked up from his desk, his face wearing an expression of confusion and outrage. He looked from Lau to Fung and back again. "What are you gabbling about? Do you *want* to be fired?"

Lau took two steps to his boss's side, grasped his shoulder, and pulled him back from the desk, chair and all. Shum reached for his sidearm, but Lau was too quick. He intercepted Shum's hand before he could draw the gun free of its holster, and tossed it toward the doorway. Fung took a step into the room and fielded it neatly.

Lau wrenched the security chief from his chair, inciting a litany of abuse.

"Take your hands off me! I'll have your job for this! Fung. My gun. *Now*."

He held out his hand as if he honestly expected the guard to comply. Fung did not comply; he turned the weapon on its owner.

"What is this? A coup? Is that it? Do you think you'll get away with—"

"Mr. Wen has requested your presence, Mr. Shum," Lau told him, his voice just loud enough to cut through Shum's snarled protests.

"Mr. Wen?" Shum straightened his suit coat. "Yes, by all means, let us go see Mr. Wen. When he hears how you have treated me, you will realize what a huge mistake you have made."

Lau inclined his head toward the office door; Fung stepped to one side to let Shum Kuo pass. With a black scowl at the two bodyguards, Shum straightened his suit coat yet again and stepped out into the hallway.

* * *

Sipping her cappuccino, Valentina studied the large display on her desk, her eyes darting between the dozen or so windows she had open; some were ticker-taping endless streams of share prices, while others showed trading news live as it happened. She had Shing Hai's Instagram page open, and watched with intent as he extolled the virtues of the New World Entertainment Group for anyone wishing to make a sound, wise investment in restaurants and gambling. In another corner of the screen was Lyn Song's beautifully radiant face as she explained into an interviewer's microphone how much gratitude she owed Asia Lion Entertainment for her new contract with a major Hollywood studio.

All in all, it had been a good—if somewhat destructive—morning's work for Valentina Vittorio. Valentina read with satisfied interest how shares in JLM asset Holdings Limited had unexpectedly reached an all-time record high of HK$89.73, and caught Golden Harvest Group on the scrolling subtext—it was trading nicely at HK$5.66; a whole bunch of people out there were getting incredibly rich off her subterfuge.

She glanced up as Jimmy Wen's twin bodyguards marched their boss into Wen's office. It seemed to her a good idea to be elsewhere for the time being. Rising from her chair, Valentina reached for her purse. It was time to check in with Kate Bennett again.

CHAPTER FORTY-SIX

S hum Kuo looked small as he sat on the couch in Wen's office sandwiched uncomfortably between Fung and Lau. Small, but defiant . . . and confused.

Lucas had vacated the seat to stand over by the exterior window, watching the scene from the corner of his eye. He knew better than to do or say anything that might look like pushback when Jimmy was on one of his tears. He would remain still and silent until this was over.

"How could you double-cross me like this? After everything I've done for you?" Jimmy demanded. "How?"

Shum met his boss's furious gaze. "I don't know what you're talking about, Jimmy. I have served you loyally since you brought me on here. What *exactly* are you accusing me of?"

"Don't play dumb with me," Jimmy snarled. "Why are you fucking with my money, Kuo? What are you playing at? You think you can get richer than you already are by betraying me?"

"I'm not playing at anything! Nor am I betraying you. I don't understand—"

"Then how the fuck do you explain the emails you sent out this morning?" Spittle flew from Wen's lips as he ranted and rained down onto Shum's immaculately pressed pants. "How do you explain the increased trading on the Golden Six since Zhang's repayment deadline?"

As Shum shook his head, his bewildered gaze darted across to Lucas, ever Jimmy Wen's voice of reason. Lucas recoiled from the glance and turned his eyes back to the cityscape beyond the window.

"All this time you've been digging out supposed SFC informants, and you've been doing *this*!" Wen leaned down to look Shum in the eye. "Are you working for the regulators, Kuo?"

Shum started to get to his feet but was persuaded to remain seated by Wen's bodyguards. He glared up at his boss, his face red with seemingly sincere fury. "Seriously, Jimmy? You think I'd ever be a snitch for the SFC? This is a setup. Surely you can see that."

Wen pointed at his computer. "The proof is right there. The emails sabotaging this company—sabotaging *me*—were sent from your office. Without question. You were the only one in there at that time." Wen straightened and began to pace. "I've had my suspicions about you ever since you threw Chrissy Huang under the bus—I'm thinking that maybe she was just a smokescreen for your own dealings with the regulators."

"This is insanity, Jimmy! Just listen to what you're saying! Tell him he's being crazy, Vaughn!"

Lucas looked across the room and saw how terrified Shum Kuo was. Fear—surely an alien emotion to one who was used only to causing it in others—radiated from him in waves, notwithstanding he was struggling to keep his face schooled to its usual impassivity. Lucas recognized his own dominant emotion as satisfaction. There was something viscerally gratifying in seeing this smug little terror-monger lose it.

"You have to admit," Lucas said, "that it's pretty fucking incriminating, Shum. You've personally removed employees on far less evidence."

"Evidence I have not been allowed to see," Shum protested.

Jimmy stood back and pointed to the flat-screen display atop his desk. "Come look."

Shum did, puzzling over the text of the explosive email, assimilating what the IP checker told him. Lucas caught the moment when it all came together in the man's head. He looked thunderstruck. There might be some truth to his suggestion of a setup, but Wen had to blame someone—someone to take out his panic and paranoia on, and as far as Lucas Vaughn was concerned, he would much rather it be the head of security than Valentina Vittorio, who'd, after all, saved his life.

Shum straightened and turned to look at Jimmy Wen. "Someone is trying very hard to frame me. I would never do such a thing to you. What motive—"

"A better job for more money?" Jimmy suggested. "Perhaps working for a man with no scruples who is more in your league when it comes to his love of violence?"

He meant Zhang Bo, of course. It made a certain amount of sense, Lucas had to admit. If Jimmy Wen went down because of his idiotic attempt to expand his corporate wealth at Zhang's expense, chances were good that Shum Kuo would be a frontline casualty. For him to go to the Triad with a deal . . .

"Get this bastard out of my office." Wen narrowed his eyes at Lau and Fung. "And arrange his suicide."

* * *

Lau strapped Shum's wrists together with white cable ties before he and Fung escorted the head of security from JM Wen Limited's offices via the back stairs.

"You're making a big fucking mistake!" Shum shouted. He kicked and struggled against the bodyguards as they dragged him down the concrete and steel staircase. "Whoever set me up will silence you bastards too—both of you!" His strident voice bounced from the bare walls and echoed down the stairwell.

Lau sucker-punched him hard in the gut. When Shum doubled over in pain, he gave him a shove that landed him awkwardly on the concrete floor of the landing.

"Have some honor, Shum," he growled and cocked an arm to hit his boss again.

Fung laid a large, blunt hand over his partner's fist. "In what suicide does the victim beat himself up before he takes his life?" he asked reasonably.

Lau considered this. "You are correct, of course." He grasped Shum tightly by the upper arm and yanked him to his feet, then turned a sly smile to Fung. "Of course, a man so overwrought with emotion might experience difficulty with staircases."

Fung shrugged, conceding the point.

When they finally reached 2IFC's basement level, which let out into the underground VIP parking lot, Shum was in a far more submissive mood. Years of tyranny had been knocked out of the man who'd run JM Wen's security operation with the same brutality and fear he'd nurtured during his years at the Chinese state police force.

"No."

This was the only word Fung heard Shum say as he and Lau donned nitrile gloves and bundled him into his beloved Volante, which sat idling in the middle of a broad aisle with its engine compartment open. There were few other cars on this level, which was for JM Wen executives only. The lot had just been closed at the behest of Shum Kuo—or so the garage staff supposed.

Fung, who had the soul of a car mechanic, had made some quick modifications to the vehicle, disabling the brakes and tinkering with the accelerator sensors. He completed these tasks while Lau cable-tied Shum's wrists to the steering wheel and looped a thick metal towing chain around his neck. Shum had made their job easier by leaving the soft top down that morning.

Once behind the wheel and encumbered by the chain, Shum spoke again. "Please, I have money."

"As have I," Lau informed him. "Such a shame about the car, though," he added, then moved to secure the other end of the chain around a concrete pillar twenty yards and change across the parking structure.

"Fung!" Shum seemed to have gotten his second wind. "Don't do this, Fung, please. I can disappear quietly. You can tell Wen you burned

my body in the furnace or threw it in the harbor. Nobody need know—
I can pay you."

"I am sure you could, but what would I tell Lau?"

"We could take him if we work together," Shum suggested, his voice a low growl. "If you give me my gun back . . ."

Fung paused in the act of reaching into the engine compartment, then looked over at Lau, who was tugging at the chain. "What do you think, cousin? Should I take Mr. Shum up on his kind offer?"

"I think we're good to go," said Lau.

Fung gave his soon-to-be ex-boss a polite smile. "Sorry, sir, but no."

The younger man reached beneath the hood and goosed the throttle. It was as if Shum had stomped the gas pedal to the floorboards. Tires squealing, the Aston Martin accelerated down the center of the parking lot, trunk slamming shut as it did. Shum Kuo's horrified scream rose above the roar of the engine, only to be cut short when the chain reached its limit. The car continued for a short distance, crashing into the wall at the end of the parking lot with a thunderous impact and the shriek of rent metal. The garage shook, though there was no ball of flames, no dramatic explosion. Fung couldn't help but feel a pang of disappointment. This was nothing like the movies.

As Lau removed the cable ties from the dead man's wrists, Fung scanned the parking lot. He saw crimson splashes of blood spattered along the concrete like Jackson Pollock graffiti. The building's regular security team would be down there any minute, as even Jimmy Wen only held so much sway at 2IFC. Let them find the traitor's head; he'd had more than his bellyful of unpleasantness for one day.

CHAPTER FORTY-SEVEN

Valentina kept a close eye on the stock markets and, by midmorning, the share prices of each one of Wen's Golden Six were riding wonderfully high—especially Asia Lion Entertainment, following Lyn Song's monumental announcement of what was now a three-movie deal with Paramount. The week was going to finish strong for those lucky enough to have invested in any one of those companies, and Zhang Bo would be expecting one hell of a payday.

Oliver and Anthony were out meeting with clients, at least one of whom had been on Sofia Reller's list of leads, while Daylen, Nadim, and Lam were hitting the phones hard to fix up closing meetings for the following week. Wen's urgency had been infectious and created a desperate atmosphere around the office; even the lowly assistants were walking on eggshells.

She could see Wen in his office. The stress of his impossible situation was etched all over his face as he scrutinized his desktop computer and the wall of screens while making phone call after phone call. Lucas hadn't left Wen's office all morning, and was no doubt trying to keep a lid on his boss's explosive temper and penchant for erratic behavior when stressed. As a consequence, Lucas hadn't said more than two words to Valentina all day, and that suited her just fine.

Of course, Wen had instructed his market manipulation office to ignore the email they'd received and quit trading immediately on the Golden Six. The instruction had come too late, though; the damage had already been done.

Just after noon a rumor raced through the office that something had happened in the executive parking garage. When building security and a handful of Hong Kong's finest turned up not long after and sequestered themselves with Wen, it seemed to confirm the rumors. The police fanned out to interview JM Wen staff after that, but as the three of the four closers in the sales room were lodged at the Four Seasons and had never even seen the inside of the parking garage, and Lam didn't own a car, they'd been of little interest to the cops. They focused their attention on the corporate executives and security staff.

Valentina pondered sending another confusing email to Freddy Tseng in an hour or so—this time with the IP redirect switched off; with Shum out of the way, she was comfortable enough to allow the proxy software to do its job and reroute her online activity via anonymous servers in Amsterdam and Canada. It was likely Freddy Tseng would call to confirm with Wen that he'd actually sent the email, but at the very least it would serve to rattle the man's already frayed nerves still further. If what had happened in the parking garage was what she suspected it was, then Jimmy Wen would be facing the prospect of having murdered a loyal employee.

In the meantime, Valentina kept herself busy by systematically working her way down the list of outside manipulators she'd recovered from Wen's hidden files. There were dozens upon dozens of them, and each one was more than capable of causing irreparable damage to JM Wen's finances by trading shares based on little more than the trending market and false rumors.

* * *

Wen slammed the phone down on its cradle so hard it made Lucas jump. "Looks like something's going our way at last." His eyes flitted to the market reports that scrolled relentlessly across his computer screen.

"Alex Sun is on board?"

Wen nodded and ran a hand over his head. "He's been wriggling for weeks now, but he's finally ready to deal. Sun-Lin Systems is on its knees, and he's running out of cash fast."

"That's encouraging," Lucas said. "How much?"

"Nine hundred million Hong Kong, give or take. He'll have the paperwork ready for me this afternoon."

Lucas grimaced. "The great Jimmy Wen making house calls—Sun's gonna think he's king of the hill."

Wen fiddled with the ridiculously expensive pen on his desk. "Desperate times, desperate measures. We don't have time for niceties—given what day it is."

"I thought Zhang bought your whole Valentina-creaming-off-his-money gambit?"

Wen closed his eyes and sighed. "Who knows what he bought, Lucas? I'm not going to take any chances. At least I can prove that Shum was manipulating the market. What I can't explain is why that should matter. When the Triads call in a debt, they always collect—one way or another. You know that."

A chill ran down Lucas's spine—like a goose just stepped over his grave, as his grandmother was so fond of saying. He'd lived in Hong Kong long enough, and seen plenty Triad activity firsthand, to know precisely what Zhang Bo and his cohorts were capable of.

"We need a way to convince him that Shum was responsible for the evaporation of his money."

"I think that ship has sailed, Lucas. Once we have control of Sun's shares, we can sell them to raise capital for Zhang; we can at least pay him back the initial value of his own and tell him the rest is on its way."

"He wouldn't buy that. He can look at the market himself and see what those shares are worth now."

"If he doesn't buy it, there's always the *Morning Cloud*." Wen managed a wry chuckle.

Lucas gave his boss a sidewise glance. Was he talking about selling the boat or something else entirely? Wen's history of disappearing from the scene of his own messes and leaving others to carry the can was no secret to his righthand man. After all, that was what had brought him back to Hong Kong in the first place. Only this time, if Wen were to vanish, Lucas Vaughn would be the first one in the firing line, and he didn't care too much for that idea.

CHAPTER FORTY-EIGHT

K ate Bennett checked her watch as she pushed through her office door and stepped out onto the street; one thirty p.m. —she was already late, and the rowdy crowd of protestors cluttering up the sidewalk with their placards, chanting, and not-so-good-natured singing certainly weren't going to help.

"I already told you the informant has all the information now," she barked with impatience into the cell phone she had pressed tight to her ear. "She has names, dates, transactions, clients, proxies—the lot."

Kate listened intently to the response as she forced her way through the placard wavers; they may have been a noisy, ill-tempered bunch, but at least they were polite enough to do their best to shuffle out of her way.

"Yes, I know I've not passed along everything. As I've *already* explained, that's because she hasn't given me everything she's dug up yet." Her impatience was quickly turning to irritation; if there was one thing she truly hated, it was having to repeat herself. "Oh, come now— we all knew she'd hold something back for insurance against our possibly ulterior motives. She's not stupid, and I'd expect her to do no less."

She reached the edge of the crowd and scoured the bustling street for her car; he should have been waiting for her by now—she'd called him over ten minutes ago.

"Listen to me," she snapped, "you don't have to keep telling me she's going rogue—I'm the one feeding you the bloody intel . . . Yes, I know she has her own agenda with Wen, which is why I need to get this whole affair wrapped up ASAP. Going by what she's given me so far, if the rest of it is even half as good, I'm thinking we not only get the bank, we'll also have a chance at Zhang. Bringing a Triad gang down will make putting Jimmy Wen away look like amateur hour. That, my friend, would be a far more valuable feather in Interpol's cap."

She turned and made her way toward a small side street; sometimes her driver waited for her there, away from the crowds. *Et voilà!* She caught sight of the rear end of her car down the narrow side street that led off the main road and quickened her step. "Look, I have to go," she huffed. "You're making me late."

It wasn't quite a lie, but the greater truth was that she was tired of having to justify her actions. She had been one of her division's best agents for two decades—always getting results. Now in her late forties, her handler had begun to act as if she was in danger of losing a step.

Kate hung up the call with a jab of her thumb, slipped the phone into her pocket, and pulled open the car's passenger door. She leaned her head in.

"Really, Xinyue, you could have let me know you'd be waiting here—" The words stopped in her throat. Something was wrong.

Her driver was slumped, motionless, his forehead resting on the steering wheel, and as her eyes adjusted to the gloom, she saw his face was a wet, glistening mask of fresh blood.

"Xin!" She straightened and reached for her phone to call 999.

The car that hit Kate Bennett was an old beat-up Honda Accord that had once been red. Its momentum took both the agent and her car's door with it. When it smashed into the wall at the dead end of the street, the force of impact all but severed her legs midthigh; it was a small mercy that the agent was in the padded wool of shock before the impact. The driver, a small, anonymous man wearing a grubby gray hoodie with a blue bandana across his face, clambered out of the car and ran full pelt back to the main street. There, he quickly disappeared among the noisy protestors and the bustling crowds.

Kate Bennett lay sprawled across the crumpled hood of the wrecked Honda, her body a broken, bleeding mess; she would be dead by the time the emergency services arrived.

CHAPTER FORTY-NINE

Valentina tapped gently on Wen's door with her fingernails and stared directly at Lucas to have him come over. She had little desire to get herself embroiled in whatever drama the two of them were involved in. She had seen for herself the anger and pure desperation in Jimmy Wen's face from across the office.

"Yes?" Lucas was curt; all pretense of being the perpetually relaxed citizen of Oz was gone.

"I have a client meeting at the Monastery," Valentina lied. "I'm heading out now."

"You could have texted me that."

Yeah, I could have. Valentina looked over his shoulder at Wen and forced a smile. "My bad. I'll remember that for the next time."

"Make it count, Valentina." Lucas closed the door in her face and returned to Wen's desk.

Out on Finance Street, Valentina pulled the burner phone out of her bag and dialed the one number it contained. She pressed the phone tight to her ear to counter the street noise as she strode away from 2IFC; she'd hail a cab once she was out of sight of the building. She didn't want to take any chances this late in the game.

"Pick up, Kate," Valentina growled at the phone. "Where the fuck are you?" The call went to voice mail.

Cursing beneath her breath, Valentina decided against leaving a message at the tone as the generic female voice instructed. Instead, she hung up the call and redialed. She gave up after her third redial.

Well, Ms. Bond. So much for Interpol's unwavering support.

Figuring she'd put enough distance between herself and 2IFC, Valentina scanned both ways along Finance Street for a taxi. Intent on her cell phone, Valentina at first failed to notice the plain white SUV that pulled up beside her.

She gave it a glance as the side door slid open. It was Japanese—the exact brand and model was impossible to discern as it was devoid of any manufacturer emblems and badges—and looked like so many others of its type that occupied Hong Kong's crowded streets.

Two smartly suited men climbed out, and by the time Valentina had registered what was happening, they had her by an arm each and she could feel the hard, persuasive jab of a gun prodding at her kidney. Valentina let the burner phone fall from her hand, thanking God that neither of the goons escorting her noticed it. She covered the sound of it hitting the concrete by pretending to stumble.

"Don't do anything stupid, Miss Vittorio," one of the men whispered; his breath was warm against her ear. "We will shoot you if necessary."

Panicked now, Valentina looked around. The street was full of people but may as well have been deserted; everyone was going about their own business and paying no attention whatever to the anonymous white SUV, the pretty brunette, and her two companions.

As the men relieved Valentina of her bag and maneuvered her toward the open door of the SUV, she contemplated screaming for help, or at the very least putting up a fight. But for what? To be ignored by the countless passers-by or gut-shot for her trouble? No thanks. It was best to play along. As Bennett had so sagely informed her, what seemed a lifetime ago, if whoever these goons represented wanted her dead, she'd be bleeding out on the sidewalk already.

Valentina clambered into the SUV and the door slammed shut behind her. "Who the fuck are you people?" She snarled at the suit who sat himself beside her—a little too close for her liking. His huge, meaty thigh was pressed against hers, and his hidden gun dug into her bruised side.

Remaining silent, the man stared blankly out through the windshield as the SUV pulled away and merged into the Finance Street traffic. Valentina snorted and settled in for the ride; she figured she'd find out who the hell had the audacity to snatch her off the street in broad daylight soon enough.

CHAPTER FIFTY

Valentina had heard about Dragon Lodge. In fact, it had been another attraction high on her bucket list to visit before she left Hong Kong, though the old, abandoned house was strictly out of bounds to tourists. However, she hadn't envisaged seeing the place in this circumstance.

The SUV eased to a stop outside the trashed back door of the imposing gray stone building; the door's warped, flaking wood was decorated with faded graffiti tags and hung loosely in its frame. Much of the lodge's rear facade was covered in a straggly mat of dead vines, which reminded Valentina of the filthy, unkempt beards of the destitute men back in New York—a homeless house. From inside the car, she peered up at the building's steep, faded, red tile roof, which was in far better shape than the damp-stained, graffiti-marked walls that held it up; Valentina thought the whole place looked like it was ready to collapse at any moment.

Dragon Lodge, she'd read on the tourist sites, was purported to be one of the most haunted buildings in Hong Kong. It had borne witness to a number of previous owners dying in mysterious circumstances, along with a group of nuns who had been decapitated on the front lawn by the Japanese during WWII. Valentina wondered if she was going to become the lodge's newest haunt.

"Out." The guy with the gun opened the SUV's door and indicated with a brusque nod and wave of his weapon that Valentina ought to do as she was told.

She got out.

The two men escorted her through the back door, along the damp ruins of the ground floor and up a rotting staircase that wobbled and creaked as if getting ready to crumble beneath her feet. As she walked, Valentina surreptitiously inspected every possible place to hide, anything she could use as a weapon, and any potential escape routes; in such an expansive, derelict place as Dragon Lodge, the opportunities had to be endless.

Zhang Bo was waiting for her in the master bedroom, a large, gleaming meat cleaver in one hand. Anita Kwok stood still and obviously terrified next to a cheap plastic lawn chair in the center of the room, her mouth sealed with black tape and her hands secured behind her back with a blue cable tie. The hardwood floor and the chair were smeared with dark, dried blood; someone had attempted to wipe the floor down but had succeeded only in massaging the blood into the herringbone pattern in the hardwood.

"Miss Vittorio." Zhang inclined his head toward her. His voice, as always, was well-modulated and deceptively mild. "It is a pleasure to see you again, although I wish the situation was more . . . amicable." He paced across the bloodied parquet floor and pointed at the chair with the meat cleaver. "Please, take a seat."

In no position to refuse, Valentina did as instructed, her gaze going to the grimy picture window. Everything she'd read about Dragon Lodge had been true: its views of the city from The Peak really were quite spectacular . . . and possibly the last thing she would ever see. She felt a bizarre sense of calm; on some level, she had resigned herself to her fate. That didn't mean she wouldn't take some means of escape if it presented itself, but she was far from hopeful.

"I take it you know Miss Kwok?" Zhang said, by means of an introduction.

Valentina nodded and looked up at Wen's assistant; her hair, makeup, and smart office attire were as pristine as ever, despite the gaffer's tape and cable ties. She caught a whiff of Anita's floral perfume; it did not quite overcome the scent of her fear.

As Zhang stood over Valentina, his tall, graceful frame seemed tense and ready to strike; he oozed with the menacing confidence of a king cobra. When he spoke, his tone was flat and matter-of-fact. "I want my money, Miss Vittorio."

What the hell is he talking about? "Jimmy Wen has your money."

Valentina's gaze flitted to the Triad henchman who stood guard in the doorway. He was holding her Hermès bag in one hand and his gun in the other. It was comical, and she felt the absurd urge to laugh; she turned the giggle into a cough.

Zhang followed her gaze, his mouth twitching with suppressed humor, then bent over and leaned in close, his face just inches from Valentina's. "That's not my understanding, *American.* Do you have any idea who I am?"

Valentina frowned. "Of course. You're Zhang Bo. A leader in the Triads . . . and CEO of Asia Lion Entertainment."

"What made you think it was a good idea to steal from a leader in the Triads?"

Valentina held Zhang's gaze. "I haven't stolen anything from you." A flush of cold adrenaline suffused her veins. *What the hell was going on here?*

Zhang kept his icy black gaze fixed on her. "Wen has provided me with documentation that shows you have been siphoning my money —*Triad* money—into your offshore accounts."

"Offshore accounts? I don't have any offshore accounts." Valentina didn't try to mask the incredulity in her voice. Still, she knew she could protest her innocence as much as she liked, but if Wen had set out to frame her, faking a bunch of false bank accounts and money trails through foreign domiciles would be a walk in the park for him.

"Mr. Wen has informed me otherwise. As has his assistant." Zhang straightened, turning his attention to Anita Kwok, who stood mere inches from Valentina's bloody chair. "Are you suggesting that Miss

Kwok is lying to me?" He traced the contour of the woman's smooth, tear-streaked cheek with the cleaver, and Anita whimpered.

Valentina shook her head. "She'll only know what lies Wen has told her. And he's been lying to you all along. Just as he lies to all his clients. I don't have your laundered money, or your shares. But I know what happened to them."

Zhang shot her an unreadable look, then—in a movement that was almost dance-like in its grace—lashed out at Anita with the cleaver. A thin, red gash appeared across the girl's throat, and a bright sheet of blood poured down the front of her immaculately starched shirt. Knees buckling, Anita Kwok dropped to the dirty floor beside Valentina, where she writhed and choked in the spreading pool of her own blood. It was all Valentina could do not to throw up. She'd been in three bloody fights since she'd come to Hong Kong, and nearly blown up twice, but this casual, dispassionate violence against the innocent and helpless—this was a different order of magnitude, a deeper level of horror.

Zhang waited patiently for Anita to die, then dropped the cleaver onto her lifeless body before turning back to Valentina, hands thrust into the pockets of his trousers. "I want what is mine, Miss Vittorio. You say you know what happened to my property. Very well. Tell me *your* lies. And believe me when I say I can make this process excruciatingly unpleasant for you—far more so than I did for Miss Kwok." He looked down at the dead girl with a bland expression. She might as well have been a discarded toy, no longer of value.

Valentina felt her emotions come back online with a stab of outrage so sharp it brought tears to her eyes. Did this man value nothing but his money and his power? In what way did he imagine he was any more a man than Jimmy Wen? She clamped her jaw shut, imprisoning her rage.

"I'll tell you the truth," she said through gritted teeth. "But first I have a question: Why did you kill Anita? She'd done nothing to you. She'd cost you neither money nor honor. She bore no responsibility for the sins of her employer."

Zhang fixed her with a curious stare, then began to pace the room.

He reminded her of a panther she'd seen at the Bronx Zoo when she was a kid.

"Justice demands sacrifice, Miss Vittorio. Someone must pay for the embarrassment I was forced to bear in the eyes of my clan. Then, too, people like Jimmy Wen—like you—need to understand that there are consequences. There are always consequences. Now, give me your story and I will decide if one sacrifice is enough."

Valentina took a deep breath, silenced the urge to snarl at him, and began to tell her story. "He calls them the Golden Six. Asia Lion Entertainment is a favorite of his, as is New Horizon."

Zhang quit his pacing to look at her. "My companies, yes. Go on."

"He sold them."

The Triad stood motionless in the center of the killing floor, his eyes never leaving Valentina's face. "What do you mean, he sold them?"

"The shares he bought on your behalf." Valentina struggled to keep her jaw from quaking; her fingers gripped the flimsy arms of the chair until they hurt. "He loaned you seventy-five percent against them as part of the process of cleaning your dirty money—"

"I know how the deal works, Miss Vittorio," Zhang snapped. "I was the one who set it up."

"Yes, you did. And Jimmy Wen sold all those shares *the day you signed them over.*"

"He sold . . . my shares?"

Now you're repeating yourself. She kept her voice low, even, expressionless, and laid out the whole scam in simple terms. "What those shares are worth today would pay back your loan *and* make you a handsome—and spotless—profit . . . but Wen *can't* give you back the shares, because he doesn't have them anymore. He's already sold them."

He was no longer looking at her, but was staring, unfocused, at the floor near her feet. The metallic smell of Anita Kwok's blood made her own blood feel like molasses in her veins. Valentina ground her teeth against the desire to scream insults in Zhang's handsome face.

"It's what he does," she added tersely. "How he makes his money.

And he usually gets away with it. Either the clients default on the loan or Wen buys the shares back at a lower price—once he's tanked their value, of course—and hands them over."

Zhang shook his head. "You are lying. Jimmy Wen wouldn't dare to cross me."

She ignored him. "It only became a problem when the Golden Six's prices started climbing. Wen doesn't have the money to buy them back to hand over to you. I have proof . . . if you'd let me show you? I'll need my phone." She looked across at the goon holding her ludicrously expensive bag.

A nod from Zhang and his bodyguard dug through Valentina's purse. He plucked the cell phone out from amid the Interpol-issued tampons that littered the bottom of the bag and tossed it over to Zhang.

Zhang caught the phone midflight and handed it over to Valentina. "Show me."

Valentina turned on her cell phone, her fingers skittering nervously across the touch screen as she opened the files she'd unearthed on Wen's servers. She held the phone out to Zhang.

"Look."

She tried to make her voice sound certain, almost commanding. Zhang was used to people groveling in fear. From what she'd seen of him in their brief acquaintance, he disdained weakness. Flinch and you die. She tried not to flinch as she showed Zhang the spreadsheet that contained transaction data on each of the six companies.

She pointed at a date column of dates. "This shows when the stocks were purchased."

Zhang nodded.

"And this"—Valentina pulled up a second file—"this shows the date of sale for each one."

Zhang snatched the phone from her hand. She recoiled, her entire body tensing, her fists clenching reflexively, her lips drawn back in a snarl. Zhang's bodyguard crossed the room with terrifying speed, his gun drawn and pointing at her temple.

"I wouldn't try anything if I were you, Miss Vittorio," Zhang said as he studied the files on her phone. "There really is nowhere for you to go."

"I'm human. I have reflexes. So sue me."

The corner of Zhang's mouth twitched, even as he studied the data that exposed Jimmy Wen's faithlessness and stupidity. When he'd digested what he'd seen, he turned back to Valentina, his jaw tight with suppressed rage. She prayed earnestly and sincerely that it would not be vented on her. If she could get him to see Wen as the real enemy . . .

"So." Zhang folded his arms across his chest. "You've stolen my money, and now someone is manipulating my shares upward to destroy Wen?"

He dismissed his bodyguard back to the doorway; Valentina noted the guy didn't put away his gun.

"I have stolen nothing from you," she reiterated with a firmness that surprised her. "And they are not your shares anymore—Wen sold them. You've seen the proof."

"Yes, I have, indeed. I'm very curious, though, about why and how you are able to show it to me. Why collect all of this? For your friend at Interpol? Or are you secretly working for the regulators?"

She was startled by his knowledge of Kate Bennett, but refused to let it show. "I have my reasons. Secret agent lady found out what they were and thought we might help each other."

"To ruin Jimmy Wen. Why?"

Valentina let some of her anger bleed into her eyes and voice. "Jimmy Wen ruined my father. My father . . . took his own life because of it, and my family was destroyed. Completely and utterly destroyed. I'm the only one who even charitably could be called a survivor."

He stared at her a moment longer, his black gaze as unreadable to her as a Chinese street sign, then he nodded. "Yes, you are . . . a survivor, aren't you, Valentina? Until now."

She held his gaze, refusing to flinch or cower at the implications of those two words.

A cynical smile played across Zhang's perfect lips. He shrugged. "If there's no money, no shares, and your Interpol friend has, regrettably, taken early retirement, what use are you to me?" He dropped

Valentina's phone onto her lap and turned back to stare out the window.

Valentina's body quivered and her mouth went completely dry. There was no doubt in her mind as to what the gangster meant by *early retirement*. It explained why Bennett hadn't picked up her call; Valentina could only hope that her death had been as quick and relatively painless as Anita's. She forced herself to look at the other woman's body and felt rage beginning to build up again. Kate and Anita, Sofia and Chrissy . . . Yan—none of them had deserved to suffer. And, as much as the Brit had been a pain in her ass, Valentina realized she liked her. Admired her.

She bit back the urge to rage at the Triad lord, kept her voice calm and sure, and said, "I know where all the bodies are buried. Jimmy Wen's financial skeletons, I mean. I also have a foolproof way to get you your money back—all of it. I'd call that useful."

Zhang spun around and glared at her, savagery leaking through his civilized facade. "And just how do you intend to do that when it's all gone—unless you really are the one who has stolen it?"

Looking into those eyes, Valentina had a small epiphany. Impotence. Zhang Bo hated to feel impotent. Feared it. When things were out of his control, he needed someone to blame. But for the love of God, did he really think she'd just made a confession?

"If you're going to kill me, fine, but please don't insult me. Wen has a billion left—a billion and half at the most, plus whatever he can scrabble together today. But even if you take every cent, it hardly puts a dent in what he owes you."

"And you can get it back?"

"All of it."

"Why should I trust you?"

"What more do either of us have to lose? Well, I could lose my life and you'll lose face. But that doesn't have to happen. I know the business, I know the right people, and, as you can see, I'm extremely good at digging." She nodded at the cell phone in her lap, which still displayed Jimmy Wen's incriminating files.

"How will you achieve this without your Interpol handler?"

Valentina thrust her anger aside. She needed to survive. Retribution could come later. "I did all of this on my own. Kate Bennett was just hitching a ride. But for what comes next, I'll need your help with a few things. All I ask is that you let me get done what I came here to do—without any hindrance."

Zhang studied her for a handful of beats then shook his head. "I make no promises, but it costs me nothing to let you try. I do this because it amuses me."

Profound relief suffused every cell of Valentina's body. She came close to crossing herself—something she hadn't done much since her father's death. She let none of that show.

"I'm tickled you find me amusing." She crossed her legs and sat back in the chair. "Okay, what's next?"

CHAPTER FIFTY-ONE

Lucas Vaughn's cell phone vibrated in the gilt-edged bracket that held it to the dashboard of his car. He pressed a button on the steering wheel and Wen's voice boomed out through the Tesla's eight-speaker sound system.

"I just left Alex Sun."

"Did you close him?"

"Of course I closed him." Wen sounded genuinely offended. "I have the collateral in position—now you need to ride Freddy Tseng until the share price hits three-fifty, and then we can sell before Sun's payment is due to leave our account."

Lucas had an uneasy feeling about that part of the deal; with the corner Wen had painted himself into with Zhang Bo, he knew damn well Alex Sun wouldn't be seeing any money at all, let alone his precious shares.

"Okay—I'm there now," he told Wen as he swung his car onto Kam Wa Street and pulled it to a silent stop in front of the run-down tenement building.

Wen's voice sounded distant. "I'll meet you there when I've finished up at the office. Did you hear back from the American girl? She was supposed to be going to a client meeting."

"No, actually, I haven't heard a peep out of Val. As a matter of fact, I was beginning to wonder where the hell she's gotten to. She should have wrapped up already." He didn't mention that she hadn't picked up either of the calls he'd made to her cell on his way over to the market makers' office.

"Like I need one more headache," Jimmy groused, and hung up.

Lucas pocketed the cell phone and switched off the car. The dingy old building always made him nervous. Drug addicts and street gangs that served them ran rife in the neighborhood. From the MTR station to three blocks beyond the tenements, this was prime real estate in which to be carjacked, mugged, or worse. That made it the perfect place for JM Wen's market makers; even the cops were reluctant to venture this far along Kam Wa Street.

Vaughn pushed open the main doors, the steel plates that covered them cold against his palms, and made his way to the makeshift office on the second floor. It was empty. All the desks were there. Each one held an active laptop and a wheeled office chair, but not one had a person sitting behind it. It looked as if everyone had just gotten up and left; there were even half-filled tea cups on some of the desks. It was like walking onto the ghost ship, *Marie Celeste.*

"Where the fuck is everybody?" Lucas's raised voice echoed in the empty, high-ceilinged room. "Hello?" He moved from computer to computer; maybe he'd have to manipulate Alex Sun's shares by himself. "Hello?"

A faint rustling noise pricked Vaughn's ears. It seemed to be coming from the office in the far corner of the large space.

"Freddy?"

The noise again—definitely coming from Freddy Tseng's office. Bracing himself for a fight, Vaughn marched across to the office and pushed open the door. "Freddy? Where the hell is everybody?"

Freddy Tseng was in no condition to reply. Sitting behind his desk, his face beaten so badly as to be unrecognizable, the man was barely conscious.

Lucas froze in the doorway. *No, no, no, no, no. Who would have done this?*

He reached for his cell and dialed Wen, his gaze going unbidden to Freddy, taking in the fact that Freddy Tseng's hands had been screwed to the desk, each one with three black, fat-headed screws through the upturned palms.

"Lucas?" Wen's voice startled him.

"Jimmy." Lucas voice shook so badly, the name came out garbled. He tried again, "Jimmy, there's something really, really wrong. The place is abandoned and Freddy is—he's been—"

"What the fuck do you mean *abandoned*?" The fury in Wen's voice grated in Lucas's ear like fingernails on a chalkboard.

"Looks to me like they've been scared off; the place is fucking deserted, Jimmy. But Freddy—"

"Zhang."

Heart pounding loud enough to drown out Jimmy Wen's voice, Lucas eyed Freddy Tseng and wondered how on earth the man was managing to sit upright. "Zhang, yeah. Look, I gotta get Freddy to a hospital—they made a real fucking mess of him." He looked around for a screwdriver, a knife, anything that would get the screws out of Freddy Tseng's hands.

"There's no time for that. You need to hit the markets, Lucas!" Wen screamed. "You need to hit them now!"

Fuck you, Lucas thought. *Maybe in the desk drawers . . .*

Across the main floor, a door slammed and he tensed. Darting out of Freddy Tseng's office and between the deserted workstations, Lucas fully expected to confront some ragtag druggie out to make easy money from the unattended computers. It didn't occur to him until he was halfway to the door that it could just as easily have been the same vicious bastards who had screwed Freddy Tseng's hands to his desk.

The door was locked.

"Fuck!" Lucas rattled the handle until it felt loose in his hand.

"What's going on over there?" Wen's voice boomed through his head.

"We're locked in!" Lucas snapped. "Someone locked us in!"

Somewhere behind Lucas a window shattered and he felt sudden heat across his back. He spun; the front corner of the office was engulfed in a rapidly spreading sheet of fire. Something flew through the broken window and exploded amid the flames. Lucas leapt backward as glass and flame sprayed across the room and the old, dry walls caught fire.

"Jimmy, get help! They're fucking torching the place!"

He didn't hear Wen's reply as he wended his way across the office space to the scarred and pitted door opposite Freddy Tseng's office. There was a fire exit sign above it—Chinese characters, not illuminated. It was his only hope.

"Are you hearing me?" he yelled at Wen. "The goddamn place is on fire!" Coughing against the thick, black curls of smoke that snaked behind him, Vaughn made it to the fire door and pushed on the metal bar at its middle.

It didn't budge. Of course it didn't. And there really was no way out.

As the heat licked at his back, Lucas kicked at the door with every ounce of strength he could muster. The damn thing didn't so much as wobble. He peered up at the windows, but they were too far away and there was no way to reach them.

At some point in his frantic assault on the fire door, the phone fell from Lucas Vaughn's hand. Jimmy Wen's voice, tinny and distant, drifted up from the floor at his feet.

CHAPTER FIFTY-TWO

Jimmy Wen listened to Lucas die and then returned to his office with the screams ringing in his ears. There was no time to mourn, not that Jimmy was particularly prone to sentimentality. There was much work to be done; he had Alex Sun's shares to dispose of. If he had lost his main team of market manipulators, there were others he could call, and he'd have to work with what he could make on them in the short term.

"Why aren't you on the fucking phone?" Wen snarled at Chun Yeung Lam as he stormed into the sales office with Lau and Fung in tow.

The closer snapped his head around, his face flushing, as Oliver, Nadim, and Daylen looked up from their respective desks. "I . . . I just finished up a call, Mr. Wen," he stammered. "I have an appointment with the CEO of Hang Chu Properties next Thursday—"

"Next Thursday?" Jimmy stopped dead in his tracks. Looming over Lam's desk, his face a hand's span from the guy's terrified face, he sneered, "Don't you realize next week is too fucking late? Didn't I instill in you—in *all* of you—the urgency of our situation here?"

"Yes, sir?" Lam cowered as far back in his chair as he could manage.

He looked confused, and Jimmy saw something in the kid's eyes he recognized. Fear.

"I . . . I can try to bring the meeting forward to . . . to Monday or Tuesday," Chun stammered.

"Not good enough."

Jimmy turned to address the entire office. "I want big numbers on my desk before close of trading *today—no fucking excuses!*" He stormed out of the room, Lau and Fung on his heels.

Where the hell was the American? She'd been the only one with balls enough to bring in the really big clients thus far.

Back in the sanctuary of his office, Jimmy slumped into his chair. With Lucas and the traitorous bastard Shum gone, he was entirely alone. For the first time since founding JM Wen Limited, there was no one he could trust. Except Fung and Lau, who was his new chief of security. They were the only bulwark he had against Zhang Bo when he came to collect.

"Don't just stand there," he barked at the two bodyguards, "take these to the closers. Tell them they will get these people to talk to me today or else." He tossed a fistful of sales leads at them. They caught air and fluttered to the carpet.

As Lau and Fung scrambled to retrieve the sales leads from the office floor, Jimmy grabbed his desk phone and dialed the first number on his list.

"There's still time to do this," he murmured, pretending that Lucas Vaughn was still there to care. "If we plug Zhang's deficit as much as we can, maybe he'll give us more time."

"Chris Kai!" Jimmy put a smile into his voice. "We need to talk about bridging the gap on your stock loan." He only half listened to the bleat of surprise and anger from the other end of the call. "Yeah, I'm sorry the shares tanked; we had no way of knowing that was going to happen, but what can you do? Political unrest like this is always going to create a volatile market."

His nervous fingers fiddling with the Montblanc, Jimmy Wen did his damndest to screw more money out of the hapless Mr. Kai. God, but he hated that ugly pen.

"You do know what will happen if you default on the loan?"

Now Kai unleashed a blistering tirade that Jimmy had heard a number of times before. "Yes, I appreciate that, but what the hell is your board going to say when you tell them you raised money against the shares—*illegally*—and then lost them all?"

An uncomfortable silence settled across Jimmy's office as he stopped talking to listen to Kai's tirade. Lau and Fung quit sorting the sales leads and stared at their boss.

"I hope they fucking hang you for it!" Jimmy slammed the phone down and hurled the pen across the office. It smashed against the door and left a fat splash of black ink against the thick glass. "What are you looking at?" he spat at Lau and Fung. "Get those leads to my team!"

Turning to his computer, Jimmy trawled his database for clients he knew had been primed for parting with more of their company's shares. Market uncertainty—and his own manipulation—had created much low-hanging fruit; the trick would be in persuading them to throw more money at their loan rather than defaulting and letting him keep the shares he'd already sold behind their backs.

Jimmy dialed another client. As the phone rang, one of the screens on the wall caught his attention. TVB News was running a breaking story; its usually stern-faced anchor looked relaxed in shirtsleeves and loosened tie. Beneath him, a chyron proclaimed the merger of Asia Lion Entertainment with an industry giant.

Jimmy grabbed the remote and raised the volume.

". . . although unconfirmed by Chief Executive Zhang Bo, Asia Lion Entertainment is rumored to be on the verge of merging with New World Entertainment Group, which would be one of the biggest company mergers in the past ten years. It comes in the wake of Asia Lion's announcement of Lyn Song's lucrative multimillion-dollar signing with Paramount. The share prices in both companies have more than doubled in reaction to the news. Asia Lion Entertainment is up to HK$138.18."

"Fuck." Jimmy put his phone down, gaze riveted to the screen.

It was over.

He knew in his churning gut that news of the merger would be fake and put out there to inflate the share prices. Even so, that wouldn't stop the market clamoring to cash in. The shares would continue to rise, and JM Wen's debt to Zhang Bo would grow. The Triads would certainly want their pound of flesh, and Jimmy Wen was all out of time.

Lau and Fung had returned to the office, having completed their task. Jimmy stood, closed his laptop, and unplugged it.

"Get Leslie Man on the phone," he barked at Lau. "Tell him to have the boat ready in thirty minutes. Minimal crew." He turned to Fung. "You—bring my car around. Back entrance."

As Fung left the office and Lau jabbed away with grim determination at his cell phone, Jimmy stared out into the sales office; it was a hive of activity . . . too little and too late. He knew he should have brought them in sooner, but how the hell was he supposed to have predicted the Golden Six would climb so damned high? It was Staten Island all over again.

He grabbed his briefcase from beneath his desk and made his way over to the wall safe, which was concealed by a genuine Mondrian. He typed in the code, waited for it to click, then swung open the door. He rolled the combination locks on the briefcase and clicked it open—the habit meant he always kept the thing locked, even though it was empty. He set it down on the floor by his feet.

Inside the recess sat fat bundles of American dollars, bonds, certificates of deposit, a handful of fake passports, and a small thumb drive containing the details of every one of Jimmy Wen's overseas accounts, properties, and shell companies. Quickly, efficiently, Jimmy grabbed everything from the safe and bundled it into the briefcase; he had more than enough to enable him to start again—once he was safely out of the Triads' reach.

"We're going," he told Lau as he scooped Alex Sun's contracts from his desk, stuffed them in the case, and clicked it shut. He would sell those when he was safely offshore and stick the money in one of his Cayman Island accounts. To avoid leaving a trail, he'd have to put the transaction through LCSSC, and he'd have to trust Li Jiang not to screw him over. The thought of trusting the crooked old banker worried Jimmy greatly, but he had no other option.

Wen straightened his suit coat and his tie. He ran a hand over his already smooth hair. It would pay to keep up appearances—the sales team would assume he was on his way out to another important client meeting. His paranoia whispered at him that any one of those industrious young people could be in Zhang's pocket, and that one phone call could all too easily undo his escape plan.

CHAPTER FIFTY-THREE

The marina was quiet. As it was a Friday, the owners of many of the yachts moored there had either taken them out for a long weekend at sea or were enjoying a late lunch at the Gold Coast restaurant, which was exclusive to the marina's wealthy clientele.

Fung and Lau followed Wen along the jetty and up the gangplank to board the *Morning Cloud IV*. Lau had offered to carry his boss's briefcase when they'd left the car, and in response, Jimmy had all but bitten his head off. He'd been glued to the stock market apps on his cell phone throughout the entire journey from 2IFC, and still had his nose buried in them as he made his way onto the yacht. He was watching his business—and his life—circling the drain.

Jimmy Wen, you are a morbid fuck.

"Where's Man?" he growled as he eyed the empty deck. Protocol dictated the captain was always there to welcome him aboard. "You *definitely* spoke to him?" Jimmy shot Lau an accusatory look; his suspicions were running out of control and he was seeing traitors, moles, and gangsters everywhere.

"He said he'd have the boat ready and waiting, Mr. Wen."

"Check the bridge."

Lau did, but returned empty-handed. "Maybe he's below decks, sir?"

Jimmy glared at him.

"I'll just go see," Lau said. He pulled out his gun and set off down the narrow, polished teak stairs that lead to the cabins.

Jimmy had Fung check the salon, which he found to be empty, while he stayed put on the open deck, clutching his briefcase and cell phone and keeping an eye on the gangway. Until his bodyguards located the captain, he wasn't about to take any chances.

* * *

Lau paused for a moment to allow his eyes to adjust to the gloom. His occasion to venture below decks on Mr. Wen's yacht being few, he had no idea where the light switches were.

"Hello, Captain?" His voice was soaked up by the narrow corridor between the cabins. He spotted the cabin with the captain's name on it to his left and rapped on the door with the muzzle of his gun. "Hello?"

The attack came from nowhere. Lau's head snapped forward from the powerful blow delivered to the back of his skull, and white flashes of light flared behind his eyes. Reeling, he staggered a few steps along the corridor and barely managed to stop himself falling by grabbing hold of the cabin doorframes on either side. Shaking his head to clear it, painfully aware that the stitches in his temple had torn open and were bleeding, Lau forced himself to turn around and point his gun at where he guessed his unseen assailant to be.

Another blow came out of the gloom, and this time it dealt his knee a painful blow. Lau yelped in pain as his leg buckled beneath him. He collided with a cabin door that flew open, dumping him on the carpeted floor of the cabin. Struggling to his knees, Lau caught a blur of movement in his peripheral vision. He fired off two shots and was about to take a third when his arm was grabbed and brutally twisted behind him and up his back. He managed to hang onto the gun, but his finger had parted company with the trigger. Growling like a wild animal, his attacker wrenched the arm again, and his shoulder dislocated with a loud, wet pop. Lau's body lit up in searing agony, his mouth dropped open, and he dropped the gun. His roar was cut short by a resolute chop to his throat. Gasping to draw breath through his collapsed larynx, Lau slumped forward and hit the floor face first.

* * *

Up on deck, at the sound of gunfire from below, Fung came running while Wen skittered toward the bow.

"Fung! Get me the hell away from here!"

Wen hugged his briefcase tight to his chest and ran. Or rather, he tried to run. His Guccis slipped and slid on the glossy marine finish of the deck, threatening to topple him. He finally scrambled into the forward part of the salon and huddled in the lee of the bar.

If the circumstances had been less fraught and he had been less a professional, Fung would have laughed at the sheer comedy of it. Now, he ignored Mr. Wen's antics and slowed his pace as he rounded the cabin stairs. Clearly, the immediate danger lay in the belly of the boat. He considered telling his boss to run, but that would have left him completely without protection. Holding his gun in a steady hand, Fung aimed it down into the gloom of the companionway.

"Lau?" he called. He received no answer. The only sounds were the cries of gulls and the rhythmic slap of water at the hull of the boat.

He frowned and took a half step toward the companionway. A sudden blur and he was knocked backward and almost off his feet. Sliding on the deck, he fought to maintain his footing as his attacker emerged from the shadows and scooted to his left. Fung's spine made an audible cracking sound as he twisted awkwardly, intending to shoot.

It was a woman. Not just any woman, but the American girl who worked in their sales office. One of Wen's rainmakers.

Fung hesitated. It would not be his last mistake.

* * *

The bodyguard was more nimble than his size suggested. Despite the power behind Valentina's attack, he'd managed to stay upright and keep hold of his gun, and now he was bringing it to bear. His eyes widened when he saw her, clearly recognizing her, and he hesitated. In that split second of confusion, Valentina went low and lunged forward, grabbing Fung's hand. She twisted his wrist to point the gun away from herself and hooked an ankle behind his knee. As he toppled, she gave him a solid kick that sent him skidding backward along the deck.

She leapt after him as he was trying to regain his feet, his leather-soled shoes hampering his efforts. As she reached him, intent on getting the gun out of his hand, he surged upward and swung his fist into her face. She ducked too late and his thick knuckles caught her a glancing blow to the cheek. Dazed, seeing stars, Valentina staggered backward. Fung raised his gun and took a chance shot in her direction.

His wrist had been weakened, though, and he missed, the slug biting into the deck by Valentina's foot and sending splinters into her ankle. Fortune smiled; the big man was off balance and the gun's recoil sent him back to the deck. Valentina was on him in a heartbeat. She kicked out at his solar plexus, but he blocked her leg with his knee and returned a kick of his own to her hip.

Valentina groaned as Fung's foot hit home and the hip spasmed. It took all she had to stay on her feet. As Fung finally regained his feet, she seized her chance. Blocking out the pain that knotted her muscles and ached bone deep, she reached for Fung's wrist and lashed out with her foot at the bodyguard's balls.

This time there was nothing to save Fung from the brutal kick. He let out a loud, rumbling wheeze and collapsed to his knees, bile shooting from his nostrils. Valentina took the man's thick wrist in a two-handed grip and twisted. Finally, the gun flew from Fung's hand, flipped over the railing, and splashed into the water below.

Fung hunched at the top of the companionway, trembling in agony. Valentina delivered a single kick to the side of his head and sent him thudding down the stairs into the gloom below. She loosed the companionway's storm hatch, wrenched it shut, and battened it down.

She looked up toward the stern. Wen, now hovering in the salon, took one look at her and made a run for the boarding ramp.

Valentina pulled the fallen Lau's gun from the waistband of her pants and went after him, her bare feet giving her the advantage of traction on the sleek surface. Just clear of the salon, she aimed the Glock and fired. The crack of the gun scattered gulls and smaller birds, filling the sky with flapping wings.

Wen had made it as far as the railing by the gangplank when he was felled by the bullet's mule-kick to his leg. As he went down, his briefcase hit the deck. Its hinges parted and it spewed its contents onto the deck.

Valentina was by Wen's side in seconds. He was ignoring the bleeding wound in his leg, instead scrambling about to scoop up the money and bonds that lay scattered around him.

God, was there ever a clearer portrait of the man? "Leave it," she told him.

Wen looked up at her, his eyes wide with disbelief. "*You?*"

"You're done, Jimmy." Valentina pointed the gun at Wen's face. "Your business is ruined and the Triads are closing in on you—I guess that's what you get for ripping off Zhang Bo. He'll be here in a bit. I just wanted to spend a little quality time with you first."

"*You* did all this?" Ignoring Valentina's order, Wen picked up a wad of blood-spattered banknotes and tossed them into his briefcase. "Kuo was right about you."

"Perhaps you should have listened to him. For someone with your history, you really have made it far too easy for me."

Wen grabbed at the stack of blood-smeared passports with shaking fingers, eyeing the muzzle of the gun. "I can pay you. I have money hidden away."

Valentina raised an eyebrow and cocked her head to one side. "I know where *all* your offshore accounts are, Jimmy." She pointed at the thumb drive that had managed to stay in Wen's briefcase. "And by the time you use *that*, they'll all be empty."

Wen looked physically ill. Understandable. Without the fortune he'd secreted around the world's tax havens, he really would be finished.

"There must be something I can do?"

"Not unless you can resurrect my dad."

"I . . . I . . . what? What are you talking about?"

"Oh, yes, what's the crazy *Lo Fan* talking about?" Valentina felt an overwhelming sense of calm. She was cold inside. Glacial. "Staten Island, ten years ago. You took every penny my father had."

"I can't remember everyone I've had dealings with—especially ten years ago. Business is business, American."

Calmly, Valentina put a bullet in the decking within inches of Wen's good leg. Wen squealed as splinters sprayed the exposed skin of his hands and face. He clutched at his damn briefcase and looked around frantically, maybe hoping his bodyguards would rush to his rescue.

"My father killed himself because of you," Valentina continued. "My family lost everything because of you. Our lives fell apart because of you. All because of Jimmy fucking Wen."

"I don't know who—"

"My father's name was Federico Parisi—perhaps this will help you remember him?" The gun jolted in her hand and a neat tear appeared in the right shoulder of Wen's jacket. The bullet continued on to embed itself in the dock. She had four shots left—that is, if the magazine had been full when Fung started shooting at her.

Wen howled with pain and indignity and clutched at the shoulder wound as blood seeped into the fabric of the ruined jacket.

"Coward. I only grazed you. You remember Federico Parisi?"

"Parisi? You—you're Fred's daughter?"

Valentina gave Wen a grim smile. "Vittorio is my mother's maiden name. You should be more thorough in your research, Mr. Wen; maybe if you'd looked beyond the money I was bringing in, you'd have found me out."

"You have it all wrong, Miss Vittorio—Valentina." Wen looked up at her with defiance in his eyes. "I didn't steal your father's money, and he sure as hell didn't kill himself—is that what this is all about?"

Valentina shook her head. "I did my homework on you, Wen. I've tracked you all the way here—you're not going to lie your way out of this." She pointed the gun at his face.

Wen held up a hand. Was that the faint hint of a smile on his face? "Your father was my—my business partner! He screwed people out of their money just as I did—I guess he never told you how many of his friends he turned over before we went bust."

"That's bullshit," Valentina growled.

"Why? Because he was an honorable man? All he was ever interested in was the money—it was always all about the money with Federico. Sure, he made with all the big talk about affording fancy colleges for you and—and Sylvia, but all he really wanted was to get rich."

The sound of her sister's name upon Wen's lips hit Valentina like a punch to the gut, calling up the image of her poor, broken sister, who'd never learned to navigate life with her father dead, her mother consumed by grief, and her sister without the resources to keep them together. Was it possible Wen was telling her the truth? Sure, Dad might've mentioned his daughters, but would Wen have remembered that detail about some faceless mark he'd conned for over a decade?

What was she thinking? Of course he would. That was the art of the con; make the marks think you care about them. "I'd advise you not to say that name again, Jimmy."

He didn't. He set off again on a different tack. "The Vaccarellis got to him in the end," he said. "Not long after I got out of the country. Two junior partners disappeared about the same time." Wen winced as he tried to scoot backward on a ramp slick with blood from the leg wound. "You remember the Vaccarellis, Valentina?"

Of course she did; they were the biggest crime family on Staten Island and were accorded the corresponding amount of media coverage when they ran afoul of the law. According to everything she'd read, they ran everything from illegal bookmaking and drugs to trafficking and prostitution.

Wen cast a glance at the handrail. "I heard he was escorted off the side of the ferry by Mr. Vaccarelli himself—now that's an honor; that man only ever got his hands dirty for those who *really* got him pissed."

"You think that would make you any less guilty, Jimmy? If you corrupted my dad the same way you corrupted Lucas Vaughn—the way you've corrupted everything and everyone you touch—just makes you more of a monster than I thought."

Wen uttered a laugh that was more a whinny of pain. "Lucas Vaughn? You think I corrupted Lucas Vaughn?"

"Lucas Vaughn is a stand-up guy at the core, Jimmy. I've seen it over and over again. He has . . . human instincts, not a monster's. Stop trying to distract me."

"*Was*," said Wen. "He's gone now. Dead. Zhang got him."

Another gut punch.

Wen plowed on. "Just like he's going to get you. He thinks you stole his shares and his money."

"I know. You see, I had a little chat with him earlier today. We . . . have an understanding."

Wen's face lost all of its remaining color. His eyes fixed on the muzzle of the Glock, currently aimed at the deck.

"So, there it is, Jimmy. You took everything my family had. Just like you've taken everything from so many innocent families. Just as you've ruined so many gullible breadwinners who were just trying to give those families a good life. Now, it's your turn."

As she aimed the gun squarely between Wen's eyes, Valentina pictured the last time she'd seen her father alive. It had been the morning he'd died. She remembered the look of bitter desperation that haunted his eyes and the fake reassuring smile he'd given his daughters and their mother that everything was going to be okay. A kiss on each forehead and eyes that showered love. The lingering look that passed between him and Mom. That had been no act. Federico Parisi had been a fool, but he'd had a heart that beat for his family, and when he felt his life could no longer help them, he ended it. All because of Jimmy Wen.

She lowered the gun. Took her finger off the trigger.

"Aren't you going to finish the job?" Zhang Bo emerged from the salon with two bodyguards flanking him. "After everything he did to you and your family. After everything you've been through to get to this moment?"

Valentine turned to face him. A spiral of gray smoke rose from the companionway that led to the lower deck.

End game, then.

"I wanted him to suffer, and he's suffering," she told the gangster. "If I'd just wanted Jimmy Wen dead, I'd have killed him the day I got to Hong Kong. He's fucking finished; he'll suffer more alive."

Zhang pulled out his own sidearm and stepped over Wen's spilled money and documents to stand next to Valentina. "That's very noble of you, Miss Vittorio, but I'm afraid that is not the way of the Wo Hop Yee. We cannot be seen to be merciful—it would be considered a sign of weakness by the other families."

"I think you're wrong," she told him. "I think leaving men like Wen alive and in ruins is far less merciful than putting them out of their misery. And it makes a more lasting impression when everyone can look at the guy and see what his greed cost him. But, hey, who am I to argue with Zhang Bo?" She flipped the Glock's safety on and stepped back a pace. "He's all yours."

With a barely imperceptible lift of his head, Zhang summoned his bodyguards, one of whom was carrying a length of thick chain.

"Oh, no, no, no!" Wen shuffled backward, away from the approaching bodyguards—the best his injured leg and arm would allow. His uncoordinated attempt at escape was futile; Zhang's men were on him in seconds.

"An example must be made, Jimmy," Zhang said as the bodyguards wrapped the chain tight around Wen's struggling, blood-slicked body. "My clan has a reputation to uphold. I'm sure you can understand."

The bodyguards lifted Wen up and dragged him over to the yacht's starboard rail. Behind them, the smoke billowing from below decks thickened, and the acrid stink of burning wood and fiberglass filled the warm afternoon air. Zhang's men supported Wen with his thighs pressed against the low railing, as if he was just looking out at the gently bobbing boats. He shouted. Screamed. The only response was the hue and cry of seagulls.

"Who do you think owns the Gold Coast Marina, Jimmy?" Zhang moved to the rail, leaning out so Wen could see his face. "No one will come until we tell them they can come—most likely after your boat has burned to the waterline."

From behind, Valentina witnessed the exact moment when all the fight left Jimmy Wen—all the arrogance, all the pride, all the greed, everything—and his body sagged in defeat.

Zhang prodded Wen's ribs with his gun. "Are you going to finish this yourself and die with some dignity and honor, or am I going to have to do it for you?"

Jimmy Wen stared down at the dark, rippling water and chose.

CHAPTER FIFTY-FOUR

Valentina walked into the marble-floored foyer of LCSSC Wealth Management and demanded to see the CEO.

"I'm afraid Mr. Li only sees clients by appointment." The neat, efficient young lady behind the reception desk peered over her thick-framed, lightly tinted Paco Rabanne spectacles, taking in Valentina's bruised face, crumpled suit, and simply frightful hair. "Do you *have* an appointment?"

"Tell Li Jiang that Valentina Vittorio would like to see him. Tell him also that I would like to discuss his dealings with JM Wen Limited and Zhang Bo. If he declines to discuss it with me, I'll discuss it with the SFC and Interpol. I'm really not particular as to which." She gave the receptionist a bland smile. "I'm sure he will make time for me—with or without an appointment."

The bank's security guard was escorting Valentina over to Li Jiang's office before the receptionist had even hung up the call to the CEO.

"Miss Vittorio." Li Jiang offered her a seat with feigned politeness. "I'm surprised to see you."

"I imagine you are." Valentina sat herself in the plush red velvet chair. Li Jiang looked even older than he had that evening on Wen's yacht; his hair seemed a tad whiter, his face yet more pallid and wrinkled. He looked . . . faded. He wore a black armband, she presumed as a mark of respect to Gao Yanlin. She tried to feel sorry for him and failed.

"How may I assist you, Miss Vittorio?" The question was a mere formality, as Li Jiang knew precisely why the girl from New York was sitting there in his office, looking as if she'd been in a fist fight—Hong Kong's underground grapevine worked quickly, and bad news traveled fast.

"Jimmy Wen is gone." Valentina told the banker what he already knew. She suspected he knew, but it felt good to hear it said out loud. "JM Wen Limited is about to go under, all thanks to Wen's legacy and dealings with Zhang Bo."

"I'm not sure what that has to do with LCSSC, Miss Vittorio."

Valentina leaned forward in her chair and fixed the banker with an icy glare; she was in no mood to play games. "I was able to access all of Wen's secret files. *All* of them, Mr. Li." She paused to let the old man digest that, then added, "I know precisely how much involvement you and your bank have with the Wo Hop Yee clan, how you launder money, and how you purchase shares through JM Wen on their behalf. I have lists of all of the smurfs—and their handlers—plus dates, transaction amounts, and account numbers. I also have a complete list of every client you have ever passed along to Wen for his stock loan scam, along with the paper trail showing each illegal kickback you have personally received via JM Wen's shell corporations. I can't imagine MDSC Financial Holdings knows about any of this . . . what do you think your holding company will do if they were to find out, Mr. Li?"

"I could say I have no idea what you are talking about." Li Jiang was terrible at bluffing.

Valentina tilted her head to study the man's face, watching as a nervous tic twitched his left eyelid in perfect synch with the one at the corresponding corner of his mouth. "You could," she agreed, "but it really won't be difficult for me to prove how complicit you, personally, are in Wen's illegal activities." Valentina paused, allowing the loaded silence to do the rest of the talking for her.

"What do you want? Money, I imagine." Li Jiang slumped back in his chair as if he'd been punched in the gut. He seemed to fade, losing what color he had left.

In ten minutes, I'll be able to see through him.

Valentina ran a hand through the unruly mess of her hair. "I want you to compensate JM Wen's legitimate client base. All of it. You cover the company's losses when it folds, and I'll hand over every bit of data I have to you, and you alone."

The old man stared at her as if she'd run mad. "You are joking. What you ask is impossible."

"No, Mr. Li. Nothing is impossible. Just look at everything you've managed to achieve so far without MDSC finding out. I know that can't have been easy—you're a smart man, Mr. Li."

"And if I don't do as you ask?"

"I'm not *asking*. I have contacts in the SFC and Interpol who are straining at the leash for the information I have. Or I may just decide to pass it along to Zhang Bo. He already has you in his sights after the stunt Wen just pulled on him—all he needs is an excuse."

Li swallowed convulsively. "I could always disappear, or—"

"Kill yourself?" Valentina read the old man's eyes. Although he had the desperate look of a man cornered, she also saw the primal instinct for self-preservation—Li Jiang wasn't the sort of man to end his life, no matter how bad things got. "You know how the Triads work. You take either of those options, and not one member of your family would be safe. Zhang would seek retribution by proxy and you'd be condemning them all to the same fate he has in mind for you. I thought you'd be well aware of that. Zhang Bo is a monster."

"Twenty cents on the dollar," Li offered.

"Eighty."

"We're talking a lot of money here, Miss Vittorio."

"Yes, we are. HSBC was fined one-point nine *billion* dollars for money laundering," Valentina told him. "That's US dollars, of course. JP Morgan Chase, forty-three billion, Deutsche Bank, fourteen billion . . . need I go on?"

"Thirty cents. That's as high as I can go."

Valentina snorted in derision. "Are you *really* prepared to lose whatever cash you have squirreled away in offshore accounts *and* face twenty years jail time—or maybe a little less time with Zhang Bo—just to play cheap with me? It's not even *your* money, Mr. Li."

"I can't just requisition billions of dollars for no good reason, Miss Vittorio."

"Please, Mr. Li. You've covered your own dirty tracks for a long time. I'm sure you are more than creative enough to find a way. You could be out of Hong Kong and sunning yourself on a hot beach in a country with no extradition treaty before MDSC ever realizes they've paid restitution to JM Wen's clientele."

"Fifty."

"Eighty-five."

"That's higher than your first proposal." Li Jiang protested. "You cannot just—"

"I think you'll find that I can." Valentina leaned forward in her chair again. "He who pays the piper calls the tune—surely you've heard that expression?"

"I can push it to sixty cents on the dollar, Miss Vittorio. No higher."

"Sixty-five and you get to retire in peace." Valentina would have been happy enough with the sixty Li Jiang had offered, but no way was she going to let the old reptile have the final word; sixty-five cents on the dollar would be fair recompense for each of the small investors who had been nothing more than an unwitting front for Jimmy Wen's vast network of illegal activities—every one seduced by the empty promise of quick and easy money.

Li regarded her with naked hatred. "Yes. Fine. Sixty-five."

"Excellent." Valentina stood up and looked down upon the deflated Li Jiang. "There will be special dispensation for one client, though. *All* losses attributed to Wen's Golden Six are to be compensated at full market price."

"You can't be serious!" Li Jiang spat. "That's tens of billions of dollars!" He struggled to his feet.

"It's billions of *Triad* dollars, Mr. Li." Valentina plucked a crumpled slip of paper from her pocket and placed it in front of the banker to emphasize her point—it listed all of Jimmy Wen's erstwhile Golden Six companies. "This is money that has been laundered through *your* bank, and money *you* helped Jimmy Wen steal from Zhang Bo—minus what you skimmed for yourself, of course. I think you can see why this would be a good idea."

Outmaneuvered and beaten, Li Jiang sighed and slumped back into his chair. "Yes."

"Of course, I'll be watching to make sure you do as we've agreed, Mr. Li," Valentina said pleasantly as she held out a hand. "I assume a handshake still means something in Hong Kong?"

* * *

Outside the bank, Valentina pushed her way through a small crowd of protestors that had appeared as if from nowhere, and made her way along the street. That group would join others in the city, which would swell in number throughout the weekend until a quarter of Hong Kong's population—over seven million souls—had taken to the streets to make it the biggest protest in modern history.

Good for them. Sometimes it pays to stand up and fight.

She headed up Financial Street toward the Four Seasons, planning to grab her clothes from the hotel and be on the earliest flight she could get off the island. A car pulled up alongside her and matched her pace. The black-tinted rear window rolled down, and Zhang Bo gazed out at her.

She stopped walking and turned her head. The car stopped as well, and Zhang opened the rear door. Valentina hesitated, pulse quickening. Was he going back on his word?

He seemed to sense the reason for her ambivalence. "We have a deal, Miss Vittorio. *I* keep my deals."

Did he? She had only his word on that. Still, she got in.

"How did your meeting with the banker go?" Zhang asked as the car pulled away from the curb. "As well as expected?"

"Of course."

Valentina stared straight ahead, as if studying the back of the driver's head. Now that the deal with Li Jiang was agreed, she was keenly aware the gang lord no longer needed her. There was nothing to prevent Zhang Bo from making her disappear, regardless.

"Do I scare you, Miss Vittorio?"

Ask a stupid question . . .

She turned her head to look at him. "You anger me."

He laughed. All the way up to his obsidian eyes. "I *anger* you?"

"You anger me because you interfere with people's lives and end them at your whim."

"Honest. Or unwilling to admit fear. Which is it, I wonder. But it's not whim. It's a matter of commanding respect and loyalty. If that loyalty is based in fear, it hardly matters."

She shook her head. "You're wrong. It does matter. People will do for love what they will not do out of fear. They will sacrifice for a friend what they will not for an enemy, no matter how powerful."

"You are a most perverse woman, Miss Vittorio. I believe that is the second or third time you've told me I am wrong. Surely, you've learned that I can be a most dangerous enemy. I can also be a dangerous friend—it is up to you to decide which you prefer." Zhang's voice was low, insistent, and filled with implied threat.

He lifted a small box from the seat next to him and placed it in Valentina's lap. She stared at it, almost afraid to find out what it contained: A severed body part? A bottle of poison?

"Open it," he said mildly.

She did. The box contained a cell phone and a key card.

"The phone," he told her, "contains the contact information of everyone I know, everyone I have dealings with, and everyone in my clan. I believe you could use it most wisely. The key is for an apartment at Pacific Place. I think you will like it there."

Valentina stared at the phone as if it might sprout fangs and sink them into her hand. "Why?"

"You have a unique talent and a great many skills that could be of use to me and my . . . businesses. I would like for you to stay in Hong Kong, Miss Vittorio. So that we might work together . . . when you are ready."

She brought her eyes back to his face. "Is this a joke?"

"Far from it." He smiled. It was a disarming smile—sincere, charming, and infinitely terrifying, given what Valentina knew it masked. "While you were . . . negotiating with Li Jiang, I was acquainting myself with your history insofar as Jimmy Wen knew it. You are ambitious. Ruthless. A strategic thinker. And, as I said, skilled in ways that would be more than useful to me." He tapped the corner of his eye. "I see you, Miss Vittorio. I know you. We will do quite well together."

But never met this Fellow, attended or alone, without a tighter Breathing, and Zero at the Bone.

The words whispered in Valentina's memory from an Emily Dickinson poem she'd learned in high school. The poem described Dickinson's encounter with a snake; Valentina smiled at the twisted appropriateness of it.

"Is that secret smile a yes, Valentina?"

His use of her given name raised the hairs on the back of her neck. Zero at the bone, indeed. She faced him again, meeting the shiny black eyes.

"Yes," she said simply, and slipped the box into her purse.

The car slowed to a gentle stop and dropped Valentina off in front of the Four Seasons. Zhang Bo looked up at her from the limo. "You will call me."

It wasn't a question, so she didn't feel compelled to answer. She merely inclined her head, then turned and strode into the hotel.

She would not tell him how patently absurd his belief was that he knew her. He'd listened to her explain why she'd wanted—no, *needed*

—to bring down Jimmy Wen, but he couldn't comprehend it. He had no idea she'd demanded Li reimburse *all* of Wen's legitimate clients, not just the Triads.

No, he didn't know her at all. And that made her a dangerous friend.

END

ABOUT THE AUTHOR

Who am I? I sometimes find it hard to answer this question. It depends on what hat I'm wearing that day, what setting I'm in, or the venue I may be attending.

I'm Dr. Vince. I'm an international financier, investing in stocks, real estate, people, and businesses. I was a CEO of a private equity fund in Hong Kong. I've operated my business throughout the Asia Pacific Region in amazing locations such as Indonesia, Singapore, Thailand, China, Japan, the Philippines, Hong Kong, and Korea. I helped executives and businesses raise billions of dollars in capital while making a small fortune for myself. But this is all the boring stuff I do.

I am a Professor in the School of Business and Accounting at Monroe College. I love mentoring and teaching. Helping young people achieve their goals, and showing people how to make their own dreams a reality is what I'm meant to do with my life. This is the rewarding and satisfying stuff I do.

I have Doctrine in Business Administration with an emphasis in Leadership, Decision Making, and Behavior. I also hold an MBA and a Master's degree in Innovation & Entrepreneurship.

I'm passionate about writing, telling stories, and creating content. I want to bring a reader into a world that captivates them, makes them laugh, scares them, and gives them a brief moment to forget about everything else.

I've always been enamored by great stories and even more so with great movies. Yes, I love Star Wars, The Lord of the Rings, The Matrix, and other great sci-fi movies. I'm a kid in an adult body. But a great Suspense/Thriller, Mystery, or Drama also keeps me glued to the screen. Yes, I cried during Charlet's Web, The Notebook and so many other tear droppers. Who hasn't? Maybe I'm a hopeless romantic or just a sensitive soul. I guess you can say that I get moved by a great story.

I am a member of the Writers Guild of the East. I'm passionate about film and attended the New York Film Academy as well as the Hollywood Film School to learn how to film my stories.

To sum me up, I'm a dreamer who never stops dreaming that the impossible is possible. I use my real-life experiences and adventures in all my novels. I've lived in 11 countries and 16 cities. I've interacted with gangsters, CEOs, scammers, and market manipulators as well as many wonderful people from beautiful cultures. I've loved, I've been heartbroken, I've climbed the mountain of success only to come tumbling down twice. I've learned a lot and experienced even more chaotic, often crazy things in my lifetime.

I want to share these experiences with you. The good, the bad, the ugly. The full and very interesting me.

Enjoy!

www.ingramcontent.com/pod-product-compliance
Lightning Source LLC
Chambersburg PA
CBHW030915300726
48970CB00001B/171